PRETERNATURAL³

Tor Books by Margaret Wander Bonanno

Preternatural
Preternatural Too: Gyre
Preternatural^3

PRETERNATURAL³

MARGARET WANDER BONANNO

TOR®

A TOM DOHERTY ASSOCIATES BOOK

NEW YORK

PRETERNATURAL³

A Tor Book
Published by Tom Doherty Associates, LLC
175 Fifth Avenue
New York, NY 10010

www.tor.com

Tor® is a registered trademark of Tom Doherty Associates, LLC.

ISBN 0-312-87760-9

First Edition: September 2002

Printed in the United States of America

0   9   8   7   6   5   4   3   2   1

For Jake, always

For Donald Paul Wander, who told me
about Bohemia, and who lives in Tir na Nog

For Jenna, whom I never met,
but, Yes, you said you will, Yes!

and with special thanks to Delmo
(the Saint) for suggesting the title

People like us, who believe in physics, know that the distinction between past, present, and future is only a stubbornly persistent illusion.

—*Albert Einstein*

ONE

It was one of those questions people only asked when the hour was late, they'd had too much to drink, and the smallest thoughts seemed profound.

"If you had to give up one of your senses, would you rather lose your sight or your hearing?"

Karen the writer always had to make sure she understood the question. "You mean from birth? Or now?"

"Now."

Karen never hesitated. "Losing my hearing would be worse. I can visualize everything I've ever seen and remember it. But never to hear music again, or the voices of those I love . . ."

"But wouldn't you rather see their faces?" someone, usually the one who'd raised the question, would protest. Almost everyone else had decided they'd rather be deaf, but never blind.

"I can touch their faces, hear their voices. It would be better than having to lip-read, knowing if I closed my eyes they'd be gone, a vibration through the floor when they walked. I'd be afraid to sleep at night, because then I'd be blind as well as deaf. No, blind rather than deaf. No question."

"But you're a writer. How would you be able to write if you were blind?"

Too much to drink or not, that would make Karen laugh.

"Honey, a lot more easily than I do now! I'm a touch typist; I keep the words in my head. There are voice-recognition programs. I'd also be even less employable than I am now, so I'd have to go on disability and do nothing but write. And bet me the same editors who reject me now would somehow find a 'market niche' for me then. Blind rather than deaf, no question."

Be careful what you wish for! she thought now, undulating carefully to fit the full length of her pale, streamlined body between the sharp shapes of rocks in the cool waters in the dark.

If she was blind, how did she know about the rocks? How did she know it was dark?

It *feels* dark, she decided. What else she felt was that the water was the same as her internal temperature, or perhaps the other way around. In the event, comfortable enough not to have to think about. She also knew what she looked like, could see herself, as she said, in her mind's eye, a ghost-pale slender form perhaps ten inches long, suggesting snake or fish or merely a very large worm, but nothing so mundane. The palest albino pink, given color only by the blood beneath the skin, she was pallid to the point of luminescence, her face all but featureless, save for the nareless, spatulate snout, the prenatal eyes atrophied to two small protuberances beneath the skin.

Eerie, unfinished, a suggestion of a face, prototype await-ing the artist's hand to provide eyes, nostrils, something other than the trapdoor of a mouth, as if it were less a face than in fact a mask, a shield to be pulled aside, revealing the real face, winsome, blink-eyed and smiling, underneath.

"Dragon's young" some had called them, others "human fish." At first glance, a mutation, a mistake. On second thought, a marvel.

Vestigial lungs, seldom used. Instead, gills, bright red with suffused blood, fluttering feathery behind where ears might be, small puffs of feather boa or tiny earmuffs where a neck that was not so much neck as just a continuation of the spine attached the domed head to the body. Lungs, gills, and a third option, the ability, like an earthworm, to breathe through the skin. What extraordinary planetary circumstances had bereft these beings of vision, but given them three ways to breathe?

Were there more, Karen wondered, or was she the only one?

Streamline. Propel by the strength of a flattened tadpole tail nearly as long as the body, fold the tiny limbs close, straight-armed like an Irish step-dancer and swim on. Neither snake nor worm, then, to have limbs. But what limbs! Sticklike, fragile, with knobby little elbow-knees and stubby finger-toes, three in front and two in back, they would never support on land absent the buoyancy of water. Karen-creature would swim, blind, for life.

But could she hear? Was there music in the lightless underground stream she swam in? That was to have been part of the deal, Karen thought, pleased with how gracefully, how naturally she moved through the water, her long tail swaying rhythmically back and forth, keeping her on keel, even absent music. The only melody that flittered was a fragment of a phrase from a particularly annoying song she remembered from childhood:

". . . or would you rather be a fish? . . ."

"I'm not a fish, I'm an amphibian!" she wanted to shout, but wasn't sure she could. Did she have vocal cords? Yes, she remembered. Her kind could squeal, and quite loudly, when removed from the water, emitting a pitiable, almost human sound, which was how they got their name. But what was the point of shouting underwater? Who on this world would hear her, who take her seriously, who believe her story? An amphibian that never evolved to adulthood?

"It's an absence of thyroxine," Karen would explain in that schoolmarmish way of hers. "It causes the limbs to remain larval, immature, like those of a tadpole who refused to be a frog."

How the hell did she know that?

Mud puppy, she thought. That's what I'd be on Earth. A sort of salamander that chose to remain in the water rather than evolve and clamber onto the land. Her mind did riffs on salamanders, creatures the fifteenth-century philosopher Paracelsus had deemed elemental, able to live in the heart of fire. Image out of a medieval heraldry, prototype of dragon, emblem of Satan. "Well, they call me Baby Dragon, and once upon a pair of wheels . . ." (What are you on about?)

Thinking too hard was bad for navigation, and the rhythm of the tail faltered momentarily. Karen felt herself losing altitude so to speak, sinking deeper in the water than she'd planned. The suggestion of the shadow of a rock almost grazed her belly. Something like sonar warned her and she twisted her forequarters, wormlike, out of the way, the two stubby toes on one back leg brushing lightly against the rock.

Pay attention!

Reading the electrical impulses running through the varying thermal layers of the slow-moving waters, she made a course correction. A quick torsion brought her flat-snouted head around a hundred eighty degrees like an owl's, the long worm-body following, and she rose with the current to her original position.

Hungry! was her next thought, and her inner sonar guided her toward a school of minuscule crustaceans pedaling their multiplicity of legs just below and to the left of her trajectory, unaware of her presence. Gliding, she let the current take her so as to disturb the water as little as possible, and was upon them by the gulpful before they could scatter away. She had seen them only in her mind's eye, but knew that they were there.

Perhaps not so blind after all. Was it the ability to read electricity, or perhaps a talent for seeing as well as breathing through her skin? A question for Govannon, when and if this adventure ended.

For now, the important question: Was she truly the only one? The crustaceans had been the only other living thing encountered so far. Was she alone on this new world? The possibility didn't frighten her as much as perhaps it ought to, knowing it was Govannon, and not an S.oteri, that was pulling the strings this time. She could trust Govannon.

Couldn't she?

TWO

Ihat was lovely," Karen says when it's over. Her human limbs seem suddenly strange to her. "What was I, and where?"

"You were on your world," Govannon says. "You were right about the mud puppy. A rare form of newt known as *Proteus anguinus*. Its only known habitat is a series of underground streams in Central Europe. I'm afraid that's all I can muster for now."

"You don't have to entertain me," she says, feeling a need, she does not know why, to set him at ease. "What is this place? Where are we now?"

"You said you wanted to see my world," he answers.

Karen stands, arms folded, her Don't-Tread-on-Me pose, on a red-rock promontory overlooking what might have been the Grand Canyon, on a planet not her own. Her roanish, freckled self is protected from this world's sun by what seems to be a permanent scrim of high cloud. She had expected something . . . different. Something more like a science fiction writer's idea of a world not Earth. This looked more real than a studio backlot, but might as easily be a location in the Hollywood Hills as on another class-M world in this galaxy, if not another. She speaks to Govannon, knowing he can hear her, even though she cannot see him.

It occurs to her that maybe she ought to rethink that blind-versus-deaf business.

Govannon is how she thinks of him, not knowing his real name, his nonhuman name, his Before-Time name. She has known three of his human personae and is aware of a fourth, and finds them each quite special. But of all of them, the one she came to know best was the one who called himself Govannon. Thus Govannon he will be to her, unless he tells her otherwise.

As she watched, what had first scrolled out before her as a weathered, deep-cut ravine, a 3-D postcard from the Grand Canyon, began to morph from parched bare rock, cracked and crumbled into endless sharp-edged configurations, to what the Grand Canyon might look like if several generations of Japanese gardeners had gotten to it.

A dozen shades of red and black and gray burgeoned and softened into uncounted shades of green. Terraces took shape, planted in soft grasses that rippled in the breeze, gentling angles and crags. Almost painfully green shoots serpentined their way out of clefts in the rock, growing years in the moments Karen watched, becoming mature, wind-warped trees clinging, with the survival skills of great age, to rocks transformed to fairy pillows by mosses and low, springy groundcover. Small rivulets tickled over rocks whose thirsty shapes suggested they had not known water for centuries. The effect seemed to begin wherever Karen set her gaze, and roll away out toward some unfathomable horizon.

What she noticed immediately, shade-seeking creature that she was, was that unlike the deserts of her imagination, this one was not hammered with heat and light. High cloud veiled the sun, the air was pleasantly warm, the atmosphere clear, not distorted by heat shimmer or mirage. The breeze, away from the cliff edge, was crisp and clean. It smelled,

Karen thought, groping for words and coming up with none better, it smelled *green*, redolent of the foliage growing below. What had it smelled like when it had swept over bare rock? She had not had time to notice.

She had never heard such silence. There was the wind, and nothing more. She'd expected insect buzz, the cry of some raptor overhead, frogs or lizards at least. But there was only wind, and the scuff of her feet when she shifted them. The flat place where she stood remained unaltered; only the far side of the ravine had changed.

The theologians have it wrong, she thought. *Man is not made in God's image, but God in man's. Bet me every species sees its god as resembling itself, even as every s/f writer starts on Earth and creates other worlds in its image, or distortions thereof. Is this really here, or am I making it up as I go along?*

" 'And the world was called Relict . . .' " Govannon intoned, ". . . because it was what remained when they had gone.' Well? What do you think?"

His voice and the touch of his hands on her shoulders reached her simultaneously. She could not see his hands, but felt their warmth, their gentleness, as it seemed she hadn't felt them for more than two thousand years. If she concentrated very hard, she thought she might feel more of him, his chest and belly against her spine, his chin with the trim El Greco beard perhaps resting on the top of her head as he'd liked to do on her world. But in fact he was only hands and voice, reminding Karen that he, like she, like everything, was really only molecules all the way down.

Pay no attention to that man behind the curtain! she thought in spite of herself, suppressing the thought because it made her distinctly uneasy.

"It's beautiful. Did you do that? Is it a projection, or is it real?"

"It's the way things happen on our world. Sometimes we can control it, sometimes not. That wasn't always the case. Much has changed since I was here last. You might not want to stay. I can take you back."

"Is there any danger if I stay?" Karen asks immediately.

"Not to you," Govannon says.

"But to you? Or anything else? You know, the stray floating time line or alternate universe or—?"

"I don't believe so, no. But I can't promise it will be interesting."

"Will I be in your way?"

"Not at all."

Karen considers it. "Then I'd like to stay. Being with you is always interesting."

She can feel his amusement. "Really?"

"It has been so far."

"Are you sure?"

"Do you know what I'd be doing if I went back?" She turns away from the ravine to address him, even though she cannot see him. "Writing another novel for an editor who is on record as saying he doesn't understand my work, at the behest of a publisher who pays me five cents a word. These are people who like nice, short sentences. Novels filled with magic swords and space battles. Sorry, neither. And even *Asimov's* pays more than five cents a word!"

Has she really been talking loud enough to echo off the surrounding rock? She lowers her voice.

"I'd rather be with you. I said that in the beginning. I want to help you solve this thing."

"But you're not with me," Govannon points out reasonably. "You're here, I'm not. And who said there was anything that needed solving?"

Karen shakes her head. Doesn't he realize it's obvious?

"We're all alone here. There isn't anything more complex than those trees down there for miles around. You expected someone else to be here. Something's wrong, and you have to fix it."

She can feel his appreciation without seeing it on his face, the way her amphibian self could feel the shapes of the rocks in the underground stream.

"Oh, you are good!" he said. "You'll do just fine!"

•

Good afternoon, Gentle Reader, this is your Narrator speaking. Ordinarily we wouldn't interrupt your journey this early on, but we're anticipating a little turbulence for the next hundred pages or so, and we thought we'd interject some guidance at the start of our journey. We're sure you'll appreciate that one of the most difficult things for a writer of a trilogy to do at the start of the third book is to create a balance between telling too much about what went before, and telling too little. The first is boring, the latter puzzling, and we'd rather spare you both boredom and puzzlement if we can.

This *is* the third book in a trilogy. Let's be clear about that. In an ideal world, you'd have read the first two volumes beforehand. In this media tie-in, star-vehicle, Emperor's New Clothes, postcapitalist publishing industry, you can't find the first two anywhere, except maybe a library in Milwaukee, and you consider yourself lucky to have stumbled upon this one.

But let's imagine that you're one of those rare, fortunate individuals who was able not only to find *Preternatural* and *Preternatural Too* but to read them in chronological order. In that case, you already know who Karen is and how she met Govannon, and you have as much of an idea of who Govannon is as anyone does, including Govannon. All you really need to know is: What happens next?

To all three of you, we apologize for the redundancy. If you'd like, you can just skip this part. These next few pages are for those of you who just happened upon this novel and had no idea it had two predecessors. Or maybe you did read one or the other of them or maybe even both, or at least heard about them. (Both were reviewed very generously in several places on line, and the first volume also got a delicious review in *The New York Times*. And if you're curious, the writer now has a Web site: <http://www.margaretwanderbonanno.homestead.com/home.html>, where you'll find more information than you ever will from her publisher.

But given the length of time between publications, you've forgotten half of what you read, which means you're even more confused. In the event, we respect your right to know what's going on before you start this book or—and we wouldn't blame you a bit—you're not going to read any further. And we can't have that, now, can we? I mean, we *need* that Secondhand Rose royalty.

•

Mystified by that last reference? Little bit of backstory here: "Secondhand Rose" is an old vaudeville tune that Barbra Streisand revived at the start of her career. Rose, whose father was in the secondhand business . . . oh, hold up; this is more complicated than we thought. Hmm, let's see, how to explain the secondhand business . . . Do you know what recycling is? Sure you do. Only you think it's only about newspapers, bottles and cans, oh my. Fact is, humankind's been in the recycling business for as long as it's been in business. Why, in the past century alone we've had any number of names for those who collect what some people don't want and sell it to people who do want it. One man's junkman is another man's Dealer in Fine Antiques.

Alternatively, consider consignment shops. You know, where your mother goes to buy designer jeans and silk blouses for a fraction of their original price, because some rich bitch wore them once and got bored with them and either left them at the cleaners' or gave them to charity or, if they're like most of the rich bitches we've known, they're sitting at home in the current designer sweater set waiting to get their share of the selling price on the consignment label? You see? Of course you do. Unless, of course, your mother is a rich bitch, in which case, forget we even mentioned it.

Anyway, Secondhand Rose, whose father was either a junkman or a Dealer in Fine Antiques or else ran a consignment shop, depending upon such variables as his religion and which side of the tracks he does business (no, don't ask us to explain about the tracks; this is not the time), complains about how everything she owns is secondhand, right down to the family piano, which her father bought for ten cents on the dollar.

That snide remark about royalties back there means this: Next time you want to complain about the price of a hardcover (or even a softcover) book—and your complaint is perfectly legitimate; the prices are obscene—remember that the author gets ten cents on the dollar. If that. It's actually a droit du seigneur tradition among publishers of genre fiction such as s/f to dole out 6–8 percent royalties, except for media tie-ins, which can be as little as 2–3 percent. Yes, for real.

Where does all the rest of the money go? Especially nowadays when so many manuscripts are delivered electronically, eliminating the editors' characteristic gripe about the typesetters' union? Well, there are the humongous advances paid to the Big Six and the One-Book Wonders (wait for it). The rest comes under the heading of Creative Accounting. We won't go there.

•

Okay, that's enough Publishing 101 for now. Time for the re-cap, the precis, the story pitch. Take a deep breath now. Ready? Here goes:

Karen Rohmer Guerreri is an Earth human who, until recently, lived in a large urban area in the western hemisphere which, for the sake of argument, we'll call New York, on the cusp of the third millennium. Karen is also a member of an endangered species which, by the time you read this, may in fact already be extinct. This species, first identified in the latter half of the twentieth century, when its numbers were already deemed too low for species viability, was known in anthropological circles as *Scriba midlistica* or, more, um, prosaically, "midlist writer."

All right, hands down, please. If we take the time for Q&A now we'll never get anywhere. If you don't know what a midlist writer is (and where did you park your saucer, anyway?) think of it this way: John Grisham, Tom Clancy, Stephen King, Michael Crichton, Dean Koontz, Danielle Steel—NOT. Got it? If we have time, we'll expand on this later.

•

No, actually, this is important. We're going to expand on it now. According to statistics recently compiled by the Authors' Guild, the above-mentioned six novelists accounted for sixty-three of the top hundred best-sellers of the 1990s. (Ever wonder how a book ends up on the best-seller list before it's even in the bookstores? It's called Magic Marketing. We won't go there, either.) These numbers don't leave a whole lot of elbow room, especially in large chain book-stores, for the several thousand other published writers who would really like you, the reader, to have an opportunity to read their recent work, much less for new writers trying to break in.

That is, unless the newbie is a One-Book Wonder. We're not sure why exactly, but editors seem to love One-Book Wonders. Maybe it's because, since they don't intend to buy a second book from these writers, they can do even less work on these manuscripts than usual. Call it less than zero.

One-Book Wonders are found in a variety of habitats, such as the Slush Pile (see Supplementary Vocabulary), the GED program at the local penitentiary, a recommendation from someone the editor roomed with at college who now runs a writers' workshop-cum-organic New Age beansprout co-op in Sheepdip, Minnesota, operating on an outreach grant from Lutefisk University or, lately, in Ivy League law firms.

Running gag: What do you call the guy at the bottom of the law school class? The answer used to be: a lawyer. Now-adays, the answer is: a writer.

(And for those of you about to point out that neither bean-sprouts nor sheep are indigenous to Minnesota, this is my novel, okay? Go write your own! Then see how hard it is to sell it. Unless you're a One-Book Wonder.)

Yes, publishing companies love One-Book Wonders. It gives their marketing people a chance to honk back at those critics who say all they're turning out these days is Product. "Well, like, excuse *us*!" they retort cleverly. "We've basically produced, um, lots of books with, you know, like, literary merit." To which the critic, always the chump, replies: "Oh, yeah? Name one!" Which, of course, the marketing person can do. Just one. The one that was on the *Times*'s best-seller list nearly a month before it ever appeared in a bookstore, clung there for fifty-bazillion weeks, and, before the writer's laser printer had even cooled off, became an Oscar-nominated movie starring a Name who bears no resemblance whatsoever to the protagonist as described in the book, and made everybody lots of money.

By the time the movie is released, the writer has disappeared without a trace. Gone back to law school, sent up for life without parole for knifing a waiter, become a day trader, doing talk shows, or all of the above. There may someday be a second book. A "much-awaited" second book. It never lives up to the expectations of the first. Never. It's almost as if there's a law of physics predicating against it. Thus the One-Book Wonder.

So that's what you, the reader, are being told you want to read: six different flavors of Same Old Same Old by the same six authors, and the occasional Soon to Be a Major Motion Picture by the Flavor of the Month. What happens to the other approximately twenty thousand working nonscreenwriting writers in the business? Answer: Not much.

It is possible, in fact quite likely, for a midlist writer to actually be reviewed in the *Times*, have a book or two available on Amazon.com (in an actual *bookstore*? You're kidding, right?) and still not be able to make rent. Still with us? Most midlist writers aren't anymore.

Even the term *midlist* is a misnomer. It was coined originally to describe that DMZ between the high ground where the Big Names dwelt and the backwaters where blue-haired ladies wrote fillers for women's magazines and Real Men freelanced for *Field & Stream*. About as misleading as the title of Jacob Riis's *How the Other Half Lives*, which raises the question: The other half of what? In Riis's day, 10 percent of Americans owned 50 percent of the wealth. Oh, like that's changed!

•

Gentle Reader, we apologize for that little outburst. Apparently our pilot has been under a great deal of stress lately. Something about a manuscript sitting unread on an editor's desk for eight months because the editor was suffering from a midlife crisis and couldn't bring himself to return phone calls, much less do anything with the manuscript. However, don't worry your pretty little head about it. There will be no further unpleasantness, and no more lectures on the publishing industry. Just straight narrative from now on. The next time you go into a Big Chain Bookstore do not—repeat not—think about all the books you'll never be allowed to read. This is America; there is no censorship. Only inertia, indifference, and bad taste.

An obvious question: Why would anyone want to become a writer? That's a tough one. At first it's probably about discovering, maybe as early as junior high, that you can. That it makes you feel good, as if you're doing something special, maybe even important. That when you share it, other people get pleasure from it, too. Kind of like sex.

Later, as adulthood teaches you hard lessons, like the fact that the stock market rises whenever unemployment rates do, and only Rich Boring White Men Get to Be President, being a writer becomes a control thing, a need to play God. It's the only place you can grasp at the tenuous hope that, at least within the confines of your computer screen (unless it freezes on you or informs you that you've just performed an Illegal Operation [Malpractice suit? Or sounds of door being kicked in by jackboots?], or one of those other MickeymouS-DOS misdirections that are built into the system to inspire terror and an overwhelming desire to upgrade), you can actually shape something, find and free the figure trapped inside the marble, the words and thoughts written in invisible ink on the page or lifted out of the screen, leave something behind that doesn't just get swept up by the undertaker. That's until you learn about remaindering. Don't get us started on remaindering.

But until then, it's your universe. There is structure, a beginning, a middle, an end. Okay, somewhere between the outline and the finished manuscript some of the details get rearranged, but there's a road map, some forward momentum, a sense of accomplishment, a journey completed when it's over. In a good novel, that is. There are things out there that publishers are calling novels which, frankly, read like piles of—ahem—printout left in a Dumpster, but it's not our place to criticize those here. Really.

Structure, then. A sense of order. A belief, however misplaced, that things usually turn out okay at the end. Except when your characters go walkabout on you, which is, quite literally, another story.

●

When we first met her, Karen had had quite enough of Real Life for the nonce. She'd just walked out of a rotten marriage and was hoping to let her emotions heal around the edges before she examined them too closely. Instead of getting counseling, which, being self-employed, she could not afford, she applied the best sort of therapy she knew: writing a novel. However, what passed for Real Life in her everyday life kept getting in the way. As a consequence, she apparently wasn't paying very close attention to some of her subplots, because her characters did in fact go walkabout on her, refusing to stay on the page or even in the same room with her. Because, unbeknownst to Karen, they weren't her characters at all.

What would you do if you thought you were writing a

novel, but instead found yourself caught in the middle of the
game plan for someone else's civilization? That was the first
book, *Preternatural.*

•

First slide, please.

What looks to you here like a cluster of jellyfish is, actually,
a cluster of jellyfish. Telepathic jellyfish, who existed as a
group mind. Sort of like New York book editors. Interplanetary jellyfish, who call themselves S.oteri, and who believed
for the first 2 billion years of their existence that they were All
There Was in the universe. Karen thought she had invented
them, and was congratulating herself on her cleverness, when
she found out too late that not only were they real but they
were (A) furious with her for presuming to think they were
fictitious and (B) about to self-destruct as a species.

Next slide, please.

With the help of a former starlet turned New Age guru,
and a couple of aging actors from an old '60s space opera, all
of whom also seemed to be visited by telepathic jellyfish,
Karen ended up saving a planet. No, not Earth. That's been
done before, entirely too often, if you ask us, and humans
never seem to learn from the experience. No, this time it was
up to as unlikely a foursome of humans as you can imagine to
save the S.oteri's world. Which is what they did.

Now, saving a planet may sound like a cool thing to do, especially if it helps sell your book and gives you a shot at a
movie deal, except that Real Life tends to be messy. People
don't always live happily ever after. When you save a planet in
Real Life, as opposed to, say, *Star Trek,* you can't always Put
Everything Back the Way You Found It Before the Next
Commercial Break.

There were some loose ends, and a few of the S.oteri got

their tentacles trampled. Which was mostly their own fault for milling around instead of staying on their marks during the climactic Final Scene, but some of them didn't see it that way. Which is why one of them, the one we'll call Fuchsia, since that was the color s/he usually wore for weddings and graduations, took umbrage and decided to tromp on Karen's tentacles this time around. That was the second book, *Preternatural Too*.

Next slide, please. Nifty cover art, isn't it? *Preter Too* (yes, the spelling is intentional) finds Karen caught in three different time lines, trying to trace the life-thread of a man who once said he loved her.

How did this happen? It seems a third species, which we'll call the Third Thing (or TQ, for short, from *Tertium Quid*, which is Latin for "Third Thing"), had given Fuchsia the power of telekinesis. The how or why of that is still unclear, which is something we hope to rectify in this third book. And Fuchsia, being of a vindictive turn of mind, was using hir new toy to bounce Karen around like Schrödinger's Ping-Pong ball.

Next three slides, please. Here we see Karen, in the persona of a hausfrau named Margarethe, in a bomb shelter in Berlin in 1945 . . . here as an herbalist and sometime midwife named Grethe in the courtyard of one of the several castles of Eleanor of Aquitaine . . . and as Grainne, an artisan in a first-century B.C. Celtic stronghold called Avaricum, a city of forty thousand souls whom Julius Caesar, one dull summer afternoon, simply wiped off the map.

Next slide, please. There's also a distinctly autobiographical quality to the novel-within-a-novel, also called *Preternatural Too*, which Karen was working on when Fuchsia grabbed her out of bed in a Days Inn in central Ohio and tossed her back into twelfth-century France. Karen's novel, *Preter Too*, too, takes place a thousand years in the future. Her protagonist is a telesper named Gret, journeying to the S.oteri homeworld on a first contact mission. The character of Gret bears a striking resemblance to Karen in that she's pining for the pilot of the ship, who seems to have forgotten that he once said he loved her. Karen's theory was that, within the next millennium, no one, not even L. Ron Hubbard, would still be writing novels anymore, so those with creative tendencies would channel them into telepathy or telekinesis. But that's in Karen's novel, not Real Life. Just to eliminate any possible confusion.

Next slide. In what we will call, borrowing from the movie industry, the A story, the one with Fuchsia and Caesar and Hitler, oh my, Karen wasn't trying to save an entire planet, just one person. So by the end, following a series of somewhat harrowing historical adventures, she got to put everything back the way she found it.

Well, almost. There were a few contradictions. And there was Govannon. Which almost brings us up to speed. But if you're still confused, you'll just have to read *Preter Too*. Try your local library. Or the author might know where you can find a copy. She might even autograph it, if you ask nicely.

•

Your next question, obviously, is: Who is Govannon? That's a little more difficult to answer. At this point, we're certain he's a time traveler, and reasonably sure he's a Third Thing (That's TQ to you, sweetheart), but whether or not he's the only one is essentially what we're here to find out.

Next slide, please.

He first appeared on Karen's event horizon in the forest just outside the walls of Avaricum, as a sturdy, silver-haired Merlin type, wearing nothing but a pair of sandals and a golden torque. To be fair, the day was warm, and his cloak was slung over his arm. Besides, before Christianity got to 'em, the Celts walked around naked a lot. You wouldn't think, their being so light skinned and all, but maybe in the absence of anything more toxic than woodsmoke and the occasional volcano, the ozone hole wasn't as big in those days. Or maybe, because they didn't know it existed, the Celts didn't worry about it. Or maybe because they hadn't discovered tobacco, and ate a lot of fish and fresh fruit and veggies and got their antioxidants, they had a natural resistance to skin cancers. Or maybe, because as a people they had a tendency to be somewhat short-tempered and given to hacking each other's heads off (yeah, like that's changed among those of the Celtic persuasion. Just try wearing the wrong colors in Belfast. A sword's untoward, but plastique is chic), they didn't stand still long enough for all those little basal cells to proliferate.

But there he was, a time traveler in the guise of a man, smiling through his beard at her, laugh lines crinkling around eyes the color of the sky at zenith on a clear, crisp day in October. He gave his name as Govannon, which means "Thunderer." The Celts, like most tribal peoples, were very much into Names that Mean Something and, as Karen could later attest, he lived up to his name.

At first he addressed Karen as Grainne, which means "Ugly," the name her mother had given her, her mother having been someone who could have given Joan Crawford lessons, and we don't mean in acting. Later, for reasons you'd understand if you'd read the novel, he gave Grainne a different name. He called her Arianrhod, or Silver Wheel, a thing of great value to a Celt, who understood the importance of chariot wheels. The name also told her he found her beautiful. Losing herself for a time in his eyes, Karen felt her life taking one of those turns that, no matter how much of a skeptic she ordinarily might have been, made her wonder about the possibility of past lives or at least alternate universes.

Which, considering that at the time she wasn't just Karen but also Ugly, might have made sense. Especially when even as she glanced up and saw Govannon for the first time, she realized she had met him before.

•

Reader, we apologize for the continued turbulence; we really thought we'd be out of it by now. To further complicate matters, we seem to have our slides a little mixed up as well. Can we go back a few? No, a few more. Now go forward one, I think. (God, I hate PowerPoint!) There we are.

Karen first met Govannon in twelfth-century France, because that's where Fuchsia dumped her first. Since telepathic jellyfish have no concept of time, the little twit got the chronologies bollixed and started in the middle, bouncing Karen from the twentieth century to the twelfth, then back to Caesar's time, then forward to 1945.

In the twelfth century, Govannon was not yet Govannon, at least in Karen's mind. He existed as the memory of Grethe's late husband, a deep-voiced, powerfully built man in a linen shirt and hose known as Jacob the Brewer, one of the countless artisans employed by the Plantagenets to run their castles, till their fields and, in Jacob's case, keep the peasants supplied with beer.

Later, she met him earlier, as Govannon, in the fifth century B.C. Clear so far? Later (next slide, please), she encountered him again, in Berlin in 1945, only this time his name was Johann, except it wasn't, and he was involved in some sort of black market under-the-rose (that's sub rosa to you; see Dictionary) activity Karen was never clear on because, as Margarethe, she wasn't in Berlin long enough to do anything except tangle a single time line.

Last slide: There's some debate about whether or not she also encountered him, on her TV screen at least, when, finally returned to her own time, she was half watching *Nightline* late one night and found herself staring into the bluer-than-blue eyes of a man named Jake Bower, who would have been a child when Johann was a mature man, and yet they were unmistakably the same person. Or were they?

The answer is: That's what we're all—you, me, Karen, and Govannon—here to find out.

•

So what's a nice girl like Karen doing in a place like this? It was her own fault. Once she'd returned to her own time and place, she discovered it tired her out even more than all those other centuries. She'd simply been through too much too soon, and thought it might be restful to go somewhere where there was no time, unless she wanted there to be, so she asked Govannon if she could tag along with him for a while.

In retrospect, mucking about in Plantagenet Europe hadn't really been all that bad. Karen knew a little about medieval history and had expected it to be dirty, but it was even dirtier than she'd anticipated, and more than a little frightening at first, because she kept expecting something to give her away, someone to suspect she wasn't who they all thought she was, i.e., Jacob's widow, Grethe. But somehow they'd never suspected. Her cover had been foolproof.

But in addition to the constant watchfulness, there was also an undertone of dread, of thinking she might have to live out the rest of her life in a place where only rich people were allowed to shit indoors. Besides, she missed her kids, and she had a manuscript to finish. But knowing the S.oteri were behind her displacement was somehow perversely comforting. They were given, she knew, to fits and starts, and as long as they didn't forget where they'd put her, they'd eventually put her back. She hoped.

The only truly scary part was the midwife bit, being called upon to deliver a baby out of Grethe's knowledge, not her own. But she'd comported herself well, and mother, baby, and midwife had all been doing well when she felt the pull of what she knew was an S.oteri yanking her out of Eleanor's time, and she assumed she was on her way back to her own time. Hoohah. Would you believe 50-something B.C.? But that's where she met Govannon.

She'd tumbled headlong into the depths of his eyes and swum their blue waters for a small eternity. She told herself afterward that she'd only slept with him because he was destined to die on the morrow. Then again, they all were, if the Romans breached the walls. But Govannon didn't wait for the battle, but volunteered himself as sacrifice to the gods to make the Romans go away. It hadn't worked. The Romans destroyed the city, Karen ended up in Hitler's Berlin, but either way she had lost Govannon, without even a chance to mourn him.

But he kept turning up again and again, and when she finally got back to her own time and recognized him in two different people simultaneously, she knew something was wrong, and she would not rest until she understood it and, probably, would have to be involved in getting it straightened out. Because, for one thing, she thought she might be in love with him.

THREE

Seascape, with figures. A beach on the Côte d'Azur, though the predominant color is gray. A gray sea flows seamlessly out of a gray sky; there is no discernible horizon. The effect of this absence of color is cool, almost chilly; the viewer might as easily be on the Baltic or the North Atlantic.

The male figure is seated on a dark blue blanket spread on the dun sand in the lee of a small outcropping. He wears shorts and a soccer jersey, and his bare toes are dug deep into the sand at the edge of the blanket. A clump of nearby sedges bends in the same offshore breeze that ruffles his hair, and a faint screed of footprints can be descried threading through them, left by the small seabirds indigenous to the region.

The male contemplates the female, who stands between him and the shoreline, her dark hair and the gauzy robe flowing from her shoulders blown by the same breeze which moves the sedges. She has been in the water for a brief, furious swim, but that was an hour or more ago, and now her bright racing suit is barely damp.

Her companion sits like a small boy—knees drawn up to his chest, arms wrapped around his legs, chin resting on knees. He is remarkably flexible for a man approaching sixty, with the compact, sinewy body of a dancer. His ancestry is

Asian, Japanese to be precise. His jet black hair is frosted with silver at the temples and his eyes are mischievous, as if he laughs often.

He is remarkably somber now.

The female figure is somewhat younger, past fifty but youthful. Perhaps it is the delicacy of her figure, a woman's body in miniature—she is scarcely more than five feet tall—the clear delineation of the bones of her spine beneath her thin skin which suggests not deprivation but a natural slenderness unaffected by time or childbearing or even gravity. Perhaps it is that her eyes are large and dark and dominate her oval face the way a child's might, or perhaps it is the luminous intelligence behind those eyes which keeps her from aging. Her neck is not as firm as it was at thirty, and she will admit to coloring her hair, but in all other respects she defies time.

The clear, dark eyes are raw and red rimmed, though not from the salt water. She has been weeping. There is a tautness to the pronounced bones of her spine which her companion likes not at all. Several times he has started to speak and each time thought the better of it. He is a dancer, and thinks best when he's on his feet. To have to sit so still for so long clearly wears on him. Yet there is that in his posture which suggests he will not violate his companion's solitude.

There is a third figure, conspicuous by his absence.

•

There will be a blindfold, Anna thought, watching the repetitive caress of sea on sand without seeing it. There will have to be a blindfold. There always is.

"It's all right to admit you're scared," Peter said, reaching out for her. Anna gave no evidence she had heard him and, with her back to him, she didn't see the gesture. "Anna—?"

"I'm not scared!" she said at last, turning on him, hands in the pockets of her robe. "I'm—stunned. Furious. They want to use Jake as a decoy and you're acquiescing to it!"

"They're using you, too," Peter pointed out. "I don't hear any complaints about that. Besides, I'm going along to make sure they do it right."

"I don't trust them!" Anna said, eyes blazing.

"Do you trust me?"

"You know I do," she said, kneeling beside him on the blanket. "With my life, and Jake's. But you're right; I am scared. When did it get so complicated?"

Peter touched her face with the back of his hand. "Has it ever been anything else, for you?"

Behind the clouds, unseen, the sun was setting. That same sun was still shining on Jake, regardless of what they'd been told. Anna willed it so. The wind quickened. Peter rubbed his arms vigorously, and Anna knotted the robe around her girl-thin waist. It only now occurred to her that Killian and the other one might still be watching from the house. She and Peter had pointedly seen their car out of sight down the curve of the main road, but that was no guarantee they hadn't returned, watching, which was what their kind always did.

They had told her Jake was dead. Not the two who had been here today, but two others, equally bland of character, though with the same stamp to them, as if there really were a factory somewhere in the woods around Langley, Virginia, that produced them, each model slightly different in detailing but, at the level of bone and brain, the same.

The first two had appeared on Anna's doorstep in the early Alexandria morning to tell her that her husband of thirty years, who was supposed to have been traveling on business between Prague and Vienna, had instead driven his car off a mountain road near a town called St. Anton am Alberg in the Tyrolean Alps. Today two more of them had somehow tracked her down at Peter's summer house, where she'd sought refuge while she decided what to do next, to tell her that the first two had been mistaken. Yes, a car rented in Jakob Bower's name had burst into flames near St. Anton, but the body pulled out of the wreckage was not Jake.

"We think you know where your husband is, Mrs. Bower," the one who had identified himself as Killian had said; his companion was silent. "We'd like you to tell us where to find him before someone else does."

If Jake was still alive, Anna knew exactly where he would be. But it was a matter of whether she would tell these people or not. Then there was the matter of what else they wanted from her, something that involved negotiating with the kind of people who trafficked in codes and aliases and blindfolds. And Anna was an expert on blindfolds, at least. The thought of having to go through that again, even for a short time, filled her with terror. But if it would bring Jake back, she could bear it. Just.

After Killian and his nameless companion were gone, she'd spent the rest of the day on the beach with Peter, forming a plan. She told herself she ought to be elated that it hadn't been Jake in that car, but what she felt was nothing. Because after the momentary shock of being told he was dead, she had recovered herself and refused to believe it.

Denial. Most people, maybe even Jake himself, who trafficked in therapists' terms, would have called it that. But Anna told herself she would have known if anything had happened to Jake, would have stopped what she was doing the moment that car went off the road, and *known*. The fact that she'd gone on with her life even when she didn't hear from him that night only proved, long before Peter and the other two confirmed it, that it was not Jake who died in flames on a hairpin turn in the Alps.

Two days ago she'd been a widow. Now she wasn't anymore. For the moment. No, she told herself. Stop that! Listen to his mind inside your mind, feel his life connected to yours after all these years. If you'd had the time, if those—those *people* hadn't gotten to you so quickly, you might even have been able to get to him and bring him home before the shadow people got involved! But now that they were involved, she had to give them her trust. If she made the wrong decision—acted too swiftly or not swiftly enough, didn't act at all—they might find Jake and kill him for real this time. It was up to her.

It was a nightmare, and she *was* scared. But Peter was right; her life had been complicated since before she was born.

There'll be a blindfold, she thought. *Again. Can I survive it— again?*

You're the only one who knows what you're capable of, my darling, the only one who really knows how strong you are!

That was Jake, teasing at the inner recesses of her mind. It was how she had been certain he was still alive even as she listened to a couple of strangers with all the right credentials telling her otherwise.

Don't do it for me, my darling. Do what you need to do for you.

Bastard! she thought lovingly, dashing tears off her eyelashes. Leave it to Jake to know before she did what choice she'd make. Never marry your therapist, Anna thought. Too late. A lifetime too late.

"You're leaving tonight?" she asked Peter as he shook the

sand out of the blanket, folding it meticulously.

"Uh-huh. I'm meeting Killian and Silent Sam in the village at ten."

"Thank God you didn't say 'rendezvous.' " Anna laughed nervously. "Spy talk!"

"*Star Trek* talk," Peter suggested, just to hear her laugh again. "No, I don't 'rendezvous' with men like Killian."

"Is Killian gay or straight, do you think?" Anna was suddenly curious.

"I don't think Killian's anything. I don't think about men like Killian."

"But you work for him." It was an accusation.

"I work *with* him," Peter said a little archly. "And his organization. From time to time. When I choose. But they don't own me. Give me that much credit, please."

Anna didn't answer.

"I'm sorry I've kept it from you all this time," Peter said. "Don't know why. God knows I tell you everything else."

How much did Jake know? she wanted to ask, but Peter had tucked the blanket under one arm and taken her hand, which meant they'd have to stop talking about it now, in case—in case there were watchers, listeners.

They moved up the beach to the house, which was warm and beckoning—all the lights on, logs set in the fireplace, a bottle of the local white chilling in a bucket of ice on the marble countertop. They walked with their arms around each other, like lovers.

"It's okay," she told him now. "I always knew you were up to something. Now I simply know what."

Peter laughed out loud for the first time since he'd gotten the word about Jake. It was the sort of raucous laugh that could carry above the polite hum of any opening-night crowd in the largest performance space; he was famous for it.

"My dear, you don't know the half of it!" he said.

"Tell me one more secret?" Anna teased at him like a child, squeezing his ribs, her mood lighter than she'd expected it to be. "Nureyev . . ."

Peter shook his head.

". . . was before my time. Although I think his courage might have been partly what inspired me. No, Rudi acted on his own, always. He was pure heart." He squeezed her shoulder. "Like you."

Anna had nothing to say to that, even if there had been time to say anything. They crossed the flagstone path and stepped through the glass doors into the kitchen.

She almost expected them to be waiting for her already. But the house was empty except for Margot, Peter's long-haired dachshund, who began her ritual dance about them, tail whipping furiously, entire body trembling, peeing on Anna's feet in a paroxysm of welcome, as if they'd been gone forever, and not only a couple of hours.

"Silly dog!" Peter scooped her up and she licked his face furiously. "You could have come with us if you weren't so fussy about getting sand between your toes. . . ."

Of course, Anna thought. Margot would have given the alarm; we'd have been able to hear her barking from the beach. Margot thinks she's a Rottweiler. Talk about pure heart. They'd have had to silence her, give themselves away. Unless, like the CIA men, they'd known she was here. But no, trust Margot; they're not here yet. Not inside the house, at least.

"Who's going to look after Margot?" she asked, as if that were suddenly the most important thing.

"All taken care of," Peter said. "You would think of that, wouldn't you?"

"I'm thinking of everything," Anna said, clutching the damp hair at the nape of her neck. "Everything . . ."

Peter sat on one of the two couches flanking the fire, Margot in his lap, and motioned to her to sit beside him. They held each other for a moment, the dog snugged in between them. Then, on the assumption that the watching had already begun—neither had ever been more aware of how much glass the house was made of—Anna went to wash the salt and sand out of her hair while Peter concocted a desultory dinner. He set the table in the dining area with the glass window-wall giving out onto his formal Japanese garden—trust Peter to compose a Japanese garden on the coast of France—plainly visible to anyone who might have reason to walk up the half kilometer of private road from the highway, enter the garden through the weathered bamboo gate, and blend in with the foliage artfully placed behind a five-foot fieldstone wall.

It was a flawless performance. They talked and laughed and gestured, though neither would remember what about. They also managed occasionally to look just sad enough, as the wife and best friend of a man who'd vanished but whom they'd just been told was still alive, to convince anyone. Unless the room was bugged—and Killian had assured them it wasn't, though how he knew for sure without bothering to check was something Anna had asked him without being answered—no one would recognize it for what it was: mis-en-scène, a performance by two old pros.

Only someone actually in the room with them would notice that neither really ate much, but merely moved the food around on their plates, picking at it artfully. They did, however, finish the wine.

Anna wondered if that was wise, considering what each of them would be facing in the next few days. But they were both riding on adrenaline, and the wine had no effect on them.

At a little after nine they simultaneously rose from the table, cleared the dishes and brought them to the kitchen. Peter set the dishwasher, then went upstairs to change, taking the stairs two at a time, Margot bounding after him. Barely five minutes later, car keys in his hand, he kissed Anna on the brow as if he expected her to still be there when he returned, and took the Jag, leaving her the ancient Peugeot as if she actually had the freedom to drive into the village afterward should she get bored or, if he made a night of it, use it to run errands tomorrow. The pretense was perfect; Peter had thought of everything. Their eyes said what their faces could not.

Anna continued to play out her part for her unseen audience long after the sound of the car had faded down the drive. She'd changed into jeans and a thick cotton sweater, armor against the inevitable assault. She assumed they would search her; goose bumps rose on her arms at the thought. She hated it when they touched her, asserting their right to be in charge, but by the time they did she'd have steeled herself not to react.

She would teach them to respect her in the end.

She sat close to the fire, the dog asleep in her lap, doing crosswords, Mozart and the snap of pine logs a background to her heartbeat.

When at last they came, they insisted on a blindfold.

•

"That's Anna," Karen says quietly as the scene dissolves. This one had definitely been a projection, appearing suddenly between her and the other side of the ravine, seeming fully dimensional while she watched it, yet vanishing like fog. "Anna Bower, your—Jakob Bower's wife. A real person. And yet, it's also fiction. Mine. Outline and sample chapters for a novel, long before I met you or the S.oteri. I've written this."

"Have you?" Govannon asks mildly, his tone suggesting he knew it all along.

"Yes," Karen says.

She's gotten used to his not being here, though she can't say she likes it much. Come to think of it, she hasn't seen him, the him she is familiar with, since two thousand years before she was born, which was much too long ago. Well, unless she counted the Big Blue Thing.

•

When all the brouhaha with Eleanor, Caesar, and Hitler was over, TQ had put Fuchsia on trial, and Karen had been asked to attend. Not to testify, merely to be there. TQ, however many of them there were at the time, had summoned her . . . somewhere. The problem had been in trying to synchronize her sensory input with their output. Kind of like trying to read a Mac file on a PC, or vice versa.

At first all she got was blue screen, and a sense of her own self, as seen from a distance, small almost to the point of being indistinguishable, poised out over nothing. Not nothing as in standing in midair looking down into a chasm, but nothing as in *nothing*.

"Hey!" she'd shouted, to make sure she could hear at least, though her voice sounded slightly muffled and there was a hint of bounceback, as there might be on a foggy day. But there was no fog. She'd stretched her arms out and touched nothing, reached down as if to touch the palms of her hands to the floor and, though her feet were planted solidly, her hands touched nothing. Even when she crouched and reached under her feet to try to figure out what she was standing on, she found nothing.

"Is anybody out there?" Karen had tried next.

When no one answered her, she kept exploring, finding the atmosphere a little cooler than was strictly comfortable, though not chilling. There was neither taste nor smell to the air she was breathing; it wasn't damp, either, because she couldn't feel the cling of it on her arms or see her breath on the exhale. For some reason that seemed important.

She had walked around a little, unable to tell how far she'd gone or in what direction, because there were no landmarks to help her get her bearings. Remembering stories about people getting lost in blizzards not ten feet from their back door, she decided it might be better to stop moving and sit down.

That had been a mistake. She had slipped out from under herself and started spinning on her own axis, slowly, but aware that she was completely out of control, as if she'd tried sitting down underwater, tumbling like a circus performer, terrifying.

She'd struggled to rebalance and stand straight again, but couldn't remember where she'd left that solid surface she'd been standing on. She'd started to flounder, thrashing like a nonswimmer in deep water, which only made it worse. There wasn't even the give of water to hold on to. She'd let out a yell, hugging herself, and rolled into a little ball, but the ball had started spinning, faster than before, and she couldn't stop it. She'd shut her eyes then so she wouldn't panic, hearing her own breathing, her own heart, the opening and closing of every valve, the rush of blood behind her eyes. . . .

Puzzled that Karen's sensory input had somehow been scrambled, TQ had intervened, conjuring a backdrop she could feel safe against. A seashore, a sunset (or was it a sunrise?), waves lapping. Granted, the colors were off, the sun too green, the sea too blue. But the sounds and smells were right, the sun warm, the breeze gentle. Then the Big Blue Thing had risen out of the sea. At least, Karen had thought of it ever since as the Big Blue Thing, though at the time it was standing between her and the greenish sun, so it could have been any color. If asked, she'd have said it *felt* blue, just as the cave where she'd swum as a proteus had felt dark. Which wouldn't have made sense unless you were Karen and had been through some of the things she'd been through at the time.

The Big Blue Thing, then. She was standing at the waterline with her toes in the wet sand when the surface of the ocean, just in the center where the sun's reflection was brightest, had begun to roil and patter, as if beset simultaneously by heavy swells and incongruously gentle rain. A *something* rose out of the turmoil, long and tall and attenuated at its stellate ends, rather ponderous in the center, its color darkish if indistinct against the greenish sunlight, its shape and displacement, as it held itself in place against the waves dancing about it, denser than the gravity of the place might suggest.

The Third Thing? Karen had wondered at the time. That was all she knew to call it. It wasn't until later that it— they—devolved down into *he*.

•

He. Govannon. It was the embodiment of him Karen liked best, the one that had, shall we say, touched her most deeply. So much less impersonal a naming than "the Third Thing," or even TQ, which had a friendly, accessible sort of nickname quality to it, but wasn't specific to him, since he wasn't the only one of his kind.

At least they both hoped he wasn't.

What brought her with him from Earth to here was the touch of a hand, the resonance of a voice, and a great deal of trust. She still doesn't even know where "here" is. "Relict," he had said. Was that truly the name of his world? Had it always been? She has so many questions, but:

"Tell me more about your novel," Govannon says before she can ask.

"It was a thriller about the Amber Room," Karen says almost offhandedly. She'd rather talk about how a barren hillside became a garden as she watched, how she had become a blind, transparent mud puppy. The idea of her fiction overlapping someone's real life—again—is beginning to wear on her. "You shared Jake Bower's life, you know about the Amber Room."

"Tell me anyway," he prompts her. "As if I don't."

Karen sighs, goes into Omniscient Author mode.

"The Amber Room was a gift from Friedrich of Prussia to the Tsar, a room constructed entirely of amber from the Baltic Sea. Walls, floors, tables and chairs, cabinets, all constructed like mosaics out of little puzzle pieces of amber, from the clearest transparent stuff to the opaque milky kind, and every variation in between. There were mirrors inlaid in the walls, brass and crystal candelabra, brocades on the chair cushions. The whole thing looked like it was made of caramel, good enough to eat."

She's hoping he's had enough, but:

"Go on."

She sighs. "It took decades to construct, became the life work of some of the best artisans in Germany. Its net worth today would be in the billions. It was shipped in pieces to the Tsars' Summer Palace in Tsarskoe Selo, near what was then St. Petersburg. Under Soviet rule, it became a museum, open to everyone. Then came the Second World War, and the Nazis invaded and stole it. Carted it off in crates, loaded it on a train and, under the order of Joseph Goebbels—who was Minister of Culture, excuse me—installed in a castle in Königsberg in what was then eastern Prussia, on the very Baltic Sea where the raw amber had been mined centuries before."

"Wonderfully ironic," Govannon muses, playing the critic. "And—?"

"Haven't you had enough?"

"Not until you've told the whole thing. You've built the suspense. Now cut to the intriguing part."

Karen sighs, resigned. A planetful of book editors had yawned in her face when she pitched this one, but Govannon was rapt.

"Königsburg Castle was bombed by the Allies in the final weeks of the war. Fragments of amber were found after the fire died out, but not enough to have comprised the entire Room."

"Amber is really only tree resin," Govannon points out. "It burns."

Karen shakes her head, the thing captivating her in spite of herself. "Still not enough. Evidence was that the Room had been removed. Almost as if Goebbels, or somebody in charge, had known the castle would be targeted. The Room has never been found. People have been searching for it ever since."

"And you find the subject fascinating," Govannon prompts her.

"I did when I started writing it. But no one bought the

book, and that was five years ago, and I've been mucking about with S.oteri ever since. I've been bounced around in over two thousand years of Earth history, and here I am on a for-God's-sake whole 'nother planet, and I don't want to talk about dead manuscripts anymore. God, I miss you! I wish I could see you."

"You will. Tell me more about the book."

Does she only imagine she can see the blue of his eyes against the cloud cover? They are exactly where they would be if he were standing here with her.

"Does it—is it important?" she asks with a sudden insight. "The fact that real life, Anna's and yours, overlaps with an unsold story of mine—and I can't understand why I'd forgotten that until now—does it have anything to do with what's happened here?"

"Please," is all he says, and she takes a deep breath and goes on.

"I submitted the outline at the time when the Swiss banks were making headlines for refusing to open their vaults and return the possessions the Nazis had stolen from Holocaust victims. This wasn't the same thing, but a smart editor could have coattailed on the publicity. Few people know or care how much stuff was stolen and restolen by both sides in that war. It would have made an interesting story. And whatever else can be said about me, I've never written a bad story. If I'd been an editor and a writer brought this to me, I'd have jumped at it.

"It was something I'd never tried before. Under my own name, I mean." Now she is warming to her subject. "Which is not to say I couldn't do it—I've ghostwritten a couple of thrillers for other writers, often for the same editors—but they've had me typecast in science fiction for so long they couldn't see it."

New York book editors! she thinks. *Egotists, despots, and fools, oh my!*

"Frustrated wannabe writers, most of them. They've all got a book in the desk drawer, but they know it's nowhere as good as what's on top of the desk waiting for them to do their job. So they treat us like cannon fodder. And, oh, they're all so overworked! They produce more alibis than books.

"Clods!" She dismisses them. "Simpleminded folk who like nice, short sentences. Since they couldn't seem to find a niche market for what they'd allow me to write, I wanted to try something new."

Her voice is even, the bitterness at bay. From here on the edge of an otherworldly precipice, it all seems so long ago and far away.

"What happened?" Govannon asks, genuinely interested. He listens better than any human she's ever known.

For a moment he flickers into partial visibility, though Karen can still see the sky through him, no more than a sketch of a suggestion of her own private Merlin, high of cheekbone, wistful of smile. Wolf white teeth, a wisp of beard, the bluest eyes in all the world. Strong shoulders, long arms, those incredible hands. The almost-sunlight catches highlights in his silver hair.

Karen laughs and reaches out to him, tries to put her arms around him. Her hands slip through him, a feeling running up her arms as if she has buried them in ice. She pulls back, hugs herself until the chill disperses.

"I'm sorry!" they both say simultaneously. Karen: "Did I hurt you?" Govannon: "Are you all right?"

"What—?" She shakes her head. What was she about to ask him? "What happened just now?" She knows as much of the answer as will make sense to her human brain: She cannot touch him; he is not here. He told her that. Nevertheless, she had to learn it for herself. "I—I'm all right. You?"

Still tenuously visible, he shrugs. "You didn't hurt me. I didn't feel anything. As I told you, I am not where you are."

"Then where—?"

"That's a little difficult to explain right now."

She will never know why she asks this. "What does it feel like where you are?"

"Nothing," he says, too quickly, shrugging it off. "Blue screen."

"The way I felt before you created the seascape? Oh, Govannon!"

He is shaking his head. "Not frightening, for us. Did it all the time. First through the Gats, then from within. Used to it. Did you ever finish it? The Amber Room?"

Does she only imagine a tinge of urgency in his voice? She wants to ask him how his kind manages that transmigration thing that they do, wants to start at the beginning and ask him everything. Why is he fixated on her novel-that-never-was? It must be important, she decides.

"I might, someday," she says, thinking *If I didn't need to make rent. If I could stay here, for instance, find something meaningful to do. What are the book editors like on your world?* "Unless you're living on a trust fund, there's no point in writing something no one will buy. Instead, you pitch them something that doesn't threaten them, and write that around the Day Job because the advance is so piss-poor.

"They said it wasn't 'hot.' It 'didn't move them.' " She can see the rejection letters scrolling across her line of vision. "The real answer was, they didn't want me writing it. Another writer maybe, but not me. It was deemed 'too ambitious' for me.

"You know what's ironic? A year later, pieces of the Room were found. Part of a wall panel and an inlaid chest that the son of a former German army officer was trying to sell. But you were Jake Bower; you know all this.

" 'Too ambitious'!" She is suddenly angry. "What the fuck does that mean? They say whatever comes into their heads. They have no respect for words or the people who write them. They placate some of us, the Big Names, the ones they've decided beforehand to pour all the money into. The rest of us they just ignore."

She shakes it off, her jaw stubborn.

"That book was just one of several that died aborning. Another x number of months spent researching and writing on spec, another concept relegated to the pile of broken promises and dreams deferred."

"For now," Govannon suggests.

"For now, unless . . ." Karen's smile is wicked. She is getting caught up in her own story in spite of herself. Who'd have thought her own life could be so interesting? "Unless I disguise it. Slip it in as a subplot in an s/f novel, and the same editor will buy it, without even remembering he rejected it once before. I get to tell my story, and he thinks he wins. Not that any of it matters, because it will still never get into the bookstores.

"But that's not important, is it?" she asks, convincing herself. "We've got work to do. Who am I on your world?"

Govannon has faded a bit while she was talking. Now all she can see is a glimmer of Earth-sky blue where his eyes should be, a brighter patch against the gray of cloud beyond them.

"You are yourself," he says. "Why? Who else would you be?"

"When you were on Earth, you were at least three people

that I knew. Maybe many more that I didn't. And each time we met, it was because I was living part of someone else's life. I just assumed that would be the case here, too."

"It's a totally different situation here. You are yourself. As you always were, even when you were living someone else. Especially when you were living someone else."

"But . . ." Karen starts to say, then lets it go, goes with it. She arrived here in the same clothes she was wearing when she left; her face is the same, her hair is the same, her toenails are still painted acid green, a recent affectation. There are no blue Celtic tattoos spiraling about her arms, no missing teeth or unshaved leg hair as in Plantagenet times, no hausfrau's apron with ration coupons and American cigarettes in the pockets. Just Karen Rohmer Guerreri, middle-aged midlist writer, in medias res as usual.

And who are you today? she wants to ask Govannon, but there will be time for that, she hopes.

·

"You're living two overlapping lives," she'd accused him back on Earth. What remained of him then was a voice in her mind, running slipstream on the carrier wave of her own thoughts, and as familiar. "You're Johann, the mystery man I met in a Berlin cellar in 1945 who, even if I believed in reincarnation, which I don't, could still not simultaneously be Jake Bower, who would have been at most in his teens in 1945. I doubt even you are talented enough to be two people at the same time. You're the Third Thing, aren't you?"

"That's TQ to you, sweetheart!" he'd said in his best Bogart. "Tell me, if you could do anything at all right now, what would it be?"

Without the slightest hesitation, she'd told him all her hopes and dreams. Start with the simple desire to find her books, advertised, marketed, distributed so that people could actually find them and buy them and read them. She seemed to remember a time when such things actually happened. Or had that been in an alternate universe?

"I want to be taken seriously," she'd concluded, and then, almost hesitantly: "I want to be with you."

It seemed to take him by surprise. "Really? But you don't know who or what I am."

She'd shrugged. "So? Does anyone ever really know another person, except in fiction? I'll take my chances."

He seemed to be weighing something. "Why?"

"Because I want to see the worlds you see. I want to know the things you know. I want your wisdom. I want you."

Had she only imagined that last statement had given him pause? Gifted actor, TQ of a Thousand Faces, he'd covered for it, extending one big strange hand to her. Their fingertips touched, and she held on.

"Come on, then," he said. "This is going to be fun! We're way beyond jellyfish now, baby."

She arrived on his world with no more fanfare than a breeze amid the trees, safe and whole and not a hair displaced, but he was gone.

FOUR

Vienna, 1996: City buses were red and white, the sides covered with huge ads for a local condiment company. An open jar of strawberry jam larger than he was enticed Jake Bower glossily as he climbed aboard. The bus seats were laminated wood, like school desks. Jake wasn't sure why he noticed this especially, until it occurred to him that he could not recall ever riding a bus in D.C.

You've gotten spoiled! he told himself. *And lazy. You walk whenever you're overseas. Have to remind yourself when you get home to walk more.*

Two schoolgirls were eyeing him, whispering and tittering, from across the aisle. College age or *gymnasium*? Jake wondered, automatically thinking in European terms, where an American would think "high school." Funny how his mind shifted gears either side of the Atlantic. They were younger than his daughter, anyway, which made their ages indeterminate as far as he was concerned. Stagily he brushed his hair back with one hand and flirted with them. The titters grew into giggles.

"*Grüss Gott, Opa!*" the bolder of the two girls said. Jake tried not to wince at being called "Grandpa." "*Bitte,* do you speak English?"

"Englische oder Deutsch," he offered affably, twinkling at her over the tops of his glasses, playing the dirty old man. "Which would you like?"

"English, please. I am trying to practice," she reported as her friend hid her mouth behind blood red nails, convulsed with giggles. "My friend here wishes to know, please, are you British or American?"

"Your friend wishes to know, but you don't?" Jake asked, teasing. This evoked fresh giggles.

"Yes, I also."

"American," he said as the sillier of the two who, Madonna wannabe, let her dark roots show through her platinum hair, whispered something in her friend's ear.

"My friend says you don't dress like an American," the bolder of the two said. Her hair, by contrast—Jake could tell from her pale eyebrows—had begun a light brown but was now Joan Jett black, with green highlights and spit curls on the sides. "No cameras, no Disneyland, *nicht war?* Myself, I thought Canadian."

"But not German?" Jake asked, disappointed, wondering what it was that had given him away.

He was not to find out. There were more whispers, more giggles.

"My friend says you are very sexy for such a, how you say—?" the dark-haired one searched for the right words.

"Old fart?" Jake offered, knowing the word was the same in both languages.

This evoked near-hysteria.

"Nein, nein!" the dark-haired girl spluttered. *"Nicht so* 'old.' Ol*der, vielleicht, und auch* handsome. How you say, *sehr vornehm . . ."* Her English seemed to have deserted her. *"Ich weiss nicht . . ."*

"Distinguished," Jake supplied, watching the street signs

for his stop, enjoying this. By now he and the girls and a few pensioners were the only ones on the bus. Almost reluctantly, he touched the signal and stood up in the aisle, waiting for the bus to stop.

"Just so!" the dark-haired girl said as he drew closer, on his way to the door. "You are reminding her of the American film actor."

"*Als* Vincent Price," the blonde said, the only words she would speak to him.

The bus slowed to a stop in front of the Opera House, and Jake gave them both his best smile.

"You're both very sweet," he said, kissing the tips of his fingers and touching each girl's cheek in turn— "*Sehr lieblich. Vielen danke. 'wiedersehen . . .*"

—and stepping down to the pavement. The two girls waved as the bus moved away. The interlude had offered him a moment's calm, a chance to drop his guard after nearly a week of waiting for something to happen.

•

First there had been the problem with the landing gear on the way into Frankfurt, which resulted in a rougher than usual landing. Then there were the endless delays getting everyone off the plane, asking each passenger the same questions with that obfuscative German efficiency.

"Were you hurt, sir? Please, have you suffered any ill effects? Do you require to see a doctor?"

Asking him first in German, then, guessing him to be American, in English; Jake's replying in German put them at ease. No, he did not require to see a doctor. He stopped himself from telling the flight attendants he was a therapist; the airline would have their own personnel available to soothe the nerves of frightened passengers, and he really could not allow himself to be sidetracked just now. What he most wanted was to leave the holding area where they'd all been herded and make his appointment on time.

That had proven to be the magic word. *Herr Doktor* Bower had an appointment! A most urgent meeting with a colleague attending a medical convention in their most hospitable city. There were effusive apologies, a taxi was called, his luggage retrieved ahead of everyone else's.

He'd gotten to the Frankfurt Intercontinental in time to be informed that David had checked out ahead of him. All that remained of him was a manila envelope with Jake's name on it left with the desk clerk. The envelope contained a first-class rail pass and a cryptic note reading: "Prague, Wednesday, 'Harriet's,' 2400."

Today was Wednesday, it was already after two. Obviously David meant next Wednesday, but the train ride only took a day. Somehow Jake was expected to play tourist in Prague for nearly a week without attracting attention. He'd been looking forward to seeing Prague again, hadn't been there since that time on the cusp of the Velvet Revolution when Anna was with him and their hotel windows had been shot out, wondered what magical changes the city had undergone in the interim, but there were the clients he'd left behind, colleagues who'd have to be contacted to cover for him. And Anna, of course. He hated being away from her so long, even after all these years.

"Minor details!" David would wave them away with his usual lack of apology. David often had several projects going at once; this change of plans was more typical than not and didn't necessarily mean anything alarming. Still, David was already gone and there would be no explanation until they met up in Prague. At least, Jake had thought gratefully, he'd be out of Frankfurt before the start of Oktoberfest, streets crammed with beer-swilling, brawling, puking adolescents and surly skinheads, a two-week saturnalia designed to relieve the pressure in the otherwise staid German brain so that the rest of the year could be devoted to business as usual.

He'd called Anna when he knew she'd be having breakfast, calculating the time in Alexandria automatically after decades of practice, told her all was well so far, but that David was sending him on another wild-goose chase and he'd try to call her from Prague, but . . .

He heard her bubbling laughter, light as a girl's.

"You'll call when you call," she told him. "We agreed long ago there's no point in worrying in the interim."

"I love you," he said, hearing his own voice echoing on the line in a way that he found unsettling.

He'd had the concierge check the train schedules for him the night before, then gotten up early to take the Zapadian Express, the antique and slightly seedy coach linking Paris and the reunited Germanies with Eastern Europe. Intermittently reading, napping, and watching rolling hills interspersed with factories and ironworks pass him from Nürnberg through Plzen into Prague, Jake arrived in Hlavni Nadrazi, Prague's main station, only an hour late.

He found that Cédok, the Czechoslovak State Travel Bureau, still handled all travel in and out of the new Czech Republic just as it had in the old days, but their offices were closed this late in the evening; he'd visit them in the morning and arrange for a full-day walking tour, pretending he was new here, though he knew parts of this city that would never merit mention in a Fodor's guide. It would give him a chance to see if he was being followed. He might even be able to determine whether Harriet's was a four-star restaurant or a topless bar or a bookshop or even a dog groomer's. Knowing David, it could be any of these.

Jake skipped the big hotels and checked into an immaculate *Gasthaus* with ironed sheets, German cooking, and a lavatory down the hall, not the same one where he and Anna had been shot at some years earlier, but its kissing cousin. He called Anna again, hearing echoes, then walked the cobbled streets aimlessly in the dark, long after the flower sellers and the street musicians had packed it in, making sure to show himself in case he was already being followed.

He didn't expect to be, until he connected with David. Someone was always following David. But Jake was thorough and wanted to be sure. When he'd strolled the length of the Charles Bridge twice without seeing anyone too obvious he'd turned back, had a late dinner complete with a complimentary glass of the local pilsner and live accordion music, courtesy of the night manager's brother-in-law, and gone to bed.

The next morning early he'd tucked his Fodor's guide under his arm, stopped at Cédok to exchange some currency, then dutifully strolled to Hradcanske Namesti to climb the parapet of the ancient castle and survey the city meandering through eight centuries at his feet. A voice behind him was accompanied by a light touch on his shoulder.

"Five minutes," the voice said in Savile Row English. "The old cemetery."

"David, for Chrissake—" Jake turned and there was no one behind him.

Spy games. Silly. Not the sort of thing grown-ups did, except in the movies, but David insisted on rituals. Feeling sheepish, Jake waited five minutes, thought about taking the Metro but decided to walk instead, taking the long way along the riverbank to the Old Jewish Cemetery in Stare Mesto.

It wasn't the only cemetery in the city, but he'd known which one David meant. The British accent notwithstand-

ing, David ben Shahan had been born on a kibbutz in the
shadow of the Golan. Jake found him pretending to read the
inscription on the tomb of Rabbi Loew.

The Old Jewish Cemetery in Prague dated from the four-
teenth century. For the next four hundred years, every Jew
who died in Prague was buried in a space barely a block
square, the twelve thousand graves with their tilted, often
indecipherable tombstones layered twelve deep. Kafka had
lived just down the street. Rabbi Loew, born Jehuda ben
Bezalel, the reputed creator of the Golem who haunted Jewish children's nightmares, was buried here, his tomb a fre-
quent stopping place for pilgrims who wrote prayers and
wishes on bits of paper that they stuck into cracks in the
grave marker hoping they'd be granted.

Watching David's back, Jake wondered if he'd written out
a wish. David was oddly superstitious sometimes. Jake
stepped up quietly and stood beside him.

"There is no Harriet's," David informed him without
glancing up from his reading. "How are you, Doctor?"

"I suppose I'd have figured that out eventually." Jake
sighed. At least he might be able to leave Prague today instead of a week from now. "Just fine, Doctor. And yourself?
How was the conference?"

"Boring as spit," David said, then proceeded to elaborate.
Two therapists talking shop. They'd met at a dozen or
more psych conferences around the globe over the years, and
that was their cover. But David, blunt-handed and surprisingly muscular under a layer of fat he fought unsuccessfully
to lose, had a characteristic watchfulness not entirely explained by his experiences in the '67 War. And a long time
ago, the two men had been introduced at a party in Washington by a Nisei ballet star and sometime spy named Peter
Kato, who also had a summer house in the south of France.

"All right, tell me," Jake said finally. "What am I doing in Prague?"

David glanced at his watch and took Jake's arm. "For starters, having a coffee with an old friend . . ."

•

"Is this the only way I can see you?" Karen asks as the Old Cemetery disappears as completely as Peter Kato's summer house, and she is back overlooking the Grand Canyon. "As a human, on Earth, but not here?"

"It's one way," Govannon says cryptically.

How strange is it to see her writing realized in three dimensions? In one reality a book of hers was made into a movie, which would have been bizarre enough, if the movie hadn't also been based on a reality only she and a handful of other humans knew was real. In that sense this was déjà vu all over again, quantum physics or magic or a bit of both (interchangeable in her right-brained mind), but at least back in the land of S.oteri there had been human elements at work. Lights, camera, action, the making of a film. This projection of an image, like a dream, without any visible agency except the mind . . .

It comes to her. *Purple Rose of Cairo,* she thinks, the only Woody Allen movie she could stand, the one where a lonely woman spends all her time in a movie theater until the characters on the screen step out into her life and begin to live around her. Or, better yet, *Sunday in the Park with George,* the Sondheim musical that, because no one but tourists and people with expense accounts could afford Broadway tickets anymore, she had seen when it was filmed for public television. Pick a more obscure subject than the nineteenth-century French painter Georges Seurat, and turn his brief life into a multimillion-dollar theatrical production.

No miniminded book editors on Broadway, Karen thinks.

The smallest stories were producible, if your name was Sondheim. Ahem. Focus and click. What she remembered best about the play was the way the characters seemed to step in and out of the painting, while the painting itself, which was really a stage-sized scrim that could disappear into the flies, appeared alternately solid and transparent depending on how the stage lights shone on it. Could Govannon's world be one big stage set with, so far, Karen as the only player? The Actor's Nightmare in spades.

On Earth, at the mercy of the S.oteri, her transitions through time and place had been lurching roller coaster rides, leaving her dizzy, nauseated, often retching when she reached her destination. From Earth to Relict, there had been only a dreaminess, a viscosity to the air, like silk against the skin, as if she and her surroundings moved at different speeds, she at normal, the rest of the universe in a kind of syrupy slo-mo.

The canyon is the template, Karen decides. Everything else she's seen so far has appeared against it and then vanished. Her adventure in amphibia, the scenes out of Anna and Peter and Jake's world, are projections, out of another time, an alternate universe, a truth hidden in a fiction wrapped in a larger truth, *Purple Rose of Cairo* meets *Sunday in the Park with George*. *The Amber Room*, a thriller by Karen Rohmer Guerreri.

When she looks across the canyon again, even the landscaping has disappeared, leaving only parched and weathered rock. Karen frowns. She had thought this much, at least, was real and now.

"Olduvai Gorge," she suggests, never doubting for a moment that Govannon is still here. If he goes away, she's really lost. "Is that why you're showing this to me? Is this where your kind began?"

"It may have been," he answers. "Though I can't be certain. You'll find our world changes almost as much as we do."

"Then why are we here?"

"Because it's one of the places where the rocks remember," he says.

"Tell me," Karen says.

"Tell you what?"

"Everything. As much as you can remember. From your kind's Olduvai Gorge to now. Or at least until you started messing with jellyfish and humans."

"Can't do that," he says. "Our time isn't linear. More like a Möbius strip."

That's when Karen notices what the landscaping hid before. She edges closer to the cliff edge to get a closer look.

Try not to think in terms of every cliché in every sci-fi novel you've ever read, she cautions herself.

"What happened here?"

"You tell me," Govannon suggests.

"It looks like burn marks." She nods in the direction of the shadowed places where the filtered sun doesn't quite reach this time of day (midmorning, late afternoon?). "Almost as if the rock is melted."

"And if you were writing this, what do you suppose might have caused that?"

"Volcanic activity? More recent than the rest, because it looks like glass; it hasn't had time to weather."

"Or—?"

"Nuclear lakes," she says without thinking. This was how other writers had described the glassy pools of molten rock caused by ground-zero impacts. Deadly hardened puddles of radioactive death, unfathomably deep and shiny as jet, their half-lives measured in millennia and longer. They could, she supposes, just as easily be some natural formation, a lava flow, perhaps even something created out of it, some art form native to this world. She counts four of them, maybe five; it is hard to see from this angle. She tries to guess their size, but can't gauge the canyon's depth or how far down the formations are. Not a time to judge. "Some sort of weapon?"

"Don't ask me, tell me."

"I don't know!" Karen says a little testily. "It's your planet, you tell me. I'm not going to make something up just to— oh. I see. I think. You want me to extrapolate, to see how closely it conforms to what really happened. Because I'm stuck again, aren't I? Writing a fiction in my universe that's reality in someone else's. Déjà vu all over again. Jellyfish all the way down."

Govannon's smile is benign, revealing nothing. Like the Cheshire Cat, it is only partly there. "Maybe."

"*Was* it about jellyfish? I know TQ changed its mind and took the telekinetic power away after Fuchsia failed the test."

"No," Govannon says. "The S.oteri came later. Or was it before?"

"Okay," Karen says, eyeing him carefully. "If I were writing this—if—I would surmise that there was a battle. A war. Though whose and why I don't know. Not among yourselves, surely? Or—?"

She doesn't want to ask *Not you against another species? Did they invade you, or was this a counterstrike?*

"There was indeed a war," Govannon begins. "Not our war, but that of two others, taking a shortcut through our space. Which is not to say we were not involved, because in fact we caused it, in our way. What you have seen me do on Earth, 'borrowing' the lives of others, living in their skins for a time, is what my kind have done for so long we cannot remember a time when we did not. . . ."

•

"Fourteen generations," Hoatzin said grimly, watching the interplay of Two ships and the One on his screen and for the first time realizing the true hopelessness of it all. He ought to be grateful, he supposed, that whatever fell out of atmosphere was falling in the high desert and not over the cities. The city shields had not been used for so long no one was sure if they still functioned. As for finding anyone, after fourteen generations' peace, who knew how to operate them . . . But that, Hoatzin reminded himself, was not what this was about. "How could we not have foreseen that this would be the likely outcome?"

Listening to his musings, Plaitha wanted to scream. His words made no sense. The fourteen generations they had *not* entered the Gats was not what had caused the Two to invade their space in pursuit of the One, but the twelve generations of intervention before.

"What have we come to?" Plaitha responded. It was the most neutral thing she could think of to say. Anything else would start them quarreling again.

But: "Is that all you have to say?" Hoatzin demanded, seeming the more determined to quarrel the less impetus Plaitha gave him. "This is not about us, but about the Two."

That did it. "Not about us? And who was it that brought the Two together with the One? They would never have met if it weren't for Klinth."

" 'Never'?" Hoatzin repeated, his most annoying habit, reiterating a single word, out of context, to show her how foolish it sounded. "Are you so certain of every possible permutation of incidence and coincidence between two civilizations in two adjacent star systems as to say with certainty that only Klinth's passing through the One's world was the cause of—" He gestured at the readouts. Starbursts of imploding ships littered the monitors, scatterings of debris like so many embers from a bonfire almost seemed, impossibly, to hiss and spit as they tumbled through vacuum and disintegrated. "—all this? Not their own lost ships, not the transmissions intercepted by both sides, not simple curiosity about roads and cities visible from space? Only one busybody from a third world caused all of this? And you say my words make no sense!"

"Mind the monitors, spouse," Plaitha said, turning on her heel. "I think you'll find the battle growing closer."

In the time they had been quarreling, four more bursts had brightened a heretofore dark screen behind Hoatzin's shoulder. Was it possible some of the ships were daring atmosphere? Out of control, or on some suicide mission?

In spite of himself, Hoatzin felt compelled to watch, even as he wondered: What was the point? They no longer had any defense if anything bigger than dust survived atmosphere. The best he could do was send a warning to the city below, as if everyone weren't already watching, as helpless as he.

And if the Two and the One wearied of their air war and came to ground? Or made truce to their quarrel in order to, by Plaitha's thinking, combine against the primal cause of all of this? What then? Hoatzin returned to his monitors. Lacking Plaitha to quarrel with—he could hear her footsteps fading down the hall—there was nothing more he could do.

As he watched, two of the One's ships, beleaguered by as many as a dozen Two ships (just as they had conducted the ground wars on their own worlds, teeming thousands of Twos against a handful of Ones), fell out of sky and went to

ground in the far canyon, melting to glass. The impact, three
sectors distant, was so severe that it was felt in the city, and
caused Hoatzin's monitors to flicker.

Plaitha must have felt it too, was Hoatzin's final thought
before the room went dark.

•

"An old-fashioned space battle," Govannon observes as the
scene fades. "That ought to keep your editor happy."

"Too many long sentences," Karen says dryly. This last
scene had had the narrative quality of a radio play. The figures of Hoatzin and Plaitha had been only dimly realized,
the "reality" of the canyon still visible through them. If this
was what TQ had originally looked like, she was no closer
to seeing them than before.

"What you saw just now was an account of the War Between," Govannon explains. "The Two and the One—
which is how we became known, in their histories, at least,
as the Third Thing—became embroiled in an air war over
our space. Two ships from the One side lost navigation and
came in under atmosphere, an entire squadron of fighters
from the Two following in low to try to finish them off.
Incoming fire caused the scars down there. The Two realized
their heat shields were frying and veered off. The damaged
One ships tried to keep flying, but one went to ground on
the other side of that rise just beyond the ravine. . . ."

Karen hadn't noticed the rise before. And does she only
imagine the ghost of a city behind it?

"It hit so hard there was nothing left to salvage. The other
got some altitude and almost made it back out of the gravity
well, but was picked off out where we could only watch on
instruments and do nothing. The debris burned up before it
reached the ground. Oh, maybe somebody caught a dust

mote in the eye later that afternoon, but that was all that was left."

"I see," Karen says. "How much are you allowed to tell me?"

Govannon has gone invisible again. Karen makes a point of looking where his eyes should be. What she sees instead is more red rock, stretching out in tumbles and potholes and sandy patches dotted with desert scrub, to where it vanishes in a kind of ground fog, real or imagined, about a hundred yards away. What, if anything, lay beyond it?

"Meaning—?" His voice is amused. She imagines him tilting his head to study her, eyes twinkling, enjoying her curiosity, her need to see beyond the next hill, however illusory.

"Oh, you know, the Prime Directive. Don't reveal anything to a less-evolved species that might alter its progress in a way it wouldn't have gone on its own."

He chuckles. "Do you see yourself as a less evolved species? Your kind has different skills than ours, that's all."

"I hadn't thought about it that way. Too many sci-fi clichés. Humans are always inferior."

"Well, we're going to change that perception. As for the concept of a Prime Directive, it's a little late for that, don't you think? You already know about my people. Not to mention telepathic jellyfish. Not too many other humans do. Has knowing there are at least two other species beyond your own altered your evolution?"

She thinks about it, shrugs. "Probably not." She chooses her next question carefully. "Tell me about Klinth?"

"One of ours," Govannon says too quickly.

"One of 'our' what? A person, a ship?"

"That's not the way to tell you about this."

Karen sits on the ground, chin resting on her drawn-up knees, not unlike Peter Kato on the Côte d'Azur. Azure, she thinks, the S.oteri who started all this. Maybe there's a connection. Her mind is doing that writer thing, tripping the light fantastic. She's onto something here. She's also wondering how she knew Hoatzin and Plaitha's names, when they never addressed each other by name. There is something more to this than visuals.

"They're all gone, aren't they? Your people. They're lost in the in between, just like you."

She sees the flash of blue again, against the grayer sky, that would have been his eyes, realizes he is on her level, as if he has taken a seat, too, prepared for a long narration.

"How do you know that?"

"Because you are. Gone, I mean. It was one thing for you to be invisible on my world, in between taking on other people's lives. But I'm here and you're not. And I think you expected someone to be here to meet you, and they're not."

"Keep talking," he says, and she definitely sees his eyes then, blue against the gray of sky.

"I don't know even where that came from," Karen protests. "I have no idea what I'm saying. I was just thinking like a writer. Like a midlist sci-fi writer, to be exact. This whole thing, watching the landscape just roll out like a carpet, the beach morphing out of blue screen the first time I saw the Big Blue Thing, there's a sense in which it's all just F/X. I need to know what's real."

"You are. I am," Govannon says.

Karen shakes her head. "That's not good enough." For some reason she knows it is important to keep her tone very gentle just now. "You have to tell me everything you remember."

His voice takes on an elegiac quality so solemn that soon it is the only thing Karen hears. His eyes and, through her writer's imagination, the rest of him, conjured out of her memory of a lover so exactly in synch with her she could not have invented a better one, become the only things she can see. She no longer knows or cares if it is morning or evening, sunrise or sunset, whether this wild place contains bandits or snakes or predators or sudden storms or precipitous drops in temperature at night. She listens, rapt. And, as is her wont, though she arrived here without so much as a scrap of paper, she makes note.

"We are, or were, or may be, an interspatial species, a species given to transmigration, from place to place and time to time, for reasons not always easy to explain," Govannon begins. "We were not always thus, at least as far as we remember but, in situ, we are.

"Did we originate on another world than here, or only in another time? Or both, or neither? It all happened so long ago, we no longer remember. All we knew is that it was a given that each of us, when we came of age, would be taught the science and art of slip-sliding through time and space the way a human slips into a fast-moving revolving door and out the other side.

"There were passageways on this world that led to other places, other times. Rabbit holes that led Through the Looking-glass. If you understand quantum physics, it's a wonder they don't exist on every world. Or perhaps they do, and it's only a matter of knowing where to find them. Some were just tunnels leading out of caves underground or underwater. Later, when we ventured into near space, we discovered more of them there as well, and that was where it got interesting. Eventually we learned to find them within ourselves."

Karen wants to ask what that means, but something tells her to wait. The leap from simply crawling like Tom Sawyer through a cave and slipping into another living being's skin is something she needs to understand. But the writer knows the narrative has to unfold at its own pace.

"Some of the Gats were immutable, always leading to the same time and place," Govannon is saying. "Others could change in a variety of ways, sometimes turning up in a different place than previously, or vanishing altogether, making it impossible to return. At first we thought those were the most dangerous, because they sometimes took one or more of us with them. But there was more. . . ."

•

Sevorsid lay half-conscious in the strange place. A taste of metal in her mouth. Something gummy in her eyes, making it impossible to open them. Fingers exploring ("Don't *rub!*" A parental voice, scolding); if she was careful it crumbled at the edges and she could free her eyelashes one at a time. Had just gotten the far corner of one eye clear enough to distinguish light from dark when the figure was standing over her.

"You shouldn't be here."

"I know." Her voice calmer than she was. "I only wanted to have a look, then go back. Kept most of me inside the Gat so it wouldn't close on me. Read about that . . . somewhere."

The figure was letting her talk. Wanting her to talk? Something said: *Be careful.*

"Was just going to peek, then go back. Go home." Don't mention home; don't say it's where you come from, where there are others like you. Don't want them following it back, capturing others. "Wouldn't have touched anything, hurt anything. Just wanted to look. Didn't think about not being

able to breathe here." Stop *babbling*! "Should have anticipated, in case. Read about that, too. Somewhere. Felt my
throat closing up, don't remember . . . anything else."

Sliding her eyes back and forth beneath the lids to try to
unstick them a little more, failing. Somehow she thought it
might be unwise to pick at the gummy stuff with the figure
watching her. Bad manners, if not some local religious taboo.
Skin prickling, warning of danger.

"I can breathe here," she finished. Brightly, she thought.
Hoped. Trying to convey gratitude, just-let-me-go-home.

The figure made a gesture she took as assent. Agreement?
Seeing it from her point of view? Or only confirming to
itself something it has suspected when it, and perhaps others,
dragged the unconscious Sevorsid out of the mouth of the
tunnel and—what? She felt her body with her mind. Except
for the sticky eyes and a rawness in her throat that was probably from the adverse effects of the air, she seemed whole.
Well, her garments were gone, but maybe that was the cus-
tom here; she couldn't see the figure well enough to tell if
the feathers were clothing or a natural part of it, or even if
they actually were feathers. Couldn't determine gender either, in this light, or even if it had one. Her insides felt the
same as when she'd left home. Not violated, then. Yet.
Would that be the price of freedom?

She was puzzling—marveling, really—over something
she'd just realized as the muzziness cleared, which was that
the figure spoke her language, or at least they understood
each other. It was almost enough to make her forget her
caution, her fear. Continued to marvel over it, was about to
mention it, even as the fist drew back (her last impression
of it was as a clenched fist) and drove into her midsection,
ruptured vitals, killed.

———————

"Ultimately the Gats became our ethos, our way of life," Govannon is saying, even as Karen shakes her head, wondering if that last one had happened in front of her eyes or behind them. Sevorsid had looked like the Big Blue Thing, though neither as big nor quite as blue. "We could not resist them. Through them, we learned the doorways of the mind. From that point on, even the least adventurous of us could not but go Inside.

"Any of us could travel through space, step into a Gat and end up elsewhere. Some of us could travel through time as well. We brought back different gifts, telekinesis chief among them. Parlor tricks at first. Think about lifting the cup from the table and carrying it across the room, and it happens. Think about planting a garden, and after half a day of sitting in your garden chair thinking very hard, it was done. But there were sometimes . . . unpleasant consequences. . . ." (Karen has a sudden vision of King Midas starving in a room full of golden fruit) ". . . so we learned not to squander the gift, not to use it frivolously. We turned the power within and learned to shape ourselves."

He stops. "You have a thousand questions. Feel free to ask."

Karen shakes her head. "I'm listening."

"You're not bored?"

"Just the opposite, but—shouldn't we be doing something? Looking for the others, I mean."

"We are," he assures her. "But I'm beginning to bore myself. There's never an Omniscient Author around when you need one. . . ."

FIVE

All right, Gentle Reader, we resemble that remark. Remember, you asked for this. With apologies to Rudyard Kipling, O my Best Beloved: "How the Third Thing Got That Way."

It began as a lark, as these things often do. What would you do if you discovered a way to move from here to there merely by thinking about it?

No, we're not talking about some sort of winking out, Schrödinger's cat, genie in a bottle, transporter effect. No jumping between two moving subway trains, that kind of thing. It had to do, at least in the beginning, with real, corporeal bodies stepping into a specific place and ending up somewhere else. Quite simply, the Third Thing learned to move from Here to There.

Start, then, with a collection of interspatial anomalies scattered about in TQ's space, some fixed, some fluctuating occasionally, as if marking time to their own internal tides. Some underwater, some in near space, some in their own backyards. Some big enough for a blimp to pass through, some no more than rabbit holes in the woods surrounding their crystalline, ever-growing cities. All intriguing, enticing, luring like magnets the iron filings of the mind.

Ever notice how some science fiction writers feel obligated to reinvent the universe before they can tell their story? It suggests they haven't much story to tell to begin with. To tell you how TQ evolved from whatever they were to whatever they became would be like starting with lemurs and going all the way through to Homo sapiens sapiens before you can write the kind of novel with Fabio on the cover. We're not going there, and you can't make us.

Brief synopsis: Having discovered that they could move about in other times and places, TQ became convinced that they must. Because what they found on the Inside was, for the most part, quite disturbing. They'd started out just curious, wanting to know, to explore, to play, and there were innumerable species, including those who taught them the art of slipping into another's skin, with whom they could do just that. But even the most benign-seeming worlds, examined closely, exist in fact in a state of precarious balance, if not downright shambles bordering on chaos, and too often TQ found themselves cast in the role of Responsible Adult because no one else wanted the job.

Wars, plagues, domestic quarrels, take your pick. Unlike the S.oteri who, you might remember, got their jollies mostly by watching, then by making a mess of things, TQ found themselves playing, shall we say, intergalactic tweaker. Because, well, for instance, take the case of the Intelligent Fungi:

•

7616Mycelia worked alone in the lab that night. Her husbands had concurred in taking the children, distributing them equally among them, keeping them safe in their pouches. At least, as safe as they could be in this time of Plague. 7616Mycelia was free to go on working.

She tried not to think of the impromptu ceremony conducted just before her departure, where her seven mates had formed the Ring around her, palps extended to each other to close the Ring protectively. They had then begun exuding the parenting pheromone so that the children, from 76161Mycel, who was nearly mature, down to the triplets, who were barely weaned, would know that it was safe. They had scattered away from 7616Mycelia then, toward the waiting males. The sound of their palps detaching from her ancillary frills in a succession of suction-breaking pops might almost have been humorous under ordinary circumstances. 7616Mycelia remembered laughing with 8325Mycel one night about how his daughter 83256Mycelia made more noise than any three of the others combined.

How long had it been since they had all laughed together? How long had the Plague been with them?

7616Mycelia watched without outward show of feeling as the children broke away from her, scattering toward the males, some to their birth parent, others to a favorite surrogate, the rest, especially the littlest ones, to whichever male was nearest. Anticipating, the males had opened their maws invitingly and swallowed each of them down until all were securely enclosed.

"Safe now," 4949Mycel, the First Spouse, whispered throatily. "We will keep the watch." The others concurred with their eyes, murmuring contentedly. 8325Mycel, especially, patted his rounded gut happily. "Do what you have to do!"

7616Mycelia had nodded solemnly. The ceremony was ended. She must go. Surrounded by her family, safe in the center of the Ring, she had never felt more alone.

She also tried not to think of 49492Mycel's inflamed mucosa, which might only mean another case of School Crud, of which he'd had three bouts since the semester started (if only he would use a handkerchief instead of wiping his nose

on whatever he could find!), or could signify the first onset
of Plague. She had not stayed inside the Ring long enough
to run the necessary tests or even take his temperature. She
truly did not want to know. What kind of scientist, much
less mother, did that make her?

If he had Plague, she reasoned, it was already too late, not
only for him but most of his classmates. His siblings
wouldn't catch it as long as they stayed in the pouches. At
the very least, 7616Mycelia chided herself, you could have
mentioned his condition to 4949Mycel and asked him to
keep an eye on the boy. What if her fifthborn died while
she was away? She could not think of that now. If tonight's
cultures were successful, the Governance had promised her,
her family would be the first inoculated.

7616Mycelia forced her weary body to move from her
office to the rear of the lab, where the cultures greeted
her with their throbbing purplish glow. Row upon row of
rhomboidal containers, seventy-seven in all, each one containing the hope that it would be *the* one. Scrolling readouts
danced in 3-D suspension above each one. 7616Mycelia
moved methodically from one rhombus to the next; they
glowed yellow-orange, fading to red and back to purple as
she first neared, then passed them.

7616Mycelia willed one of them, any one, to show sufficient growth against the culture medium to indicate that it
had responded to the recombinant protocol, and could be
tried as a vaccine. Not one would oblige her.

•

Now, honestly, what would you do? Let's say you had the
ability to slip into 7616Mycelia's skin, to look at the world
from under her mushroom cap and worry about all those
husbands and offspring, even for a minute. This was how

TQ evolved from watchers to participants. They traveled alone, and each had at least one story about arriving in the middle of a crisis, and feeling as if they had to do *something*. And, each assured the Arbiters during their debriefing, it was something they found within the person they were walking in, something that person would have done anyway, if only they hadn't been so tired, distracted, etc. In fact, some of the more persuasive ones argued, who was to say that the person they were walking in wouldn't have done that exact thing even if TQ hadn't been there?

As we say, tweakers. Not police or mediators exactly, and certainly not your cliché sci-fi dei ex machinae, but sort of behind-the-scenes fixers, transtemporal Lone Rangers riding into town just in time to give the townsfolk a hand with what they could have accomplished themselves anyway, if only they'd been paying attention. . . .

•

For reasons no one understood, children kept within the nurturing pouches were immune to Plague. It was the only thing known to stop it thus far. There was no physiological, biochemical, or even psychosocial explanation for it, yet some of 7616Mycelia's colleagues had argued for reproducing the exact components of the pouches in artificial environments and enclosing the entire population in them in order to stop the spread. No one said how long that might take.

The whole concept troubled 7616Mycelia. In not knowing what made the pouches safe, might they not alter the entire signature of the Plague, leaving them all that much more vulnerable after whatever hiatus of months or years they spent suspended in their artificial pouches? Were they to put the entire Citadel in a pouch and bring progress to a standstill? If it took years, what devastation—starvation, at least, in the absence of a working agriculture—would they find when they emerged?

Yet the Governance had already made allowance for certain populations to be suspended in the artificial pouches. The elderly, those weakened by other illnesses, and of course the wealthy, were first on the lists. Pressure was being exerted on the scientists to, if they could not find a cure, at least hurry the production of more pouches. No one seemed to have considered what would happen if more than the idle rich were pouched; the suspension of industrial and political leaders was already, even in theory, having devastating effects on the infrastructure. One way or another, the Plague was having its way with them.

7616Mycelia was among the last to insist that cure was the best option. She maintained her lab's integrity as a place for research, refusing to let it become an assembly line for the production of pouch-enzymes, as so many others had.

Had she ever felt more tired?

Until yesterday, she had had six assistants. All gone, within the day it took for the contagion to spread from one to the next. By the time the sniffles and the fever evidenced themselves, it was already too late. 7616Mycelia had watched helplessly as, in a matter of hours, the blood blooms spread over the entire surface of their bodies and the delirium boiled their brains. She'd done what could be done to make them more comfortable, providing black-market painkillers when the legal ones no longer worked, held each of them in her arms as they died, then waited for it to claim her. When it didn't, she wondered. Had she been spared for a reason, or only randomly?

She also wondered if the contagion had originated within the lab. Someone grown careless about sterifields or proper cleanup. And with a cold methodology that surprised even her, she had prepped each corpse herself, taking tissue samples for comparison before consigning them to the ash-units.

She had gone without sleep for days now. As she moved away from the cultures, which remained stubbornly unchanged no matter how often she checked them, she could not even say how long it had been since her eyes had closed. She was beyond pain, beyond feeling, but not beyond fatigue. Was it better to soldier on until she collapsed, or to rest? For a moment, only a moment . . .

How was she to know that Culture 89003425607 would choose that very moment to mutate, hold its form for about four seconds, then revert? The sensor alarm, detecting some change, did bleep for precisely one of those four seconds, but 7616Mycelia was lost to slumber at that very moment and did not hear it. The duration of the mutant form was not sufficient to record more than a minor hiccup on the printed readout, and—

How many times had she cajoled, threatened, pleaded to be given one of the newer digital recorders, only to be told it was not yet in the budget? 7616Mycelia would cling to that oversight even as she watched the blood blooms on her extremities and sealed herself off in the lab to wait for the end, the message from the substation that 4949Mycel and all his offspring were also affected clutched in her lower left palp, her brain conjuring paranoias in every corner as she lost her grip on consciousness.

"If I'd had the proper equipment," she told herself over and over again, "my own weakness would not have mattered. If I'd had the proper equipment . . ."

•

Now, suppose you were a passing TQ, watching this tragic scene unfold? Would you just duck back into the nearest

Gat, telling yourself "It's not my problem"? Or would you do something and, if so, what?

Well, as you might guess, serious reader of science fiction that you are, TQ did intervene wherever it seemed expedient, but then sometimes had second thoughts afterward. Reports started coming back from worlds that were revisited that suggested it might have been better to leave things alone. The Arbiters tried to put the genie back in the bottle by decreeing that from now on travelers could only watch, not participate. As if it could be that simple.

•

On Govannon's world, the cities grew.

Now, there's a boring sentence. Self-evident, too. Of course cities grow. They start as little muddy river crossings or a cluster of huts along a waterfront, sacred springs where the god dwells or places where miracles are reputed to have happened, a place deemed good for trade, hostelries along the Silk Road, stage coach stops, Greyhound depots, 7-Elevens just off the Interstate that expand outward over the land. People are born and die, usually more of the former than the latter, except in times of war or plague, and if the water supply holds up and people have things to trade, the little collection of huts becomes a city.

Roads are paved, sewer lines dug, stock exchanges evolve from places where sheep and slaves are traded to places where they do the trading. Folk dancing evolves into lap dancing, better music is played in the streets than in the opera houses, back alleys become black holes where people disappear without a trace. Slums proliferate on the outskirts until, crossing some undefined border where the passengers on the commuter trains grow successively paler and more blond, they are magically transformed into suburbs. Of course cities grow. Nothing mysterious about it.

In time, certain mysterious forces take place which change the shape of cities. There is the mysterious force known as redlining which, though invisible, has the power to divide a city into Us and Them and form a stranglehold around the heart of any major urban center until it literally cannot hold. Certain areas, usually known as downtown (except in New York, because downtown is where they keep Wall Street; it's uptown the cabbies are afraid to go. Everything's different in New York), begin to crumble and die back. Arson fires, like forest fires, destroy everything in their path.

Sometimes there is rebuilding, sometimes not. Sometimes the blight is unseen, unknowable, and cities seeming untouched are left vacant, emptied of life as if by a neutron bomb, sometimes so thoroughly that, though it seems incredible, even those who once lived there no longer remember where the city was or what it was called. Ever wonder how humans can just walk away and "lose" an entire city? There are doubtless those who carry the genes of Troy and Atlantis and the Anasazi nation to this day, but they haven't got a clue. Who's to say it's any different on other worlds?

What was different on Relict was that the stones grew.

•

Okay, Fan Boy, settle down. You're about to say something clever like "Duh! Rocks are inorganic. They can't grow!" Wanna bet?

Remember those crystal-making kits you had as a kid? You bought these Magic Rocks, put them in water in which you'd dissolved the Magic Chemicals, and the rocks would grow, like stalagmites, until they reached the top of the water. Sometimes they'd spread out from there, forming little islands. Let's zoom out and take the idea to a larger plane:

Limestone caves. Stalactites and stalagmites and all that jazz. The steady Chinese-torture drip-drip-drip of a few million years of mineral-rich water creates underground cathedrals, Carlsbad Caverns, the Hall of the Mountain King, Plato's Cave.

Zoom out farther. Hawaii. (Just fine, and you?) Undersea volcanic eruptions, lava floating to the surface and forming some of the best soil for orchids and pineapples you can imagine. Except you don't even have to imagine; it's there. Archipelagos. Get the idea?

Quick question: What's the one thing all three scenarios have in common? Right: water. Impossible to make the Magic Rocks grow without water, because the Magic Chemicals only work in solution. And a very good thing, too, or they'd be growing right there in the box before you brought them home from the hobby shop, sawing their sharp-edged way through the cardboard, making your mother shriek reflexively: "Be careful, you'll poke your eye out with that thing!" And so back on the shelf they'd go, while she tried to persuade you toward something safer, like how about a nice tank of tropical fish?

Further: Impossible to leach the limestone out of the rock strata to form the drip-drip-drip that shapes the subterranean cathedral, either, without groundwater, good old H_2O. So neither of these analogies is all that helpful, except in establishing the possibility. Now consider this:

Volcanoes. Not all of them are underwater, right? However, isn't it interesting that some of the more recent theories about the evolution of organic matter from the inorganic suggest that this unwitnessed but no less remarkable shift took place around the edges of underwater volcanoes. (Makes sense. You want primordial soup, you need water and heat, right? What's so complicated?)

Nevertheless, lava can form the most fantastic shapes in any medium; you only need water if you want to make islands (or new life-forms), because the lava needs some-where to float and pool so it can harden and cool. But if you just want the effect of a pool of glass or a suspended-in-midflow flow or some pillow lava or your basic bed of aa-aa, then you don't need water at all.

Not sure of the spelling of that last term, which is bound to give the proofreader fits. (Assuming there are any proof-readers left, either; most of them were being hunted to ex-tinction even before *Scriba midlistica*.) We do know that it's Hawaiian and that Hawaiians probably have as many words for lava as Eskimos have for snow. It's used to describe the particular form of lava that hardens into erose (bet you've never seen that word outside a crossword puzzle, eh?), jagged edges as opposed to smooth or rounded forms. Easiest way to remember this is to think of the sounds you'd make if you tried to step on it without shoes. (Ouch, [expletive de-leted], ow!)

Now, stretch your mind a little more and try to imagine a very special kind of lava that might exist on another planet. It isn't too hot to touch, in fact it's rather pleasantly warm in the blooming stage, and most of it spreads very slowly, forming different shapes as it oozes out of the ground and gradually solidifies.

Some of it is crystalline, unfolding in flat, micalike plaques that tend to make odd little clacking, overlapping noises, especially at night. Some is oozy like toothpaste, some tends to puff like muffins rising, suggesting it might be hollow inside, but that's deceptive. Still other varieties unfurl like fiddlehead ferns, or split into petals like daylilies.

See it? There now, that wasn't so hard, was it? Except it is hard, most of it, once it's finished blooming. There are as many different types of it on this particular world as there are, say, types of hardwood suitable for building on Earth, or names for snow. Some of it, the stuff used to build garden benches, for instance, is relatively soft, almost foamlike, with enough give to it to make it comfortable to sit on and then reshape itself once the sitter is gone, but the structural stuff is as hard as diamond and about as indestructible.

Over the centuries, it is clear from what is left behind, the inhabitants learned to sort and classify and cultivate the different types, sometimes mining them out of the ground and moving them about, but often simply letting them sprout where they were and guiding them into various shapes and purposes before snipping them off and waiting for the next batch to grow. The hardest varieties were used where Earthers would use structural steel, the shiny mica types for windows, rougher textures for walls, and smoother ones for paving. Some forms were left to freeform on their own, then transformed into gardens where plant life as strange as the rock flourished exuberantly, and little springs bubbled up in trills and rills and rivulets and sometimes quiet pools. The results were sometimes startling.

Now, imagine what it would be like to travel through space and sometimes time as easily as finding your car in the underground parking at the mall, mixing it up with S.oteri, Mycelia, Earthers, the One and the Two, and maybe some we haven't even told you about, places where, whatever else changed, at least the stones remained the same. Then you took a long, hard look at where you came from and wondered why it was that if you ignored the kitchen wall for a week or more, you found it creeping into the family room. Travel often enough on other worlds, and your own doesn't feel like home anymore.

Most crucial of all was the time line thing. If you could travel through time, end up in the past (or even the future?) of a world not your own, inhabit the lives of various individuals who lived there, what was the likelihood that at least two of those time lines might cross, and you'd meet yourself coming and going?

Because Karen's made a mistake, again. She thought Govannon couldn't be Johann and Jake Bower simultaneously, but that's because she never took physics in high school and still doesn't get it. So once again she's acting on a false premise. But this is about more than Karen right now.

•

Back to TQ, and what came to be known as the Middle Era, the time when Gat travel had become the norm and not the exception. Somehow it all started moving too fast. It became almost impossible to keep their time lines straight, and some of them found themselves looping back over themselves until they no longer knew where they began. Some felt they were losing their identity. Others got into some scary situations on the worlds they were visiting. Like the boneheaded notion of giving telekinesis to a jellyfish, or the intervention that precipitated the War Between. It's hard not to change history when you're not sure whether you're coming or going. Which was Klinth's argument at the trial, but later for that.

Besides, while most of the population was off being somewhere else, their homeworld began to suffer. Dust settled in the corners, infrastructure began to crumble. By the time someone in authority decided they ought to give all this quantum travel a rest, the place they came home to was not what they remembered, and they couldn't be sure if it had changed or only their memories of it had. A little thread of insanity crept into TQ thinking, almost at the genetic level. It was time and past time to stop.

When the Arbiters first decreed the ban against active participation, most TQ decided they could no longer travel the

Gats. To simply stand by when they might have helped was not in their nature. But even that was not enough. The Arbiters went so far as to declare a moratorium on Gat travel. Temporarily, everyone agreed, even though roughly 37 percent of the population had lost all sense of time. The Gats were closed to travel. Until they sorted things out, everyone said. Got back on track, caught up with themselves. Too late.

Because, you see, they had changed things on those other worlds, and those changes would come around to bite them in the butt. There was no way to seal themselves off completely from the times and places they had been. Sooner or later some inkling of a repercussion from Out There was bound to reach them, and they would have to decide if they were going to involve themselves again.

That was when the Two and the One arrived in TQ's space, owing to some meddling by a TQ named Klinth, millennia or only days ago. For the first time TQ had to intervene to save itself. This not only pulled the entire species out of its decline but gave it a direction for the future—playing Interplanetary Arbitrator whenever two others, like, for instance, humans and jellyfish, started circling around each other muttering "This galaxy ain't big enough for the both of us!"

And if we were the sort of writer who had to reinvent the sun every time we began, this story might go off in that direction. Fuzzy physics and nice, short sentences. But we aren't, so it won't. So there.

So on that subject, O my Best Beloved, that's all she wrote.

"And now," as the little blue furry guy used to say, "on with our story. . . ."

———

Margarethe sensed rather than heard Johann's footsteps on the stairs leading up to her flat. For a fairly large man, he was remarkably light on his feet, not even touching the place where the sixth step creaked for anyone else. Margarethe moved the bureau away from the door and waited for him. Not a vain woman, she still could not help touching her hair and smoothing her dress as she heard him stop for breath on the second-floor landing. The ability to obtain a bar of soap in this time and place signified a return to civilization. It was important she look her best for him.

"Are you sure that's safe?" was the first thing he said, eyeing the bureau and the open door. "The stairway is dark. You could not be sure who it was."

"I knew it was you," she said with a prescience he had come to expect of her, her smile with the discolored front tooth brightening a face wan with fatigue and chronic hunger, the face of postwar Europe. "No one else walks the way you do. Come in."

•

Karen makes a little involuntary sound in her throat when that one vanishes.

"You said you wanted to see me," Govannon offers.

"But I didn't want it to stop—!" she protests. "It was just getting interesting. Can't you—oh . . ."

She feels dizzy suddenly and decides it would be best to sit down. If she knew where she was, maybe she could find something to sit on. They are not in the desert anymore, but seem to be in some sort of garden. There is a stone bench; she grabs for it and lands harder than she planned. The stone gives beneath her slightly, shaping itself like a cushion.

This is the first time she's seen Margarethe from the outside. For a moment it was like watching herself on video, herself playing a character out of a war movie, except that when Johann crossed the threshold into the flat, she was sure she could feel him brush past her, the touch of his hand, the heat of him, feel the doorknob in the small of her back as she stepped back to let him pass, the unevenness of the floorboards beneath her thin-soled shoes.

There was the scent of him too which, now she thinks of it, is the same clean scent, like a small child's hair in sunlight, that she's associated with every human form he's taken in her presence. Sensurround, then, olfactory and tactile impressions as well as audiovisual. If it had lasted a little longer, she thinks, she might have slipped back into Margarethe's skin. Would she have wanted to? Before she could decide, the image vanished, and she was here, which wasn't the same here as it had been before. . . .

"Too much input," Karen says, her smile a little wobbly. "Where are we?"

"In the garden," Govannon says, in a way that gives her no clue whether it is just any garden, some prototypical Garden, Edenic, private, public or otherwise, or perhaps, if she hears a proprietary emphasis on the word "the," a garden that holds memories for him. Whatever the case, it is a pleasant place. Perhaps a little overgrown with ferny, tendrilly things in need of training or trimming, but framed within a well-kept fieldstone wall, divided by a flagstone path winding toward what looks like a house or several half obscured by shrubs and fading evening light.

There is more. A memory intervening between this stillness, this twilight, this garden and what a moment ago had seemed an immediate memory of Margarethe's flat in postwar Berlin. Frowning, Karen remembers a dreamlike sense of flying, more like Super Grover than a bird or plane, over vast crystalline cities, laid out in a grid seemingly composed of scalene triangles, puzzle pieces interlocked like the stones of ancient walls in earthquake zones on Earth that fitted together without mortar. Rapid, flittering images, too many to process at once and, as they faded into memory, Govannon's voice against a silence so profound that for a moment she wonders if he has forgotten the audio this time.

"I was afraid of this," was what he'd said.

He hadn't sound alarmed, just disappointed. Karen had waited for him to finish his thought, as more of him became visible. The eyes first, always. Then that mouth, gifted at shaping itself to thoughts and words and . . . other things. Flash of teeth, glint of silver hair, curve of jaw and cheekbone, slightly off-center nose.

"Broke it playing football in school," he'd explained at some point. Back in Avaricum? As Karen recalled it, that was the only time they'd been together long enough for small talk. "Not once but twice. Guess I was a slow learner. European football, not that tight-pants-and-helmets stuff Americans play. Ran face-first into the goalie, or he into me, depending on who was telling it. I was either Jake Bower or Johann at the time, but I don't remember which."

"Maybe you broke it once for each," she'd suggested.

"It doesn't quite work that way," he had answered vaguely, in whatever lifetime that was. Thinking about it now, she understands how TQ must have felt when their various identities began to blur. Isn't that what's just happened to her?

Behind him now, through the translucency of him, trees and horizon are sketchily visible. The effect is unsettling.

"You were right," he says at last, having listened for something that is no longer there. "They're all gone. I'd hoped at least a few of us might have been caught here. Someone was always supposed to remain behind."

He sighs. "Something has happened. Something—time, space, both, neither—hiccuped, at a point where each of my kind was either in transition or away. It might have been a natural phenomenon, or something one of us caused, but it's never happened before. And whether the rest of us are trapped on the other side of whatever it is, or scattered through time and space or, like me, caught in some Between Time, I don't know. But it is my belief that none of us can get back to Here until that glitch is mended. And that mending falls to me."

Karen's next question is very careful. "How do you know all of them are gone?"

"Because I can no longer hear them," he says, as if that explains it.

"And how do you know you're the only one who can set it right?"

"Because I'm the only one who's been able to return even this far."

"Except for me," Karen says quietly. But he seems not to hear her.

"Something is wrong, and I have to set it right," he is saying. Wherever he is, he seems to be pacing; the effect from where Karen stands is like watching a balloon bob back and forth. It might have been funny, if it weren't so serious. "Find the others, if I can. Maybe we're all doing the same thing, trying to find each other, even working at cross-purposes for all I know. But I have to do something. After so long living along multiple time lines, each one looping back over itself and others, I no longer know for sure where or when I am. I have to assume I'm the only one able to solve it."

"Okay," Karen says. "Where do we begin?"

"Well, as you pointed out, Jake Bower's life overlaps with

Johann's, and I have been both men, in overlapping time lines. Which is not impossible, by the way. Quantum physics, again." He stops, as if he's only just registered the last thing she said. "And what you mean 'we,' Kemosabe?"

"Don't play games with me!" Karen says a little sharply. "You know I don't understand physics of any kind, quantum or otherwise." She seems to deflate, shrink into herself, grimacing. "I'm here on a false premise again, aren't I?"

"What do you mean?"

"I thought it was impossible for you to be Johann and Jake simultaneously. I was wrong, wasn't I?"

"Not wrong exactly. You just didn't have enough information."

"So it's just like when Fuchsia and I went back through time looking for Raymond, and I thought he was Ryalbran, but he wasn't. The time line ran through Aoife and her baby."

"Exactly," he says. "Then there's also you and Margarethe."

"What do you—?" Karen frowns, and then she gets it. If Margarethe had survived the war and the occupation, she'd have still been alive when Karen was born. "Oh. My God. That's even weirder than a TQ borrowing a human. It's . . . I can't even think about it; it makes my head hurt."

"Happens all the time in the movies," Govannon tweaks her. "Witches, ghosts, shape-shifters. Special effects. Don't you go to the movies?"

"No, I don't!" she snaps. "And anyway, that's fiction."

He lets that go by. "The important thing is, you did succeed in straightening out the time line, regardless of whether you understood the reasons."

Karen considers it. "So maybe that's the case this time, too. It doesn't matter why I'm here, just that I'm here."

She can see the outline of him sit beside her on the bench. Does she only imagine she can feel his warmth as well?

"Maybe," he says.

"All right, then." She is on her feet. "I am here, and I'm part of this. And unless you send me back, which you won't"—he does not ask her how she knows this—"then you're stuck with me, and I'm going to help. So it is 'we,' Kemosabe. Deal with it!"

SIX

"Navajo skinwalkers," Karen says. "The Celtic Tir na Nog, where the dead are visible to the living through a veil or fog. Every human culture has some similar legend. As you say, witches, ghosts, shape-shifters."

"Vampires," Govannon adds, knowing all this. He can't resist making fangs at her. Does she only imagine they grow longer for a moment, then return to normal? Hard to tell when he's still only face and hands and those transparent.

"So which were you?"

"You mean which am I?"

The real question, Karen thinks, is knowing where to begin. She thinks of the Caucus Race in *Alice in Wonderland*: "It had no beginning, it had no end. It just went around and around." If she wondered why Govannon retained his human shape, she wonders no longer. At first she thought it might be because she was comfortable with it, but surely he knows her well enough by now to realize that whatever form he took, she would accept it.

So is it possible, she wonders, that in addition to being caught between Here and There, he's also, in at least one time line, still on Earth?

"I'm not sure how to phrase this," she begins. "And if the

whole issue is about being outside of time, my next question might not make any sense, but when did this glitch, this 'hiccup,' happen?"

"As nearly as I can tell, *something* happened while I was making love to you in Avaricum." *Did the Earth move for you, too?* Karen thinks, and quashes the thought immediately so he can't even read it in her mind. "At first I thought it was just my time line. In that case it would have been a simple matter for one of us here to pull me back. But then I brought you here and could not return myself, which meant it was larger than that. Then when I realized all the others were also gone . . ."

"But if you were with me in Avaricum," Karen starts to say, "wouldn't you have been trapped there? Instead, you're—oh."

She sees it even as she says it. Time as Möbius strip, turning back on itself and somehow ending up in a different place each time. How he can be Govannon and Jacob and Johann and Jakob and Govannon-in-Between all simultaneously. Was there someone else in her place even now, Karen wonders, interacting with another Govannon? She can't think about it. It's scary enough being the only thing more complex than a plant on an entire world. If she thinks too hard, she might panic and ask him to take her back to Earth.

And do what? Leave him in the in-Between? Abandon him and return to Earth for five cents a word? Not hardly.

Besides, his world is beautiful, in exactly the way she would have designed a world if she were one of those s/f writers who was compelled to write about things because they did not know how to write characters, to fill their pages with flora and fauna, genotypes and phenotypes, intricate descriptions of comm and propulsion systems or vague references to badly thought-out archetypal political structures because they didn't know how to write about what mattered (a quote attributed to the ex-wife of a former President: "Ask him what time it is and he'll tell you how the watch was made"), to describe the setting in order to avoid describing those who moved in it, much less what they were feeling, because they don't know how.

It's not that this two-dimensionalism is limited to science fiction, only that there are so many varieties of it in this, of all genres. Ironic, if you think about it, that those who supposedly write about offworld experiences so often end up being flat-worlders all the way down, obsessed with tungsten and condiments. Karen always thought condiments weren't sufficient sustenance in and of themselves. She only used them to spice up the primordial soup.

Govannon's world, then, which is neither Rocannon's nor Christina's, though perhaps a bit of both, is most primordially Relict, That-which-was-left-behind. A temperate climate, a sun more often than not obscured by cloud. On the rare occasion when it does venture through in its fullest splendor, its rays are mild and warming, beneficent. No melanoma or cataracts here. Rain falls only with darkness, as if the clouds lie in wait along a particular point on the ecliptic, to open themselves at the same time every night, pouring forth a steady teeming rain that falls straight down, just long enough to saturate the soil, then stop.

Nights are still. The breeze begins at sunrise and endures till dusk, caressing. Enough to ruffle the hair and sway boughs and branches of growing things in soft minuet, but never chill. Enough to dance a wind chime, if there had been wind chimes. The very feel of the breeze convinces Karen she can hear them.

The air is scented, sometimes with the things that grow,

other times simply with its own freshness, a suggestion of a sea nearby. There are plants everywhere, some strange, but many reminiscent of those Karen knows from her world, though in large or miniature. A predominance of climbing things. She classifies them in her mind as *ur*-honeysuckle, *ur*-bougainvillaea and the like.

"They look as if someone's been tending them," Karen muses, touching their leaves lightly as they walk the flagstone path, she making room for Govannon even though where he is he doesn't need it.

"Genetically engineered that way," he explains. "Most of them, anyway. If you wanted something in your garden to trim and fuss over, there were those, too."

The retaining wall surrounding the garden grows a new crystone before their eyes. Unfolding in slow motion with an audible *clack!* it fits itself neatly into the stones surrounding it, giving off a scent of lemon. The trees sough rhythmically, leaf-shadow fluttering on the flagstones leading up to the house; there are further scents of jasmine and of jacaranda. Karen closes her eyes, inhaling deeply, aware that Govannon is watching her. He seems pleased that she enjoys his world, she thinks, but also a little melancholy. Was it like looking at old grainy photos of cherished places for him, so near and yet so far?

"Would you like to come inside?" Govannon asks her, and for a moment Karen thinks he's talking about the Gats. But he gestures toward the house half hidden by the foliage.

"There is that about the nature of time travel," he continues—Karen swears she can feel his arm around her shoulder—"which alters memory even as one is remembering it. The singer becomes the song, or is it the other way around? We discovered too late that too often traversing time and space, especially both together, altered the very engrams etched in our brains, creating different, often contradictory, versions of the same event in a single individual's mind.

"Then there was the matter of living other beings' lives, however briefly. Were the memories we retained ours, or theirs, or something both or neither? I think you might know something about that."

"Grainne and Grethe and Margarethe," Karen supplies.

"Yes."

The three women's lives she had lived, in three different centuries, for as little as an hour or as long as several months, have a dreamlike quality now, yet she remembers returning to her own life trailing subtle talents that weren't there before. A knowledge of herb lore, the feel of wet clay shaping itself into a pot beneath her hands, the confidence that she could deliver a baby or survive a war or rescue a child from certain death if need be, are things she cherishes, no matter how she came to experience them.

Yet her life was brought into conjunction with these women's against her will. She can't imagine the kind of courage required to choose this kind of life, to crawl into a cave without knowing where it leads. She'd have worried about vampire bats, rattlers, and bears, oh my. And about losing her direction, or getting stuck, or having the roof cave in. Practical considerations, quite apart from the realities which lay on the other side. If she'd somehow been persuaded to go beyond the entrance, she for sure would have gone no farther than where she could see the light and remember how to get out. Anyone who's ever read Mark Twain knows what happens to kids who go exploring too far in caves. They invariably end up in the dark, out of candles, almost out of air, and prey to pirates.

And what Mark Twain with his dirty fingernails and Victorian proprieties couldn't tell you, is what pirates do to little boys and girls once they've been captured. Add the dimension of time and space, and one could just imagine.

Govannon is watching as she puzzles all this out. He is still transparent to her, the suggestion of a face, a miragelike shimmer displacing the air where his body would be. Still, she knows him well enough to supply the body language which suggests he enjoys looking at her. This pleases her.

•

Plato's cave, Merlin's, Govannon's, oh my. The door apparently operated on some sort of sensor, and slid open as soon as Karen approached it. Now she stands in the entrance foyer, uncertain what to do next.

"Is this yours?" she asks.

"It may have been."

The rooms leading out of each other are empty. There is nothing resembling furniture or personal effects, no carpets or throw pillows, paintings, flowerpots, children's toys. Just walls, ceilings, windows, floors, open doorways neither rounded nor quite rectangular. But something said it had been well lived in once; there were resonances of laughter in the walls. Karen accepts it, as she had the hut in Plantagenet France she'd shared with Kit and a pig, or Sequanna's open-hearthed and many-peopled house built into the great wall of Avaricum, or the basement of a bakery in Hitler's Berlin.

Govannon's house, then, to fix it in her mind. It is low to the ground, though built to accommodate the terrain, rising and falling where the land does, comprising seven different levels in all or, at least, seven changes of level, accomplished by something neither steps nor a ramp, but an undulating hybrid of both. A softness to all the angles, floor to wall, wall to ceiling, window frames, no sharp edges or corners. The size of the rooms, height of ceilings and doorways, suggests inhabitants somewhat taller than most humans, but Karen will make no assumptions. Set an alien down in Versailles and he'd assume humans were three meters tall and bred like ants, to need so many rooms.

"Ergonomic," Karen remarks as she walks up and down the ramps, fitting her feet to the undulations by only slightly lengthening her stride. "Very practical."

"I thought it would appeal to you," Govannon says knowingly.

She can see his face entirely this time, though disembodied, floating just above her shoulder level like the Cheshire Cat's. He walks with her from room to room.

The entire structure, not surprisingly, is of stone. Even the roof tiles have a dressed-slate look to them. The walls are smooth, unmarked, of varying shades of grayish mauve or greenish gray. Different from the retaining walls or the bench in the garden, Karen thinks, though she isn't exactly sure what she means. Where it is actively growing, mostly in the room she would come to think of as the kitchen, and in a side hall off the main entrance, it is a particularly appealing shade of green, like milky jade.

"Put your hand flat against it," Govannon suggests.

"It's warm!" she says, marveling. It gives a little at her touch, like foam rubber or the surface of an angel food cake, then seems to grow liquid and shape itself around the starfish of her hand. She watches, fascinated, determined not to pull away unless it starts to close around her. It begins to glow a dull orange around the edges, and does she only imagine it seems to be getting warmer?

"What will it do?" she asks warily. "Does it know when to stop?"

"How much do you need that hand?" he teases, and she pulls away. The orange glow fades, but the shape of her hand, down to every etching of fingerprint, remains. Karen is too intrigued to even scowl at him.

He guides her through the rooms, silent, watchful, interested in her reactions. She stands by the long windows, first studying the gardens, then the windows themselves, which are made of one of the translucent crystalline types of stone and seem grown into the surface of the surrounding opaque stone with no way to open them, yet somehow a breeze wafts through. If there had been curtains, they'd have floated gently into the room from dawn till dusk. Absent curtains, Karen is conscious of an intermittent softness against her skin that is a breeze somehow transported into the room.

When Govannon stands between her and the window, the not-quite-sunlight suffusing him, she can see more of him, a silhouette displacing the light. Sometimes Jacob the Brewer's slightly twisted spine, sometimes Johann's ramrod posture. But always the same width of shoulder, the same definition of muscle in the arms, the same hairless smoothness of his skin, not seen so much as remembered.

She wishes she could see him whole and fully dimensional, touch him. Instead she conjures what ought to be there. Can she tell from a mere silhouette that his shoulders, arms, and legs are bare? Is he naked? A surreptitious glance tells her no, though what covers him is not clear. Designer underpants, a loincloth, a cloud? His feet are bare, possessed of the familiar "witch toes," webbed between the second digit and the third, that she remembers were Jacob's and Govannon's. She remembers a birthmark just above one knee, but when he turns toward her and she looks for it, the whole of him vanishes again.

"Govannon—!"

"I'm still here." At least his voice is. "I'm afraid I can't always control the fading in and out. But even if I disappear entirely, you're still safe. Do you understand?"

Karen exhales, exasperated. This is starting to get on her nerves. "Not entirely, but—"

"Are you hungry?"

She wasn't until he suggested it. "Is that important?"

"Is it important?" He flickers on again. "I'd be a bad host if I thought otherwise!"

The room where she'd left the handprint is in fact the kitchen. What had she expected? Appliances, countertops, spice racks, an ostentatious array of copper-bottomed pots? A microwave, shelves stocked with canned tuna, a breakfast nook? Had their equivalent ever occupied this clean and airy but otherwise empty room? How long has it been empty? Centuries, millennia, a day? An aperture slides open in one wall, side to side; a slither of cool air wraps around her wrists as she reaches inside. A working fridge, after all this time? Don't question it. Within, a blue stone platter, not quite round, its surface pebbled, offers something that looks disappointingly like cubes of tofu.

"What's your favorite fruit?" Govannon asks her. Parts of him are reappearing again, face and hands, a displacement of the air like heat shimmer where his body should have been.

Before she can answer, the colorless cubes become slices of mango, sections of black plums and mandarin oranges, fresh blackberries, dates the size of her thumb.

"It can be chocolate, if you like," he offers, and she tastes it. "Or caramel corn, or ice cream, or sirloin or sauerkraut or even tofu," he goes on, and each flavor lingers briefly on her tongue. "Your first impression was accurate. It's got the nutritional value of tofu. You can live on it. But it doesn't have to taste like tofu. Or, in the case of tofu, should I say *not* taste like it?"

"I'm perfectly happy with this," she says, catching a blackberry before it falls on her shirt. "Aren't you going to have something?"

"Not hungry. Part of the process. Which reminds me, if you ever start feeling not hungry, or in any way 'unreal,' you'll let me know, promise?"

She nods, swallowing. The dates, especially, are wonderful. "Is it important?"

"It's unlikely to happen, but if it does, I'd like you to tell me."

It's apparently all the answer she's going to get.

"Promise." She stops gorging, realizing she's thirsty, hasn't bothered with niceties like napkins, is making a proper pig of herself. Something tells her she will find a handleless mug of the same pebbled blue stone in the fridge where the platter had been. Has it just materialized or had she simply not noticed it, hidden behind the platter? The liquid inside looks like water, but could, she knew by now, taste like anything from grapefruit juice to Diet Coke to a good merlot.

"Unless you'd prefer something hot," Govannon suggests, enjoying the fact that she refuses to act as astonished as he knows she feels. For a moment the aroma of coffee is there, then faded.

"No magic mushrooms?" she wonders wryly. *"Alice in Wonderland,"* she says off his blank look.

"Ah," he says.

"So, when and where do we start?" Dinnertime chat, even if there's no dinner table, and she's the only one eating. "Just jump on the merry-go-round or, I'm sorry, into the revolving door, and see if we can run into one of your peers? Where is the nearest Gat, anyway?"

"No one but TQ has ever been able to enter the physical Gats. Not successfully, anyway. A few others have tried, against our advice, and the consequences have been—well, disastrous for them. Reassuring for us, in that they couldn't follow us, which is why the Two and the One had to travel through space to find us, and even that was accidental."

"So what's the plan?" Karen has finally eaten her fill, wonders if there's a dishwasher, or a way to hand-wash these; the one thing she hasn't noticed is anything that resembles plumbing. "What do we do next?"

"Just put those back inside," Govannon says, meaning the dishes. Karen puts them back in the fridge where she found them; the aperture closes as soon as she takes her hands away.

"I meant—"

"I know what you meant." He looks as if he's going to give her an argument about the "we" part of it again, so Karen heads him off at the pass.

"Tell me about your first time."

"My first time?" He twinkles at her. Then, like most men, he dodges the question. "At first I imagine we were just curious to see where they went. Then we began to see a pattern to them, which suggested we had arrived here from somewhere else. This suggested we ought to try to get back there, wherever 'there' was, just to see."

"I meant you personally," Karen starts to suggest, then lets it alone. She must allow him his ruminative style, his inside-out narrative. It seems to work best for him; he is clearest when he can start in the middle of a story.

"At first, in the Before Time, the earliest Gats were little more than caves, crude passageways underground or under-water, so crude we couldn't tell if they were natural or artificial.

"There was a necessary training period. Not compulsory, not in the sense that any of us *had* to enter the Gats, though I don't recall a single instance of anyone's not wanting to. The training was necessary before we could go. The hardest part was waiting to be old enough. It was the first game we played as soon as we could walk. Every family had a story about some young one getting stuck in a culvert or under a foundation playing at Gats. . . .

"By the time I came of age, the training was codified and rigorous, endless days of simulators on everything from the simple holes in the ground to the most complex space/time Gats. Then trial runs on the stable ones before you were allowed to go solo. There was so much more at stake by then than our individual lives. At least that was what the Formularies stated. It had always been about more than our individual lives, but it took them that long to see it. . . ."

Karen waits, but he seems to lose that strand.

"I remember the smell and the feel of it more than anything else. Isn't that odd?"

•

Do all species refer to the loam between their digits by the name of their world? Dirt, yes, granted, but don't humans in s/f novels refer to themselves as Earthers more often than Dirtballers? Besides, the second has more subtexts and connotations, some of them unpleasant ("You did it in the dirt!? Yuck! Why didn't you just use your hand?" And then there's the story of King Midas whispering his secrets into a hole in the ground, or was that actually a metaphor for something else?), than we care to examine right here.

Thus he, not yet called Govannon, having scrabbled dutifully through the mock-up tunnels on the training ground until his knees were callused over callus, was finally pointed toward one of the tamer Gats and told: "Go!"

He knew this one would not close up on him, unlike the mock-ups, which were programmed for Anything-Can-Happen and, depending on whether that day's instructor was in a sadistic mood, often ended up clamping down and squeezing various body parts more than was strictly necessary for Escape Training. This one really was a tame Gat, never been known to vary its shape by a hairsbreadth, in fact well worn with the footsteps/knee prints of a thousand thousand others before him.

You'd think, he thought, *they'd at least rake over it once in a while, to restore the original shape, try to make it look more natural!* It was actually hardpanned almost to the consistency of crystone in places, though not as slick, and even that got him thinking.

"You think too much. There are times for thought and times for action!" his Preceptors were wont to lecture him.

"What if there are times to do both together?" he'd answered back, and none of them called him timid after that, but chose different adjectives instead.

But right now, seeing the roof of the tunnel slope down and, more to the point, seeing the footprints turn to knee prints just a little ahead of where he was standing and wondering how long he could continue walking, even stooped, before he'd have to crawl, he was thinking: *Why are the Gats the one place on the planet where crystone doesn't grow?*

Because he'd had a momentary vision of himself, having gotten to the Other Side and then turning back as he'd been instructed (though no one told him how far it was to the Other Side or what was there or why he couldn't stay a while and, like all trainees, he'd taken the Secrecy Oath not to tell another trainee about it, ever), had this vision of dutifully turning back and finding his way blocked by an overgrowth of blooming crystone, and having to—what? Dig his way around it? No tools of any kind were allowed in this Gat; he'd known that going in. Dig out barehanded, if he could, or go back?

Too late to think about that now. He made a mental note

to remind himself when he got back, if he got back (did he recall any instance of casualties in this Gat?), he would ask about the stone.

For now, feeling the roots of things brushing the top of his head, some of them long enough to tendril into his eyes, he gave up stooping and resigned himself to crawl. In front of him, he became aware of a vague luminescence and a sense that the walls got even closer. No twists or turns that he could see, just a straightaway, but narrowing. He wasn't claustrophobic—at least he hadn't been when he'd started out—but wondered how far he was expected to go. He was almost full grown, but not as big as some adults he knew who'd traveled the Gats, so it couldn't be that he'd get stuck.

Could it?

It was damp here, too, and smelled of relict. That is, of the stuff between his fingers. Dirt, soil, loam, the synonym for what they called their planet then, which wasn't Relict yet because it wasn't yet. Which was to say that all of them still lived there, except for the ones who were Away, and so their name for their place, which might even have been Place or, like Earth, named after some ancient god, if they'd in fact had ancient gods, their name for the planet they lived on was not yet That-which-was-left-behind, but simply Place, soil, loam, dirt, earth/Earth, stuff underneath your fingernails, if you have fingernails, what you'll scrub out with a nail brush when you get home but which, for now, smells rather nice.

Sweet, fecund, almost warm, reminding him of other things in his experience that were sweet and warm and fertile and smelled nice. Good for growing things. Especially good for growing things, to judge from the number of roots hanging in front of his eyes by now. You'd think (he thought, thinking again) with all the trainee traffic down here the roots would wear away as much as the soil, or someone would get impatient and break them off as they went. There weren't any regulations against that, as far as he knew. Well, maybe they had in fact been cut back and just kept growing. Fecund. Tickling his nose and ears, grabbing at him. But the smell, the feel, of Place beneath his hands and knees, was comforting. Damp enough to soak through to the skin now; he could feel it even through the calluses. An urge to stop and muck about in it like a child. Was there enough oxygen in here? The giddiness he felt wasn't entirely physical.

For some reason he would never understand, he raised one muddy finger out of the muck and tasted it, licked the sweet soil off it. That would be his trademark from thereon. Wherever the Gats took him, he would taste the soil.

•

"Interesting . . ." he muses now, touching his fingers to his lips thoughtfully. "In the Pit in Avaricum, I had the strangest sense of déjà vu. I'm not sure if it was claustrophobia—I'd never been claustrophobic before, not after so many lifetimes in the Gats—or if it was because the soil on Earth tasted like the soil here."

The Pit. One of those subterranean shafts found in certain pre-Christian Celtic settlements, some dating back to the Bronze Age, dug straight down as much as forty meters deep, filled with bones and broken pottery and deemed "mysterious" by some later scholars. As if the sharpened tree trunk set upright at the bottom and the traces of human blood didn't suggest what they had been used for. A perceived need to propitiate the local gods had sent Govannon to the bottom of such a pit, with Karen helpless to prevent it.

Now she is breathing hard, remembering. Yes, the carnage that followed, forty thousand dead, including deaf Sequanna, who had been her closest friend, and possibly Ryalbran her almost-lover, and so many more, yes, all that was with her, too. But Govannon's death most particularly, though she never witnessed it, though he was here before her, clearly alive, haunted her more completely. The others were doomed by history, dead millennia before she was born, but Govannon had chosen his fate.

"So you did go through with it." Is there a trace of accusation in her voice? Criticism, at least. *Look what you put me through! And for what?* "I thought you might have magicked your way out of it at the last minute. Considering that everyone was going to die anyway, everyone but Aoife and the baby . . ."

"And Grainne, who was called Ugly, though she was not," he reminds her. "No, I had given my pledge to the Old King, and I kept my word."

"Did it—" Even as it escapes her mouth, she thinks: What a stupid question! "Was it . . . painful? Did it hurt?"

"Of course!" He crosses his eyes at her, teasing, to tell her it's all right, more than two thousand years past as she understands time and no longer important, but she will not be comforted. "Impaled through the liver by a sharpened stake as thick as my wrist, and you ask me if it hurt? And you slept through it!"

He is teasing her, trying to get her to express the anger she invariably turns inward, transforming it into grieving. For what he has in mind, that will not do.

"And whose fault was that?" she snaps. This is anger. Good. Her fists are clenched, her voice shrill. "While we're on the subject, you did something to me. That was no natural sleep. You—I don't know—cast some sort of spell on me to keep me out of it, make certain I wouldn't be there. You—"

Her own rage, at being duped not once but twice, amazes

her. Are they having a lovers' quarrel? A bit one-sided, if that's what it is.

"What would you have done if I hadn't?" he asks gently.

He has a point. She couldn't have rescued him. The gods and the Old King had spoken and, after all, he had volunteered. The sacrifice would have transpired no matter what she did, the Romans would have attacked the next day regardless, everything would have turned out as it had. What could she have done? Borne witness? Could she have stood there and watched him die, or would she have made a scene?

"I don't know what I would have done," she says at last.

"You see?" he answers.

SEVEN

Far more dangerous than any physical Gat was the Gat of the mind. Even though we turned away from the Inside, we retained the gifts we had learned, to shape ourselves and our world. With enough mental effort, we no longer needed tools, vehicles, anything but power of mind. As long as we could teach these skills to our children, we thought we would be content once the last of the travelers was dead.

"Those who had been exclusively space travelers seemed to accept their retirement. They became raconteurs, historians, tellers of tall tales, invited to every social gathering, as merry as the storytellers about Gwylwyd's hearth in Avaricum."

Karen sees the lost pre-Christian city against a backdrop of flame, first the tame fire of the Old King's hearth, later the fire she herself, in her role as Grainne the Ugly, set as a manner of funeral pyre for the forty thousand the Romans slaughtered. This time the scene does not appear in the air between her and Govannon, but does she only imagine the reflection of those long-ago flames in his eyes?

"No family gathering was complete without some grandparent shape-shifting to entertain the kiddies." Govannon chuckles, as if at some particularly memorable event. Karen is confused. He must be speaking historically; he can't possibly have been there. If the War Between happened after the Gats had been sealed for fourteen generations, how long ago was that? "But there was also envy, growing unrest among the young ones coming up, who had never been permitted the opportunity to go Inside themselves, but had to be content with secondhand tales, hand-me-down skills. There were . . . incidents.

"Those who had been time travelers were less fortunate. Uncertain of their memories, many of them slowly went mad. Some could not free themselves of the shapes they had assumed on the Inside, others reverted to their trans-species selves as feeling more familiar than the selves they had been born to."

Were you one of them? Karen stops herself from asking, reminding herself that however many times he may have retraced his own and even earlier time lines, he was born long after all of this was over.

Wasn't he?

"Even after the last of them had died, a kind of narrow streak of psychosis ran through all our civilization, because too much had changed. Our cities continued to rebuild themselves, but our arts and sciences grew moribund, our population dwindled. The only things that flourished were weeds, and argument. And then came the War Between, and we were forced to get involved again."

Karen suppresses a yawn. Govannon notices. Before she can explain that it's not boredom but an inability to keep the time lines straight, he says: "You're exhausted. And being very brave about it. As you said yourself, too much information at once. There's no rush. And you need sleep."

She hadn't until he mentioned it. Suddenly everything else is forgotten. The rooms that a moment ago had held no furniture suddenly suggest that, at the far end of one of them, there might be a very comfortable bed, with clean sheets and a fluffy quilt, and a *makura* pillow identical to the one she'd left at home. As she passes the wall where her hand-print had been, Karen notices it is gone.

•

7616Mycelia forced her weary body to move from her office to the rear of the lab, where the cultures greeted her with their throbbing purplish glow. Row upon row of rhomboidal containers, seventy-seven in all, each one containing the hope that it would be *the* one. Scrolling readouts danced in 3-D suspension above each one. 7616Mycelia moved methodically from one rhombus to the next; they glowed yellow-orange, fading to red and back to purple as she first neared, then passed them.

7616Mycelia willed one of them, any one, to show sufficient growth against the culture medium to indicate that it had responded to the recombinant protocol and could be tried as a vaccine. Not one would oblige her.

You had to mention magic mushrooms! Karen reminds herself, trying to banish Disney movies and the strains of Tchaikovsky from her mind and failing.

The new day's breeze had woken her, or was it a hand caressing her face? Once more Govannon's eyes and teeth were the first thing she saw. The rest of him might have been sitting on the edge of the bed, watching over her. She sat up, yawned, stretched, thought *Good morning, did you sleep well?* She'd been trying to convince herself that if she squinted hard she could see more of him, when suddenly Mycelia and her laboratory were projected flat against the far wall, like an old-fashioned 8-mm home movie.

Karen accepts this with as much suspension of disbelief as she possesses. This can't be yet another Relict projection.

She's not awake yet; it has to be a dream. Telepathic jellyfish were one thing, but walking fungi in lab coats?

"No, it's real," Govannon stage-whispers in her nearer ear. Does she only imagine his hands on her shoulders, like yesterday at the canyon? "And I appreciate your skepticism. They don't really look like that."

"Then why—?"

"To protect their privacy. As much as we would yours if we found it necessary to share your history with another species."

"But—" she begins, then realizes he is reading her mind again. She twitches her shoulders beneath his invisible hands. "Please don't do that! And why are we whispering?"

Before them, "onstage," as it were, Mycelia—Karen refuses to use the numerical prefix—rubbed her eyes and sighed. At least, she used one of the palps around what Karen assumes is her mouth to stroke an area in under the rim of her mushroom cap which sparkled from time to time, suggesting visual organs, and her defeated posture suggested exasperation.

"Don't do what?" Govannon asks.

"Read my mind. I mean, I love you, but speaking of privacy . . ."

"Sorry!" he says. "Sometimes I lose the boundaries. Do you really?"

Govannon's breath is definitely tickling Karen's ear; she fights the urge to scratch.

"Do I what?" If Mycelia could rub her eyes, Karen can scratch her ear. She does.

"Love me."

Karen isn't playing. "Shh, I'm watching this." Then she realizes something else. "*Have* you 'shared' humans with other species?"

"Shh," Govannon replies in kind. "I'm watching this. . . ."

The projection shimmers for a moment, almost like Govannon, then refocuses. For the first time it occurs to Karen that she arrived on Relict without her glasses and doesn't seem to need them.

•

7616Mycelia had gone without sleep for days now. As she moved away from the cultures, which remained stubbornly unchanged no matter how often she checked them, she could not even say how long it had been since her eyes had closed. She was beyond pain, beyond feeling, but not beyond fatigue. Was it better to soldier on until she collapsed, or to rest? For a moment, only a moment . . .

No. She inhaled sharply, drawing as much of the laboratory's rarefied air into her lungs as she could to cleanse herself. Something inside her seemed to shift, a wave of nausea swept over her, then passed. Nausea was not one of the symptoms of Plague, she reminded herself distractedly. She inhaled again, feeling strangely stronger, fresher, ready for another shift, or three, or however many it would take to solve this. There was also a realization, from what source she did not know, that she could, *would* solve it.

She returned to the cultures, her glance drawn, for reasons she would never understand, to #89003425607. It *moved*. Actually changed its position in the dish. Not some subcellular pavane visible only under the 'scope but an outright pirouette, visible to the naked eye, then gone so swiftly it might have been imaginary. Except that the alarm bleeped. Beyond the chronic buzz of weariness in her ears, 7616Mycelia heard it. And grabbed for the paper printout and saw the hiccup, barely a hairsbreadth different from the surrounding field.

More energized than she had felt since her first mating, 7616Mycelia locked the 'scope in place and ran the recorder back, saw the dance again. And, replaying, saw it again and again and again. Knew it for what it was, and ran the schematics to duplicate it. Within a day she would have sufficient culture to begin purifying it for an experimental vaccine. After that, others could take over the inoculations and she could sleep, although her excitement was such that she thought she might never need to sleep again.

•

The movie ends. Karen half expects to hear the flap of loose tape against the reel of an unseen projector.

"That was you, wasn't it? Slipping into Mycelia's skin, helping her stay awake those few extra minutes."

"Not me personally, but one of us," Govannon replies, taking shape as he speaks. Face and hands, arms and legs, a kind of shadow where his torso ought to be, the window framing the garden partly visible through him. "That might have been Pangolin, one of the few who was able to go transgender. Came in handy on worlds where it wasn't as simple as male/female. Always promised to show me how he did it, but somehow he never got around to it. Bit of a bullshit artist, very cagey about his trade secrets. As for why we were whispering, this one frightened me just a little. It's the first time I know of that a memory has intruded within a private dwelling."

"Is it dangerous?" Karen asks, not for the first time. She's been wondering with a small corner of her mind where this wonderfully soft one-piece garment she's wearing has come from, and why she feels as if she's already showered, washed her hair, and brushed her teeth before she's even gotten out of bed. Obviously Govannon has somehow caused all this while she slept. Probably a mere bag o'shells for a shape-shifter, if he were here. But since he isn't—and come to think of it, how did last night's dinner change its shape if he didn't, couldn't, touch it? It's making her head hurt again. He sees it.

"Not dangerous. Impossible."

That's gotten her attention.

"The stone that grows cannot retain memory," he explains, as if it's something he learned on his first day of school, and it's only now occurred to him that this is something she might not know. "Because as it grows, the molecular structure changes and the memory is lost. So that scene should not have presented itself here, even if it had been my personal memory, which it wasn't."

"Maybe the stone on that wall has stopped growing?" Karen offers, arching her back, stretching, getting out of bed, wondering what to do next. "The projection did seem very flat, against the wall instead of three-dimensional like the others. Okay, I'll shut up now," she says against his silence. When it goes on too long, something else occurs to her, a little connection in her brain, an almost audible synaptical snap. "Govannon? Maybe it's part of the same glitch that sent all of you away? The way you winked out for a moment yesterday . . ."

He nods. "That's occurred to me, too."

"It's a mystery," she suggests. The long silences are making her nervous. She tries to make light of it. "Maybe you should have gotten a mystery writer instead."

"I did," Govannon says vaguely, still studying the wall where Mycelia had been. "She didn't work out. . . ."

•

Karen gapes at him.

"There have been others?"

Does she mean other writers or other women or other

women writers? Yes. It was the kind of question she might ask a human lover, the kind of question, pre-AIDS, that Dear Abby and Ann Landers adamantly insisted one should *not* ask. But Karen always thought it was the kind of question that, given the proper lead-in, one ought to ask. One could always be told it was none of one's business, and that was when one could, and should, back off.

"Yes," he admits, giving her a sidelong look. "It was important to have someone with me who was firmly rooted in a single time line. I made the assumption, after only a few lifetimes among your kind—arrogant of me—that most humans were."

" 'Someone'?" It is difficult for her to ask: "Just anyone?"

His face softens into a smile at the corners. "Well, it helps that you're a writer. I've always admired writers, those who possess the flexibility to bend their imaginations around the fictionally possible without losing the here and now. And writing, fictional or otherwise, as you can surmise from the circumstances under which my kind evolved"—he gestures at the walls, implies the planet as a whole, the stones that grew, and those that didn't—"was not an art we developed overmuch.

"But it also helps that you're you, Karen. You're very strong of character. Never underestimate that. I watched how you wove in and out of time in your fiction and in life, without ever losing sight of who you are. I especially admire that about you. . . ."

She'd hoped he would say something like *Because you're unique in all the world. Because you're the only one who can help me. Because I love you.* Well, maybe not all of them. Two out of three would have been acceptable. Even one, any one of the three, Karen thinks, though she's partial to *I love you.* But any one of them would be fine. Really. Unless that was what he meant by what he said, or is she projecting?

"But it didn't necessarily have to be me," she persists. Why can't she just let it alone? "Any writer with a 'sense of self' would have been fine."

"No, not any writer, a *good* writer!" he insists. Karen sets her jaw, waiting. "And, I'll admit, it helps that you're a woman. I *like* women. . . ."

"Obviously."

Govannon chooses his next words carefully. "I have to be honest with you. There were many. Don't ask me for a number; what would it mean to you? Accept that I say 'many' and leave it at that. Understand, I never . . . made the overture. Each of them always asked me first. Just as you did. 'Let me come with you' or 'I want to come with you,' only to change their minds once they saw what was entailed. No one of them but you has made it this far."

"All of them women?"

"Yes. Does that surprise you?"

"Not in the least."

"But it offends you."

"No. That was the past. . . ."

". . . Which suggests that you'll be the only one from now on. Please don't make that assumption, because I can't be sure. What I have to do, finally, is larger than—I don't say more important than—but more encompassing than, any individual who assists me with it. Do you understand that?"

Her chin quivers. "Entirely!" she snaps, thinking: *Just once I'd like to find a male of any species who will love me for myself and not just for what I can do for him!*

"I'm sorry," he says, and she knows he means it.

•

Well, what did she expect? Maybe she's secretly been writing one of those novels with Fabio on the cover after all. If she hadn't jumped in the sack with him in Avaricum, would she be so eager to get him back into her—um—time line now? Did she really believe that between them they'd come up with some solution to bring him back to Relict? And then what? Would she move in with him in a house that grew new walls and live on tofu that tasted like blackberries? Even if he returned to his original form, which she is more and more convinced really was that two-meters-tall blue thing that looked like a sea cucumber?

As opposed to what? Writing novels that never left the warehouse?

"It's all right," she says, suddenly needing to blow her nose, the first physical discomfort of any kind she's felt since she came here. She sniffles once, and the sensation is gone. "Hell, no, it isn't, but I suppose having some of your attention is better than all of anyone else's. So what do we do now?"

"What do you mean?"

"I mean, how do we find the rest of TQ? That *is* why we came back here."

"No," he corrects her. "It's why *I* came back here. You are here because you asked to come with me."

"And if I said I wanted to go back to Earth, you'd find someone else."

He doesn't answer immediately. "Maybe."

"So you really can't do this by yourself. Look—" she says before he starts protesting again. " 'If you write it, you will know,' right? Déjà vu all over again. It's past time we got started."

"What you mean, 'we,' Kemosabe? This has nothing to do with you."

Here we go again.

"The hell it doesn't!" And now, at last, she is angry. If he were here she might even take a swing at him. "You tricked me into coming here, like you did all those—others. Made me think it was my idea—"

"But it *was!*" he protests, all innocence.

"Yes, of course, it was. But it was yours as well. And if you think you're going to just dump me back on Earth and go off trying to solve this on your own—"

"—or with someone else—"

"—or with someone else—"

"You're jealous!" he says almost gleefully.

"Fuck that! Don't change the subject. I'm not going back without at least having a shot at it."

"A shot at what?"

"Writing your damn novel, obviously! You've been testing me. Deciding if I'm worthy. Seeing if I've got the Right Stuff."

"Not deciding if you're worthy, no. Never that. You are more than worthy, Karen. But as to the Right Stuff—"

"Auditioning me!" Karen fumes. "Just like every fucking petulant-child editor I've ever worked with. 'I don't know what I'm looking for, but I'll know it when I see it.' Three chapters and an outline that'll sit on your desk for eight months unread, because I'm so low on the food chain you know you can get away with it. What's next? The form letter with the line about how it 'does not suit our needs at the present time'? Or is it even about that? Is it more a question of my paying the price for all the other women in your life who 'didn't work out'?"

He is a little boy with his hand in the cookie jar. He chews his lip, tries to look contrite. Karen is having none of it.

"It *is* about me," she insists. "You want me to write it for you."

"That much, yes," he admits at last.

"And it's very possible I'm the only one who can."

"Possible, yes, but—"

"I'm not asking you for likely. Possible will do."

"Possible," he concedes at last. "If you will."

Shit, Karen thinks. *Here we go again!*

•

If she will. How can she not?

"If you write it, you will know." It was what the S.oteri had wanted from her. Or was it Max Neimark the Famous Director who first suggested it, after the S.oteri had decided she was altering their reality and tried to stop her? Or had she thought of it herself? Or was it all a series of layers— S.oteri manipulating humans, TQ manipulating S.oteri, whoever built the Gats manipulating TQ, and she at the heart of the onion?

Once upon a time, she had saved a planet. The next time it had been a single human being. What now?

Save Govannon? Yes, absolutely, no question. Save the rest of TQ if she can? Of course. But save them how, from what?

The first hundred pages are the hardest, she reminds herself. Could she handle the physics this time around? Time as Möbius strip, memory as *Rashomon,* everyone's version different?

Why couldn't she have been one of those facile s/f hacks who turned out potboilers like litters of kittens, one of those writers whose editors actually called *them* and asked them to write novels about singing spaceships or spacefaring elephants? Why did it always have to be so complicated?

Shit.

"I am an actor absent a script," Govannon suggests. "Oh, a talented actor, certainly; I can improv for days, but not for an entire lifetime, much less several. And it may come to that. If I cannot find the rest of my kind, and then find my

way back, the only path I can see clear is to choose one of
the lives I have lived in the past, and live it through. In the
event, I will need structure, narrative, character development, plot, and theme. I need to know what happens next.
And since, in some alternate universe, you found an editor
smart enough to buy your story about Anna . . ."

". . . who in real life, or at least what passes for real life in
any writer's life, is a real person who just happens to be
married to one of the humans you were . . ."

"Exactly."

Exactly what? Karen wonders. She sighs, in lieu of tearing
her hair out.

"And if I write it, I will know. Okay, I surrender! I mean,
what else have I got to do?"

•

"You must have kept records," she suggests over breakfast.

"Records?" For an instant, the image of an old hard-
plastic 78 on a hand-cranked Victrola, complete with oversized audiohorn, conjured out of Johann's memory or
perhaps Jakob Bower's, hangs in midair between them.

In spite of everything she's seen so far, this catches her off
guard. First she giggles, then she sighs.

"Histories, archives," she corrects herself, and the image
dissolves like smoke rings. "Something . . . written down."

"Mostly we kept it all in our heads. Eidetic memories. In
the Before Time."

"Like *Fahrenheit 451* in reverse," Karen says.

He considers for a moment. "That seems right. I think
Jake Bower read the book, or saw the movie. I don't remember which now; if I think about it, sometimes I see
images, sometimes words. Well, maybe he did both. Read
the book and saw the movie. But I know what you mean.
It never occurred to us to record it anywhere"—he watches

her wait for the Victrola to appear again, enjoying her re-action when it doesn't—"not in written form, because we assumed either we or the stone would always remember it. Shortsightedness at the least, maybe a touch of arrogance."

"And by the time you realized your memories were being altered by the very act of traveling, it was too late."

"Exactly. There are places, like the canyon, where some memories are stored, but we can't be sure of their reliability, because they change, depending on who's remembering them and when. For instance, Mycelia's story."

"In one version, TQ—let's say it was Whatsisname. Pangolin?—stood by and did nothing and she never noticed the growth in the petri dish. In another, he intervened and she was able to save her world from Plague."

"Perhaps. You see, it's not my memory, so I can't be sure. But it is a perfect example of what went wrong. At first we just acted on impulse, the way you did, through Margarethe, when you rescued that little girl in the cellar in Berlin. But, just as you did, we had second thoughts after we had acted."

Karen notices that today he seems more "present" when he explains things. She can actually see all of him, wearing the same kind of garment he's dressed her in, more trans-lucent than transparent, more a saintly apparition than a ghost, on this second day here. Maybe if he just keeps talking the thing will solve itself?

"As we got more sophisticated and began calculating long-range permutations and realizing, for example, that having saved one-quarter of the population of Mycelia's world from Plague in her time, we hadn't taken into consideration her species' incredible proliferative capabilities. Unchecked, they'd have overpopulated the planet within a century. Those who survived the famines and droughts and oppor-tunistic infections would most likely have begun to slaughter each other which, their weaponry being what it was, would leave ninety percent of them dead. Unless, of course, we intervened again."

"So what actually happened?" Karen wants to know. Or does she? What if he told her TQ had gone back to Mycelia's world and restored the Plague? Or that maybe the first time line was the way it happened after all? But before she can withdraw the question, she sees a look of genuine distress flicker across his features like heat lightning. It alarms her. She's never seen him angry or afraid, and doesn't know which would concern her more. "Govannon?"

"I don't know!" he says, sounding suddenly like a bewildered child being asked to perform a task clearly beyond him. Hearing his own tone, he stops, breathes, gathers himself. "I'm holding two versions in my mind. One in which we did nothing, and the Plague killed a third of the population. Another in which one of us helped Mycelia stop the Plague and the planet was overpopulated within two generations . . . now a third, where we intervened again to stop the food riots and . . ."

He blinks, frowns, shakes his head. "There's also a fourth possibility. That Mycelia's world is fiction. A speculative novel written during our so-called Middle Era, if there was such a thing . . ."

He sits with his hands clasped between his knees, looking as close to defeated as Jacob the Brewer did when his beloved wife, Elspeth, died. Karen reaches out to him now as she did then, though this time her hand stops just short of his shoulder as she remembers just in time.

"I'm here," is all she says. And then she's not.

EIGHT

French sky above Japanese garden. Anna and Peter sat on the couch by the fireplace, exchanging glances as the little melodrama played out. Of the two strangers who'd arrived silently through the garden, not even setting off Margot who, all eight pounds of her, would otherwise have flung herself at them in a barking frenzy, the one who'd identified himself as Killian did all the talking. His unspeaking companion, who hadn't identified himself at all, pretended to study the garden through the sliding glass doors leading out of Peter's living room.

"Dr. Bower took a meeting with David ben Shahan in a coffee shop in Prague on Thursday, then dropped off the radar," Killian said. "The assumption was that ben Shahan had some information for him about a contact in Vienna who could lead him toward what he was looking for."

For someone who'd had two violent shocks in the span of only a few days, not to mention a lot of cloak-and-dagger stuff in between, Anna felt surprisingly giddy. *I'm trapped inside an episode of* The X-files! she thought, crossing her eyes at Peter—it seemed the only reasonable response to the drivel coming out of Killian's mouth—and for the next few moments Peter had trouble controlling his facial muscles.

"We have no idea where he was or what he was doing

until we picked up his trail in Vienna four days later," Killian concluded humorlessly, completely unaware that he was being mocked. "Did he call you at all during that time, Mrs. Bower?"

"He called me when he arrived in Prague," Anna said carefully, wondering if even that was revealing too much. The giddiness was gone as quickly as it had arrived. "We don't necessarily speak every day when he's away. Sometimes it isn't convenient."

"Convenient for whom?" Killian challenged her.

"Either of us," she shot back, too quickly.

"So after that initial call from Prague, he did not call you again until he turned up in Vienna?" Killian asked, attempting to lead her, but Anna was not to be led. "I'll take that as affirmative," he said off her silence. "Right. Did he call you from Vienna?"

"I was in New York," she said carefully. "Consulting for a gallery. I'm an art historian. I also do restorations," she started to explain. Needlessly.

"We know who you are, Mrs. Bower. So he didn't call you from Vienna?"

"He knew I'd be traveling that day, coming home. Cab to the airport, the flight, cab home. Six, seven hours in transit and, no, before you ask, I don't have a cell phone. Hate the damn things. So the most he could have done was leave a message on the answering machine, which I wouldn't have picked up until I got home, because I've never mastered the art of picking up calls by remote." Which was their usual procedure when both of them were traveling simultaneously, and when she had run through the messages and not found one from Jake, she had been concerned, but Killian didn't need to know that. "Then with the difference in the time zones, one or the other of us would have been asleep. Besides, he was due back home the day your two goons showed up. . . ."

She was talking too much, saying too little. They all knew it. Giddiness squelched, as if it had never occurred, replaced by a dead still solemness. Anna looked to Peter, who'd been sitting with Margot in his lap, long fingers lost in the little dog's silky hair. He was telegraphing. *Shut up, Anna!* she told herself, where Peter never would.

"They weren't *our* 'goons'—!" Killian said impatiently, then realized he was saying too much and snapped his too-square jaw shut. Did Anna only imagine his silent companion, who still had his back to them, suppressing a guffaw? She was sure she'd seen his shoulders hunch, as if with silent laughter.

"So whose goons were they?" she demanded.

"I'm not at liberty to say. All you need to know is that coming here was possibly the worst thing you could have done."

Anna thought of the circumstances under which she and Peter had bolted the States and arrived here. She doubted that very much.

"And why is that?"

"Once more: Dr. Bower got off the bus in front of the Opera House, disappeared down an alley, and then nothing," Killian temporized, as if to say he was asking the questions, not answering them. "A day and a half later, two men claiming to work for us turn up on your doorstep, and inform you that he's dead. You contact Peter, the two of you leave the States and end up here."

"For the third, and final time, yes!" Anna said wearily. Something occurred to her. "Do you have proof of what you've just told me? If you had people following Jake, you'd have photographs, at least."

Killian's silent partner had abandoned the view of the garden and was examining the room, fingering knickknacks like an ill-mannered child. Anna wondered why Peter, always particular about his things, didn't say something.

"We weren't following him," Killian said. "It was passive observation. Your husband was traveling between two hot zones. Our surveillance people have more to do than devote themselves to one aging art collector. Ben Shahan's people told us about the meeting in the cemetery."

Scratch David from the guest list from now on! Anna thought, keeping her face neutral, expectant.

"Dr. Bower made all his travel arrangements in his own name," Killian went on. *Amateur!* his tone implied. "We knew from his previous trips that one of his contacts in Vienna has a law office near the Opera House, so it was easy to pick him up there. But no photos."

"They've all got Palm Pilots now," Peter said quietly. "They message each other. I'm not quite sure how they scramble their messages, but there's so much crap flying around out there it probably doesn't matter."

"Thank you!" Killian said drily, brushing Peter off like a mayfly. "Mrs. Bower, we want to find him as much as you do. I'm going to ask you to help me fill in what went before."

•

It had begun, Anna wanted to say, though not to Killian, in their living room, spinning out to encompass, it seemed, the greater portion of the post-Soviet world.

Two or three times a year, Anna and Jake threw a party, for no other reason than that it was time to throw a party. They were always careful to avoid holidays and anniversaries and people's birthdays. It was a Mad Hatter sort of party— not quite an unbirthday party, but an unparty party.

This particular one was a summer's-finally-over party. Anna had cranked up the town house's air conditioning to compensate for the usual humid torpor oozing out of Foggy Bottom and across the river into Alexandria and refused to open any of the doors. No, they would not go outside to mill about on the patio and get eaten alive by mosquitoes the size of bats, or dive-bombed by bats the size of 757s. They would sit on her comfortable chairs in her spacious living room and talk and laugh and listen to Mozart and admire Jake's collection of paintings by artists no one else had ever heard of—

"Yet," he would caution them, raising a finger didactically. "No one's heard of them yet."

—and eat delightful small appetizers someone else had prepared, followed by a sit-down dinner without place cards so that anyone could sit beside anyone they chose.

The only rules were that there were no rules. Dress the way you want, talk about anything you wish, except politics. Anna's were the only D.C.-area parties where no one was allowed to talk politics.

And who were her guests that night? A couple of Jake's fellow therapists and their significant others, a few people Anna knew from the Smithsonian, a handful of friends of friends invited to tag along because they happened to be in town, Peter of course with one of his dancers, and Anna's sister Caitlin, an attorney, who also happened to be in town, testifying before a Senate subcommittee.

Anna, having told the caterer's people to go home early, had been in the kitchen with Caitlin, spooning caramel sauce onto a breathtakingly beautiful flan, neither of them wearing aprons, daring the fates to spill something on their little black dresses, listening to the tinkle of laughter and cutlery from the other rooms.

". . . can't believe he's wearing that cape in this weather!" Caitlin was saying about Peter. She was tall and rawboned, with a redhead's high coloring, though at her age the red hair was the result of having a very creative hairdresser. Looking at her, Jake's two young film buffs on the bus in Vienna would have said at once "Katharine Hepburn, *nicht war?*" and convulsed in giggles. No resemblance to the petite woman beside her despite the shared last name; even as a child Anna hadn't had to tell strangers, "Oh, I'm adopted."

"He says it's my fault," Anna confided, licking caramel sauce off her thumb. "Should we have warmed that, do you think? You know, cold flan, warm caramel?"

"Too late now, unless you want to lick it all off and start over," Caitlin remarked, considering it. "If you'd asked the caterer before he left . . . What does he mean, it's your fault?"

"Because we've got such a gorgeous entrance foyer, he says. He feels obligated to wear something flamboyant so he can swing in and out of it and do justice to the entrance foyer."

"He's just trying to do justice to that cupcake he brought with him!" Caitlin snorted. "Isn't he plucking them rather young these days?"

"Oh, he's not sleeping with Justin," Anna said confidently. Peter told her everything. "He says he's just trying to teach him table manners. The kid's from Wisconsin or some-place. . . ."

Just then Jake appeared, wearing the Look.

"Uh-oh," Anna stage-whispered to Caitlin. "Time to haul out the suitcases."

She'd seen Jake head-to-head with someone she knew, just by feel, was one of his clients, and wondered why the man had been willing to accept an invitation to his therapist's dinner party, much less why Jake had extended it. Ordinarily Jake was ironclad about keeping his various worlds separate, and Anna had had a watchful eye on him and his guest, who barely spoke to anyone else, all evening. Now when she saw the gleam in Jake's eye she realized all his worlds had just converged.

Or collided. She heard Peter's raucous laugh from the dining room and watched as caramel dribbled as if of its own will over the lip of the serving dish and onto the countertop.

"Careful!" Caitlin covered the awkwardness of the moment with a flourish of the dishtowel. She saw the sparks passing between Jake and Anna, wordlessly after all these years, and knew it was time for her exit. "May I take the dessert with me, at least?"

Anna's hand on her arm stayed her. "Don't run away just because of us. Jake? Outside?"

"Better," he acknowledged. Anna followed him outside to the mugginess on the patio.

She felt the air press in on her from all sides, tropical, the silk of her dress clinging as perspiration rose to the surface of her skin. She lifted her shoulder-length hair up off her neck, as if that would make a difference. Hot weather destroyed her. Most years she wouldn't even be in D.C. in August, would wangle a commission in San Francisco or Calgary just to get away. She'd scheduled things badly this year. She took Jake's hands in her own and tilted her head up to meet his eyes.

"This is a big one, isn't it?"

"Maybe the biggest one yet."

•

Cross-fade: "Interior: Home Life: The Second District. Believed to have been completed sometime in the artist's middle period, circa 1933–38. The Second District referred to is the so-called Jewish Quarter of Vienna as it existed in the artist's time. No longer quite a ghetto, it was by this time inhabited mostly by religious Jews and émigrés from the Hungarian countryside. Prosperous Jews had begun to enter the mainstream of Viennese society decades before; the bourgeois and the very poor remained in the Second District until Hitler's time.

"The work depicts the parlor and a view into the kitchen of a middle-class flat. The excess of furniture, shabby with wear but of good quality, suggests a certain prosperity. While the artist does not identify the figures, later critics have judged them to be mother and children, the fine quality of the woman's dark dress precluding the possibility that she is a servant, despite her placement in the kitchen.

"She is turned away, her face obscured. She appears to be kneading bread dough at the wide table. A girl in her early teens works beside her; clever brushstrokes highlight the young woman's long auburn hair, worn braided down her back, which indicates she is not yet old enough to consider marriage. In the foreground, two boys, one about eight or nine, the other somewhat younger, tussle over possession of a small toy horse, while a third, barely a toddler, stands watching, imprisoned in the room beyond, doubtless a bedroom, his prison bars formed by the backs of two dining chairs laid sideways and lashed together. The look on his face is that of longing, suggesting a desire to join his two older brothers, regardless of how rough their play. . . ."

•

Karen is no longer surprised by the sudden changes of scene, the shifting images, a sensation not unlike stepping in and out of a painting that simultaneously begins to move, *Sunday in the Park with George* all over again. She feels a shift in the ambient temperature, the particular warmth of a parlor in a cold climate, heated by a coal stove. She has read somewhere that the stoves in Vienna were notoriously elaborate, great ponderous enameled things, decorated in swirls of color like bone china, dominating a room on their stout legs, emanating heat from their glowing bellies, causing smuts of coal dust to settle on every surface in even the cleanest households.

The writer's eye notes that the double-glazed windows beyond the net curtains are steamed with condensation, the result of too many people breathing in too small a space. Diapers spread over the top of the stove to dry only add to the humidity.

Beyond the glass, snow swirls in desultory flakes caught on an updraft in the courtyard between this flat and the ones on three sides, surrounding. An ancient, ringed city, its fortifications built to withstand invasion by the Turks, Vienna could not expand outward no matter how its population grew; some of the older districts, like the once-named Jewish Quarter, were especially overcrowded.

It was not a poor household, Karen judged, at least not in material goods, though the overstuffed furnishings with their spidery antimacassars, the heavy velvet drapes layered over the sheer net curtains, the small area rugs scattered over the larger room-sized Kirman to hide the worn places were, if not the stultifying Victoriana she'd expected, rather a more Middle European version, much too ornate for her taste. Despite the overall stuffiness, the room seemed barren, lacking.

She can smell goulash cooking in the kitchen, hear the rumble of what was probably a tram in the street below, the muffled sound of church bells, distorted by the snow and the closed-tight windows. The heat of the stove is more noticeable on the left side of her face than on the right. This scene is more "present" than any of the others so far, yet though the action is taking place all around her, she knows she is not actually in the room. She cannot feel the carpet beneath her feet; a hand stretched out to steady herself against the back of an armchair passes through it like a ghost's. There is a sense that she has been in a situation like this before, but she can't remember where or when.

She knows those in the room cannot see her; if she speaks they will not hear. Yet she studies them with a kind of reverence, wanting to know who they are and why, especially the youngest boy. She'd recognize those eyes anywhere.

He stands in the doorway of what is probably the master bedroom, perhaps the only other room in the flat. Trying to peer inside, Karen finds she cannot move, except to turn in a circle. She is a camera, at the mercy of some unseen cameraman. The mother in her wants to intervene and make the two older boys stop fighting; curiosity makes her wonder about the kitchen. And yet it seems she is here only to watch the baby.

Was there ever a more solemn child? Karen judges him to be about eighteen months old, an age when most children ware never still—crawling, walking, climbing, exploring, chattering to themselves and others. It would not surprise her if, being a younger sibling and a boy, he did not talk yet, but somehow she knows that this uncanny silence is his place of safety. His blue eyes very wide, his hair in soft dark waves almost as long as a girl's, he stands very still, watching, making no sound at all.

"I don't think my mother ever looked at me. . . ." The voice is Govannon's, from somewhere behind her, outside the frame, so to speak. "I don't remember ever demanding it. You know how babies are, how they get your attention by making little sounds and smiling, or tugging at you if they can reach you, or, failing those, by crying?"

Transfixed, Karen nods. She can't take her eyes off the child.

"Normal children, normally nurtured, that is. It never occurred to me to try, never occurred to me that I had the right to convey to her: 'Mama, notice me! Pay attention to me! Love me!' Her eldest son had died before I was born, you see. She was afraid to bond with me. Afraid I'd be taken from her, too, I suppose."

The scene dissolves, they are together again. At least, Karen is present and Govannon is somewhere in between, mostly transparent, but improving.

"Whose life was that?" she asks him.

"Mine," Govannon says immediately, then corrects himself: "Johann's. The man you met in the cellar in Berlin."

"Was your—his name really Johann?"

He shakes his head. "That was cover. I spent the war hidden in plain sight. Not the only Jew to do so inside the Reich."

"You were part of the underground, helping to smuggle others out," Karen suggests quietly. Even knowing she can't be overheard, she can't help whispering.

Govannon looks genuinely surprised. "How did you know that?"

Karen shrugs. "I'm extrapolating. Margarethe had American cigarettes in her apron pockets to use for barter. Or bribes. She was out after curfew, looking for someone. That someone was you."

Govannon has grown very still, studying her.

"Sorry!" Karen murmurs, thinking she's stepped over some invisible line. "Too many war movies."

"No, you're exactly right. I knew I'd chosen well this time." Before she can ask what he means, he changes the subject. "Johann's given name was Yakov. My sister Minna—that's she helping my mother in the kitchen—used to call me Yankl. It was Minna who raised me, after my mother died.

"Yakov for Jacob," he muses quietly, as Karen notes how he has slipped through the barrier separating himself and Johann/Yakov, not "him" but "me." "Jacob the Supplanter, born to replace Benjamin, the favored son. Not that I imagine my father loved even Benjamin when he named him. He never loved anyone, least of all himself. As for my mother . . ."

His voice has taken on not quite an accent but a cadence Karen remembers from Johann's speech.

"It was an arranged marriage. Raisl—that was my mother—Raisl's older sister served as matchmaker. Their mother died when Raisl was born. What does that do to a woman, I wonder, knowing her own mother died giving birth to her? Not that it was so terribly uncommon in those days, but to carry that guilt, for something you did not do, from birth . . . what fears must it have put in her mind about her own capacity to live through childbirth? Yet she kept bearing. And then to lose her own firstborn . . . no wonder she couldn't look at me. But a child doesn't know that. A child thinks he's somehow to blame. . . ."

He seems to have forgotten Karen is here, looks at her in bewilderment, suddenly all too human, wearing the expression of an old man who can recall D-Day as if it were last Tuesday but doesn't remember his children's names.

His face begins to alter, a kind of superimposition of older, younger faces, morphing perhaps into every human whose life he'd ever lived, short-term, long-term, down the centuries. Maybe other species as well, Karen thinks, wondering if she'd recognize them as such. Aspects of, dimensions of, in any event, his many incarnations. It might have alarmed her if she hadn't intuited what it was. Now she wonders how humans got by within the limitations of their faces.

"He used to shout at him all the time. . . ." he murmurs, his voice gone deep and mournful. Karen feels the scene around them shift again. "My brother Herman, his second son . . ."

•

Herman's twisted face loomed above the little one.

"Die, die, die!" he chanted in a whisper, spittle flying from his damaged mouth, knobbly fingers poking the baby wherever he could reach him through the slats of the old-fashioned crib, knowing the baby would wince and shy away, though not enough for his little hands to let go of the bars of his prison, but wouldn't make a sound. Wouldn't retreat, either. Something in him had to stand here, the only place from which he could watch them, see the world the Big People inhabited, from which he was, for some reason he could not understand, excluded.

"Die, you little bastard, die! If you get sick and die like Benjamin he'll be too sad to think about me. He'll leave me alone for a while. Too busy to come after me, if you die!" The older boy began shaking the crib, trying to knock the baby off his feet, chanting: "Die, die, die!"

"He was cross-eyed and had a harelip," Govannon explains. "My father loathed the sight of him. . . ."

Johann, Karen thinks. Or rather, Yakov, the baby behind the prison bars. Though even from the tiny bit of the scene she can see, she knows this is not the same apartment. Or is it? The dark bulk of the stove in the corner looks familiar, but she can't be sure. The room is dark; the two boys are alone, the light around them seems artificial in its brightness, like a follow-spot. More like theater this time than a painting or a film. Karen is outside the scene once more. She can't even make out the pattern on the carpet to determine if the furnishings are the same even if it's a different flat.

Herman is about eight or nine years old, loose limbed and awkward. He wears knee pants, his socks are falling down, his shirttail torn and half tucked in. Was it he who had been scuffling with the younger boy over the toy horse before? Karen had only seen him from the back then, hadn't seen his face. She would have remembered his face.

His eyes are the same bright blue as the baby's, but turned cruelly inward with strabismus, almost as if they were staring at each other and not at the world beyond. The bilaterally split upper lip made it impossible for him to close his mouth completely; the loose flesh flaps horribly when he breathes. Does Karen only imagine she hears the chanted schoolyard taunts in Herman's mind, superimposed, soundtrack within a flashback, on the minimalist scene before her?

Most small children would have been terrified at the sight of him, but the baby only stares, dodging the older boy's poking fingers, but then returning, with a kind of stubborn territoriality, to stand in the same spot each time. He shows no fear. Or else he knows there is greater terror yet to come.

"He'd come in with the dark at night, after all day in the shop, the measuring tape still draped around his neck. . . ." Govannon's voice continues. " 'Papa.' What a mockery that word, applied to him! No matter where Herman was, he'd find him; the poor fool never learned to hide the way the rest of us did when we heard his footsteps on the stairs. He would stalk through the rooms looking for him, ignoring my mother's pleas to sit and eat something, rest himself. It was as if his day was not complete until he found someone to torment, someone worse off than he, a scapegoat for his misery.

" 'Monkey!' he'd shout at him. 'Monkey, monkey, monkey!' As if Herman had asked to be born that way! As if he were nothing more than God's joke on the man who had fathered him, and not a human being at all."

"Poor Herman!" Karen whispers, hearing the echoes. "Poor Yakov!"

"No, not Yakov," Govannon is whispering too. "This is Jake. Jakob Bauer, whom you knew as Jake Bower, Anna's husband. Yakov was born before the Great War. This is '36, much later. Within two years the Nazis would be in Vienna. Some of Jake's family would disappear into the Nazi maw; the others would emigrate in '38, first to England, then the States. And at the same time that you see Jake here at this age, Yakov—or Johann, as you knew him—has surmised what the future will bring and begun to learn the geography of the alleys and cellars of Berlin."

Fade to black. Lights up. As if the whole thing were no more substantial than a movie. For the first time, Govannon looks as solid as if he were truly there. He shakes himself all over, his spine and shoulder joints making little cracking noises. The multiplicity of faces recedes from their hold on his features, leaving only himself.

"You're here!" Karen says, reaching out for him.

"Not yet." Her hand passes through him as it did through the chair in Vienna. And the "here" has shifted, too.

"Um, Govannon? Where are we?"

"Oh." He seems to notice the surroundings for the first time. "In the Museum, naturally."

"Naturally," Karen says.

NINE

It looks, she thinks, steadying herself after all these journeys, the way the inside of a very large monastic beehive cell might look, or perhaps a Byzantine cathedral half buried underground, the dome of the Hagia Sofia absent its Moorish arches, a hundred feet high, all of a piece and completely unadorned. Or a Brobdingnagian child's mud-pie house, or the inside of any hollow sphere cut in half and set down on the ground.

The writer notices that the surface seems to change depending on whether it is looked at directly or out of the corner of the eye. Front-on, the walls are adobe-smooth and about the same color as warm brown mud, still with a wet-looking sheen in places, a suggestion of trowel marks here and there. Glanced at obliquely, parallax, they seem to be made of carefully fitted fieldstone, like the so-called beehive cells, characteristic of ninth-century monasteries, that dotted the countryside in remote parts of Ireland. Govannon said the stones that held the memories did not grow. But these walls seemed almost to be breathing.

There's nothing on the walls, either practical or ornamental, not so much as a light switch, a crack, a nail hole, just the smoothness or roughness or both together rising in what, to Karen's untrained eye, seems perfect symmetry to a dome several stories high, suffused with the kind of indoor light one associated with old museums in major cities, though the light has no apparent source. Perhaps the stone itself contained the glow.

There also didn't seem to be any way in or out but, still thinking in s/f terms, Karen assumes it simply isn't visible to her inexperienced eye just yet. They'd gotten in somehow, hadn't they? She isn't quite ready for transporter beams.

The floor is a separate sort of marvel, comprising inlaid tiles of something that looks hard as stone but gives like carpet when stepped on. It also iridesces from what Karen thinks of as its dormant color, a swirl of dark seashell colors like the inside of a mussel shell, to lighter pearlescent "active" hues wherever she sets foot. There is a subliminal sound to it as well, almost of bells half heard from far away on a foggy morning, musical.

The effect is immensely pleasing. Karen finds herself grinning, poking her feet here and there in little dance steps, resisting the urge to spin around and run up and down like a child until she has made her mark everywhere in the huge structure, like an Aborigine singing the landscape of Australia as he walked, so that the thousand thousand generations that came after him would be able to find their way along the same path simply by singing the same song.

She becomes aware of Govannon's Cheshire Cat smile, and stops. Govannon, she notices, leaves no footprints.

"Don't stop," he tells her. "Run or dance, or both if you want. Please."

"The Museum," she prompts, standing very still, intent on seriousness.

"For want of a better term. I suppose it could have many other names—Archive, Library. The place where we kept the knowledge, anyway."

"But you said there were no records."

The Victrola appears again in the space between them, its image projected in several places on the walls around them.

"Tell me you're not doing that on purpose!"

The original image vanishes first, the ones on the walls lingering like echoes for a few seconds longer before they too blink off.

"Just trying to make a point," he says. "Looking for short-cuts, a way to explain to you that just because it wasn't written down doesn't mean we didn't save it. This is another of those places where the stones remember. Only it's more focused than the canyon. The canyon only saves the mem-ories it chooses. The Museum, because we built it, remem-bers everything. Any of us could come here with the knowledge we had gathered elsewhere and 'think' it into the stone. Only as a backup, because at first we kept everything we knew in our minds as well."

"So that when repeated time travel made some of you doubt your own memories . . ." Karen says, chiming her way across to one of the walls and laying her hand against it to see if it will change the way the walls in Govannon's house did. It doesn't. ". . . the stones would retain a 'truer' version of events than your memory might."

She envisions it. With a combination of telekinesis and eidetic memory, who needed card catalogues, microfiche, databases?

"Exactly."

"Wow. Talk about being written in stone," Karen says, as if daring something to appear on the walls. It doesn't. "So what are we doing here?"

"If I were actually here," Govannon says, "I could pull up any memory I chose, mine or anyone else's, and give you a better perspective on our history. But from where I am, I can't seem to draw them out. You don't photograph well, do you?"

Now, there was an odd transition. She didn't. Always ended up grimacing or with one eye closed. Should she be surprised that he knows this?

"No, I don't, as a matter of fact. It's enough to make me wonder if I'm part vampire. How did you know?"

He shrugs. "Because those we 'borrow,' when we're living them, don't photograph well either. However close the match, our personae never exactly match the hosts we're inhabiting. That's why I thought at first you might be one of us."

Karen grows very still, almost afraid to breathe.

"You see, if the host match is good enough, we very seldom recognize each other when we're away from Relict. So we've worked out codes to identify ourselves to each other, words that would be meaningless to anyone else. But even though you didn't respond to the codes, I couldn't help noticing that there's something about you that's out of synch with other humans. . . ."

Karen's always known this. It's been hurled at her ever since the schoolyard, but never offered as a compliment before.

"It might be nothing more than the gift you have of slip-sliding through time in your writing," Govannon is musing, "yet it made me wonder. . . ."

"Is it possible," Karen says slowly, "that I could be one of you without knowing it?"

Even as she asks it, she's not sure what she means. An orphaned TQ left on a human doorstep as a child? Unlike those human children who developed the seeming irrational fear that their birth-parents were not truly their parents, she remembers wishing she was adopted so the pod-people who called themselves her parents would send her back to the pound, give her a better chance at a normal family the next time around.

She knows she's no TQ, but she asks the question anyway. Why not? Why couldn't she be Karen/TQ or TQ/Karen as readily as she had been Grainne and Grethe and Margarethe?

"Doubtful," Govannon says, almost regretfully. "But I did entertain the idea briefly, given how often our paths seemed to cross on Earth."

"But that was the S.oteri. In fact, I'm wondering if this whole thing has to do with S.oteri. Them and their inability to cope with time. Some sort of revenge for taking the telekinesis away. How did you get tangled up with them in the first place? Is there a Gat that leads to their world?"

"Actually, they found us." Does Karen only imagine Govannon is sitting, genielike, in midair? "Same way they found humans. Just reaching out with that telepathic group mind until it intruded on someone else's."

"TQ must have known they weren't ready for telekinesis." Karen's not about to try the midair thing. Since there's nowhere else to sit, she leans her back against the curve of one wall and makes herself comfortable on the floor, which chimes slightly as it settles around her. "Whose idea was it to give them that?"

"It was something of an expediency," Govannon says vaguely. He is chewing his lip in that thoughtful way of his. He looks so solid! Karen wishes more than anything that she could just put her arms around him. "A way to distract them from . . . something they shouldn't have been doing. Another one of those situations that needed tweaking, only this one was more critical than most."

"Meaning—?" Karen prompts him.

"Meaning I can't tell you any more about it. Do me a favor? Try one of your memories."

Karen frowns. "I'm not sure what you mean."

"You hear voices on battlefields."

She has absolutely no recollection of having told him this, but how can she be sure? Their lives have crossed three times in the human past—at least three times that she knows about—and not always in chronological order. Were there other lives she can't remember? She suppresses the very real memory of the Battle of Avaricum, where she arrived too late to hear any voices but those of feral dogs and carrion birds, though she saw and smelled and felt everything else.

"Yes," she says, not wanting to go further.

"Would you like to tell me about it?"

"Not really. Is it important?"

"It might be."

He doesn't say "please," but she hears it.

"All right. My parents—the pod-people—were into bat-tlefields. . . ." she begins, then hesitates. Of what possible interest can this be to him?

"Keep talking," he says, though he is not looking at her but at something she can't see.

"Civil War, Revolutionary War," Karen warms to her subject. "Anyplace within a day's drive where we could tromp around in the hot sun without paying an admission fee, reading plaques and listening to the mother-pod, who considered herself an expert. Ever notice the less some people know about certain things, the more they like to talk about them? . . ."

Early summer 1962, Gettysburg, Pennsylvania. Next July will be the hundredth anniversary of the battle, but Karen's mother will have none of it.

"It'll be nothing but crowds," Gloria Rohmer had announced with what she considered a brilliant line of reasoning. "And everything'll be more expensive. I'm not falling for that!"

Whatever. Karen didn't especially want to be here, but at twelve she has been deemed "too irresponsible to be left home alone while we're away," whatever that might mean. On the cusp of puberty, she is hypersensitized, susceptible to many things, including the migraines her mother will insist she's inventing just to get attention.

"You're making that up!" Gloria said as they left the doctor's office some months earlier, shoving something into her purse that Karen will later deduce is a prescription slip for Cafergot she has no intention of filling. "Flashing lights and feeling sick to your stomach! Dr. Butler says you got that right out of a medical textbook. He says you're making it up so you can get out of doing your homework."

Which medical textbook? Karen wondered at the time, and, later, wondered how her mother imagined a child her age would have access to such a thing. She knows even then that Dr. Butler never said any such thing, or he wouldn't have written the prescription. This is one of countless instances of Gloria's role as revisionist historian.

Dr. Butler—no relation to Rhett—is tall and blond and a southerner, which, to Gloria, who had committed *Gone with the Wind* to memory when she was a girl, were perfectly valid reasons for choosing him as the family physician. Listening to that molasses-laced voice had done more to ease her labor pains than the anesthesia.

The thought of those thick, ungentle fingers, which have poked and prodded Karen through a host of childhood illnesses (he even took it upon himself to do her appendectomy in lieu of a more skilled surgeon) reaching up inside Gloria and dragging her jaundiced and scrawny self out into the light two months prematurely was enough to—

But we digress. The appendectomy scar bears mute testimony to Dr. Butler's relative skills as physician and surgeon. Even its location—why a paramedian incision, when the standard, and less apt to stretch or keloid, was a McBurney?—was sufficient to suggest that some people got by on charm when skill would have been preferable. Not all butchers are found behind the meat counter.

As to butchery, we give you the Battle of Gettysburg, the one and only major battle of the Civil War that transpired north of the Mason-Dixon line. Considered the turning point in the war, just as the Battle of Saratoga was in its time, four score and not quite seven years earlier, considered the point where the British lost it and the Continentals started to gain ground.

Gettysburg had Karen fooled at first, because she thought the sounds she heard were coming from a recording, perhaps from the little audio stanchions set at intervals along the road that wound through the battlefield, a tinny little voice explaining this monument or that plaque, accessible to people in their cars willing to rent an audio set at the Visitors' Center.

"We don't need that!" Gloria Rohmer had announced when Karen's little brother, Ricky, whined about it. "You can read the plaques yourself. It's nothing but a gimmick to make people spend money."

Karen, melanin-challenged as always, just wanted to find someplace out of the sun.

Her father has parked the car near one of the several monuments dotted about the battlefield, which otherwise might just look like fallow cornfields. Dick Rohmer, less than interested—the trip was his wife's idea; he'd seen more than his share of battlefields in the South Pacific, thank you—but not about to argue ("unless you've got a better idea," she'd said, which he hadn't; hasn't really had too many ideas of his own since his wedding day), leans against the hood of the car lighting his pipe. Little Ricky is craning his skinny neck at the bronze officer on his bronze horse while his mother reads to him about Pickett's Charge; when they get home she will coach him in learning Lincoln's Gettysburg Address as a parlor trick to impress the relatives. Karen, unnoticed enough not to warrant the Don't-go-anywhere-where-I-can't-see-you! speech, slips into the shade of a nearby copse of trees.

The local birds, who'd been making some sort of sparrowy group-mind racket as she entered, grow silent, watching her. When she stops to stand more still than the trees—she doesn't shimmer her leaves in the ghost of a breeze the way the trees do—they resume their very important conversation. Braced to hear Gloria's crow-caw ("Karen, get back here this minute or we'll leave without you!"), Karen instead hears other voices.

First, horses. A '50s kid, reared on westerns, she knows the sound, thunder of hooves and jingle of harness, the human shouts and bugle calls, that signify a cavalry charge. There are rifle shots now, waves and waves of them like sheet lightning, and the ground-shaking roar of cannon. A horse screams, echoed by another, then by human shrieks and shouting, sounds of bullets ricocheting, trees splintering with cannon-shot, though nothing moves but the breeze in the canopy.

Karen shades her eyes and squints back toward the sun-bleached road, where she can just make out one of the audio units, a metal post with a squawk box on top, sheltered from the elements by a little rustic roof. The whole thing is distorted by heat shimmer, and about a hundred yards away. The noise can't be coming from that far. Could there be loudspeakers among the trees? And wouldn't the noise bother the birds? They're still gibbering in the trees. Even as she searches, the sound seems to gather itself and Doppler past, as if horse and man have simply ridden through her and passed on.

Wisely, Karen says nothing to the rest of the family when they pile into the broiling car. ("Air conditioning drains the battery, and it costs money." Gloria again.) Later, when they have stopped at the Visitors' Center, she studies a diorama depicting Pickett's Charge. The recorded sounds summoned when the visitor presses a button beside the plaque are similar to what she heard back in the trees, though tinnier, two-dimensional. Karen considers asking one of the park rangers about loudspeakers, but can just hear Gloria carrying on all the way home about her "showing off." Besides, she already knows the answer. What she heard was not a recording.

The following year's battlefield is Saratoga. The contrast with Gettysburg is interesting. This is a low-tech battlefield. No recordings or room-sized dioramas, no outsized bronze and granite monuments, just a smallish visitors' center on a rise overlooking the battlefield, and lines of fence posts marking the British and Continental lines along the rolling hills of Upstate New York. The fence posts are about four feet high, the lower half painted white, the upper half painted red to mark the British lines, blue for the rebels.

Red, white, blue, amid verdant grass green and the darker almost black-green of pines, against the summer-long blue-white of sky in a humid climate. Yes, it is summer again, but even under the hammering sun, thirteen-year-old Karen is feeling chilled. She stands alone just inside one of the blue lines that straggle away over the hills in either direction, ignoring the gaggles of tourists that include her own kin. She is long ago and far away.

Where she is, it is October, and late at night, the air so crisp one could almost snap it off like icicles. There is a campfire, its orange glow perhaps replicated elsewhere on the surrounding hills, though Karen cannot see any of this, only feel it. Her back is chilled by the night air, but the fire warms her belly, face, and hands. She hears two voices talking.

It is difficult to make out their words, which are not the English she knows but the half-Dutch Knickerbocker accent that's the norm hereabouts in 1777. Still, enough words are familiar for her to get the gist.

The speakers are young, two boys not much older than she. What they thought when they signed up would be little more than a prolonged tramp through the woods has long since begun to pall. They know from the nearness of the British fires on the other side that they will fight tomorrow. They do not know if they will live.

Karen hears the creak of saddle leather, the scuff of feet, the snap of burning twigs, what sounds like something being stirred in a cast-iron pot, and then one boy asks another:

"Skeered?"

A grunt of negation is the other boy's answer, followed by a silence.

"Yeah," the first one says with a short laugh, "So'm I."

"So'm I," Karen echoes him.

————

"I'm here," Govannon says when it's over.

Karen knows what he means. It helps.

She shakes it off, like a medium coming out of a trance, a Vulcan emerging from a mindmeld, only to find it there all around her on the walls, Pickett's blue-clad cavalry cutting a caper around Hessian mercenaries in their beetle red cutaway coats over snowy breeches, easy targets for the motley-clad Continentals on the next hill. How, Karen the housewife wonders, did they ever manage to keep their whites so white, marching through rain and snow and mud, washing in river water? One of those historic imponderables, like why the armies of the time marched up to each other in nice, tidy lines until they were close enough to play shooting gallery and obligingly dropped down dead in neat, regimented rows.

Men and their rituals! she thinks. A woman's army, she thinks, would have hunkered down and picked the enemy off from behind rocks and trees, preferring to stay alive. Or simply gone home and made mulled cider and put their feet up and let the men siphon off all that testosterone with grapeshot. Which was why women like Helen and Cleopatra and Catherine the Great might start a war, but it was always men who finished them.

"Did I do that?" she asks, turning slowly to view the scenes in their entirety all around them.

"Molecules all the way down." Govannon winks at her as she watches the collage of war scenes interchange and overlap. "You weren't far off when you told your fifth-grade nun that you could see the molecules moving inside the wall."

"Did I pass?" Some of Pickett's horses gallop through a Continental army tent without so much as rippling the canvas; the images are starting to muddle and dim, until they finally march or gallop or melt off the edges and disappear.

"Pass?"

"The final exam. Before we collaborate on our novel about the Gats. I hate that name, by the way. Can't you come up with something better?"

"It's what we've always called them," Govannon says simply. "Why? What's wrong with it?"

"There are too many resonances. It can mean too many other things. It's too close to 'gate,' which some overzealous copyeditor might decide it's supposed to be, and change it throughout the manuscript. Well, at least they would have, before all the copyeditors went extinct. Which was after the proofreaders vanished and before the midlist writers started to go. Anyway.

"It's also slang for a weapon, a gun. Abbreviation of Gatling gun, I believe, although why it subsequently came to mean a handgun, I couldn't tell you. Then, for the crossword aficionados, it's going to remind them of 'ghat,' which is a Hindu word for—"

"I know what it's a Hindu word for!" Govannon says a little impatiently. Karen looks surprised. "At least Johann did. In all those respects, the word 'gat' is appropriate, because for us the Gats were sometimes gates, ways to get from here to there unaltered. Over time, some of them became stairways to the sacred river, or the river of death, which were sometimes the same river. Others became weapons, which we had, knowingly or inadvertently, turned upon ourselves. . . ."

He drifts for a moment, and she waits for him to return.

"Ultimately, of course, you may call them something else if you like. But that was our name for them."

"Oh, all right. Then that's what we'll call them for now,"

Karen concedes. "Okay, let's go back to your first time. Your first Gat. What was on the other side?"

She had witnessed the crawl through the tunnel through his eyes, literally. The image of what he was describing had begun to form itself before her as he spoke, scenes of a dirt-walled tunnel moving out ahead of her as if viewed through a handheld camera from Govannon's POV. Any hope she might have had of seeing *ur*-Govannon's young self, absent human form, was not to be realized.

"Earth," he says simply.

"Always Earth?"

He nods. "Sorry to disappoint you. I know how you feel humans are inferior to other aliens and all, but they aren't. Mine was Earth, always. And always the same place, though at different times . . ."

He stops and is moving suddenly, defensively, as if he could put himself between Karen and something on the walls, an expression of genuine horror on his face. Karen is compelled to look where he does not want her to look. This was a man who could laugh and make love to her on the verge of death. What could possibly frighten him?

"Oh, no, not this one . . ." he is almost pleading. "Not this one, not now! Don't look!" he says harshly, reaching as if he were actually solid enough to shield her eyes with his hand, knowing her well enough to know she will look anyway, but wanting to warn her it will be terrible.

Impatiently, Karen brushes at where his hand would be, aware that there is something half blocking her vision, blurring it. "Why?" she demands. "Why 'not this one'? After Avaricum, what could be so terrible?"

•

The scene is dark. After the brightness of the flames, it takes Karen's eyes a moment to adjust. There is the same stage-set quality of Mycelia's world and little Jake's. Karen supplies the stage directions: interior, a small space, most probably a clothes closet. A solitary figure half kneels, half sits on the floor, her wrists bound, arms raised above her head by the rope pulled half-slack, half-taut and looped over the hanger rail.

Patty Hearst! Karen thinks, conjuring an old memory of something she never saw, that no one in the civilized world ever saw, but only read about when it was over. But it wasn't Patty Hearst. It was Anna, a much younger Anna, but no mistaking her.

She half sat, half knelt in the center of the closet floor. She had no choice; the rope binding her wrists was just short enough to make it impossible for her to sit down completely. Her only other choice was to pull herself upright by the rope and stand for a while. She'd tried that at first, just to be able to move a little, stretch the cramps out of her calf muscles, give herself the illusion of some modicum of free-dom, some control, get her bearings. She'd practiced sliding each foot in turn first forward, then sideways, then back, until it struck the walls or the closet door; this told her how small her space was, what the limits were. But she couldn't stand forever. She'd slid back down to the floor then, trying as many positions as she could in order to ease the ache in her arms.

They'd already warned her about the blindfold.

"Take it off, bitch, and we take your eyes out," Leon had said the first time he caught her groping at it.

And because, with the blindfold on, she couldn't tell at first when they were watching her and when she was alone, she didn't dare take the chance. But as silent as they were, she'd learned by now to feel the change in the flow of the air when the closet door was open instead of closed, and so had come to know that most of the time she was alone. Unless there was a camera. One of the women, the impatient one with the smoker's voice, had planted that idea in her mind early on.

"Closed-circuit TV, like they have in banks. You might say we're experts on banks."

The others had laughed then, for some reason Anna couldn't understand. She'd honed in on the individual sounds in that split second, trying to guess how many of them there were. Not many, she thought. Four, maybe five. That didn't mean there weren't others, coming and going all the time. When they left her alone her hearing was hyperacute, and she'd learned to distinguish them by their footsteps as well, knew how many were in the room beyond the closet, heard them thumping up and down the stairs, or maybe only felt the vibrations through the wall. She'd read somewhere that that was how deaf people experienced music, by putting a hand on the surface of the piano or even the speaker of a record player and feeling the vibrations. At the time she'd read it, it had seemed ridiculous, sad. How could anyone be satisfied with so little?

Now, blinded, hearing too well, she thought of how little it would take to satisfy her, if only she could be free again. Really, that was all. To be free again.

For now, focusing on the minutiae of her surroundings, the detail of her captivity, kept her sane. . . .

•

"You don't have to watch the rest of it," Govannon says softly, a half-pleading timbre to his voice that Karen hasn't heard before. It makes her angry.

"Don't I?" Karen is whispering, too. "Anna keeps reappearing. She's a recurring theme. It could be important. How are we going to solve this if—?"

She catches her breath with a hiss as the closet door is thrown open, flooding the little space with light. But Karen is with Anna, flinching in the dark behind the blindfold, knowing her captors have returned by the rush of air, the scuffle of feet and the heat of bodies, the closed-in funk of those who smoked too much and bathed too little. Their breath on her face, their hands on her body. How many this time?

"Please—!" she hears Anna whimper, just once, as soft as a sigh.

Don't! Karen wants to shout. *Don't plead with them. Don't let them hear you, or they'll think they've broken you. Take it from me; I know! If they think they've broken you, then they have you, they've won, and it will only get worse. . . .*

By the time they have finished, closing the door behind them, Karen is digging her nails into her palms, the muscles in her back so taut she feels as if someone has been pounding on them. She can feel the fear-sweat in her armpits and at the backs of her knees. But she has borne witness, to all of it.

TEN

I couldn't stop it, Karen. I'm so sorry. I didn't evoke it, it popped up without warning, and it wasn't even my memory. Anna told me about it— told Jake, anyway—but I've never actually seen what happened. Until now."

"Any more than you've seen so much of what's happened to me, yet you know about it." Karen is careful not to make it sound like an accusation. The just-vanished scene has in fact disturbed her more even than the Battle of Avaricum.

"I wish there had been more time to prepare you," Govannon says, watching her warily. "I'm so sorry."

"Why?" was all Karen said, but he knew exactly what she meant.

"Go on."

"Why is it so much harder to watch someone else suffer than endure it yourself?"

"Is it?" It's a therapist's question, and she wonders if he is playing at Jake Bower, or if he really doesn't know.

"You know it is. Didn't you ever, when you saw your father terrorizing Herman, didn't you wish—well, first of all, you wished he'd stop. You'd say it to yourself or to God or whoever inside your mind: 'Stop it, stop it, please God, make it stop!' Then if that didn't work, you'd think 'If it were happening to me instead of him, I could stand it more easily. . . .' "

She stops herself. Where is all this coming from? Oh, she knows where, but how can she explain it to him? Once more, it isn't necessary. Images forty years past materialize in the space between them: a little girl being dragged across a room by her hair, which is clutched in her mother's two little clawlike hands, the man whose jawline is the same as hers sitting ponderously on her bed, patting his knee with one hand, announcing "Come on, let's get this over with."

"You were terrorized, violated. Not even by strangers but by your own kin." The visuals dissolve beneath Govannon's voice. "There are dark closets aplenty in your mind."

"Yes." Karen says softly, hearing footsteps on the stairs, the rush of doors wrenched open. "He always spanked me with his left hand. . . ." she murmurs, a bemused look on her face. "He claimed he was left-handed when he was a kid, but his teachers forced him to write right-handed. Apparently that was common in those days. A lot of left-handed children became stutterers or bed-wetters. I wonder if Hitler was left-handed?"

"He wasn't. Keep talking."

"My old man . . . that's how he refers to himself, on the rare occasion when he speaks. Messages on my answering machine. 'This is your old man calling. Your mother and I want you to . . .' Fill in the blank. He hasn't had an original thought in fifty years. But after he's had a few beers on Thanksgiving, somehow the conversation always comes around to his being left-handed. He'll say: 'There are some things I still do better with my left hand. For instance, I can handle a hammer or a saw better left-handed.' I always watch him very closely when he's making that speech, wondering if he remembers what else he used to do better left-handed. Something only I know."

She grimaces. "The left hand of darkness. None of it ever really happened, you know. Because there were no witnesses. I wouldn't cry. I never made a sound. . . ." She is trembling, tears are streaming down her face. "Why was I so stubborn? Why didn't I scream at the top of my lungs the minute I saw the doorknob turn? Especially in the summer, with the windows open, the neighbors would have heard. Maybe someone would have done something. At least it might have embarrassed him enough to make him stop. Why was I so *stupid*?"

"Not stupid." Govannon's arms are around her. She wraps her own arms around him and holds on, burying herself in the solidity of him, the strength of him. "Never stupid, never. You were a child, a child betrayed. There was nothing else you could have done except survive, bear witness, treat your own children differently."

"I don't know why watching Anna triggered all that." Her voice is muffled against his chest.

"Yes, you do." She can feel his breath in her hair, his fingers caressing her face. "Keep talking."

"I think . . ." Karen begins, having trouble with her voice. She clears her throat, starts again. "I think there is a sense in which we can forgive a stranger more easily, because it's so much easier for them to objectify us. They don't know any-thing about the person they're abusing, haven't formed a bond, so why should they care? There's been so much writ-ten about it, especially since the Holocaust. How the Nazis were taught to 'objectify' their victims, see them as vermin, less than human. Parents, though. Why a parent can do what some parents do to children . . ."

" 'Why'?"

"What?" She has broken the embrace, frowns up at him, drying her eyes.

"You said 'why,' not 'how.' Wouldn't most people put it that way? *'How* a parent could do that to their own child . . . ' "

"Oh, I understand how!" Her voice shakes; she forces it under control. "It's the *why* I've spent my whole life trying to figure out. If they could give me a reason, I might be able to . . ."

She trails off, realizing for the first time what's happening here.

"Govannon?" Her hands touch his face, his shoulders, his arms, his chest, his face again. "You're real, you're here! I can touch you!" She laughs, hugs him, wants to whirl around the room. "We did it! You're here!"

•

"No," he says. "It is you who are Here."

She braces for another instance of blue-screen-all-the-way down, but it doesn't happen. They are standing together in the Museum, in the exact center, under the highest point of the arch. Body and mind communicate again, and she processes it, then finds that when she moves, the scenery does not move with her. She is "stuck," like Govannon. With Govannon.

And? she asks herself. *Isn't that what you want, to be with him? That's halfway to getting him back where he belongs.* She shudders violently, like someone startled out of a deep sleep, but holds on, and begins to laugh.

"Then we've done it! All I have to do is hold on to you and I can pull you through to my side. . . ."

Even as she says it, she is aware that she's losing him again. No point in questioning which of them is melting out of the other's reality; the outcome is the same. Her hands are cotton and he is fog and even though everything else is as solid as when she left it, she feels dizzy, nauseated, and suddenly has to sit down again.

"Are you all right?" He is watching her carefully.

"Yes. No. I don't know!" She waves him off, impatient, though whether with him or with the situation she cannot say.

He waits, patient.

It is very still. The Museum, its walls blank for quite some time now, seems darker, even cold. The myriad-color floor seems to have dimmed. Closing time? Should they go now?

It's the last thing she remembers thinking about. She has a vague impression that Govannon might be carrying her somewhere, a vague memory that he had done this once before, when his name was Jacob and hers was Grethe, and she was only a child, and somehow a pitchfork was involved. The rest is darkness.

•

"It would help if I had an eidetic memory!" Karen announces, settling herself in what she has decided is the living room of what she will always think of as Govannon's house. She doesn't remember how she got here. She's more than a little annoyed with herself—she has never fainted before in her life—but the aftermath seems to be a remarkable clarity. Her thoughts are clearer now than they have been since she got here.

"You will," Govannon assures her.

He has conjured a freestanding fireplace in the center of the room, not dissimilar to the one in Peter Kato's summer house in southern France. Now, for effect, he waves his fingers like a magician and there is a fire. There are also two comfortable chairs, with footrests, arranged at such an angle that one can sit with an equal view of the fire or of one's companion.

Karen's answer is a wry look.

"Right," she says.

"I'll be your memory." He "sits" in the second chair, tapping his temple. "Got it all right here."

"Uh-huh," she says carefully, damping down skepticism. But what else can she do, after all? Carve it on crystone, write it in the sand? Preserve it in the Museum, perhaps? That seems the most hopeful. Maybe as long as they stay on the same time line he'll be able to retain it.

"Nice!" she remarks, feeling the warmth of the fire. "Where do all these things come from? The food, the furniture, the fire. If you're not here—"

He has to think about this. "Their memory is in the house, just as the histories are in the Museum. A different kind of stone. They're resonating with you, not me."

"Great! So if you can instruct them to provide me with a PC or a good, old-fashioned Selectric, or even a legal pad and a cheap Bic pen . . . No, huh? Because they don't have the memory."

"Precisely."

"So I have to."

"It's all in there," he assures her, tapping his forehead and pointing to hers. "Keep talking. Unless you'd rather rest some more."

"No. I'm ready. Here's what I've come up with so far. The outline and three chapters, if you will: TQ are beings from a world where there are—portals—called Gats, that lead to other worlds. Some of them also lead to other times. In those other worlds and other times, TQ developed many skills, including telekinesis and the ability to inhabit other beings, to borrow their lives for varying times. Eventually some even learned to travel the Gats within their minds. Okay so far?"

Govannon considers. "Overly simplistic, but not bad for a first draft."

" 'Overly simplistic'!" Karen mutters. "If you're so damn smart, why don't you—?"

"What?"

"Nothing. Time travel as revolving door, to use your metaphor," she suggests. "Clarify something. The time Gats, like yours, always ended up in the same place. The space Gats could end up in different places, but always at the same time?"

"It depended on the resonance it picked up from the individual. Some could diversify to different worlds, others remained fixed on the same world. Some were fixed as to time, others fluctuated. Eventually we learned to manipulate some of that. To explain would require more physics than I think you'd feel comfortable with."

"Okay. But you always came back here? It wasn't a question of finding other Gats on those worlds that led to other worlds? Or entering the same Gat and ending up elsewhere than Relict? Or finding time changed when you got back here, like *Planet of the Apes*?"

She watches him process the reference, courtesy of Jake Bower's fascination with science fiction.

"That was the intriguing part of it. We could jump from here to, say, Planet A and back here, then jump from here to Planet B or G or Z, but never from Planet A to anywhere but back here. At least, some of us could. Some were limited only to certain types of planets, certain species to inhabit. All of this suggested a design, controlled by a designer. Something with a purpose, a reason for leading us to the Gats, wanting us to explore them. Something more advanced than we. Or maybe some aspect of us that had moved on, leaving us behind. At least, that's what we told ourselves in the First Era.

"But, yes, each of us would end up back here, except for the ones who never returned. And, no, no one ever went after them. It wasn't—possible."

He closes his eyes, winces as if with physical pain. From somewhere Karen hears what she somehow knows is a woman, weeping inconsolably.

"Govannon? You lost someone once, didn't you?"

He opens his eyes. "Always returned to where we had started, and at the same moment we had left. Nor did we age while we were gone, though we might have lived an entire lifetime on the other side. You see?"

He wasn't going to answer her. Karen makes note. "I think so. Okay, let's talk about you personally. Your Gat always led to Earth. You were always human?"

"Mm-hm. And always as you see me. This body, replicated in each of the humans I was." He seems to be working it through as he explains it, as if it's never occurred to him quite this way before. "I have the memories of younger versions of my varied selves, though whether I actually lived them all the way through, or simply borrowed them as I borrowed everything else about Jake and Johann and Govannon, I no longer remember."

"Could you have chosen another world if you'd wanted to?"

Govannon shrugs. "Earth was where my Gat led me. My talent was time, not space. I only resonated with one Gat, and it always sent me to the same place at different times. Besides, humans underestimate how truly interesting they really are. . . .

"There is a cave in a forest deep in Central Europe, carved by subterranean rivers that have never seen the light, in one of those places where the borders shift as many as a dozen times in a century, where the inhabitants speak several languages, because they never know who's going to ride into the village and demand tribute or their women or their lives, where children born in times of strife don't always look like their fathers. Does any of this make sense to you?"

"All of it!" Karen says. "Every human has at least one rapist in the family."

Govannon chuckles grimly. "I never thought of it that way before."

Wars are playing out in the space between them, nightly news footage, firelit, primeval. Afghanistan, Armenia, Bosnia, Cambodia, Chechnya, Kazakhstan, Somalia, Uganda, as easily list them in alphabetical as chronological order. It amounted to the same thing: Was there ever a species more gifted in feeding on itself?

Outside, the nightly rain has started; Karen hears it beyond the crackle of the flames. On Earth, in Avaricum, there was torrential rain on the day Govannon died.

"Does this place have a name?" Karen wants to know. "In my time, let's say?"

"The cave opens out of an outcropping deep in a forest known simply as the Wood in any of several local languages. It is not far from a place where, in the early twenty-first century, as often before, the borders of three countries meet. Beyond the mouth of the cave there are forest trails, deer tracks mostly, that the locals know, but that are otherwise unmarked. That much has been true since the human Govannon's time. The nearest inhabited place within your lifetime, beyond a hunter's shack or two, is a town called

Salzheim, so small you won't find it on any map. Purportedly it is built on the ruins of a much larger Bronze Age village that lay along the Salt Routes."

"What are the Salt Routes? The Silk Road I know, but—"

"Older, and running north to south rather than east to west," Govannon says, gazing into the fire. "Wait for it."

"A Bronze Age village? Wouldn't Govannon know that for sure?"

"How much would you know about an Indian village on Long Island two thousand years before the white man came?"

"Not much, because I'd rely too much on what was written down. But the Arverni were preliterate. They had a rich oral tradition, told tales around the fire that were generations old, perfectly preserved in minds uncluttered by the printed word."

"I know," he reminds her. "I was there."

"So was I."

She wants him to take her back further, and he knows it.

"You're relentless!" he grumbles. "How do I know you won't turn this into a fantasy novel? This would be just the place for some elves or a magic sword. If I must disappear into somebody's narrative, please don't let it be a fantasy novel! Although," he ruminated, "it might satisfy your editor. Fantasy being more gender-specific. Girls write fantasy, boys write spaceship battles, if I understand his thinking."

"Nothing I do satisfies my editor," Karen snaps. "And I don't do swords and silliness."

"Well, now that we've established that . . . yes, there was a fortress city of various names, as early as the Hallstadt era, from about 3000 B.C. forward. Its people were mainly horsemen, which meant warriors, cattle-raiders, bronze- and bead- and pot-makers, salt miners and traders, just like their later brethren, the Arverni, whom you and I both knew. Their market town was ideally situated to trade the copper and tin and salt they harvested from local caves, for furs and Baltic amber brought from the lands to the north, silks and jade from the east. . . ."

Karen sees it in the fire as he speaks.

•

First, actually, were the smells, of cured hides and wood-smoke, of braising meat and the tang of fresh-sliced onions, of mud and cow dung. Then the hubbub of a human gathering, laughter, singing, the twang of some stringed instrument answered by a reed pipe, the bubble-and-shriek of children careering about in some chasing game, market day in any land. A haggle of voices whose language began alien in Karen's ears, the vowel sounds throaty or spliced into diphthongs spoken high in the nose, an odd voicing of certain fricatives and the virtual absence of others. Karen swore she heard someone mutter something about "Turdy-turd Shtreet," before a shift in her brain made it possible for her to understand.

Finally the visuals. First the food vendors, their wares arrayed on either side of a tamped-dirt aisle wide enough for a steer to pass without his cropped horns disturbing the pyramidal heaps of rosy crab apples and tiny green-gold pears and brown-skinned onions, the bronze-bellied braziers glowing with the heat of charcoal fires where chunks of new-killed meat, perhaps kin to the very steer who passed, led by a small boy toward the auction block where the aisle opened out into a well-trodden field, were offered up on skewers, interspersed with bits of sweet onion and root vegetables. Herbalists sheltered under hide tents hung with wreaths and bunches and streamers of their leafed and flowered and fungal and twigged and hairy-rooted wares.

Piles of animal pelts, some stiff as cardboard, some furred, others butter soft and reeking of tannin, occupied the next stretch of booths made from loose-flapping curtains of similar stuff, with potential buyers fingering and musing over them. In a logical progression, the leather-workers offered belts and boots, garments and carry-bags, quivers to hold bronze-tipped arrows, and bronze-bound leather shields to accompany them.

Next, by some leap of local logic, the salt traders displayed their deceptively simple offering, as valid a currency as gold in that time, if somewhat bulkier to transport, uniform rows of casks filled abrim with nothing more than blue-gray or bright white or yellow-tinged crystals ranging from fist-sized chunks to fine powder, the single compound most essential to human health and safety in the thousand thousand years before refrigeration. Here there was no haggling. In contrast to the rest of the din, this space seemed unnaturally quiet. Potential buyers merely studied the substance as its quality and purity were touted by the sellers, who displayed the merchandise by taking a scoop out of a given barrel with a rounded wooden hand-scuttle and letting it cascade with a sighing sound back into the cask. Occasionally, one would proffer the brimming scuttle to a wavering buyer to wet a finger and take a taste.

Those intent on purchase scratched lot numbers with bits of charred sticks on palm-sized sheets of birchbark or made cryptic knots in cords at their belts, then moved on to the auction field to conclude their purchases.

Cattle, horses, slaves of course, each in their segregated pens arrayed on either side of the auction platform, each comporting themselves according to species: cattle docile and chewing, horses champing and skittish, humans wearing a dozen shades of emotion from resignation to defiance to woe. Karen lingers here only so long as the hidden camera requires her to.

And where is she, exactly? As she was in all the previous scenes: Not *in camera,* but *I Am a Camera*, outside the frame, unseen. The flash of sunlight on silver hair catches her eye. She turns.

"Govannon—?" she starts to say, then realizes he probably won't hear her. If it is in fact he.

Like most matters Celtic, this marketplace is not built along straight or perpendicular lines but circularly, meandering about itself like an illumination out of the *Book of Kells*, so that while the auction block seems to be the pinnacle of the day's events (well, unless one counts the horse racing going on at the far end of the field), it is possible for human passersby, unlike the ox, who has reached the part of the arc where he must disembark, to continue beyond it, back into the moil of beings moving slow as cattle, gawking at the additional wares on offer.

Bronze pots, alloyed from the local tin and copper, sized and shaped for a variety of purposes and bearing the distinct look of what later historians will call the La Tene culture, can be seen set up on a long trestle table at the curve of the arc where Karen began, between the fruit stalls and the leather dealers' tents. On a smaller table, one of the bronze-makers, an enormous woman in a leather apron, her frizzy hair exactly the color of the wire worked between her hands, has set out several dozen pieces of bronze jewelry.

Between the jeweler and Karen's POV, a camel. Not your *Lawrence of Arabia* one-humped dromedary but a shaggy two-humped bactrian, rhythmically chewing, clearly belonging to the flat-faced Asian trader in the fur-trimmed rawhide clothing and hat, all of whose wares are contained in two saddlebags cinched neatly to either side of a small saddle blanket nestled between the camel's humps. One side holds jade, the other amber. Raw, uncut chunks in every color each mineral possesses, the jade from common to uncommon greens, to rarer whites and yellows and rarest-of-all rose, the amber from milky opaque through cloudy through glass-transparent clear, and of that latter every hue from urine-yellow to claret-red, with every variation on the indefinable color called amber in between, some of it bubbled with gases trapped a million years ago or more, much of the clear displaying perfect specimens of leaf or twig or insect wing captured when the world began.

The jade the Mongol has brought from his home province, along what will a few thousand years hence be dubbed the Silk Road, but which is now mostly long stretches of flat, waterless land, too hot in summer, too cold in winter, and mountain defiles whose main inhabitants are goats and bandits, where surefootedness is de rigueur. Hence the camel. The amber he has gotten in trade from other merchants he has met along the way, their paths running perpendicular, his east to west, theirs north to south, and often the twain do meet.

> "The one-humped camel
> She's a treat.
> The two-humped camel's
> Very neat.
> But lifetimes will your soul entrammel
> Before you'll see a three-humped camel."

The speaker is a bead-maker, his small table aglitter with his handiwork, displayed loose in shallow wooden bowls or strung in multicolored strands. He has been haggling with the Mongol in his own tongue for a handful of amber chunks the size of walnuts and the color of honey, a piece of rose jade as wide as his palm, and some odd bits of common green jade, all of which, beneath his touch, will be transformed into earrings, pendants, and the portable wealth of necklaces.

He is indeed another, far earlier, avatar of the Govannon Karen knows, possessed of the same intermingling of wistfulness and whimsy that characterizes all his personae, the same sad eyes and warm smile. He recites his bit of doggerel not to the trader but to the spot where Karen would be standing if she were there.

"Did you know," he goes on, "that jade is always cool to the touch? Wear a jade pendant against your skin on the hottest summer day and, while it will warm to the heat of your skin, when you take it off it will feel cooler than the surrounding air. Amber, on the other hand, holds hidden fire. Strike two pieces together in a dark room, and they'll spark, and the sparks will give off a scent like lemons and honey."

"Yes, as a matter of fact, I did know that." Market and camel and jade and amber vanish, and they are back on Relict. "Research for the book, remember? What I didn't know was that you weren't being honest when you said the first human whose life you lived was Govannon."

"Not true. You didn't ask me which Govannon. There were several Jacobs," he reminds her.

"So why not several Govannons? And, as with the women in your life, I'm not supposed to ask you how many."

"It would be counterproductive," he suggests.

"And you can be Johann and Jake Bower simultaneously?" Karen demands, just to make sure.

"Yes."

"And Govannon, both of them, and Jacob the Brewer

and whoever all else, all at the same time." She isn't asking.

"Yes."

"No wonder you're so confused!" she says, though neither of them finds it funny. "So I know I'm repeating myself—or at least I think I am, because if I hang around with you long enough I think *my* brain will turn into a Möbius strip—but I'm pretty sure I've done it again. Gone blundering into a situation on a false assumption. Looking for Raymond, thinking he was Ryalbran—or was it the other way around?—saving Aoife's baby instead.

"And, all right, I was in Avaricum for the wrong reasons, but everything worked out in the end." Karen is on her feet, ready for action again. "But that doesn't mean I'll get it right a second time. That only happens in fiction. But Anna, Anna keeps cropping up the way Raymond did, in life as well as fiction. Tell me more about her."

"What do you want to know?"

"Why was she kidnapped? And how did she survive it to become the strong, assertive woman I saw on *Nightline*? Or did she? Was she instead the woman I met, the woman who took Raymond's place?" *Because if she was*, Karen thinks, *then she wouldn't be married to Jake, which means . . . well, I'm not sure what it means, but—*

"She survived it," Govannon assures her. "Though not easily. And it was neither the first nor the last such ordeal for her. I know. Before I married her, I was her therapist, briefly. . . ."

ELEVEN

"E*s brennt...*" Anna murmured, falling into German as Jake took her back in time, down into her earliest memories. Her voice was that of a small child. *"Es brennt!"*

"It's burning?" Jake prompted her, switching languages as easily as he switched realities; German had been his second language, after Yiddish and long before English. "What is? *Was brennt?* What's burning, Anna? Tell me. . . ."

•

"I need a favor, old friend." Peter Kato never identified himself to his friends on the phone, assuming his deep, well-modulated voice to be easily recognizable, distinct from anyone else's. To Jake, it was.

How had they first met? What strange juxtaposition of events had brought together the young émigré therapist whose clients consisted mainly of Holocaust survivors and their children, and the highly visible nisei ballet star who had spent his growing-up years in a dusty detention camp in Arizona?

The answer was that Peter Kato was not only a media darling, flamboyant lead dancer, and sometime choreographer of a world-renowned avant-garde company—which might have been enough to exercise the energies of any ordinary mortal, if Peter had been only ordinary—but he had a secret life as well.

Well, two secret lives, to be exact. The first secret was that Peter was gay, which in '60s America required almost as much cloaking as the second, which was simply that when certain international incidents either happened or didn't happen, Peter Kato, perhaps coincidentally, seemed to be in the vicinity. People who lived between worlds knew things, heard things, sensed things that ordinary people missed. Peter Kato knew where the bodies were buried. He had things to trade for information, and information to trade for things.

Jake Bower had a passion for salvaging what Hitler had tried to destroy. Foremost, his clients and their children, and secondly whatever treasures—paintings, photographs, family mementos—they'd had to leave behind in their flight.

He'd begun by making inquiries through official channels to sources in France and West Germany, the Soviet countries being out of reach, and found that, as with most human endeavors, one thread connected to another and another and another. A client's father had been a painter in Linz before the war, his work banned as "decadent"—i.e., Jewish—by the Nazis. He had entrusted a portfolio of sketches to a Gentile friend before his arrest, and had died of typhus in Theresienstadt in the winter of '42.

The dead man's daughter had heard a rumor that the friend was still alive, somewhere in what was now East Germany and, if he could be contacted . . . she had heard from a friend of a friend that Dr. Bower had done similar things in the past, and . . .

Dr. Bower had been making what he thought were discreet inquiries through sources he had contacted before, making arrangements for a short visit overseas if necessary, when he found himself accosted by a dapper young Asian in a very expensive suit who sidled up to him at a charity event at the National Gallery. Peter had come right to the point.

"If you can see your way clear to laying off the search for another couple of weeks, I can make it a lot easier for you," he'd said so quietly no one else in the shifting crowd could have heard him. "Let me buy you a drink and I'll explain."

"I'm not sure I—" Jake had begun, when his elbow was taken with surprising strength by a man a good four inches shorter and forty pounds lighter than he. A good therapist, and curious in spite of himself, he'd let himself be led.

"Assume I'm with the Good Guys," Peter said, flashing a smile full of perfect teeth when they'd found a bar noisy enough so they couldn't be overheard even when they were shouting in each other's ears. "I won't ask for your sources if you don't ask for mine. Although," he said with a subdued version of the raucous laugh that interviewers claimed could be heard across three states whenever he let it loose, "it doesn't really matter, because I already know most of your sources, and you'd have no way of checking mine.

"Let me make it simple for you: Your client's drawings do exist, and I can get them for you. But her late father's friend lives in an area where there's too much activity going on at the present time for you to be blundering about on an American visa playing at James Bond. That's my job."

Jake found himself wondering how a Japanese could move around Eastern Europe unnoticed, but was too polite to ask.

"Once my little errand is over, I'll get the drawings for you. All I'm asking you to do is stay out of the way."

Jake thought it over. "I guess I can do that."

"Thought you could!" Peter grinned again, clapped him on the shoulder, said "I'll be in touch!" and melted into the crowd.

Three weeks later, the wife of a research chemist who had

escaped from East Berlin a year earlier was suddenly reunited with her husband in the West. A week after the headlines shrank away to nothing, a large, sturdy mailing tube covered with East German stamps was delivered to Jake's office. The next day Peter showed up to make sure everything had gone smoothly, and this time Jake paid for the drinks. The bond was instantaneous, and for life.

•

Which was why when Peter called this time, Jake's immediate response was: "What can I do for you?"

"You've heard about the Fallon kidnapping?"

"Heard about it? Shit, Peter, what else is anyone talking about?" Jake's voice was unnecessarily rough. From the moment the story of the young woman's kidnapping had broken, he'd been obsessed with it. It wasn't just that the group taking credit for the kidnapping, the New Front for National Socialism, made his blood boil simply in their choice of name but that he had a fair idea what their victim would be going through.

And, all right, he'd told himself, if it had been some fat-cat industrialist locked in a car trunk and made to sweat, or some left-wing/right-wing politico blindfolded and shot in the woods somewhere, he wouldn't have let it spoil his breakfast. But the Front had given no reason for Anne-Marie Fallon's abduction, though the media had speculated that her adoptive father, a retired army major, had been one of the founding members of the OSS just after World War II. There was an even more bizarre rumor that she might be the biological daughter of an important Nazi leader.

But if the Front believed that, why had they terrorized her, dragging her off at gunpoint in the middle of the night? Whatever the case, it had nothing to do with Anne-Marie Fallon herself, only with what she represented to the kind of people who wore balaclavas and brandished automatic weapons.

Finally, it was not just Anne-Marie Fallon's innocence but her ethereal beauty that had moved Jake more than it should have. The media kept harping on how small she was. "The petite, dark haired beauty, at five feet tall and ninety-five pounds, was no match for the ski-masked captors who broke in to the youth hostel in the predawn hours where she and her sister, on a cross-country bike trip with a group of fellow students . . ." they went on. And on and on and—

"You know we've got her," Peter was saying, and Jake didn't even ask who "we" was. "Broke down some doors and broke some heads early this morning. There was a press conference at noon."

"I had clients all morning," Jake said. "I haven't had the TV on. Thank God, though. Is she—?"

How did he ask: *Is she all right?* when he knew what the answer would be? Even if she were physically untouched, and he doubted that very much, the psychic damage would take years to heal. He knew what Peter was going to say next.

"That's what we'd like you to tell us."

Jake took a deep breath, didn't hesitate. "Where is she now?"

"At Walter Reed. Under sedation and under an assumed name. But it won't be long before the newshounds sniff her out. How soon can you see her?"

Jake had cleared his calendar for the next day.

•

Peter brought her in a car with tinted windows, a coat over her shoulders, his arm around her. It had been he who had been the first through the closet door, and the only one besides the doctors she would allow to touch her. Dark glasses concealed her eyes. Jake knew she'd be experiencing visual disturbances after so long in the dark.

She walked like an invalid, looking frail and tinier than even Jake had imagined. How much weight had she lost in the fifty-one days of her captivity? When she took off the glasses, blinking slightly, it was as if she had stepped out of a time warp, might have been Anne Frank somehow saved from Auschwitz and suspended in time, her luminous dark eyes burning into his with that same otherworldly intensity.

"It's Anna, not Anne-Marie," she said before either man could say anything. "That was Eleanor Fallon's idea when she and Frank adopted me. Let's get that straight from the beginning."

Jake suppressed a nervous bubble of laughter; it was the last thing he'd expected of her. Her voice was low, flat, almost mechanical; after such an ordeal he would have been surprised if she hadn't shown a lack of affect. But the fire behind it, the determination to be taken for who she was, amazed him.

"Anna," he acknowledged almost humbly, taking the small hand in his own when she offered it, and they began.

•

He held three sessions a week with her at first, drawing her out of what was at first an almost catatonic, staring silence to where she could at least recount the events in some sort of horrible clarity, her voice dead, removed from it all.

"It's as if it happened to someone else," she explained after nearly three months, her voice brightening for the first time. "If I don't look at it that way, I'll go crazy. If I'm not already."

Jake hadn't said a word, had offered her a silence in which to continue, but she hadn't.

"I'm stuck," she said finally, not intimidated by the silence, not driven to babbling the way a lot of his clients were. Then she'd shrugged. "I can't do anything more than just keep telling you what happened. You keep asking me how I feel about it. I don't. I don't feel. Not that, not anything, don't you see?"

"That's perfectly natural," he'd said from the lofty distance of a young man's bravado, which passed for self-assurance, though he'd found his professional distance eroding with her from the beginning. Her being "stuck" worried him. "Have you always felt this way?"

"You mean not felt this way?"

Again her way of putting things made him want to laugh, but not out of amusement. "All right. Have you always *not* felt this way?"

She cocked her head, listening to something inside. It was a slight movement, almost birdlike, but because she usually sat so very still, as if afraid too much movement would cause a shattering—of her composure, herself, the world around her (had she been that way before her captivity? Jake wondered)—it was startling.

"I don't know," she said at last.

"Perhaps it might help if you talked about something else. Perhaps what your life was like before the kidnapping."

" 'Perhaps'," she'd echoed him, not mimicking, just seeming to savor the way he spoke. "I don't know anyone else who says that. You weren't born in this country, were you?"

"No, I wasn't," he'd answered, surprised that she'd noticed, although why should he be? She had that watchfulness, that hypervigilance of abused children; she noticed everything. But he thought he'd lost all trace of the various transitions his accent had gone through as his family's exile had dragged his child-self from Central Europe to England to the States. Perhaps, then. Perhaps not.

"Neither was I," Anna said, offering the ghost of a smile for the first time.

Jake sensed a gift being offered him, and reached for it, tentatively. "Would you like to talk about that?"

"I wouldn't mind," she clarified, a frown crossing her face. "Except I don't remember most of it. . . ."

•

That was when he'd suggested hypnosis. She'd agreed almost eagerly, or with what passed for eagerness in her shut-down state, then had slipped almost immediately into a deep trance under his lightest induction; had he been less experienced, it would have frankly alarmed him. She sat pressed back into the farthest corner of the sofa, knees drawn up to her chest, arms wrapped tightly around them, holding herself in, as small as a child.

"Es brennt. Es stinken. . . ."

"It won't hurt you now, Anna. It's very far away. A picture in a storybook," Jake soothed her. "A make-believe," he added, using a term he'd heard an eight-year-old client use recently. "Tell me the make-believe. . . ."

She'd rocked herself and begun to cough, her voice a little girl's.

"Stinken . . ." Wrinkling her nose, her whole face twisted. Tears coursed down her cheeks. Emotion, or only sense memory? She seemed unable to go on.

"Yes, I know it stinks," Jake prompted. "Tell me . . ."

He would follow her child's mind down the burning paths, see through her eyes the houses crumbling instantly to dust, a world come tumbling down, a sky that shrieked and split into fragments of death, earth that heaved and smoked. The smoke filled his nostrils and closed his throat, and he wept too.

Wept for his own childhood of overcrowded rooms and mourning women, of constantly being moved about, of wearing clothes that smelled of strangers. Wept for the poverty of cold dank flats that stank of cabbage, whispered secrets, voices that paused in midsentence when he entered a room, people he would never see again. Damaged Herman, taken as a "defective" in the first round, schoolmates removed from their classrooms, aunts and uncles and all his cousins gone, a world burning, and his mother dead of a stroke, or only despair, not long after they got to England. Wept for lost childhoods, wept for them both.

"How did you survive?" Anna asked him, genuinely curious. Brought out of the induction, she saw he had been weeping, and asked him why. Surprised once again, Jake found himself telling her about his own past.

"By being the no-good bum my father said I was," he replied, trying to make light of it. "I used to cut school and hang around the train yards. That day they were full of soldiers . . ." He'd stopped himself. "Well, you know the rest. It's in all the history books. I think my father must have paid a large sum of money to someone to get us out. Why he didn't act right after they took Herman . . ."

His voice trailed off. She was studying him with those big, dark eyes. "You were how old?"

He shrugged. "Seven or eight."

"A 'no-good bum' at seven or eight . . ." she said, shaking her head in disbelief. Again Jake found himself amazed at the things she focused on. Not the Holocaust, as if, the human race being what it was, that was a given, but the fact that his father hadn't loved him. Who was counseling whom? Before he could voice the thought, she had settled back against the cushions again, signaling that she was ready for another induction. He led her through the images of fire once again.

•

Brick burns, if the fire is hot enough, if the brick is old enough and friable, if there's enough straw in the mix of sand and red clay. In Dresden a hundred thousand people died in the firestorm, many of them literally pulled off their feet as they fled the bombing, sucked into the maelstrom, bodies fused together, corpses shriveled to doll size, as many as ten collectible in a washtub in the days that followed. In Berlin the destruction was, like everything about Berlin, less neat, more erratic, arbitrary. Block after block was reduced to burning rubble, yet here and there a house survived without so much as a shell-pock. Some people survived, too, enduring nothing more traumatic than food shortages, a stolen bicycle. Most emerged from the burning never knowing what they might have been in its absence. It is this that the artist attempts to depict in this otherwise difficult work, limned mostly in blacks and reds, its brushstrokes almost frantic in their urgency. . . .

•

". . . the world was burning. And Mutti would not let me climb out of the pram. . . ." Anna's voice was prim, a little older this time, perhaps a ten-year-old looking back at her younger self with something like disapproval. "I kept insisting I was too old to sit in a pram, and trying to climb out. She would slap me and scold: 'Sit back down this minute and don't bother me! I have enough else on my mind. . . .' "

As she said it, imitating a mother's voice twenty years in the past, Jake could see her. The image of a petulant blonde in a dirty fur-collared coat, wearing lipstick and laddered silk stockings so late in the war, sprang uninvited into his mind, seemed to hover in the air between him and Anna, too vivid, startling. He shook his head and found his client watching him.

"When——? How did you——?"

"I don't know. I seem to be able to come up out of trance as easily as I go in," she said, diffident. "But I can see her, for the very first time, and remember that I called her Mutti, except when I was frightened or very tired, and then I called her Mama. She has blonde hair, almost white, like cornsilk. Maybe it was bleached; I don't know. But my hair was very light, naturally so. It only darkened as I got older. I don't know if I actually remember that, or it's just that my adoptive parents told me. . . ." Her voice took on a dreamy, sing-song quality, though she was not in trance. "But I can see myself sitting in the pram as if it were yesterday. . . ."

She drifted for a minute, then came back. "She must have found it or stolen it or traded for it, because I was much too old for it, but it was easier than waiting for me to walk. We used it to transport everything we had, a bundle of clothes with me sitting on top. I remember that now. I can actually see it. It seemed like she walked forever, pushing that pram along these dusty roads, so many other people all around us."

She stopped, shook her head, looked to him for guidance. "Now, do I actually remember that, or have I seen it somewhere? Newsreels, movies about the war, even?"

Jake chose his next words very carefully. "I'm not sure I know how to answer that."

"That's as far back as I can go," Anna said then. "Everything after that is just what the people who adopted me told me later. When my mother was killed in the bombing, I was turned over to the Red Cross and . . . do you want to hear all that now?"

They were almost out of time. And more than that, he didn't want to complicate pure memory with hearsay.

"Maybe at your next session. You have a lot to process from today. It's much more detail than ever before," he reassured her.

Her smile this time was anything but tentative. "It was good, then?"

"You're making excellent progress," he said, hating himself for sounding so pompous.

He'd sent her home in a cab, determined that during their next session he would tell her he thought it best to refer her to someone else. He could no longer be her therapist; he was in love with her.

•

"You've heard the latest rumor," Peter didn't ask as much as tell Jake when they next met for a drink.

"I don't suppose I can stop you from telling me."

"She's supposed to be the illegitimate daughter of Joseph Goebbels."

Jake winced and put his drink down too forcefully. Was this bar noisier than the others they'd been to, or was he only more sensitized to noise, experiencing it the way Anna did, after the closet? ("I don't so much hear it as feel it against my skin," she'd explained. "If it's too loud, it feels like sunburn, or even like something coarse rubbing against my face, my arms. I know that sounds bizarre, but—" And he'd said: "No, no, not at all. Keep talking.")

"That's a pretty sick joke."

Peter shrugged. "No joke. It's what the one Front member we managed to hold on to said when she started to spill."

"What happened to the others?" Jake asked, not really interested, but hoping to derail the other topic, at least for a little while.

"All but Marielle had not only foreign passports but warrants outstanding in their countries of origin. We had to ship them back." Peter didn't bother elaborating on who "we" might be. "Interrogations were supposed to be coordinated, but that broke down almost immediately." His tone suggested this was to be expected. "So we concentrated on Marielle, without telling her she was all we had left. She didn't know much, but she knew that."

"Knew what?"

"That their leader, whoever he might be—and Marielle was too low on the food chain to have been told—was livid when he found out how Anna was being treated. She was supposed to have been treated like royalty, given who she supposedly was, not trussed up in a closet. Marielle claimed they were going to untie her and begin to 'rehabilitate' her the very day we busted them. She was in the kitchen preparing an elaborate meal for Anna's 'welcome party' when agents broke the door down."

Jake dismissed it. "She was just saying that to try to make them look good. Mitigating circumstances. 'Oh, yeah, we blindfolded this woman and tied her up in a closet for over a month, terrorized her, sexually abused her, but what we really *meant* to do was . . .'"

His mouth had gone dry, recounting it. The scotch tasted medicinal; he pushed it aside and asked for a glass of water.

"We thought of that," Peter assured him. "But Marielle wouldn't let it go. There's a point where you realize you can't break them down any further, so what they're telling you is as close to truth as they understand it—I know, I know," he said off Jake's upraised hand. "Too much information. But the suggestion has taken hold. Inquiries are being made."

Jake sighed. For Anna's sake, he was going to have to know. "Can we continue this conversation somewhere else?"

"Sure."

•

They walked around the Reflecting Pool, hands in their pockets, their breath forming plumes around their heads. The silence made Jake's ears ring. It was winter, not too many others crazy enough to be strolling in the shadow of the Washington Monument on a night when the temperatures were well below freezing, which was exactly what Peter had been counting on. Jake remembered, or thought he did, a night in a cave, his child's eyes alit with torchlight, when the air had been even colder than this. He suppressed a shiver. Peter walked briskly, as impervious to cold as he was to most physical challenges.

"The Russians have the body, you know," he was saying, looking straight ahead as he walked; anyone more than three feet away would not have even known he was speaking. He was cocooned in a knee-length dark overcoat and a sable hat with earflaps (Soviet import? Jake wondered with a corner of his mind, wishing he'd brought a hat; his ears were freezing), the lower half of his face swathed in a cashmere scarf that exactly matched the color of the coat. His voice, muffled by the scarf, was precisely loud enough for Jake to hear. "There's some controversy about whether they also have Hitler's—some sources say they do, others say he and Eva Braun were burned to ashes or buried in the subsequent shelling—but they definitely have Goebbels. Soviet troops were the first ones in the bunker.

"They found Goebbels and his wife, Magda, in the garden." Peter's voice had taken on a theatrical tone, like a Greek chorus. "The bodies were partly burned but still recognizable, especially his. He still wore a brace on his right leg, because of the crippled foot. They'd taken cyanide, Goebbels and his wife. The only mystery was whether or not he'd also shot himself. They found a Walther pistol by his side. . . ."

Jake shivered this time, though not from the cold. He was about to ask what the Russians had done with the bodies, but Peter wasn't finished.

"Inside the bunker, there was one room with bunk beds, three and three against the walls. It was where the Goebbels kids slept. He and Magda had six, you know, five girls and a boy. The eldest was twelve, the youngest three. They'd been tucked into their beds and given cyanide; they looked like they were sleeping. I've seen photos. There was a family Christmas card from 1940, I believe. Beautiful kids, in a spun-sugar kind of way. All blondes with dark brown eyes."

"Anna told me she was blonde when she was little," Jake murmured, almost to himself.

He wondered what would have become of the Goebbels children had they lived. Executed by the Russians as "enemies of the state," demon seed? Turned over to the British or the Americans as trophies? Were they better off dead? As for Anna . . .

No, the idea was monstrous. He stopped, listening to the echoes of his footsteps off the surrounding monuments.

"Look, I'm told Goebbels was a notorious womanizer. Half the 'Aryan' kids in Germany could have been his, and probably a few Jewish ones as well."

Peter had stopped a few feet ahead of him, turning with a dancer's grace. "That's as may be. But it's important to know for sure about Anna. To rule it out, if nothing else. The Soviets could help us with this, but they've already refused."

He turned again and kept walking, forcing Jake to jog to catch up with him.

"What could they do? The Soviets, I mean."

"As I say, they shipped the body back to Moscow after the war," Peter explained. "It's safe to say they've had it in the deep freeze ever since. Maybe autopsied, looking for some organic explanation for this particular variety of madness. Who knows? But you can believe they've held on to it. If we could get them to give us some blood and tissue samples . . ."

"For what?" The whole conversation struck Jake as macabre, but he had to know. For Anna's sake.

"Ever hear of human leukocyte antigen testing?"

Jake shook his head.

"Forensics experts have been using it for a couple of years now. It only works some of the time, but it's sometimes possible to match tissue samples for solving crimes. For instance, say a killer cuts his thumb on broken glass climbing through a window to get at his victim. If the police have a list of likely suspects, and the blood on the window matches one of them . . ."

"I'd think fingerprints would be more accurate."

"They are," Peter acknowledged. "But HLA testing sometimes works when there are no fingerprints, for crime solving. It's being used in medicine, too. Now, it's that much trickier trying to prove paternity, since a child would have only half of the father's genetic material, but they're working on that, too."

Again, Jake knew enough not to ask who "they" were.

"Ever hear of DNA testing?" Peter asked.

"Alphabet soup," Jake replied. His feet were numb, his face stiff. He'd tried inviting Peter back to his place, knowing Peter assumed his own apartment was wired, but Peter wanted to keep this conversation outdoors, out of the range of microphones real or hypothesized. Jake wondered, not for the first time, if his multitalented friend had ever seen a therapist, and if so, what a therapist would make of him. This was years before Watergate.

"Deoxyribonucleic acid," Peter said.

"Like I said, alphabet soup," Jake repeated. "Oh, wait. You mean gene testing. I did read something, in one of the medical journals. But it's all just speculative."

"Right now, sure. But in a few years, who knows?" Peter shrugged. "Anyway, the Official Thought is that the Front intended to try to prove Anna's paternity."

"And then—?"

"Who knows? Start a Fourth Reich with her as Fearless Leader? We're not talking about grown-ups here."

"The whole thing's ridiculous!" Jake snorted. "Even if they could prove it—"

"Of course," Peter agreed. "But it's the fact that they tried that has alerted the people I work for. And I'm not supposed to tell anyone, but I wanted you to know."

Jake picked up his pace. He'd heard enough; he wanted to go home to his warm apartment and a bed he was suddenly too acutely aware of being empty.

"I'm done," Peter called after him. Now it was Jake who turned to look at him. "Need to know, my friend. You'll want to check the shadows in the corners and under the bed for the next little while, not only in your professional capacity but to keep the young lady from further harm."

Jake wanted to shout after him, to thank him at least, to let him know that his professional and personal care for Anna were now one and the same, but Peter kept walking, his heels sharp on the frigid pavement. How did he find time to train, rehearse, dance, choreograph, travel, be seen at all the right parties, and still play spy games? Jake wondered, not for the first time.

And carry coals to Newcastle, he thought, remembering a phrase from his Liverpool secondary-school years. *Anna's mine to look after from now on, regardless. At least now I have an idea of the shape of some of the demons I'm defending her against.*

TWELVE

Anna is the key," Karen insists, finally having something to grasp at. "She displaced Raymond when my time line first wrinkled. She showed up in my fiction at the same time she was living a real lifetime with Jake Bower. And being the little girl in Johann and Margarethe's past. Her life crossed two of yours and one of mine."

She can hear Govannon considering it, as if only now remembering that humans tend not to be able to do this. "I think you may be right."

"How long were you together?"

"Anna and Jake? Thirty years and counting."

"No, you and Jake. What I mean is, how long do you inhabit each life? My impression at first was that it was like my experiences: weeks as Grainne, months as Grethe, hours as Margarethe. But in each instance, I was aware that whatever memories I had were theirs, not mine. All I could truly share with any of them was the Now, the time where our lives overlapped. But you talk about each person as if you've inhabited his entire life."

"I think," he says, in lieu of answering, "that tomorrow we need to go back to the Museum."

Somewhere between the lines Karen hears the thought:

Sooner rather than later. All this time they have been waiting passively for each bit of information to come to them. Now it is time for action. Finally!

"We can go now. I'm not tired."

"No." His voice steadies her, the hand he reaches out might be present enough to rest on her shoulder. "Let's go back to your novel."

His tone is mild, it's-up-to-you, but the resonance underneath says: *Please, it's important.*

"Are you sure? It seems to me the sooner we get started . . ."

"There is no time," he reminds her, and she has to stop and read between the lines.

"Meaning it's too late? Or meaning that because there is no time where you are, we have all the time in the universe?"

"There is no urgency. Not in the sense you understand it. Three chapters and an outline," he prompts.

•

September 17, 1941: Nazi storm troopers invade the former Summer Palace of the Tsars near St. Petersburg. The palace, Tsarskoe Selo, had been transformed into a public museum by the Soviets, and contained the Amber Room, the single most valuable artifact the tsars, and later the Soviets, ever possessed.

Designed by Andreas Schlüter, architect to King Frederick I of Prussia, and presented as a goodwill gift to Peter the Great of Russia in 1716, the Amber Room was constructed by German artisans entirely from Baltic amber and took decades to complete. Not until the reign of the Empress Elizabeth in 1770, when it was enlarged by the addition of six more panels and rococo friezes, was it considered finished.

Empress Elizabeth frequently had diplomatic visitors in to

tea, hoping to impress them with the opulence of the Room and, by extension, that of the Russian Empire. Thereafter the Room graced the so-called Catherine Palace, the tsars' Summer Palace in Tsarskoe Selo, for over a century and a half before the Nazi onslaught.

Consisting originally of twelve wall panels, later eighteen, carved over six decades from amber sometimes no more than an eighth of an inch thick, fitted together like a jigsaw puzzle, with the addition of mirrors, intricate Florentine mosaics depicting pastoral scenes, carved and gilded wooden friezes, brass and ormolu candelabra which held over five hundred candles, and a highly polished parquet floor, the worth of the Amber Room in materials and workmanship could, prior to the outbreak of World War II, be estimated in the hundreds of millions; its worth as an artifact to the Russian people—who, after the revolution, were allowed for the first time by special permission to tour the palace—was beyond measure.

Jake and Anna were convinced it still existed, and they were determined to find it.

•

The *Führerbunker,* Berlin: May 1, 1945: Adolf Hitler had killed himself and Eva Braun the day before. Joseph Goebbels's wife, Magda, poisons her six children by placing cyanide capsules in their mouths, after a doctor injects them with morphine to make them sleep. She writes in her diary: "The world that will come after the Führer and national socialism won't be worth living in, and that's why I've brought the children here. They're too good for the life that will come after us, and a merciful god will understand me when I give them salvation myself."

Shortly thereafter she and her husband commit suicide. Goebbels's charred body, found in the garden outside the bunker by Russian soldiers the following day, is removed to Moscow, along with that of his master, Adolph Hitler.

The postwar era: Numerous neo-Nazi groups spring up in the decades following the war. Perhaps the most enduring is a group which calls itself Reinheit, the German word for "purity." The group's premise is a bit unusual. While they revere Adolf Hitler as their Führer, they believe that the true genius behind the Reich was Joseph Goebbels.

Raising funds for their cause by trading in stolen artworks, gunrunning, and the occasional contract killing, Reinheit naturally intends to establish a Fourth Reich. Its figurehead will be a direct descendant of Goebbels himself.

A notorious philanderer, Goebbels might very likely have fathered at least one illegitimate child during his travels for the Reich. Agents of Reinheit spend decades tracing rumors from the USSR to the U.S. Only one likely candidate emerges. Found as a small child in the rubble of Berlin, adopted and raised in the States with no idea of her origins, she will be summoned when the time is right.

But there are some who are less patient than Reinheit. When an innocent young woman is kidnapped in the late '60s by a pack of unwashed neo-Nazis calling themselves the New Front for National Socialism, and held incommunicado for over a month before being rescued in a predawn raid by odd admixture of police, FBI, CIA, and one slightly daft civilian, the rumor somehow gets out that the victim is ostensibly the biological daughter of the Nazi propaganda minister. But the rumor makes no sense in view of the way she was held prisoner, and it soon dies out.

The media has long since lost interest in the event when, one by one, the escaped members of the New Front for National Socialism meet sudden and violent death, and the only member held in custody commits suicide, reduced to a footnote buried deep inside the late edition. The kidnap victim, too, drops out of sight.

At the end of the cold war: To all appearances, Anna and Jake Bower are a successful and interesting, but not especially remarkable, professional couple. She is an art restorer and historian, an expert at spotting fakes, he a D.C.-based therapist with some powerful clients. In the prime of their lives, they live comfortably and unobtrusively, with much of their social life centering around the arts—museum and gallery showings, and the ballet. Among their closest friends is the renowned choreographer Peter Kato.

No one would suspect that each of these three attractive, accomplished individuals harbors at least one dark childhood secret.

Peter is a Nisei, a first-generation Japanese-American who spent his early childhood in a detention camp in the Arizona desert. Jake, born Jakob Bauer, a German Jew, fled the Nazi onslaught with his parents as a small child. And Anna may or may not be the illegitimate daughter of the Nazi mastermind, Joseph Goebbels. Few would connect this assured and beautiful society matron with the waiflike kidnap victim thirty years earlier, but they are the same person.

Through his work with Holocaust survivors and their children, Jake Bower has made countless contacts with government officials, art museums, and private collectors in an attempt to recover some of the countless artworks stolen by both the Nazis and the Soviets during and just after World War II. He has an inexplicable obsession with the Amber Room. For all his wisdom and experience as a therapist, he doesn't fully understand it himself. Perhaps for the very reason that he has no ethnic, religious, or cultural tie to this particular artifact, he is free to obsess about finding it, and being instrumental in restoring it to its former owners, in the interests of world peace, and perhaps greater publicity for the cause of Nazi victims and their smaller, but no less precious, treasures.

Any whisper of a rumor about the Room draws Jake's attention. Imagine his excitement when he is approached by a friend of one of his clients, who just happens to work for the State Department, and who has seen some documents from the archives of the East German state police regarding the possible location of the Room. A colleague and old friend from Israel is able to provide more information, if Jake can meet him in Prague on a certain date.

Anna has a prior commitment and promises to join him as soon as she is able. Jake leaves for Europe on his own, flying into Frankfurt, taking a train into Prague, eventually ending up in Vienna. Two days later a rental car registered in his name is forced off a narrow road in the Tyrolean Alps and bursts into flames.

Anna is packing to join Jake when two suits claiming to be State Department employees appear on her doorstep and inform her that her husband is dead. The body has been cremated, she is told, and the ashes will be returned to her per her husband's wishes. Anna is stunned. How does the State Department know Jake's wishes? What does any of this have to do with Jake at all?

Anna refuses to believe that Jake is dead. Her first impulse, once she's shown the two feds to the door, is to contact Peter Kato.

•

Peter wasn't answering his phone. Anna knew he was home; he never got up before noon if he could help it. She left a message on his machine and was looking for his cell phone number when the phone rang. Thinking it was Peter, she grabbed it.

"Peter, thank God—" she began, then stopped herself.

"Mrs. Bower?" A male voice, cultured, with the slightest touch of a Maximilian Schell accent.

"Yes!" she said involuntarily, then stopped herself. "Who is this?"

"You have just received some visitors." It was as if, beyond confirming her identity, Anna hadn't spoken. "They have given you some very upsetting news. But what they have told you is not true."

"Who is this?" Anna demanded, over against a faint humming in her head that had begun when she opened the door of the townhouse and saw the two suits there and realized there couldn't possibly be any good news in their presence.

"Who I am is not important, please. You are concerned with the safety and the whereabouts of your husband. He is not dead, but he could be in grave danger if you do not cooperate with us, yes?"

Simple words, fragments of words, rattled into place in her head. Words like "kidnapped" and, in the disembodied voice's own words "could be in grave danger." Could be. She would cling to that. Very slowly, she relaxed her posture and sat in the chair closest to the phone.

"Tell me what to do," she said carefully.

Did she only imagine a conscious effort at relaxation on the caller's part, mirroring her own?

"Very good," the voice said. "You will wait there until someone comes for you, yes? That is all you need to do. Someone will be there soon."

The caller hung up. Tentatively Anna clicked off, wedging the phone between shoulder and ear. She was reaching for the Rolodex and Peter's new cell number when the phone rang again. She started so violently she almost dropped it.

"Hello!" she all but screamed.

"Anna? Peter. Just got your message. I'm in the car. Don't say anything until I finish, okay? I'll be at your door in less than a minute. Grab your passport and wait for me outside, where you can be seen from the neighboring houses. Don't talk to anyone else, not even someone you know. Don't touch the phone again once we're finished speaking. Have you got that?"

Anna swallowed, unsure of her voice. "I think so."

She ran upstairs to the bedroom. Her suitcase lay open on the bed; she'd wanted to iron a couple of blouses before packing them. Peter hadn't said to bring the suitcase, but if he wanted her to bring her passport . . .

She slammed the suitcase shut, and was lugging it down the stairs when Peter let himself in the front door without knocking. She couldn't remember how long ago she and Jake had given him a key—probably the day they'd moved in—but heretofore Peter had always knocked.

"Passport?" was all he said, eyeing the suitcase before relieving her of it.

Anna waved the passport at him before shoving it into the pocket of her trench coat. She slung the coat over one arm, Peter took the other. His young protégé, Justin, was idling an unfamiliar SUV in the driveway while Anna fumbled with locking the front door.

"Leave it!" Peter said softly between clenched teeth. "They'll get in anyway."

"But we don't want to let them think we knew they would, now, do we?" Anna shot back. The short burst of temper was enough to steady her nerves and her hands, and she managed to get the door locked.

Peter's laugh was almost soundless. "You'll do. Not a word in front of Justin. I'll explain everything after he drops us off."

That, Anna thought as the pieces started to fit together in her mind, would be very interesting!

•

"For starters, how did you know I got another phone call after I called you?" she began after Justin left them under the restaurant awning, glancing in the rearview mirror once before pulling away. She had to wait while one waiter provided menus, another filled their water glasses, and a third poured coffee for her, tea for Peter, out of long familiarity and without asking. "I haven't even begun to tell you about Jake, but you act as if you know it all already."

"I do," Peter said, looking around him to see if anyone at the adjoining tables was watching before he put on the half glasses he needed to read the menu. He wasn't as recognizable these days as he had been when he still danced, but he was no less vain about his appearance. "At least, I know as much as you do, and a little bit more."

"But—"

"Anna," Peter managed to hide his face behind the menu but still make himself heard. "We have an eight-hour flight to Frankfurt. I can answer all your questions on the way."

It took her a moment to digest this. "You're coming with me?"

He whipped off the glasses and tucked them inside his jacket, grinning at her. "Of course."

•

"Actually, we're not going to Frankfurt," he informed her after he'd switched tickets in a sleight of hand that was surprisingly good even for him. "At least, not directly."

He'd asked to see her ticket while their waiter served the entree ("I shouldn't be hungry, but I am," Anna said with something like wonder, while Peter dismissed her qualms with a wave of his hand. "You're hungry? Good. Eat. You'll need it."), perusing it for far longer than Anna thought was normal, even with a repetition of his fussing with the reading glasses. When he handed the folder back to her, she glanced inside on a hunch. The ticket inside was not the same.

"Dulles instead of Reagan or BWI, and a domestic flight instead of Lufthansa," Anna said, keeping her voice steady. "Good thinking. I think."

"I'm assuming they've been monitoring you since Jake left," Peter said. "In that case they'd know which flight you were taking to meet him. You're supposed to be home wringing your hands, waiting for the ashes to be delivered. Or else you didn't take them seriously, and you've bolted. You'll confuse them for a little while, but then just in case your mind is as narrow walled as theirs, they'll be waiting at the Lufthansa gate at Reagan. I'm counting on their not having enough manpower to check every flight for Frankfurt. Particularly not one that stops in Amsterdam first."

"What about you? You don't have any luggage."

"It was in the trunk of the car. Justin's gone ahead to precheck it for me. I want to have both hands free. You didn't notice you have a new name," Peter added, sounding disappointed.

"I—" Anna began, then looked at the ticket again. An involuntary giggle bubbled in her throat. "Nina Kato? Am I supposed to be your wife or your sister?"

Peter gave her an arch look. "Sorry, neither. My sister-in-law, if anyone asks, which they won't. Widow of my late and much beloved brother."

"You don't have a brother," Anna pointed out, being difficult. "Two bossy older sisters, but—"

"The Customs officer isn't going to know that. Anna, don't give me a hard time."

"And I suppose Nina Kato has a passport, because I obviously can't use mine."

"We'll make the swap in the cab," Peter assured her.

The humming inside Anna's head had grown to an intermittent thrumming, like a faraway helicopter coming closer, ominous.

"I don't suppose there's any point in asking you where the passport or the ticket came from?"

"Probably not."

Anna took a deep breath. It had started to rain, and she watched as it streaked the window near their table while she composed her thoughts. She'd never really asked Peter how deeply he was involved. Now she saw she should have.

•

"Involved in what?" he'd asked innocently the day after the rescue when he came to visit her in Walter Reed.

As far inside herself as she'd withdrawn, she was still flattered by his being here. One didn't have to know anything about ballet to know who Peter Kato was. Anna was a college kid, nobody special; Peter was as famous as Nureyev.

The Somebody pays a visit to the Nobody, Anna thought, sitting up in bed and actually worrying about what her hair looked like for the first time in over a month. She hadn't seen the newspapers or turned on the TV, much less noticed the phalanx of security extending from beyond the door of her private room all the way to the lobby, didn't realize that, for as long as the media feeding frenzy lasted, she too was a Somebody.

The stark hospital light loved Peter's face, defining the planes and angles, accentuating the ivory skin, the blue-black hair, the flash of flawless teeth when he smiled. He sat at complete ease in the plastic bucket chair, his perfectly toned body, all in artist's black, turning the heads of both sexes as he strode down the exact center of the corridor and showed his ID to the guard at her door.

Anna was well-read, intelligent. Not a psych student, but she knew enough to realize the welling of emotions she was feeling for her savior was just that—a heady mix of awe, gratitude, embarrassment, a dozen other emotions she couldn't name—but none of them was really sexual attraction. Not after what she'd been through. She wondered if she could ever bear being touched by another human being again. *I feel safe with him,* she told herself, then asked the question that would put him in perspective for her:

"What were you doing there yesterday?"

Peter's eyes almost gave him away. For the briefest of moments they looked away from her, to some unseen thing in the corner of the room. It was how she knew he wasn't being entirely honest with her. In time he would learn to cover better, but Anna would always know when he was lying.

"Would you believe I was just out for a walk and saw all this commotion and figured it would be a thrill to be a part of it?"

"No."

Peter pretended to be chagrined. Dancers are also actors, and his body language was flawless, but he was accustomed to audiences watching him from beyond the orchestra pit. Close up, he was still readable.

"This doesn't go beyond these walls . . ." he began.

"What? That you're a spy?" Anna's mind was so raw, in spite of or maybe because of the drugs they'd given her to ease the trauma of the abduction, the closet, the blindfold, those dirty hands and voices, that anything seemed possible. "So who do you work for? FBI, I guess, if it's inside the

States. Although I heard accents, in the closet. They said they were connected with people in West Germany. So, CIA, Interpol? My father always claimed he worked for the OSS just after the war, but my father is a drunk; he'll say anything." Anna's laugh was brittle, and she was trembling. "So you tell me the truth."

Peter worked with dancers; he'd dealt with backstage hysterics since his teens. He suppressed the collage of older memories that threatened to intrude here, of heat and dust and barbed wire, of uniforms and guns and barracks housing, little wooden pens where whole families lived in a space no bigger than a prison cell, the sound of his mother weeping nightly, his father's repressed, whispered rage, a rage that had eventually killed him, the expression on the faces of Caucasians when they spoke the word "Jap!"

All of that was at work here, rising up again and again every time "they" asked him to help, ever since the first time, backstage on tour in Europe when the very young, slicked-back, bland-looking suit with the mid-American accent pretending to be a documentary filmmaker ("Your unique place as a Japanese-American in a classical ballet company, blah–blah–blah . . . understand your family was relocated during the war . . .").

It was the latter comment that had tipped Peter off that the guy was a fake. For one thing, how would he know? For another, the official "take" in the '60s was that camps like Poston and Manzanar had never existed; only those who had been there talked about it, and only those of his generation whispered it, furtively, among themselves, not within earshot of the surviving elders. By then Peter was really intrigued. He had to find out who the guy really was, and what he wanted.

Thoughts of blackmail crossed his mind, too. It was a

cliché that all dancers were gay, but still not something to say aloud in the land of June Cleaver and *Life* magazine.

"What do you really want?" he'd asked the guy point-blank, hoping at the worst to make him go away.

That was when he was told about a dancer with a Latvian ballet company who, it was rumored, wanted to defect, and would Peter be willing to get close to her when the two troupes met next month on a goodwill tour in France? Nothing flamboyant like when Nureyev leaped to freedom in '61, just a quiet little conversation or two to make sure she was sincere and not a plant. If so, the professionals would take over from there. Don't answer yet, Mr. Kato; sleep on it tonight. Someone will be back to speak to you again to-morrow.

Peter spent the night staring into the dark, thinking about the nature of imprisonment, deciding finally that the issue wasn't loyalty to a country that had locked him up when he was four years old; the issue was freedom, in whatever form it took. If he'd been approached by a Soviet agent who wanted to help an American dancer defect to the other side, his decision would have been the same.

He'd been young enough, and naive enough, to think they'd only use him once. But at least his celebrity made it possible for him to pick and choose his "assignments." If the suits leaned too hard, he'd make a point of chatting up a journalist friend at a party. He and the journalist might only be talking about what Streisand was wearing at the Oscars, but the suits would back off. He was useful enough when needed, and not important enough to retire or kill.

When Anne-Marie Fallon was kidnapped, Peter had vol-unteered.

Now he studied the drawn, troubled face, almost as pale

as the sheets on the hospital bed, and thought carefully about his answer.

"You know who I am," he began, and she nodded. "Well, famous people often end up knowing other famous people. We're interconnected in funny ways. I'm not a spy. I've never trained at Langley or wherever. I don't carry a gun or, in spite of the stereotype, have a black belt in karate. I just try to help people. People in situations they don't want to be in. People like you."

"Okay." Anna had been sitting with her arms wrapped around her drawn-up legs. Now she seemed to sag, yawning violently, giving in to the effects of weeks of terror, and this morning's medication. Peter took it as a good sign. She had decided to trust him. He tucked her in, brushing the hair back from her brow.

"I'm here for you, Anna," he said. "Always."

•

Decades later, in a four-star restaurant in D.C., Anna put her fork down with a clatter and touched one hand to her brow, shading her eyes.

"Peter?" she said, fighting down panic. "What about Angelica?"

She hated herself for only now thinking of her daughter, her more-visible-than-either-of-her-parents daughter, who was lead cellist with a major symphony orchestra. Was she rushing off to rescue Jake and putting Angelica in danger?

"I made another call before I got to your house," Peter assured her. "Angelica's going to have the flu and miss a few performances over the next few days. She won't be happy about it, but she'll be safe."

"As long as this is over before the twenty-third," Anna mused. "They're doing the Dvořák. She'll be furious if she has to miss that." She stepped back and heard what she was saying. "God, Peter, I think I'm losing my mind! This is like a bad B movie!"

Peter touched her hand. "It's okay, Anna. You're not supposed to think of everything. Just know that Angelica's safe."

"You know where Jake is," Anna said carefully, trying not to sound accusing. "You know there's more to this than the Room."

"I know now," he said. "As soon as you got that phone call, it was more than just the Room. And I know Jake's alive because that's why they called you, but I don't know where he is. If I did, I'd retrieve him myself. But you're safer with me." He hesitated for a moment. "They want you to lead them to him."

Anna could feel a scream fighting to get out of her throat. She controlled her voice as much as she could, but it still sounded shrill. "Then why are we playing into their hands?"

"We aren't. We're just letting them think we are," Peter said, squeezing her hand. "I know it's complicated. I'll explain once we're safely on the plane."

"Safely? You mean—?"

"I don't know what I mean." Peter slipped on his glasses and pretended to study the dessert menu. He looked at Anna over the tops of the glasses. "Just promise me that until the plane leaves the ground, you'll do exactly what I tell you, no matter how bizarre it sounds. Promise?"

"Promise."

They finished their meal in silence. The rain was coming down in sheets now, and they had to run from the shelter of the restaurant awning to the waiting cab to keep from getting drenched. As promised, Peter swapped her passport for one he had in his raincoat. Anna looked at the photo, bemused. It was identical to the one in her original passport, as was everything except her name.

Ever since the day more than thirty years ago when Peter had rescued her from the Front, she'd wondered how deeply he was involved, and what in. It was as if he'd been anticipating this day for as long as he'd known her, and prepared for every contingency. A strange calm settled over her as the rain sluiced off the cab's windshield, making Peter's face and hers look as if they were melting. Jake was alive, that was all that mattered. The rest was just a bad dream.

THIRTEEN

They were waiting at the airport anyway.

". . . so I said 'Only if I can have the aisle seat.' "

Anna laughed obligingly. She'd heard the story before, knew Peter was performing, they both were, although if he knew who the audience was he wasn't sharing. They stood within view of their departure gate, though they might as easily be waiting near the adjacent gate for the flight to Jakarta. They pretended to be relaxed. Peter, who thought through his body, was better at it, but Anna had come of age in an environment that required quick reflexes and a host of personalities, and she was no slouch either.

Peter's eyes worked the crowd. To any but the casual observer, he was looking at Anna while they spoke, but anyone watching for more than a minute would see that he was looking just past her shoulder, scanning an approximate two hundred-degree range behind her for subject or subjects unknown. Occasionally he would shift his weight just enough to move them both an almost imperceptible few inches clockwise, so as to take a different segment of the arc into his field of vision.

"That's our boarding announcement," Anna said unnec-

essarily as the flight attendant at the desk made the call for
first-class passengers.

"I hear it." Peter made no effort to move.

Anna gripped the handle of her carry-on nervously. She
wondered if it wouldn't have been wiser to fly coach, but
Peter believed in hiding in plain sight.

"Peter, shouldn't we—"

She didn't finish. He took her elbow and leaned into her
slightly so he could speak in a whisper above the crowd
noise.

"Go to the ladies' room," he instructed her. "If you stand
just to the left of the doorway, I'll still be within your range
of vision. Leave the bag with me," he said as she tightened
her grip on it. When she'd nodded and released it, he went
on. "I'll lag behind the coach passengers so I'm the last to
board. When you hear the final announcement, wait for me
to put my hand in my left pocket, then make a run toward
me. Unless something, anything at all, prevents me from
getting on the plane, in which case—"

"Peter, you're frightening me—"

"You don't have time to be frightened now."

She could feel the warmth of his breath on her face. It
focused her. She closed her eyes for a fraction of a second,
and nodded again.

"If anyone other than the flight attendant gets between
me and the boarding ramp, you walk away. Don't look back.
Use this phone card"—she felt rather than saw him slip it
into her trench coat pocket—"and call Justin. Take a cab to
his place and wait."

"Wait for what?"

"Go, Anna, now."

There was a newsstand and a bank of telephones between

her and the rest rooms. As she passed the newsstand, a tall Aryan type hung up the last phone in the bank and brushed past her. As she reached the shelter of the rest room doorway, she turned and saw him stalking straight toward Peter. His walk was not friendly.

"A 'blond, Aryan type'?" Peter would have teased her if she'd told him. "What other Aryan type is there? You can't tell me you got that close a look at him."

"It was retroactive," she would have said. "When I saw him going toward you there was this sort of hyperfocus. I never actually saw his face, but I could describe it to you, down to the strawberry mark on his neck just below his left earlobe."

Peter would have shaken his head at her. "You're too much!"

But there was no time for that now. She didn't know for sure that this man was a threat. Maybe he just happened to look like central casting's idea of an SS officer. Maybe he and Peter knew each other. Maybe he wasn't actually approaching Peter at all. All she had to go on was a bad feeling, and that wasn't sufficient.

She knew enough from her adventures with Jake that to do anything other than precisely what Peter had told her could only make matters worse. But the urge to shout and warn Peter made her press one white-knuckled fist against her mouth, earning her odd looks from the two blue-haired ladies and the mother of a toddler struggling with a stroller on their way into the rest room.

Anna watched transfixed as the blond, half a head taller than Peter, stalked toward him. How was it possible that Peter hadn't noticed him? Or had he, and was that part of the game being played? Was Peter acting as a decoy to lure him away from Anna? A too-rapid movement from the far corner of her peripheral vision yielded two suits bearing down on the *Übermensch* from stage left. Anna's head swung around, she focused with a start. They were the same two suits who had appeared on her doorstep to tell her Jake was dead.

As if in a dream, she watched the blond register their presence, then turn and move off quickly, not quite at a run. One of the suits began walking rapidly in pursuit. The second, as if all of this were perfectly normal, casually approached Peter and seemed to be striking up a conversation. Anna stared at Peter's profile, trying without success to lip-read from this distance, hoping for clues. Peter's posture was relaxed, his gestures unhurried. The coach passengers, who had been lining up moments before, were mostly on the plane by now. Some few had watched the other two men hurrying by, but their curiosity was transient.

"Attention, ladies and gentlemen," the flight attendant began in one of several languages as Anna agonized over what to do. Peter had told her to leave if there was any trouble, but all she wanted to do was rush the spook in the suit hard enough to knock him down, and run with Peter toward the plane. "This is the final boarding announcement for Northwest Airlines flight number thirty-six to Amsterdam. . . ."

A sound of firecrackers from the direction the other two had gone. It was enough to make the spook let go of Peter's arm, glaring at him over his shoulder before bolting off to help his friend. As if in slow motion, Peter smoothed back a wing of jet black hair and moved toward the boarding ramp, Anna's carry-on bag, with its wheels and long handle, in tow. Just when she thought he never would, he stopped, put his hand in his left pocket, and drew out his boarding pass.

Grateful she'd remembered her sister Caitlin's best advice ("Never wear shoes you can't run in"), Anna ran.

•

"What happened back there?" she dared when the plane was finally in the air and her heart rate was almost back to normal. Neither she nor Peter had said a word until then.

"Oh, I imagine someone got shot, though not fatally," Peter said casually, setting up his laptop on the tray table and settling his glasses on his nose. "And I imagine the Hitler Youth poster boy will be detained for questioning, which is good news for us. And I imagine some creative fictions will be provided for the media."

"Who was he? What did he want with you?"

"Beats me." Peter was intent on attracting the flight attendant's attention, pantomiming toward the laptop to know if it was okay to use it yet.

"What about the other two? Those are the same two who told me Jake was"—Anna lowered her voice—"who told me about Jake. They said they were from State. Won't they contact someone and try to stop us when we land in Amsterdam?"

"Nope." The flight attendant smiled at Peter and nodded. He turned on the laptop.

"What do you mean 'nope'?" Anna's tone was exasperated. "You've got to do better than that. You're telling me State or CIA or whoever they were can't just contact their counterparts in Europe and detain us?"

"Softly, please. They can't touch us now. They are None of the Above." Peter was not making eye contact. He was fiddling with a games program, and the reflection from the screen made planes of blue and green light dance on the lenses of his reading glasses. "They have no jurisdiction outside the States. Or inside, for that matter. Officially they don't exist."

"I see," Anna said, frowning. "Or, rather, I don't see. And you can't tell me Blondie didn't have backup. Someone to report to, someone who might notice if he got shot in the leg and hauled off for questioning."

"All quite possible." Satisfied with the games program, Peter concentrated on opening a spreadsheet in a second window.

Anna tapped her fingers on the armrest, counted to ten. Peter seemed to have forgotten she was there.

"You may as well tell me everything," she tried.

"I don't know 'everything.' I'll tell you what I know. In time," Peter said, searching for a file. "For now, you look like you could use a nap. Or maybe you'd prefer to watch the movie."

"I'm not—" Anna began, then realized what he was doing.

"Easier if we do it this way," Peter typed rapidly. "No chance someone will overhear."

Anna yawned ostentatiously. She saw his point. The first-class cabin was safer than coach. Their seats were far enough away from anyone else's so that they could probably talk in whispers, but this way was better. Too intense a conversation was bound to draw at least a casual eavesdropper. But a Japanese businessman working on his quarterly report while his female companion napped or watched some aimless comedy on the small screen set into the seat in front of her would soon draw yawns from everyone around them.

Anna watched as Peter opened a third window on his screen. One for the games program, one for a screed in Japanese that could easily be a quarterly report, and, sandwiched

in the middle, the narrative he was filling in for her. If someone got too inquisitive or merely too close, he could change
screens in a heartbeat. Anna beamed at him in admiration,
yawned again, leaned her shoulder against his, half closed her
eyes, and read as he typed.

•

Jake Bower was an indifferent chess player, but he found
himself remembering the moves as David ben Shahan let him
win the first game. They played in silence, with the fervor
of those for whom it was a very serious business. When
they'd succeeded in boring everyone else in the steamy-
windowed café into considering them invisible, they talked.

Brilliant! Jake thought with genuine admiration. David
had chosen the perfect venue, one of the myriad such places
throughout Central Europe where one could nurse a cup of
coffee and a newspaper until lunchtime, order beer and sau-
sages and talk until evening or later, without anyone's suggesting it was time to leave. Revolutions had been formed
in such places, art and music and literature created, discussed
and criticized afterward, new ideas explored. If the U.S. was
a cultural wasteland, Jake thought with a chuckle, it was
because someone else always needed the table.

He and David spoke in German, which was less conspicuous than English and, aside from catching each other up on
their respective families and personal lives, they actually said
very little. Midway through the third game, David produced
a business card and slid it across the table near Jake's elbow.

"I've worked with Tony before," Jake said, having read
the card with a puzzled frown. Anthony Nunn was an art
dealer, a British expatriate who made his home in Vienna at
the moment, and an acquaintance of twenty-plus years' duration. David knew all of this. "Matter of fact, I thought

I'd at least call him while I was over here. Got my own copy of his card in my briefcase."

"Then you won't need this one, will you?" David said, taking it back.

"That doesn't answer my question. Why did Tony contact you? Why didn't he come to me directly?"

"Who was it that said 'sometimes the longest way round is the shortest way home'?" David answered by way of not answering. "Too many people sniffing around him for too many reasons. Tony's up to a lot of things these days, not all of them entirely kosher. He prefers to avoid overlap."

"What makes him so sure they won't be watching when I get there?" Jake wanted to know.

"Aqaba by sea," David said, studying the chessboard, trying to sound mysterious.

"You watch too many movies. All right, I get it. If I'd flown directly into Vienna and gone straight to Tony's, I might be noticed. But meandering in from the East, I'll slip in behind their backs."

"Exactly." David motioned toward the board. "Another?"

Jake shook his head.

"I'd like to keep moving," he said, reaching for his wallet. "Thank you, David. You know I can't ever repay you for this one."

"Thank me if and when you find it." David put a hand over his to stop him. "Put that away. I'm still working on paying you back for saving my life."

"Ridiculous!" Jake said. "On that score we're even. But we neither of us have time to argue about it. I assume you didn't come all this way just to see me."

"You assume correctly," was all David would say, and Jake asked nothing further. Tony wasn't the only one who was up to a lot of things. If anyone with rumored Nazi ties living within a one hundred-kilometer radius of Prague turned up on the evening news on his way to trial, Jake would note David's uncredited handiwork, and draw his own conclusions.

"All right, then." The two men shook hands, as if they'd be here for chess again within the week, and not as if both were on their way out of town and might never see each other again.

•

The spy business, Jake thought from his tenuous view of the fringes, as he stood on the pavement outside Anthony Nunn Ltd. was, like academic research, mostly plod. Go here for this piece of information, there for that. A rumor here, a document there, an overheard conversation reported by a third party, an invoice, a photocopy of a photocopy, a scrawl on a scrap of paper. Fit them together into a puzzle that perhaps countless others have tried to solve before you or that perhaps had never been attempted to this point, step back and see what the picture looked like, then plod on searching for the next piece.

The reflection of the late afternoon sun on the shop window created a fandango of orange flame. Impossible from here to see inside, to see if the shop was open or closed, whether Tony was alone or with a customer, or perhaps out of town on a buying trip, and the shop being run by an assistant. From this angle the entire building seemed to be on fire. Jake would remember that image for the rest of his life.

•

"The car was rented in Jake's name," Peter typed. They could hear the dinner carts rattling. "That's what had the local police fooled. But the dental records didn't match."

"So it wasn't—" Anna had to speak; she couldn't contain herself any longer.

"Did you ever meet Tony Nunn?" Peter interrupted her, closing everything on his screen but the games program. The question was harmless enough, even if overheard above the clatter of first-class cutlery.

"Once," Anna said. "The first time Jake and I were in Vienna. Jake was understandably ambivalent about visiting the city that had exiled him when he was a child, so we'd been just about everywhere else first. Except Berlin, because that was my city of sorrows."

Peter nodded, waiting for her to go on.

"I'm afraid Tony and I started talking shop almost the minute Jake introduced us—he's got a couple of de Hooches and a Steen; obscure ones, but in excellent condition, and he wanted my advice on how to keep them that way. We've written or e-mailed on and off ever since. Holiday cards, that sort of thing, but I never got back to Vienna so we never met again face-to-face. I remembered that afternoon, though, thinking afterwards that Jake must have been bored out of his skull listening to us finish each other's sentences, but you know how long-suffering he was. Is. Oh, God. So it was Tony?"

Peter wasn't about to commit. "Describe him."

"About Jake's age, about Jake's height. Dark hair, when I met him, silvering on the sides. Rather like Jake's. I suppose he'd be completely white by now. Like Jake." The conclusion was obvious; neither had to say it aloud. "Why?"

"Why did they swap or why did someone kill him, you mean?"

"You know Jake would never knowingly put someone else in harm's way. Tony must have tricked him somehow. But why?"

Peter was typing again. "We think T gave J some info, another contact somewhere else. The next piece of the puzzle. J went on his way, maybe with a false ID T provided, not realizing T planned to create a diversion. Because T knew someone would try to follow J. Or maybe nothing to do with J. T was a very busy man."

Anna took a deep breath before she asked her next question. "Who did Tony work for?"

"Can't tell you," Peter typed.

"Meaning it's secret, or you don't know?"

"Can't tell you," Peter typed again.

"But he was . . . involved," Anna persisted.

Peter nodded imperceptibly, shutting down the laptop, clearing the tray table for dinner.

"Peter? How much was Tony involved? As much as Jake? As much as you? Or more?"

"Yes."

Anna sighed. When Peter was reduced to monosyllables, the subject was effectively closed.

"Poor Tony!" she murmured, almost as an afterthought.

Poor Anna! Peter thought, studying her carefully whenever he could without her noticing. He knew she was strong, but she would have to be that much stronger for what lay ahead.

Hours later, when she'd actually dozed a little with her head on his shoulder, he asked her: "Do you know where Jake would be if he thought he was in danger?"

•

He was entirely too comfortable in this part of the world, Jake thought, stopping at a news kiosk for copies of *Kürier* and *Der Standard*. His German was good enough to pass, and he liked to stay up on local events, if for no other reason than to see if he could guess from the headlines what else besides seeing him had brought David ben Shahan to Prague.

Jake rarely pretended to be anything other than an American, but this time was different. The documents Tony had given him listed him as a German citizen, a dealer in rare stamps and coins, permanent residence in eastern Prussia. Time to play the part.

It had been two days since Jake and Tony had spoken; he was dawdling in Vienna primarily, he told himself, to make sure no one was following him. But he was also trying to understand the feeling of déjà vu he experienced every time he came here.

The first few times he'd sought out the places he remembered as a boy, but so much had been leveled during the war, so much rebuilt and torn down and rebuilt again in the intervening decades, and even what remained was no longer familiar. It was as if older memories had so overlayered his own that they were no longer his, but those of another man, or several.

He never read obituaries in any language, so he might have missed the tiny item at the bottom of the page. But it was hard not to notice his own name in print. "Tentatively identified as," he translated, and an auto accident near Innsbruck. No sense of déjà vu there, just immediate horror and rage.

Tony, you idiot! he thought when he had figured it out, remembering the exchange of documents. ("Here you go, old boy. Better for you to be someone else for the nonce. Places you're going some people don't cotton to *Juden*, eh? Your own passport goes in the safe, all nice and tidy, till you find what you're after. Then you drop us a fax or an e-mail saying you want it back, and Mr. FedEx will pay a visit anywhere in the world, right?") The passport hadn't stayed in the safe, but had gone into Tony's pocket, for reasons Jake only partly understood.

Now Tony was dead, taking Jake's identity with him, meaning Jake was free to be whoever he chose to be for as long as it would take him to see a man about a dog in a suburb of what used to be East Berlin.

"Stasi files, old dear, yours for the asking now that the Wall's gone down," Tony had told him, fairly twinkling with excitement. "Yours for the asking, that is, if you know who to ask, and if you look as if you have the right to ask. If the East German *Polizei* don't have documentation on the whereabouts of the Amber Room, no one does.

"Thing of it is, files are a disaster. Stuffed in boxes, never properly archived. Hard to keep watch on all your citizens, bug the loo, amass reams of documentation, *and* get it all properly filed. Characteristic efficient German juggernaut bumps smack into the brick wall of Soviet indolence and do-it-tomorrow-when-tomorrow-never–comes, and you've got a proper mess. They don't know what it is they have on this particular subject, but we do. And you're going to find it, with the help of that little slip of paper you've got along with your new passport.

"Wouldn't keep it there, by the way, if I were you," Tony had concluded. "Too much to memorize, especially at our age, but you might try tucking it somewhere less notice-able."

"I will," Jake assured him. "But why give it to me? Why not go after the Room yourself?"

"For starters, my German's not nearly as good as yours," Tony had temporized, not quite able to look him in the eye. "Oh, the words, certainly, but never the accent. You can take the boy out of Hornchurch, but not the other way round, yes?"

"And—?" Jake prompted. He wanted to hear the words

aloud, to ascertain exactly how much Tony knew.

"And we both know the Room is only the first half of it!" Tony had said all in a rush and more than a little crossly. He'd squeezed Jake's arm then. "Look, Jake, it's easy enough to say that those of us who know and love Anna would kill for her, but in the end it's just words unless one puts some action behind it, right? I've an inkling who you're trying to draw out and why, and, my God, man, your courage in the face of what they could do to you—!"

"I'm hoping someone bigger and scarier than me will step in and stop them before it goes that far," Jake said.

Tony had eyed him dubiously. "Yes, well. Since I can't talk you out of it, the least I can do is give you a leg up, so to speak."

He'd done that and more, Jake thought ruefully, feeling a red rage gathering behind his eyes at the thought of how Tony had died.

Past time for a change of plans. He folded the newspapers methodically to still his shaking hands, leaving them on the table beside his unfinished coffee *mit Schlag*, and vanished into the crowd in front of the Burgtheater.

•

"Yes, I know exactly where Jake would go," Anna told Peter as the plane began its descent. "The question is, where are *we* going, and why?"

"Well, Amsterdam, for starters. Then Frankfurt."

"And—?"

"And, I'm surprised you didn't yell at me for having the wienerschnitzel. I know you don't approve of eating baby animals, but I haven't had a good piece of veal since I met Justin. Justin's a vegan, did I tell you that? I keep telling him he can't sustain a dancer's regimen on vegetables . . ."

"Peter—"

"No," he said firmly. "Jake is safe, and we're going to go get him. The rest has to wait, for now."

•

"It's not like in the movies, is it?" the old man asked his students thoughtfully. They eyed each other warily, unsure if the question was rhetorical, or if they were expected to answer. "It never is, you know."

•

Human-designated borders change. Primeval nature remains the same. In almost every country there are caves, as fixed in geography as the cave itself is fixed in the human mind.

We forget that our time in cities is measured in the thousands of years, our time aboveground as hunter-gatherer-farmers measured in the tens of thousands. Before all that, for several million years before that, there was the cave. The Garden of Eden, in whatever language, is only wishful thinking. Much of mankind's memory resides in dank, fetid pockholes filled with the stink of rotten meat and too many bodies in too small a space. Having sprung from this, is it any wonder we consign so many of our fellows belowdecks, to mines, to windowless rooms and cubicle farms, instead of allowing them to live beneath the trees?

The cave in Jake Bower's mind lay in a place most recently called Slovenia. The last time he had been here, when he and Anna were newlyweds, it had been part of Yugoslavia. The first time, he had been a child, too young to know what it was called or who had claimed it then. He only knew that it had saved his life.

After his brother Herman was taken, Jake's father had finally roused himself enough to get the rest of his family out of Vienna. Jake's memories were of dim, stuffy rooms full of weeping women, eternal train trips, long journeys on foot, then still more trains, each more cramped and shabbier than the one before. Finally, the wonder of the caves.

He would read his own history years later, learn of the partisans who hid a trainload of Jewish refugees in the Adelsberg Caverns before smuggling them across the border into Italy. He'd joked that if his Indiana Jones adventures ever got him into serious trouble, he would hide out in the caves.

From the comfort of his Alexandria living room, it had seemed so simple. Now he was not so sure.

What if the people who had killed Tony realized their mistake? Would they have the knowledge and the power to backtrack, to search Tony's place, perhaps find evidence of a false passport, and deduce who it had been given to? Jake knew Tony to be beyond fastidious, but he might have made mistakes. In that case, the passport's use was limited to a certain number of days, and to where in the landscape he would stop using it and allow the trail to grow cold.

It got him a series of second-class rail trips out of Vienna and roundabout into Trieste, where he left his good luggage with most of his clothes in a dubious-looking locker in the station, bought a rucksack and what would pass for hiking clothes from an open-air Saturday secondhand market. A travel visa for Slovenia, another second-class rail ticket into the town of Postojna, where a gaggle of hikers his daughter's age advised him on where to buy canned goods and dried beef, before joining the rest of the tourists taking the underground train ride through Europe's largest known contiguous network of caverns.

Halfway into the hour-long tour, when the guide turned off the lights to impress his visitors with the true meaning of subterranean darkness, Jake stayed behind.

FOURTEEN

Déjà vu all over again, Karen thinks, this overlap of the reality of Anna and Jake Bower's lives with what she thought was her own fiction. Been there, done that. This is her third adventure since stumbling over a jellyfish two novels ago; she's an old hand by now, seasoned. Whatever doubts she had about her ability to handle time travel were dissipated once she got out of Grainne and Grethe and Margarethe's lives and back into her own. In the event, she has work to do. After all, it was one of those women who saved Anna's life, foredooming her to that scene in the closet, and what came after.

In a previous life, Karen's fiction had become the S.oteri's reality. Could she do the same for Govannon? If the universe really was a Möbius strip, why not?

"Was I close?" she asks Govannon quietly, her voice surprisingly mellow to her own ears in the dark. The night's rain patters softly against the leafed things that gleam with a kind of diffuse light beyond the windows, as if no time at all has passed.

She hears his indrawn breath. "Uncannily."

She is almost afraid to breathe. "So what happens next?"

"You tell me."

"First I'll ask you: Did you refer Anna to another therapist?"

"What do you think?"

"Professionally, you should have, before you formed a personal relationship. But . . ." She hesitates, listening to his voice in her head, the way she always does with her characters. "I don't think you did. I think you ended your formal sessions, but continued to talk her through informally."

Govannon smiles. "Brilliant! By George, I think she's got it! Exactly right. This may be easier than I dared hope."

His eyes and teeth are all that are visible in the darkness. The fire has gone out, the fireplace vanished. Karen has been tucked up in bed, though she doesn't remember how she got there.

She lies on her side, head on her arm, at ease, her thoughts caressing the shape of Govannon's back silhouetted against the suggestion of light through the windows. There are no streetlights, she reminds herself. The night sky is overcast, raining, no possibility for moon or stars. Where does the light come from?

Another unasked question. It only matters to her because she can see Govannon in the dark, a solid presence against the half-light, though he is "gone" again, seeming to sit on the edge of the bed without displacing anything. She's almost getting used to it.

"Mm, that feels good," he says, flexing his shoulders.

"You can feel that?" Karen asks, surprised. She hasn't moved. It was her mind's hand that caressed him. (Well, if a mind can have an eye, why not a hand?)

"Mm, a little lower. Right there, on both sides of the spine . . ."

"Am I right? About the therapy sessions?" She doesn't

want to stop, wants to knead the knots out of his shoulders that she knows are there, wants to stroke every muscle of that broad back, kiss every freckle spangling his shoulders, but she also wants an answer to her question.

"Oh, all right!" he grumbles, yielding reluctantly, as if she really had been giving him the most wonderful back rub and he was savoring every stroke. "Back to business. No, I did not refer Anna to another therapist. She refused to see anyone else. One thing you must understand about Anna above all else is that once she makes up her mind, she will not be swayed. Even at so young an age, she was immovable.

"We did continue the formal sessions for a few more months until I could assure Peter that she was coping, so he could assure her government watchdogs that she was healthy enough to resume her life. After that we had what I call co-counseling sessions, each of us taking a turn talking, then listening. I can honestly say that, while I was the professional and she was not, she helped me as much as I her. Maybe even more."

Karen hears him speaking as Jake now. There is none of the morphing that transpired back when they were visited by the scenes from his childhood, but his voice and posture and manner have altered subtly for the role. An actor absent a script, indeed! Karen thinks. If he truly is, he's very good at improv.

"So you were with her then? Sharing Jake's life even that far back?"

He shrugs. "Could have been. The memories are there. Whether we lived them together, or I came in later, or came and went . . . it's not a question I can answer."

"All right." Karen nods. "Then I'll stop asking questions like that. What happened next?"

"Anna went back to school, finished her degree. She'd

been working for a local art collector as a cataloguer and restorer when she was kidnapped. She eventually started as a file clerk at the National Gallery, but she was good, too good. She had an eye. Became an expert at spotting forgeries. But you know all that from *Nightline*. Somewhere in there I asked her to marry me. Her father managed to sober up long enough to clap me on the back and inform me I 'seemed like a decent fella, for a Jew-boy.' "

He can see Karen struggling with something.

"Is it the ethnic slur that troubles you?"

"You're reporting what you heard," she doesn't quite answer.

"It's the multiplicity of detail," he suggests. "I keep forgetting how difficult it must be to keep it all in your head, particularly where not only two lives but reality and fiction overlap."

"There is that. I can't imagine how you do it. But there's something else, too, that I can't quite get to. . . ." The rain stops abruptly, as it does every night at precisely the same moment, as if God has shut off the sprinkler system. "Were there versions of Anna in any other lives than Jake's and Johann's? Even in a minor role?"

This is clearly something Govannon has not considered. Karen can see him scanning howevermany memories before he answers.

"I don't believe so," he says finally. "At least, as nearly as I can remember."

Karen settles back down into what is really the most comfortable bed she's ever slept in, her eyes still on him.

"I miss you," she says. "I wish you could lie beside me."

"Well, why didn't you say so?" He lifts the coverlet beside her. "Move over!" he commands and, giggling, she does. His shadow blocks the light from the window, the coverlet falls lightly over him. Karen closes her eyes, listens to the steady rhythm of his breathing, remembers that he doesn't snore. She can feel him beside her, feel his displacement in the bed. She accepts it. No point in questioning it, just cherish it when it happens. Keeping her eyes closed, she reaches out, and her hand comes to rest in the middle of his back. He chuckles. As she drifts into sleep, she is smiling.

•

Pretty scene, isn't it, Gentle Reader? Watching them sleep together, you're confident that they will solve it, that Karen will work some more of the fictional magic which seems to move through her the way the visions of a once and future king moved through Merlin in his crystal cave, the way Govannon's myriad lives and fragments of hers realize themselves on the cold stone walls of the Museum or on sheets of cheap copy paper, baffling her editors, dazzling the critics, frustrating readers who can find the reviews but not the books to read, and bring Govannon home again.

And when she does? Why, of course he'll have the magic to find the rest of his kind and bring them back from whatever dimension of time and space they're lost in, recalled to life, won't he? There will be much rejoicing, and they'll all live happily ever after.

And then what? Will they make Karen an honorary TQ, invite her to stay with them on Relict or teach her telekinetic travel, too? Or will Govannon elect to return to Earth with her, at least for the length of her lifetime, and forgetting that one of his incarnations just happens to be married to someone else? After all, it's not as if he can't be in two places at once. In fact, if this were an open-ended s/f series and not a grudgingly allotted trilogy, he and Karen, caught as they are in a time-not-time, could have endless adventures, and truly live happily ever after.

But we all know Karen's editor isn't going to stand for it. He's already said he doesn't understand her work, and God knows he's been nothing but a speed bump in her progress this far. So this is the end, beautiful friend. This book will be the last, Just Because. Whatever Karen wants to say will have to be said here.

As for solving the mystery, writing Govannon back into existence, saving the happy ending, have you entertained the possibility, even for a moment, that she might fail?

Don't think about it too hard, Gentle Reader. It will only spoil your enjoyment of the pages to come. We don't want that. So let's take our cue from the sleepers. When you have no time, you have all the time in the universe.

Look at them with their arms around each other, breathing in tandem, unaware that the only time they're fully able to connect with each other is within the realm of dream . . .

•

Berlin, autumn 1945: The fat man thrust the child into Frank Fallon's arms. "Her name is Anna," he wheezed in German, sweating even in the morning chill. "Her mother is dead."

The little girl reached out to the American, her tiny hands scrabbling at the collar of his uniform tunic, arms wrapping around his neck like vines. Something panicked in him and he tried to pry her loose.

"Look, buddy, I can't take her. It's not my job. You have to bring her to the infirmary." Fallon nodded in the direction of the familiar flag on the rooftop two buildings away. "Red Cross, *ja*?"

But the fat man either didn't understand English or wasn't listening.

Was it the captains' insignia that drew them, or only the deceptive openness of Frank Fallon's freckled face? At thirty-five he looked younger than some of the regular draftees, an overgrown Boy Scout, too easy to trust. It was one of the reasons he'd been plucked out of the typing pool (his eyesight too bad for combat, married with kids, too, not the kind of GI, called up in the last year of the war, that you wanted to send home in pieces) to play the poster boy of the occupation forces in post-Potsdam Berlin.

You can trust me! Frank Fallon's face said, even the wire-framed glasses like Harry Truman's and the pipe he affected suggesting intelligence, reliability. And because you can trust me you can trust all Americans. We're not like those goddamn Russkies across the road.

Whatever dubious charisma Frank Fallon had overseas, his own kids were terrified of him, and while his wife, Eleanor, included him in the family prayers every night ". . . and please, God, keep our daddy safe and bring him home from the war . . ." in her sugary voice, neither the boys nor coltish Caitlin truly cared if they never saw him again.

But here he found himself surrounded by street kids every time he stepped outdoors. They would line up by the guard shack and salute him every morning while he waited, briefcase under his arm, lighting his pipe, for the car to take him to the Allied *Kommandatura*, where representatives of all four victorious nations met daily to see if there was anything— even the lunch menu—that they could all agree on.

Because he had no languages beyond high school Latin, Captain Fallon was a minor player, an aide who stood behind the American Commandant's chair when it was his turn in the rotation and handed him papers out of the briefcase, doing a younger man's job because none of the younger men could be spared. He was only a flunky, but a redheaded, spit-and-polish flunky, the all-American OSS functionary. The street kids and the *Trümmerfrauen,* the old women who

picked through the rubble daily looking for something, anything to salvage, adored him.

Most times he only had to walk three short steps to the
jeep Corporal Timmons pulled up with a screech of brakes
at precisely 8:45 every morning, stirring the red brick dust
that still covered the cobbles, sifting over everything months
after the surrender. They'd take off for Dahlem, a ten-
minute drive if there was nothing in their path—a crumbled
building that had given up the ghost during the night, a line
of refugees plodding back from the hinterlands with carts
and prams and wheelbarrows filled with belongings, searching for homes that might no longer be there—and if he was
in a generous mood Captain Fallon would toss the kids a
few Hershey bars or a scattering of cigarettes for street barter.
What he dreaded most was being stopped anywhere along
the route; his open American face attracted them, and it was
hard to shake them off.

But on this particular morning, Corporal Timmons had
been quarantined with chicken pox.

"Chicken pox?" Fallon repeated when the staff sergeant
had rung him up to let him know. "How the hell do you
notice chicken pox on a man that color?"

The staff sergeant, who hailed from Alabama, thought that
was hilarious. Fallon could picture him scratching one overlarge red ear while he laughed.

"Beats me, sir. I've even heard Nigras can blush, but it's
not anything I've ever seen."

"Well, you keep an eye out for that, Sergeant," Frank
Fallon said with a wink in his voice. Being New York Irish,
he could swap racist remarks with the best of them.

He'd managed to hitch a ride that morning with someone
from the motor pool, but when the day's meeting broke up
and the big brass went off in their cars, he was left standing

on the steps of the imposing gray stone building that had
once been headquarters of the Nazi Labor Front, which was
somehow untouched by the shelling that had leveled one
building out of every three in the city, his briefcase empty,
wondering how far it was to walk, and whether, with neither
cigarettes nor chocolate to distribute, he could make it without being swarmed.

He was almost within sight of the barracks when the two
men seemed to appear out of nowhere with the child.

Now he could feel the little girl's openmouthed breathing
warm against his throat; her hair was fine and blond, and a
light breeze blew it against his mouth and nose like candy
floss. He didn't dare put the briefcase down; even empty it
could be stolen, and he'd hate to have to explain that. He
hooked the hard leather handle over the last two fingers of
his right hand, so he could support the kid's weight with
that hand and rest his left hand on her back to steady her.

What if she's carrying something? he wondered. Her skin
was cool, her breath sweet, but the pinprick rash of typhus
could manifest itself in minutes. How old was she? She felt
lighter than a rabbit in his arms, fragile.

He sized up the two characters who had brought her, the
fat man with his Coke-bottle glasses and asthmatic wheeze,
the older man, patrician and silent, standing just behind him,
observing more than participating, and wondered what the
story was.

"I can't take the kid," he repeated, nodding again toward
the Red Cross flag, trying to push the child back into the
fat man's arms. "Infirmary. Take her to the infirmary."

But the fat man and his silent companion were already
moving off, and the kid was holding on to his neck so tightly
he was finding it hard to breathe.

"Hey!" Frank started to shout, but the little girl jumped with fright and clung closer, burrowing her face into his neck. The fat man turned as if he'd been insulted.

"You must take her, *mein Herr*," he said evenly, as if it had been decided by someone other than himself. Neither he nor the white-haired man ever looked back.

What the hell! Frank Fallon thought once they'd picked their way over a pile of rubble and disappeared between two partly damaged buildings. It didn't mean a damn thing anyway. All he was going to do was dump her with the first Red Cross nurse who crossed his path. He headed in the direction of the flag, patting the little girl's back gently, out of long practice, sitting up nights with any of his bawling, colicky red-haired brats.

"I need my beauty sleep," Eleanor would announce, dumping the latest one in his lap and trailing down the hall. "You can at least do your share."

The war, Frank Fallon thought, his war, had been a pleasant change of pace. Well, at least by the time he got back the youngest would be out of diapers, and there wouldn't be any more. The last one had done something to Eleanor's insides and she'd needed a hysterectomy. She was still carrying on about it when he'd shipped out. Why a woman couldn't be content with five kids, Fallon thought bitterly, each of them louder and more demanding than the next, all elbows and knees and overbites and bad tempers, as different from this flaxen-haired beauty as—

She was a beauty, he thought in spite of himself, looking down at her heart-shaped face. Those eyes, though, would haunt him if he looked into them too long. He stopped just outside the infirmary. What the hell was he thinking? He was going to dump her in with all the rest of them, tumbling everywhere in the overcrowded building like so many litters of puppies, let her blend in with the rest of this godforsaken country's orphans and forget all about her.

The child stirred and raised her head sleepily.

"Papa?" she asked softly.

"No," Frank said, too quickly, in English. "Not Papa. Jesus, kid, don't go getting any ideas! God knows who your papa was. Not Papa, no."

She didn't understand the words, but he hadn't raised his voice, which seemed to reassure her. She smiled then, her whole face lighting up.

"*Schokolade?*" she ventured hopefully, tugging at the insignia on his collar.

For the rest of his life Frank Fallon would wonder what thought process was behind that single word. Had she learned to associate all men with sweets, or only men in uniform? Or had someone, her recently dead mother, perhaps, taught her this winsome little parlor trick? When in doubt, ask the nice man for chocolate.

In the event, Frank Fallon found himself returning her smile.

"Yeah, kid, that we can do. I think we can manage to find you some *Schokolade.*"

•

"Are you sure that's safe?" was the first thing Johann said when he'd climbed the stairs to Margarethe's flat, eyeing the heavy bureau that was the only thing between her broken-locked door and the world of occupied Berlin beyond. "The stairway is dark. You could not be sure who it was."

"I knew it was you," she said with a prescience he had come to expect of her, her smile with the discolored front tooth brightening a face wan with fatigue and chronic hunger, the face of postwar Europe. "No one else walks the way you do. Come in."

Immediately after the surrender, Russian troops had swarmed through the city, and no female between the ages of nine and ninety had been safe. Margarethe had abandoned the flat when the tanks rolled in, moving with the rest of the city from cellar to cellar, everything she owned in a single cardboard suitcase, the little girl with the huge, dark eyes held safely by the hand. Even now, with the city divided, and her flat safe in the American sector, a door with a broken lock needed to be secured some other way.

After however many weeks in hiding, she had returned to see what had survived. There had been no glass in the windows for quite some time, but the scraps of board she had fitted into the frames to keep the rain out had been kicked out just for spite, or else to provide more light to pillage by. They'd burned most of the books, a lifetime's accumulation, hurled the rest into a corner and pissed on them, smashed crockery and glasses, stolen the silver and cooking pots, trodden the parlor rug into a muddy pulp that she'd dragged down the stairs the first day back.

The bureau had been too heavy to smash, or maybe they hadn't had time. They'd rifled the drawers looking for jewelry, which she'd taken with her, taken one good cashmere sweater which she hadn't—a gift for a wife or girlfriend waiting in Irkutsk? she'd wondered—then gone away, leaving only the muddy tracks of their boots on the stairs. Margarethe had scrubbed the stairs as soon as the water was turned on again.

The flat below had been empty since the first bombs fell. Timothy still slept in the back room of the bakery but, with his weak heart, two flights of stairs might be the far side of

the moon. Better to barricade oneself in in the hope of keeping others out. Margarethe moved the bureau back against
the door every night, except, as now, when she sensed Johann's approach.

"Have you eaten?" she asked, shutting the door and letting him help her drag the bureau back into place. "There
is soup, and bread also. Timothy has, with his usual re-
sourcefulness, somehow 'organized' some flour."

"I'm not hungry," he said, not truthfully, knowing the
soup was thin and would get thinner each day as she added
water to make it last until the next food convoy, whenever
that might be, but that she'd still give him the lion's share if
he let her.

"Coffee, then? It's ersatz, but—"

"Nothing, please!" He raised a hand to stop her offering
him anything more. "May I sit down?"

"Of course," she said, motioning him toward the parlor's
surviving chair; the fabric was slashed and singed in places,
but it served. "You know you don't have to ask."

She waited until he was comfortable, his feet up on the
mismatched ottoman, then sat on the ottoman and began
unlacing his shoes. He looked as if he were about to object
to that as well, but didn't have the strength.

"Did it go well?" she asked at last.

"The child is safe," he answered. "The Americans will see
that she's taken care of, and the plan will go forward."

He did not elaborate on the plan or who had ordained it,
and she did not ask.

"I could have cared for her, you know," she reminded
him; the topic was not new. "Passed her off as my own. A
change-of-life baby, or a grandchild."

The thought amused him. "She doesn't look anything like
you."

"So what? Half the children in this city are being raised by people not their parents." *Including,* she thought but did not say, *those you found homes for, knowing they'd be raised as Christians, but at least that they would live.* "I would have kept her safe. They'd never have found her."

"They would have found her," he said, ending the conversation. "Killed you, and taken her. It could not be risked."

"I suppose not," she said sadly, looking away as she eased his shoes off. He thought for a moment she might cry, but then he knew she wouldn't. He watched her hunch her shoulders, heard her sigh. The eyes that met his had tears in them, but she would not let them fall. "Poor little one. I'll miss her!"

•

"Good morning. Did you sleep well?"

Karen can smell fresh coffee before she even opens her eyes. It helps her remember that at least some of the conflicting versions of reality are only dream. She sits up and takes the proffered mug from Govannon's hands, inhaling deeply before she drinks.

"How did Frank Fallon know the details about Anna's mother's death?" she asks, watching him over the rim of the mug.

"Explain," is all he says. He is sitting on the edge of the bed again, still with her.

"When I was Anna's house guest in Alexandria, that time I did the interview for her little sci-fi TV show, she told me the story about how her mother had died in the bombing, but her own life was saved by a mystery woman who protected her when the ceiling caved in. That's when I knew one of us was out of time, and the whole thing started to unravel. But neither you nor Timothy told Frank any of that."

"Ah, but which Anna was that?" Govannon challenges her. "If it was the incident in the cellar in Berlin that clued you to the fact that she had supplanted Raymond in the reality that you knew, then which Anna are we talking about? The one Timothy gave to Frank, the one in your novel, or the one you dreamed last night? Or any combination thereof."

"Shit!" For a moment Karen is crestfallen. Last night's dream had been so clear she believed it was the way it actually happened. Then something else dawns on her. "But wait a minute: She told Ted Koppel the same story. Gotcha!" she says, when Govannon doesn't answer.

"Just making sure you're paying attention," he counters. "Have you written that part yet?"

"Not yet."

That answer seems to satisfy him. Karen notices he has conjured a room service cart to hold the coffeepot, in case she wants a refill. Real coffee for her, not ersatz. There is also a covered platter of French toast, a smaller plate of strawberries and fresh whipped cream, fine linen, good silver, everything but the monogram of a four-star hotel.

"You keep spoiling me and I might just want to leave things the way they are." She beams at him, teasing.

Govannon's answer is to reach for a dab of whipped cream and threaten to put it on her nose. She moves faster than he does and catches it with her tongue, not incidentally licking his fingers at the same time. He's still here; she didn't dream it. This is good. Maybe if she's careful not to overreact, he might stay a little longer this time.

"When you're finished eating"—Govannon has to stop

himself from chuckling, enjoying this too much himself—
"we go back to the Museum."

"Back to the Museum!" Karen agrees past a mouthful of
French toast.

•

But when they get there, they can't get in.

The outside is as seamless as the interior had been. Was it
only yesterday they were inside? How many lifetimes ago
was that? Karen wishes she hadn't passed out yesterday; she
might remember something helpful now. The Museum is
constructed of what she's begun to think of as thinking-
stone; it's not as if there were some doorway that's been
overgrown by crystone since they were here last. Was the
only way in through the doorways of the mind? She stands
by uneasily as Govannon walks around the entire structure
twice, touching it as much with his fingertips as with his
mind.

"What can I do?" she asks, seeing puzzlement and not a
little concern on his face.

"Nothing!" he says too sharply, and it's the first time he's
ever raised his voice to her. "This is not about you!"

And because she knows his anger, at least, isn't directed
at her, she keeps very still and waits.

"This isn't supposed to happen," he says tightly, looking
as if he might pound on the walls. He moves restlessly, at a
loss. She has never seen him like this and it frightens her.
"If I can't get back in, it's because I'm losing resonance, I'm
losing everything. It means—" He stops, looks at Karen,
makes a decision. "It means I can't even go back through
the Gat and choose one of my previous lives. And it means
you're going back home, while I'm still able to get you
there."

"The hell I am!" Karen folds her arms, digs in her heels.

"I don't have time to argue with you—" he begins.

"Then don't waste it arguing," she snaps back. "I am not going anywhere until we solve this!"

" 'We'—are not—going to solve this," he says between clenched teeth, striving for control. "*I* am going to solve this. If you had your way you wouldn't go back at all, you'd stay here with me. Or as much of me as is here—a voice, a two-dimensional suggestion of one shape of a shape-shifter who doesn't even remember his original form."

"So?"

"No!" he says breathlessly. "That's not enough for you. You deserve better. And if I—can't—hold on to this—little foothold—" He flickers off, on, off again for a too-long moment, then on again, buzzing around the edges like a migraine aura, Karen's least favorite version of him. "—if I vanish entirely—leave you marooned here—the only thing smarter than a plant on the entire world? No!"

He solidifies with an almost audible snap, but it's as if he's standing between some unseen projector and the screen ("Down in front!"), images flickering over him, all the different versions of his borrowed lives through all their ages from infant to mature man, interspersed with versions Karen's never seen. Frightened children, tormented adolescents, solitary young men traversing barren landscapes. Bomb shelters and crystal caves, the well-tended, sun-dappled forests of Avaricum, the darker, overgrown woods near mythic Salzheim, the silent, eerie whiteness within the salt mines that gave it name. Yet another cave, stalactites dripping in the light of smoking torches, names and dates written in smoke on the walls, the First Gat, the Pit in Avaricum, the blank interior of the Museum, a womb full of stars.

In medias res, he spins around, circling his own axis aim-lessly, arms outstretched, as if the images are moving him. Has he ever, in any of his lives, been so out of control?

"Govannon . . ." Karen says quietly, not knowing how she knows to do this, but finding the him of him inside that welter. "Take my hands."

"What? I can't. Not now. I can't—I've got to—"

"Can't you?" She reaches for his hands, grasps them against a sudden vertigo, closes her eyes, opens them, and they are both Inside.

FIFTEEN

It's difficult to say which of them is more unsettled by what's just happened. Neither wants to examine it too closely.

"Tir na Nog," Karen says finally, still holding Govannon's hands. She is testing a theory, or several. The Museum is only dimly lit, the walls blank. Nothing happens.

"Gesundheit!" Govannon answers almost by reflex.

Karen sighs. Pity the first thing to recover is his sense of humor.

"I'm sorry," he says a little breathlessly. "I can't seem to resist. Tir na Nog, the Celtic Land of the Eternal Young, where it is always summer, where the world of the living is separated only thinly from the world beyond. Yes?"

"Yes. That's what Relict is. Or would be, if TQ were still here. And human lore is full of hollow hills. Caves and barrows and fairy hills where the otherworldly live," Karen says, not sure how much he knows or remembers. "Mystic lakes with islands and castles that appear and disappear by magic. Certain times of the year when the dead speak to the living. And all of these times and places connect the mundane to the Otherworld. Which is where we are right now. Because I am with you, neither Here nor There."

He only now seems to realize she is still holding his hands.

It isn't like him to be so disoriented. He slips his hands out of hers. For a moment she thinks of grabbing for him again, then reconsiders. For one thing, she knows him well enough to know he would resist. For another, it isn't really necessary. This time they will remain on the same plane. The writer knows.

"I wish you hadn't done this!" Govannon says, shaking his head sadly. "There's no way of telling if you can ever go back."

He doesn't say what he means by going back, but Karen knows. Crossing the veil back to Relict, the whatever-it-is that will take her back to Earth. She ought to be terrified. She isn't.

"Been here before," she reminds him. "The hayloft."

She and Fuchsia, the wayward S.oteri, were supposed to be retracing their steps through history, returning to the precise three points in time where Fuchsia had dumped Karen before, to try to set things right.

The first place they were headed was Chinon, Eleanor of Aquitaine's pied-à-terre in France, at the start of the Third Crusade. In hir haste, Fuchsia had overshot Eleanor's reign as Dowager Queen of England (busy lady, she), landing them instead in a hayloft in the cathedral city of Bourges on the eve of Eleanor's coronation as Queen of France, fifty years earlier. Of all the adventures s/he'd gotten Karen into, that one was the eeriest.

They were invisible, or nearly so. Karen knew she was sitting, standing, occasionally pacing, *somewhere*, but there was no true sense of the dusty solidity of the ancient planking, the prickle of straw or stink of chickenshit. The dust, however, had made her sneeze. The hens in the rafters had ruffled their feathers when she sneezed, but couldn't see her or the S.oteri, only a kind of displacement where they ought to be. A human child had come up the ladder to the loft to gather eggs and walked right through them.

Ghosts, or spirits, if Karen's childhood's religion were to be believed, her state of being somewhat similar to how she'd been taught eternity would be. Had TQ drawn that ghostly quality out of stored race memory, Jungian, the way they'd conjured the off-color seascape and the Big Blue Thing? If it was only a visual, why had she sneezed? Once again, she was integral to the puzzle, a kind of intertemporal water witch.

"Well, you're Here. I suppose I may as well get used to it . . ." Govannon's tone is resigned, long-suffering, his earlier distress either controlled or simply well disguised.

"And that means there has got to be a way through the veil to There," Karen says, not knowing how she knows this. "I still think this has something to do with jellyfish! Whose boneheaded idea was it to give them telekinesis in the first place?"

"Not mine," Govannon says, all innocence. "They were the one contact that had nothing to do with the Gats. They found us the way they found humans, reaching out with their minds until they bumped up against us. The reason they were given telekinesis—and the decision was by no means unanimous—was to divert them before they ran up against the Mad Dog. And before you ask, the one thing I can't tell you about is the Mad Dog. Not in this novel, anyway."

But Karen is only half listening. "Is it possible—? No, this is crazy—you'd know if Anna was TQ, wouldn't you?"

"She never gave me any of the codes," he says, not quite answering the question.

As if the mention of her name has triggered something,

the newsreel of Anna's life begins again. *Sunday in the Park with George* meets *Purple Rose of Cairo*. Look out!

•

Frank Fallon handed the little girl off to a skinny nurse with a mole on her chin and never gave her another thought. It was his CO who, two days later, suggested he take her back to the States with him.

"I beg your pardon?" In his befuddlement, Fallon forgot to add "sir."

"Understand you and the wife have a slew of them already," the major said. "What's one more? You can take her on as a foster kid if you'd rather not adopt. Either way, the army will arrange for a nice little compensation package. Including knocking three months off your hitch."

The suggestion was so odd that Fallon didn't process it. His mind had latched onto something else entirely. Did he really want to go Stateside three months sooner? he wondered. He'd come to enjoy the orderly predictability of military life, the absence of caterwauling children and his wife's endless little projects, the sense that once he was off duty, his time was his own. He was one of those Irishmen who could as easily have drifted into the priesthood as into the army or marriage. Absent a regular bedmate, it never occurred to him to go looking for sex he'd have to pay for, with all of its implied guilt and potential diseases, not to mention that there were other things he'd rather spend his money on, things that could be poured into a hip flask and enjoyed in solitude. As long as the shooting war was over, he was in no great hurry to go home.

Finding himself woolgathering—the flask was in the desk drawer or his briefcase when he was on duty—Fallon tried to focus on what his CO was saying. He seemed to be suggesting that Fallon adopt the little blonde girl, bring her back to the States with him. Insisting on it almost. It wasn't as if there were a shortage of orphans in Berlin, in all of Europe. What was the deal here?

In later years, the Jameson's having claimed as much of his brain as it had his liver, Fallon would swear he never actually said yes. There was a cloudy area in his memory between the start of that conversation and his recollection of walking up the porch steps of the big redbrick house in Arlington with his kit bag in one hand and the little girl, snowflakes falling on her shoulders, in his arms.

He'd set her down in the living room, where Eleanor had lined up the rest of them, from ten-year-old Frank Junior through Jerome and Matthew and Caitlin to the youngest, James. He could tell by the breathlessness and shirttails out that at least some of them had been brawling up until the minute he walked through the door. No one greeted him, none of them threw themselves at him shouting "Daddy's home!" They'd been sufficiently threatened by their mother's wrath to stand in rigid expectation until they were given their next instructions.

Fallon vaguely remembered explaining to Eleanor on the echoing overseas trunk line during their single conversation that the little one would fit nicely in the gap between Caitlin, who was six, and James, who'd just turned three. The gap, Frank didn't bother to acknowledge, left by one of Eleanor's several miscarriages; the woman was obsessed.

But Anna was so tiny compared to his gawky brood. Just as he began to think this was all a terrible mistake, Eleanor did what she always did, took charge.

"All right, everyone, I want you each to go over one at a time and say hello to your new sister, Anne-Marie."

Anne-Marie? Fallon wondered, grateful he'd thought to have one last nip before he got out of the cab in front of the house, knowing he wouldn't have another chance until all this preliminary stuff was over.

"Her name is Anna—" he started to say, but Eleanor cut him off.

"I think she'd be more comfortable with Anne-Marie, don't you, dear?" She had managed to exert herself enough to give him a little peck on the cheek after eighteen months, though she never took her eyes off the children, ready to lunge at anyone who got out of line and pinch an arm, tweak some hair, smack the back of a head, if necessary. "Now that she's an American."

Fallon didn't have the energy to argue. Besides, suddenly things began happening rather quickly.

The four boys had started circling Anna as soon as her feet touched the floor. Jimmy, the youngest, sucking his three middle fingers exactly the way he had been the last time his father had seen him when he was half this age, was exactly her height. He stood almost nose-to-nose with her, and, reaching out one finger of his other hand, tentatively poked her cheek. Anna blinked reflexively, but otherwise didn't react.

"Leave her alone, you jerk!" Caitlin yelled so that Jimmy jumped. Jerome, the loudest one, turned on her.

"Oh, yeah? Well, you leave him alone, too!"

Before Caitlin could respond, Frank Junior shoved her out of the way and yanked Jerome back by the shoulders, knocking him into Matthew, the chubby, passive one, who reacted finally, yelling and trying to kick Jerome, kicking Frank Junior instead, who began pounding him. Faster than the eye could see, the three older boys were rolling on the floor pummeling each other, while Jimmy sat down with a thump and started howling. Eleanor loomed over all of them, slapping and trying to separate them.

"Christ!" Frank Senior muttered, and retired from the fray, stalking into the dining room where the glass decanters were, a stranger in his own house.

Caitlin put her arm around Anna, who still hadn't moved, was watching the noise and tumult as if it were interesting, but not at all threatening. Compared to the life she had known, this was nothing.

"You're my *sister*!" Caitlin announced, planning to bring Anna upstairs and show her the room they'd be sharing. "I've never had a sister before."

They were halfway to the staircase when Anna noticed the fire and began to shriek.

Surrounded by that gaggle of redheads, she hadn't seen the big marble fireplace that was the living room's showpiece until now. Anna had seen fire inside houses before. She knew what it meant.

"*Es brennt, es brennt!*" she shrieked, pulling away from Caitlin and starting to run. The pitch of her voice was so incredibly high it startled everyone into silence.

"It's the fire, for Chrissake!" Fallon bellowed from the dining room, the hand holding the decanter halfway to the old-fashioned glass trembling with nerves. "Douse the goddamn fire. She thinks the house is burning down!"

"That's the most ridiculous thing I've ever—" Eleanor began. Obviously she thought wars were fought in black and white, just like the newsreels.

Only six-year-old Caitlin shoved past everybody, grabbed the fireplace shovel which, along with the poker, she'd been expressly forbidden to touch, and shoveled ashes over the flames the way she'd seen Frank Junior do when he was allowed. She wasn't going to let her new sister be frightened just because the grown-ups were acting like fools.

•

"Caitlin was Anna's savior from that day forward," Govannon tells Karen as the scene fades. Neither of them wants to mention the fact that, with both of them stuck between Here and There, the walls shouldn't have been activated in the first place. Karen looks at Govannon, who shrugs, as mystified as she. "Taught her to speak English, protected her from the boys. Frank Junior in particular had some funny sexual habits when they were growing up, I understand. Always trying to get one or the other of the girls alone and grope at her. Anna bit him on the arm once. He'd cornered Caitlin and was twisting her arm behind her back when Anna jumped him. Bit him until he bled. Left a scar.

"Caitlin was also the only one who always called her Anna, never Anne-Marie. Got an especial delight out of embarrassing Eleanor in front of strangers, no matter how often she was beaten for it later. Caitlin kept Anna safe growing up. A formidable woman. She's never forgiven herself for Anna's kidnapping."

"The first kidnapping?" Karen clarifies.

"Correct. Then Peter took over, after Anna's rescue. He took it upon himself to watch over both of us after I entered the picture. But even he couldn't keep up his guard forever."

"Which is why if Jake—if you—had been in that car in Switzerland . . ."

"Exactly."

"Jake would have died, but not you. Just as Govannon died in the Pit in Avaricum, but you're still here. What did you mean about going back and choosing one of your previous lives?"

He sighs, is about to speak. But the walls are moving again, and Karen can't help noticing he's relieved.

•

"Tell me this is a bad joke," Anna pleads. She and Peter have been traveling for so long she keeps looking out at the sunlight in the Japanese garden to remind herself that it is morning, when in her gut it feels like night. "I realize the planet is crawling with neo-Nazi groups, but surely there can't be two that are more obsessed with Goebbels than with Hitler."

"The bunch who kept you in that closet thirty years ago were amateurs," Peter says. "Reinheit are pros. And think about it for a minute. Of the two, who was the more consummately evil? The homeless street thug with his paranoid ravings, or the Ph.D. with the Jesuit education who created the myth of the Eternal Jew and fed it not only to his putative master but to the masses? Who do you think caused more death? Without Goebbels's propaganda machine behind him, Hitler would have died in the gutter with his head smashed, a nobody. And if you were a skinhead or an old Nazi looking for something to follow, who would you choose? The clown with the bad accent and the silly mustache, or the mastermind whispering in his ear?"

Anna shivered. "Well, if you put it that way . . ."

•

Peter felt strangely euphoric. He had told Anna everything. How he and Jake have been watching over her all these years. About the file somewhere in Langley with her name on it, and at least hearsay evidence that she might be the daughter of Hitler's propaganda minister by way of a minor actress or artists' model, one of several dozen women the chronically philandering Goebbels involved himself with during the war. Where he expected outrage or at least disbelief, Peter had found only quiet acceptance. As if Anna had surmised as much all along.

"How much did you know before this?" he asked her now.

Anna seemed lost in the overstuffed sofa cushions. She was looking down at her hands, as if wondering what genetic blueprint they might reveal.

"I heard things. Overheard things. I was a furtive child. The rest of them, the 'natural-born' Fallons, were so noisy— well, you know what Caitlin's like."

"Oh, I do indeed!"

"So no one noticed me lurking in corners, padding around in my pajamas in the middle of the night. And my father drank. He said things. Especially just before he died. So he *was* talked into adopting me."

Peter nodded.

"Did he really work for the OSS?"

Peter shook his head. "Not likely. Unless it was just at a clerical level. James Bond he wasn't."

Anna laughed then. The juxtaposition of the dapper Bond with the broken-down drunk who called himself her father was too much.

"And when I was kidnapped . . . they didn't realize I could hear through the closet door. They were stoned most of the time, and they argued a lot. And my hearing became hyperacute because I couldn't see . . ."

She began making a gesture Peter hadn't seen in thirty years, rubbing her hands together the way a surgeon might while scrubbing in for surgery. He wanted to grab her hands and tell her to stop, but restrained himself.

"Anna—" he began.

"Is it true?" Her voice was high, strident. "You say the

file on me has 'hearsay evidence.' What does that mean?"

"I've never seen the file, Anna," he said gently. "For all I know, its very existence could be hearsay."

"That's not what I'm asking you." Her voice had normalized again; Peter recognized the slow anger building in her eyes. Anna was the calmest person alive, until pushed. "Is there any way to prove whether or not I am Goebbels's daughter?"

Contrast a balmy fall day in the south of France with a frigid winter night in the District of Columbia, Peter thought, remembering that conversation about DNA with Jake by the Reflecting Pool. He took a deep breath, centered himself, and told Anna now what he'd told Jake then.

"And if Reinheit is as 'professional' a group as you say, then they might have ways of contacting the Russians, asking for a tissue sample. To compare Goebbels's DNA and mine."

"I know what you're thinking," Peter said. "And I want you to stop thinking it. We're here to find Jake before Reinheit does, not to walk into their trap."

"And of course whoever's tracking Reinheit isn't coincidentally following us, like those two goons at the airport, and both sides are going to let us all just go home and pretend this never happened!" Anna said dryly.

"Of course they aren't," someone said from the vicinity of the kitchen.

Are they issued those suits, like the Men in Black? Anna wondered, or just told to patronize a particular tailor somewhere in northern Virginia? The two men strolling silently in from Peter's kitchen on their composite-soled shoes were as nondescript as the two who had appeared at the airport. Except that one of them was carrying Margot, with one hand clamped gently but firmly around her muzzle to keep her from barking, and he was expert enough at it so that she trusted him and wasn't struggling. Or else they'd met before.

"Hello, Peter," the one who wasn't holding the dog said.

"Hello yourself, Killian," Peter said. Outwardly his posture didn't change, but Anna felt him coiling inside.

"Mrs. Bower, I'm sorry you had to take that roundabout route to get here," the one named Killian began as if they knew each other, keeping Peter in his peripheral vision. "Mr. Kato here has just wasted a lot of everybody's time. We'd have gotten you where you needed to go a whole lot quicker."

"You're assuming you know where I needed to go," Anna replied coolly. "And you're assuming you'd have gotten to me before the guy with the accent did. Now, why don't we start from the beginning. You know my name. What's yours?"

"You can call me Killian," he said.

It was too much.

"Oh, Jesus, this is *worse* than a B movie!" Anna exploded. "Suppose I feed you your next line. You're from the CIA, you want to help me find Jake or you want me to help you find Jake, but in any case you need my 'cooperation.' " She waited a beat. "How'm I doing so far?" No one said anything. She turned her attention to Peter. "Okay, you explain it to me. You obviously know these people. You're not terribly surprised to see them, and more to the point, neither is Margot. Did they arrange this, did you, or are you simply resigned to the fact that they can find you, and by association, me, no matter where we go? In which case, why aren't they out there finding Jake instead of here?"

"It's not about Jake, Anna," Peter said carefully. "It's about you."

•

On the night of the same day, Anna waited in Peter's living room for them to come, the dog asleep in her lap, the snap of a crumbling log in the hearth making them both jump. Before Killian left, he'd given Anna a long, considered look that she interpreted as the first real emotion he'd expressed all afternoon. The emotion was pity.

"Mrs. Bower, this is official as well as unofficial," he'd said. "If you decide to opt out, even as late as tonight, you just let us know. We have other options."

She hadn't even hesitated. "They tried to kill Jake. The next time they might succeed. Or they might go after my daughter. And since I'm the only person on the planet they won't harm . . ."

And since I don't trust your kind to do the job without someone's getting hurt or killed! she did not add. She'd waved the two men off.

"Go, please. I'll do what you ask. I need to think right now."

•

"Am I really?" she'd asked Peter when at last they were alone on the beach.

"Goebbels's daughter?" Peter had said what she could not, then shrugged. "No way of knowing without tissue samples. Which may never be obtained, because nobody outside of Moscow knows if they still have the body. The Soviets refused any cooperation as a matter of course. The new government's got enough else on its mind. Which is why part of Jake's thinking about the Room was that if he could help the Russians recover it—"

"—they'd help us find out if I really am." She simply could not say it, could not put the two words of the name together. All her life she had dismissed it as one of Frank

Fallon's drunken fantasies. Hearing her captors repeat it had only made it seem less real, something out of the *National Enquirer*, of conspiracy theories, UFOs, delirium tremens and bad acid trips, a metareality that had nothing to do with her. Now having been brought out of the shadow world into the light by the kind of people who all wore the same suit, it was, at a visceral level, too horrible to contemplate. Anna shook her head.

"Jake honestly thought he could get away with it. All by himself. That no one from either side was going to intervene, co-opt his search, detain him, kill him? Oh, Jake!"

Peter saw her about to crumble.

"Hey," he said, reaching out for her. "You're not going to fall apart on me now, are you?"

"You knew!" Anna dabbed at her eyes, her voice dead in the center. "Ever since the kidnapping. Maybe even before. Maybe that's why you were there. And Jake knew, because you told him. Did he—? No, I won't—I can't even put words around it . . ."

"Anna . . ." Peter knew her well enough to know what she was asking even if she couldn't ask it. He chose his words very carefully. "Jake loved you—loves you—intensely. It's true he might never have met you if it weren't for the kidnapping. But who knows? You were both unattached, mingled with the same kind of people. Who's to say, if you'd never been kidnapped, or even if some other therapist had seen you afterward—"

"Peter—"

"What I'm taking a very long time to say, Anna, is: No, Jake didn't marry you because he was trying to protect you. He didn't fall in love with you because there was some macabre thrill in the possibility that you might share the DNA of one of the most evil men of the twentieth century. He fell in love with you because you're you. Because your courage moved him to tears. Not in front of you, but whenever he talked to me." Peter's own eyes were brimming now. "So put those thoughts aside now, or else let me contact Killian and tell him—"

"No! I said I'd go in, and I will. I am, as I say, the only person on the planet they'd never dream of harming. I will be the decoy, keep them occupied while you and Killian retrieve Jake. As for the rest . . ." She laughed weakly. "As the saying goes, 'need to know.' I don't want to know. I just want my husband back, and I want my family safe once I get him back. And then I'm going to give him hell for keeping all of this from me!"

•

She would not think about how much Jake hadn't shared with her; she would focus instead on what he had. She thought of how well they fit together, how naturally she'd participated in that part of his life involved in tracking down stolen art. How exciting it had been, once upon a time, when he'd brought her to Europe to try to retrace the paths he'd fled in the night with his parents when he was a child, one step ahead of Schickelgruber and the camps, he'd bought a painting from an old man in a village in Austria so small it wasn't on the map, and the old man had told the nice American couple a secret.

The secret had do to with some pencil drawings smuggled out of a concentration camp and hidden in a barn loft. Were the *Amerikanisches* interested? the old man wondered. The *Amerikanisches* were very interested, and rode in his wheezing truck to the abandoned farm, where the sketches turned out to be hidden behind the faded wallpaper in the farmhouse parlor and not in the barn at all. They were delightfully childlike drawings of a vanished shtetl life, and remarkably well preserved. Jake paid the old man his asking fee and Anna smuggled the sketches home rolled up in an improbable rock poster. Once there she compared the signatures with those of a well-known folk artist from Lublin who had died at Auschwitz.

How the sketches of a Polish Jew ended up behind the wallpaper in an Austrian farmhouse no one knew, but the "discovery" made headlines, though at their own request neither Anna nor Jake was mentioned by name. The sketches were presented to the late artist's surviving relatives, who donated them to the Jewish Museum in New York. The old man who had provided the tip about the farmhouse was rewarded with a showing of his work at a gallery in Linz. And they'd all lived happily ever after.

There were other successes, most of them less spectacular, and the Bowers had tried to stay out of the headlines after that. There were the dangerous ones, too. Having their hotel windows shot out in Prague, their passports held for two days when they were trying to leave what was then Yugoslavia.

Would Jake have taken any of those risks if, in addition to all the smaller finds, he hadn't also been obsessed with finding the Amber Room?

And then what? Return it to Russia in exchange for proof that Anna either was or wasn't Goebbels's daughter? Anna couldn't begin to imagine the conversation she and Jake would have had leading up to that.

Maybe just as well! she told herself, retrieving the crossword puzzle she'd started earlier, filling the boxes with random letters because her mind wasn't on it, in case they, the ones who would be coming for her before the night was over, were already watching the house.

On her lap, the dog sighed in her sleep. Anna wished they'd come and get it over with.

SIXTEEN

So they came for her, and they blindfolded her," Karen says with absolute certainty. She doesn't need to see it to know. "Not because they didn't want her to see their faces. In fact, they simply let themselves in, one through the front door, one through the garden, and asked politely if she would accompany them because they knew where to find her husband. And even though in her heart she was convinced you were safe in your cave in Adelsberg, Anna went along with the game. Because, she assumed, Peter would find Jake, the 'Agency' would follow her, all of the Bad Guys would be rounded up, and she and Jake and their daughter would be safe. And maybe the Agency would destroy her file. And maybe, even, the Amber Room was a part of this and not a phantom.

"So the two who came for her showed their faces. They only asked if she minded being blindfolded so she wouldn't know where they were taking her. They were young, and not yet sure of her 'loyalty.' The old man who ruled them believed that blood would out, and it was only a matter of gentle persuasion before she joined their cause."

"He was in for a surprise," Govannon murmurs.

"None of this ever made the news," Karen concludes. "The paintings you and Anna recovered, the CNN headlines and the appearance on *Nightline,* all that was later. So the Room was never found."

"Is that how you would write it?"

"I need to know how you and Jake and Anna lived it."

"Just tell me how you would write it."

"And then what? You tell me how close I am to what actually happened?"

"It's no longer up to me." He nods toward what is happening around them.

Because it's no longer just on the walls. This is not the flat diorama of Karen's battlefield memories or the sensurround of Jake/Johann's bifurcate childhood, nor yet again a Bronze Age marketplace or a medieval hayloft crying out for a magic sword or a unicorn or two. This is reality, Greg. You Are There.

Karen stands behind the couch where Anna sits pretending to do a crossword puzzle. She can feel the heat from the fireplace, smell the fragrance of applewood burning. When she steadies herself with one hand on the back of the couch, she can feel the texture of the brocade. She knows she could as easily rest her hand on Anna's shoulder, but doesn't want to startle her.

Margot stirred in her sleep, paws twitching. Her small head came up, her eyes opened and stared directly into Karen's, pupils dilating. She growled.

"Not yet, baby." Anna said, knowing somehow. She stroked the dog, who settled and went back to sleep. "Not yet."

•

Ultimately, Anna thought, it was about freedom. She had been an unwitting pawn in someone else's game almost from the beginning. Whatever happened, endgame was here.

"All right," she had said to Killian in a voice she didn't

recognize. "I'll go in. But if anything happens to Jake, or my daughter—"

The dreamlike quality that had descended on her even before she and Peter had left D.C. cleared with a snap.

"Your daughter is safe," Killian assured her. "Less than thrilled at being under virtual house arrest, but she's fine. As for you, we have an agent on the inside. Tall and blond, speaks flawless German just like all the rest of them, and close enough to the leadership to be able to keep an eye on you. That plus the fact that these people revere you . . . you'll be safe. It won't be like the last time."

"Nothing could possibly be like the last time," she said, and it was done.

When Killian and the other man had finally gone, she and Peter stood looking at each other for a long moment in silence. Then she went upstairs to change, and down to the beach for a swim.

It was a brief swim. The water was still warm this late in the season, but her timing was off and she tired quickly. It was all an alibi anyway, an excuse to be alone so Peter could brief her on exactly what she was expected to do.

"Just humor them, that's all. Keep them preoccupied with me so you and Killian's people can get to Jake?"

"And tell them about the code," Peter said.

"Obviously. But tell them about it reluctantly. Make them think they're dragging it out of me as I learn to trust them." Anna shook her head to clear it. "Tell it to me again. And maybe again after that. I need to be absolutely clear. Because it has to look real, doesn't it? If they test me, take my pulse, for instance . . ."

The breeze had picked up and was ruffling their hair. Peter swept his back with one hand. He realized Anna needed to exorcise her fears, and the best thing he could do for her was listen.

"Take your pulse? What are you talking about?"

"There was a novel. Alistair MacLean, I think. *Where Eagles Dare*, it was called. I don't remember if the scene made it into the movie, but there was this American girl—or was she British?—who was passing as a German in order to infiltrate some Nazi stronghold. She was assigned to flirt with one of the officers, keep him busy so Richard Burton or somebody could do whatever it was they had to do. Blow the place up, or target it for the bombers, or help someone escape—"

"Anna—"

"Anyway, she's supposed to be flirting, but the Nazi takes her wrist and notices that her pulse is racing. He's about to shoot her as a spy when Richard Burton or whoever breaks into the room—"

"Anna, you're not a spy. You're an innocent civilian whose husband is missing, and who's been kidnapped by the people you believe may have killed him. If your pulse *weren't* racing they'd be suspicious."

She laughed then, humorlessly, wrapping the robe about herself more tightly. "You're right. It's all so crazy."

"Besides, I'm much better looking than Richard Burton," Peter muttered.

"But you won't be there, you'll be with Killian."

Peter gave her a long-suffering look. "I'd love to infiltrate, too, but I'm hardly the Aryan type."

Anna knelt on the blanket and hugged him then. "It's just nerves, darling. You understand that, don't you?"

"Of course. That's why I'm letting you talk it out. Now, once more from the top?"

Anna nodded. She sat on the blanket beside him. They watched the tide coming in and put their arms around each other's shoulders. Peter talked and Anna listened.

•

"Even Killian's people can't give names to the leadership. But they know at least one of them is old enough to have fought in the war, and maybe to have known somebody who knew somebody who knew something. In a perverse way, it all ties together. We know that Goebbels, as Minister of Culture, would have been the one who ordered the Amber Room stolen from Tsarskoe Selo in the first place. During the last months of the war, when Königsburg was being bombed so heavily, it made sense that he'd want it moved. Maybe to a place he'd had prepared in advance, because it was so huge. Maybe with the intention of retrieving it after the war, using it as a bargaining chip, who knows? In point of fact, Anna, you're going to make Reinheit believe that nobody knows better than you. . . ."

•

"Again, *bitte*," the old man said. His eyes were the color of ice, his face as droopy as a bloodhound's. The voice he used with Anna was different from the one he used with his "children," as he called them. There was more deference in it, but it was no less relentless. "Tell me this again."

"This is boring!" Anna said testily. "And you know it all already. I refuse to be tested!"

The old man pursed his lips, drawing all the lines of his face together in a pucker of loose flesh. He sat spraddle-legged in the stiff-backed chair, leaning forward, his hands clasped together on the curve of a thick walking cane. His legs were unnaturally long, his knees reaching almost to chest-level.

Anna wondered how tall he was. He had already been

seated when she was brought into the room, but she was sure he was closer to seven than six feet tall. And if she had expected some central casting Nazi with ramrod posture and a knife-edge pleated uniform, she was disappointed. The old man wore baggy corduroys and a flannel shirt. Even his hair was long enough to touch his collar in the back, and shadows in the bloodhound folds of his face suggested he might not have shaved that morning. He could have been Everyman's grandfather. Or perhaps this was part of the performance. Only the eyes were inhuman.

"It is not my intention to test you," he said in his deliberate English. His voice held the softness of leaves rustling. "I am testing the facts, not their source."

"Bullshit!" Anna had ascertained early on that he hated profanity, particularly from her, and she used it to her advantage. She wanted him to understand that she was at the end of her rope. Jake's supposed death, the flight across an ocean and half of Europe to get to Peter's house, the abduction that brought her here, wherever here was, how much more did they expect her to take?

"Would you like to rest now?" the old man asked her, reading her tone as she had hoped he might. "You really should eat something, lie down for a while. So much activity in so little time—"

"I will rest when my husband and I are safely back in our home and you are dead!" she said.

The old man seemed to find this amusing. At least the noises in his throat sounded like chuckling, though his face did not look amused. Only his eyebrows, great wiry, tufted things, shot up in surprise, and he shook his head in amazement.

"I knew you would have this fire, I knew!" he breathed. "But I did not know you would be so much without fear."

If you only knew! Anna thought, suppressing a tremor, but emending her thought even as it occurred, as if he could read it. *But you will never know. I will not give you the satisfaction!*

Her choice not to rest was deliberate. She did not want them to guess that she was stalling for time, even as she did so.

•

"All we really need is twenty-four hours' lead time," Peter had told her on the beach. "If you can give us more than that to get to Jake and brief him, so much the better. But not to where it's going to make them suspicious and put you in danger. Twenty-four hours, Anna. After that, play it however you think best."

•

"Just so, then," the old man said, settling in. "Since you will not rest, tell me. From the beginning."

"There are many rumors and theories about what happened to the Room after April 1945," she began. "Having been removed wholesale from the Tsar's Summer Palace at Tsarskoe Selo by direct order of Nazi Minister of Culture Joseph Goebbels in September 1941, it was transported across Russia and installed in Königsberg Castle near the city of Kaliningrad, ironically, not far from where the raw amber was originally harvested centuries earlier. . . ."

•

It was only yesterday that she had Peter had planned their strategy. *Yesterday afternoon,* Anna reminded herself. *As recently as yesterday. I think. They did not drug me. I neither slept nor lost consciousness on the trip here. That's useful. It was a small plane; I could tell from the sound of the engines and the turbulence, because we were flying low. I don't think it took more than a few hours to get here, wherever "here" is. That will be useful in helping them find this place when it's all over. Unless they already know.*

Stop it! she told herself, even as she continued her filibuster ("Twenty-four hours, Anna," Peter had said). *What are you doing? You're thinking like* them, *like the goddamn spies. Do you want them to find this place afterward, and do what? Ask everybody politely to put their hands up and march off to prison? Or stage a bloodbath?*

The goddamn spies. The goddamn spies who saved your life when you were a girl, held blindfolded in a closet. Those goddamn spies. The goddamn spies who, if Peter's information is correct, kept a file on you claiming you were Goebbels's daughter, which is what led to the kidnapping in the first place. Those goddamn spies. It was Peter who saved your life.

Yes, Peter who knew where you were because they knew. Because Peter was working with them. For them. Was one of them. Is one of them.

Twenty-four hours. Save Jake. Maybe coincidentally find the Amber Room, if the rumor wasn't a sham. But aren't you overlooking the most important thing, the core thing, which is: Close the file on Anna Goebbels, if there ever really was such a person? Ensure somehow that no one, ever, lays hands on me for that reason again?

Keep talking. The old man doesn't know you're stalling. He thinks he's interrogating you. He's eighty if he's a day, and he's on at least one medication, because you've seen one of those interchangeable blond boys hand him the little brown plastic vial and a bottle of mineral water, and you've seen his attention wander. Keep talking. Don't think. If you think, your thoughts will seep into your words, and you'll give yourself away.

"Königsberg Castle was bombed by the Allies and gutted by fire in April of 1945, and the Amber Room, along with hundreds of other artworks looted from museums and private collections throughout Europe, was presumed destroyed," she went on. "However, only a few fragments of charred wood and melted amber were found after the fire, not nearly enough to comprise the entire Room. Rumors of its whereabouts have persisted since.

"Was it in fact destroyed in the fire? Or was it smuggled out of the country aboard the *Wilhelm Gustloff*, a German freighter known to be carrying crates of oil paintings in its hold when it was torpedoed by a Soviet submarine in January 1945, killing over eight thousand passengers, five times as many as perished on the *Titanic*, most of them civilian refugees? Or is it even now part of someone's private collection—in England, Russia, Germany, even America? Treasure hunters and serious collectors have been searching for the answer ever since."

Like riding a bicycle, Anna thought in spite of herself. When she was in college, before the kidnapping (the *first* kidnapping, she thought bitterly. How many people had been kidnapped twice in a lifetime?), she had spent her summers with Caitlin, who had bolted for New York right out of high school. Anna worked as a docent at the Metropolitan Museum, conducting walking tours for school groups, foreign visitors, and the ladies who lunch. Her self-assurance, the pleasant contralto voice, the range of knowledge had impressed everyone, not least Anna herself. She had never lost that confidence, nor the ability to make an audience see what she was seeing. She was doing that now.

"There is even the possibility that the Room remains hidden in the basement of a museum or government building somewhere in the Russian Republic, only one of hundreds of thousands of objects, from paintings and sculptures to church bells and rare Torah scrolls, relooted by the Soviets after the war and never even unpacked, just as the Trojan

Gold was found in the basement of the Hermitage as recently as 1989."

She'd been watching the old man closely, waiting for him to nod off, as he almost had several times. But this seemed to rouse him. He was nodding vigorously, those tufted eyebrows working, the look of a snake in his eyes.

"I have seen the Trojan Gold!" he said, not managing entirely to contain the excitement in his voice. "In Berlin, in the Zoo *Flakturm*. It was hidden until the Russian occupation, and then . . ." He shook himself like an old dog. "Thieves! Go on."

"Even so," Anna did as instructed, "as late as 1991, Russian President Boris Yeltsin announced that he believed the Room was still hidden somewhere in Germany."

"Drunken fool!" the old man murmured. "Go on."

"This gorgeous creation, product of thousands of hours of devoted labor by skilled artisans, reserved only for the eyes of royalty for over a century and a half and finally made accessible to the public, looted and possibly destroyed by the machinery of war, existed for the next twenty-five years as nothing more than a handful of black-and-white photographs, some of them colorized by guesswork as to the type of amber used, its thickness and intensity of color. Yet it kept popping up in the imagination, if not in reality."

The old man raised one long-fingered hand from the head of the cane in a traffic-cop gesture.

"One thing only. I would ask you not to use such words as 'looting.' The Room was created by German workers from German materials. It belonged to Germany. And while you are even now skeptical of the facts of your origin, I ask that you speak of your father and his work with at least the pretense of respect."

"In 1979," Anna went on, ignoring him, "Russian artisans were commissioned to create a reproduction of the Room, using the same materials, but far more advanced techniques, such as computer imaging that made it possible to estimate accurately the color and thickness of each individual piece of amber in the grand mosaic. Even so, a single small table took a year to reconstruct from this most quixotic substance, tree sap transformed into a manner of stone, its workability unlike any other earthly thing. But the original remains hidden, if it in fact still exists."

"Very nice," the old man murmured, almost pleased with her defiance. "But somewhat off the subject. Almost finished, now."

Someone knocked on the closed door just behind the old man's chair, not for the first time.

"Come!" the old man would say each time, almost with a sigh.

I wonder which of them is Killian's "man on the inside"? Anna thought, watching them slipping into the small room to whisper something in the old man's right ear and receive whispered instructions in return. So far she had counted five of them, four male and one female, none of them yet thirty. She wondered how many there were altogether.

•

"We have no idea," Killian had said. "There could be five or fifty. Like most terrorists, they're subdivided into cells that don't communicate directly with each other. But by the way the exaggerate their numbers, we're assuming closer to the former. We don't even have real names for those we have been able to identify. Even the old man could be one of two possible individuals. He's known only as Opa."

Opa, Anna thought, appreciating the irony. A German child's word for "grandpa."

"How do you know even this much?" she'd asked.

Killian had grimaced then. It was the first evidence she'd seen that he was capable of human facial expressions.

"They have a Web site!" he'd explained, exasperated, as if it somehow ought to be illegal. "And make no mistake about it, they're real. They may seem small, even ridiculous, compared to the people who hijack planes and bomb embassies, but we can link them to the deaths of several individuals, and their sources of funding would surprise you."

•

I must ask to see the Web site, Anna thought now, knowing how inordinately proud most people were of such things. It could buy her even more time.

This latest bout of whispering between Opa and one of his interchangeable young men had been going on too long. Were they aware that her German wasn't as good as Jake's? Did she only imagine she heard his name, saw the old man leering at her out of the corner of his eye? Was this part of the game, to make her think they'd found him? Or had they?

•

It wasn't a bad hiding place, Jake thought, as hiding places went. He had chosen, perhaps dangerously, if anyone who knew him well managed to think it through, to camp out in the same cave where the partisans had hidden his family and so many others during the war. But then, who else knew, besides his surviving siblings, to whom he hadn't spoken in years, and Anna, who would never tell?

He remembered bringing Anna here years ago, her small hand in his large one, a halogen torch raised high in the other, showing her the names scrawled on the walls in candle smoke.

His family's was not among them. He could hear his father dismissing the possibility.

"Foolish!" he would growl, and: "What's the use?"

His despair had been so lifelong and profound, the wonder to Jake was that he'd bothered to leave Hitler's Europe at all. Now Jake, still hunted by Nazis, toyed with the idea of inscribing his name on these walls so many decades later.

The caves where the refugees had hidden were above-ground, not nearly as cold and damp as the great cathedral caves where the underground rivers ran and trams transported the tourists. A writer for *The New York Times* a hundred years ago had rhapsodized about ". . . the hollow roar of the Stygian stream . . . in this jewel of European caverns, the ghostly glimmer of its half-seen waters . . . the gloom of this shadow of death." These caves had meant not death but life to little Jake, and they would again, he hoped, to his older, perhaps wiser, avatar.

He had set up camp under the smoke-inscribed names of the refugees, on a kind of shelf of flat rock out of the way of the trickle of breeze that kept the air fresh but not a little chilly. An air mattress, a winter-weight sleeping bag, a new halogen lamp and spare batteries, food, water, notebook and pen, and a copy of Thomas Mann's *Buddenbrooks* in the original German, and his universe was complete. He would stay here until he finished the seven-hundred-page novel, or until they came for him, whichever came first.

He had made a point to set his watch alarm every hour, and to take himself outside the cave at dusk, which came earlier and earlier. He would walk briskly through the surrounding woods for at least an hour before returning. On the milder nights he stayed out longer, reminding himself of the names of stars, listening to the far-off sounds of dogs and cars and the occasional train whistle. Part of his brain feared the sudden snap of twigs that could be a stray dog or a pack of them, or the kind of two-legged dog that, in uniform or not, could mean trouble, but on the whole he was strangely unconcerned about such things. He held long conversations with Anna in his head, and just before he went to sleep, wrote them down in the notebook, a kind of journal.

The end of one of the German world's wordiest novels, or the arrival of another soul or group of souls. If no one came for him by the time he'd finished with Mann, he would venture back into the world as far as a telephone, a call perhaps to Anna's sister, Caitlin, whose number in New York, like perhaps fifty telephone numbers, he had committed to memory, a habit out of the loneliness of his youth. He would call Caitlin, who would call Peter, who would know how to get to Anna, if only. If only they were safe, and he the only one in exile. If only.

He had been in the cave for four days, three days longer than Lazarus. His beard was growing in around the sides. Would he be more or less conspicuous, he wondered, if he had to leave his sanctuary abruptly, looking like this?

He was strangely calm. When there was nothing one could do, one was best advised to do nothing.

•

The room was inordinately silent. Anna and the old man were alone again. How long ago had the whispering stopped, when had the young man left, and why hadn't she noticed either? Had she actually dozed off, or had her attention merely wandered? Or was she so stressed, so sleep deprived? *Had* they drugged her?

"I am beginning to lose patience," the old man said, almost pleasantly, giving her his full attention. "Though I cannot decide whether it is you or the children who are irritating me more."

He was leaning forward now, his chin all but resting on his hands where they gripped the head of the cane. With his outsized legs, he looked like a praying mantis.

"You have given me the history of the Amber Room. A very pretty presentation, very well presented. Now bring it down, please, from the historic to the personal. Disregarding the bombing, the fire, the *Wilhelm Gustloff*. Tell me what you, personally, know about the Room."

Anna sighed, as if the subject bored her.

"There is one more rumor which persists. That Goebbels, knowing the end was near and that the Allied bombings were inexorable, ordered the Amber Room removed from Königsberg in the last weeks of the war, with the intention of concealing it for future retrieval, should he somehow survive the war. This seems inconsistent with his ultimate fate, that of suicide, along with his wife, Magda, and their six children—"

The spidery hand was raised in the traffic-cop's gesture again; Anna noticed that, freed of its grip on the cane, it had a distinct tremor.

"Please," the old man cautioned her. "Speak only of what you know, not of what you extrapolate."

Time to crank this up a little! Anna thought. She managed a patronizing look, a mild derisiveness of tone.

" 'Please,' yourself. Are you going to tell me Goebbels is alive? Or that his death wasn't suicide? Don't insult my intelligence!"

"What you do not know about Dr. Goebbels is infinitely more than what you know."

Anna waved this away. "I'm tired of this. Where is my husband?"

The old man hesitated, only for an eye-blink, but Anna heard it. She had been right, then. Jake had eluded them and gone to the caves.

"Not important at present." The old man dismissed as she had his reference to Goebbels. "We will take you to him when you have told us what you know."

"You tried to kill him. You succeeded in killing a friend of his. Those things may not be important to you, but—"

"That was a mistake." The old man sounded as if the admission was as painful as passing a kidney stone. "We wanted to take him alive. The car was supposed to have been disabled, not destroyed. I told them none of it was necessary. The young are so cynical. I told them this was not needed, that you would work with us without such . . . dramatics."

"And after all this, you still expect me to cooperate with you?"

The old man's next statement was so ingenuous Anna truly believed he believed it.

"Yes. Because you are who you are."

•

Jake only noticed the sound of the water when he tried to sleep. It wasn't intrusive, just a gentle trickling from some ways off, like a leaky faucet in the bathroom down the hall that you don't have the energy to get up and shut off. But try as he might, he could not hear it when he was awake, only when he tried to sleep.

Even with the air mattress, he swore he could feel the hardness of the rock beneath his back. The constant chill and damp weren't good for a man of his years, either.

Had he been able to sleep here when he was a child? He had asked his father, his brother, his sister, how long they'd had to stay in the cave, had asked them separately, hoping out of a therapist's long practice to see how the different versions, like *Rashomon*, either meshed or contradicted each

other, but each of them in turn had looked at him in amazement, as if they had rehearsed it, and said, almost identically:
"What are you talking about? What cave?"

So he did not know if they had stayed here for hours or
for days, and whether or not he had slept. All he knew was
that it was difficult to sleep now.

"I've spent the night in hotel rooms that were worse than
this," he told himself aloud, to keep his spirits up. The rock
gave him back a resonance of his voice. Then he sneezed.

Wonderful! he thought. A head cold would be the final
insult!

Karen does not need to look around to realize Govannon
is no longer with her. She felt the absence of him even as
she felt the chill of the cave and the crispness of the air
during Jake's nightly walk. Govannon has slipped the veil to
inhabit Jake, and Karen is alone. But not. She too is with
Jake, inside his mind as she always is with the best of her
characters, knowing what he will do next even before he
does.

She thinks she understands now what Govannon meant
about choosing a past life. If the search for TQ does not find
them, if he cannot return to Relict, he will stay with one
of his past lives and live it to the end—human, mortal and,
most likely, lost to Karen forever.

Not if I can help it! she thinks.

SEVENTEEN

"If you truly believe I am who you say I am," Anna said in careful German, refusing to say the name, "you will show me more respect!"

She had to admit even to herself that she had played the line just right. The old man's reaction was precisely what she had hoped it would be.

He bowed his head slightly, as if she were not merely the daughter of the man he revered but the man himself come back from the dead, restored from the ridiculous shriveled corpse in the charred uniform tunic and strangely pristine boxer shorts in the garden of the *Führerbunker,* to sit before him in an armchair so high that his small feet, the deformed one disguised by the highly polished boots, barely reached the floor. As Anna's did.

"Forgive me." Did she only imagine his eyes were moist? "You are correct. This whole event so far has been a preposterous charade. Let us stop pretending. You will rest, you will eat, we will continue this tomorrow."

"No!" Anna said, with what she hoped was the proper sharpness. Surviving newsreels of Goebbels's speeches were less numerous than Hitler's, but she had seen enough of them to be able to mimic his delivery without seeming to imitate it. Goebbels's diction, she recalled, was far more refined than Hitler's *Suddeutsch* street thug's accent.

"The difference between Atticus Finch and Rocky Balboa," Caitlin had suggested once. Which, as Peter said, made the more educated man that much more accountable for the evil.

The single syllable made the old man's ridiculous face droop into something chastened, more bloodhound than ever.

"You will either bring me to my husband or him to me, or I will walk out of here right now. If I am who you say I am, you can't stop me. And you must know that if you harm Jake, you will have effectively killed your 'cause' as far as I am concerned."

The old man pursed his lips then, pondering. With white-knuckled effort he leaned on the cane and pulled himself upright. Anna's estimate had been correct. He was at least six and a half feet tall.

"All in good time," he said, slightly winded. "Come with me. I have something to show you."

•

"Don't even think of it!" Killian snapped from behind the wheel as the car slowed at the border crossing and he turned on the dome light to fumble for the necessary documentation, and Peter eyed the door locks ruminatively. "James Bond wishes he had a car this versatile. You're not going anywhere."

Peter sighed, handing his visa to Killian to hand to the border guard, settling deeper into the leather seat. "Someday, Killian, you're going to grow up. I hope I live to see it."

The guard handed their papers back with an incurious but longer-than-necessary glance at Peter, who was playing Japanese tourist for this gig. The guard was so busy wondering why a tourist would leave Italy for the grim Slovenian landscape he didn't seem to notice that Killian pocketed both sets of documents. They drove on. The sky ahead of them was beginning to lighten.

"If we find out that Mrs. Bower's sent us on a wild-goose chase . . ." Killian didn't finish.

This annoyed Peter.

"Who's 'we,' Killian? Unless you locked your sidekick in the trunk instead of leaving him back in Trieste, there's nobody here but us chickens. Mrs. Bower wouldn't mislead *me*." He leaned back against the headrest and closed his eyes, adding as an afterthought, "Hey, Killian? You ever killed anybody?"

Killian eyed him narrowly. "No. Why?"

"Shot anyone, at least?"

The car slewed around a curve. Did Peter only imagine he heard him sigh?

"No," Killian said at last, sounding disappointed.

•

There was, indeed, a Reinheit Web site, accessible to those who knew the password. Yet another of the fuzz-headed young blonds showed it to Anna proudly, his nail-bitten hands trembling at the proximity of the great one's daughter. Anna had pointedly not looked at the framed portraits lining the corridors on the way here, except to note that Hitler's, draped in crepe as if he had died within the month, had been placed second. The place of honor belonged to Dr. King Rat Goebbels himself.

Worse than a Mel Brooks movie! Anna thought as the young man complimented her on her German, and she in turn complimented him on the thoroughness of the site and the effort he had clearly put into it. Here was where she would make the gradual transition, straight out of the Stockholm protocols, from outraged kidnap victim to grudging sympathizer. From there to Daughter of the *Reichsminister* would be a more difficult transition, but she would manage it.

The old man stood behind the two of them, leaning on the oversized cane, his arthritic knees locked like a horse's as if the effort of lowering himself into and heaving himself out of a chair was more than that of standing.

At first he had beamed at them like the doting Opa he was pretending to be, but now he was growing impatient. He shuffled his feet slightly, cleared his throat. Had he begun to suspect that Anna was trying to memorize as much of the site and the links as possible?

"There is something else," he said with a final cough, nodding at the young man, who stumbled awkwardly out of the chair, his ears blushing, and hurried from the room. He returned moments later with another fuzz-head (nine of them now, counting Opa, Anna noted), carrying between them what looked at first like nothing so much as a foot-square piece of peanut brittle. They set it down, gingerly, flat on a cloth-covered table. The old man gestured Anna toward it: "Please."

Under conditions of intense heat, amber melts. Exposed to direct prolonged flame, it burns. The piece might have been authentic. Anna moved to it as reverently as if it were. The workmanship, the artistry, were of more interest to her than the material, the labor of love as much as skill that it took to carve each piece to a perfect fit with those surrounding it. She looked to the old man, who nodded that she was free to touch it, to examine it as she saw fit.

She forgot about the role she was playing for him, lost herself in the moment. Ran her fingers ever so lightly over the suggestion of what could once have been the beak and seven-feathered wing of an imperial Russian eagle, a broken portion of what would have been the head of a scepter clutched in its right claw. Her mind was telling her this is what she should see here; her eyes and fingers showed her only blurred and lumpy shapes, smoke-stained and drizzled like caramel.

If she had her acids with her, she could at least determine if it were true amber and not copal, a cheaper, more easily worked and often precast imitation. The fire damage made it all but impossible to tell if the inlays were genuine. Whether it was truly a portion of the Room . . .

"Given the condition and the circumstances, I can't tell for certain," was all she said.

"My thinking exactly," the old man said, fiddling with something in a briefcase one of the young men had also brought. "But when we find the rest, we will know, yes?"

It was a test, Anna realized. Well, wasn't everything? If she'd shown either too much enthusiasm or too much skepticism, he'd have been suspicious.

When he came toward her this time, she realized it wasn't only the amber's authenticity he was questioning.

It's an empty hypodermic, Anna told herself as she watched him swab her arm and slip it expertly into a vein. He's not injecting me with anything. He's taking a blood sample. Why? But even as she thought it, she knew the answer.

"I was a doctor once, you know," he had murmured as he washed his hands, and she thought momentarily of grabbing the hypo off the sterile cloth where he'd placed it in plain view and stabbing him with it. She let the moment pass, but had to ask: "Where? In Auschwitz?"

His smile was wintery. "No. I was on the eastern front. But please, retain your sarcasm. I don't want to win you over too easily. I wouldn't trust that."

After he'd closed the briefcase and shifted his weight to one side so as to carry it and manage the cane, he looked down at her from his great height.

"Now you will rest. And I would advise you to eat. Tomorrow we conclude this."

•

She must have slept, though she didn't remember it. She did compose her thoughts, surprised at their clarity in spite of everything. The thing that worried her was that the old man didn't seem to be in any hurry. She still didn't entirely understand what exactly he wanted from her—to assist him in finding the Room, of course, but what else? She'd expected a greater urgency. She tried not to interpret this almost leisurely questioning, interspersed with show-and-tell, as meaning she'd been wrong about Jake. Were they stalling because they had already found him, and were waiting only to bring him here, so Anna would see that he was in danger? Or, worse—?

No. He was not dead. She knew, just as she had known when she was first told about the auto accident. As long as that remained true, the rest was possible.

•

"The information your husband got from his British friend was accurate," the old man told her over a breakfast of shirred eggs and croissants and excellent coffee. Anna noted how he had to stop himself from saying "Jew-husband." That had been yesterday's tack. Today he was showing her more respect. "There is a document somewhere in the Stasi files indicating the last known whereabouts of the Amber Room. On land, not sunk in the Baltic with the *Wilhelm Gustloff*."

The old man chuckled around a mouthful of scrambled eggs. His teeth were bad, too, Anna noted, watching him chew on only one side of his mouth. "The *Gustloff* was built to hold fourteen hundred passengers, four hundred crew. Estimates were it was carrying between six and ten thousand when the Russian sub torpedoed it. There would have been no place to conceal something the size of the Room."

"Except the swimming pool," Anna suggested mildly. Her appetite was surprisingly good; her hand was steady as she poured the coffee, first for him, then for herself.

The old man was gaping at her again. "Oh, you are good!" he breathed. "How did you know there was a swimming pool?"

"A German ship without a *Schwimmbad*? Unthinkable!" She was charming him, turned it off as quickly as flipping a switch. "It would have been emptied for a voyage in such rough seas. The crates containing the Room could have been stored there."

"The swimming pool, in fact, became a dormitory for a group of nurses traveling with the wounded," the old man said dryly. "All of whom were lost. There was no room for packing crates."

"There were paintings and statuary in the hold," Anna countered. The old man blinked; he was not accustomed to being contradicted. "They were listed on the manifest. I've researched this subject thoroughly. Don't you think I would know that?"

Now who's interrogating whom? she thought. Time to make the transition to fellow conspirator complete.

"But no, I don't think it went down with the *Gustloff*, either. I admit it appeals to my sense of irony. The fact that the ship was named after a thug whom Goebbels propagandized into a hero. The interconnectedness appeals to me. It would make an interesting novel, but I don't believe it's true.

"However"—she studied the bottom of her coffee cup, amazed at the words that were coming out of her mouth— "you've squandered enough of my time. Tell me where you're holding Jake. Bring me to him or him to me. Then and only then we will discuss what happens next."

The old man's eyes almost disappeared beneath his lowered brows. "Do you really think you're in a position to dictate terms?"

Anna shrugged. "That depends on whether you really have Jake, doesn't it? And upon the outcome of the blood test. How long before you have the results?"

She had meant to play it casual, sip her coffee while he framed an answer, but now her hands were shaking. It had only now occurred to her that she couldn't wait for any test results. Because if they were negative, or even inconclusive . . .

"Where is my husband?" she asked for about the hundredth time against the old man's silence.

"First you must finish the history you began yesterday," he countered. "Your own involvement, please."

"I don't know what you're talking about," Anna said, too quickly, just as she and Peter had rehearsed it.

"What were you wearing the day you were brought to the Americans as a child?" the old man asked just as quickly.

Anna frowned, she hoped believably. "How the hell should I know? It was over fifty years ago. I don't even remember the event itself, much less what I was wearing."

"I will help you, then," the old man said, settling back in his chair as another youngster, the first woman Anna had seen (of course it was the women who would cook and serve the meals in any good Nazi household, she reminded herself), cleared the dishes away. "The day was sunny but cool, and those who had sheltered you after your mother was killed in the bombing wanted to dress you as well as they could before handing you over. You were wearing a little coat of fine wool, too small for you, as your mother had bought it the year before, but of very good quality. The color was, what is it in English—? *Rost . . .*"

"Red," Anna suggested. "No, rust. A dark orange."

"Just so. Now you remember."

"No. I'm just repeating what you're telling me."

"What was in the coat, Anna?"

She pretended to think. "I don't remember."

•

"Milk it, Anna," Peter had instructed her. "Play the whole range of emotions. Honest puzzlement, outrage when he doubts your word, a little pleading when he threatens to harm Jake. Don't overplay it, but play it. When you finally 'give in,' it has to be believable."

•

"Something in one of the pockets?" she suggested after what seemed like at least an hour of temporizing. "I honestly don't know."

"Not in the pockets. Sewn into the hem of the coat." The old man was barely whispering now. "This is not a child's memory you are trying to recall. This is what you were told as an adult, when the American Frank Fallon was, how does one say it? In his cups and trying to justify his role in guarding you. He was experiencing remorse, you see, because you had been kidnapped by those—*amateurs . . .*" He gave the word its original French pronunciation. "In a year he would be dead. He told you about the slip of paper sewn into the hem of the coat."

Anna sighed, looked down at her hands, milked it. "Yes," she said after a long moment.

"Did he give you the piece of paper, or simply tell you what was on it?"

"He didn't have it." Again she spoke too quickly, like a bad actress trying to cover for something. "He said he only found out about it later, when they told him why they wanted him to adopt me."

"Who are 'they,' please?"

"The army. His CO—commanding officer. I don't remember his name."

"Who was assigned to the OSS. And who just happened to know that this slip of paper was sewn into your coat."

"Oh, for God's sake!" Anna exploded. "Again, you're asking me something I don't know. I don't even know that my father was telling me the truth. He was, as you say, a lifelong alcoholic. On alternate Tuesdays he insisted he had worked for the OSS, that he still had ties to the CIA. In the middle of the night he talked to dead people. He saw them in his sleep. Delirium tremens, guilty conscience, I don't know. But by the time I was about twelve I refused to believe anything he said."

"But you knew he wasn't your true father."

"All I had to do was look in the mirror to know that. Five gangly, freckled redheads, and me. And when I was old enough to ask, I asked. And got the answers I just gave you."

"Just so. What did you see when you looked in the mirror, Anna? What do you see even now?"

I see a small, fine-boned woman with enormous dark eyes whose hair has darkened over time from an almost white blond to deep brown, she thought. A woman with a long, slightly off-center nose and, I used to think, a vaguely Semitic look. But I have seen photos of Goebbels's six "legitimate" children, and know that they were blond and had dark eyes, and had they lived to adulthood, their hair might have darkened, too. Please don't let me be who he says I am!

How many hours had they sat together in this room? There was a life-size photograph of Goebbels, positioned by design on the wall behind the old man's right shoulder. She could not help but see it looking back at her.

"I will make it simple for you, Anna." The old man had seen her close her eyes, deny the sight, if not the fact, of what she saw in that photograph. His voice caressed her. "The slip of paper contained a string of numbers. Handwritten. One of them, the number seven, crossed in the middle as Europeans, particularly those accustomed to the Gothic alphabet, are wont to do. Frank Fallon knew about them, because his superiors asked him what he thought they might mean, before they took the slip of paper to their new headquarters in Langley, Virginia, and added it to the file they had started on you. Because they knew who you were, Anna, even then. His brain not yet entirely rotted by alcohol, Frank Fallon, for whatever reasons, had memorized those numbers.

"His superiors tried everything to solve the mystery. Was it as complex a thing as a code? As simple a thing as the number of a Swiss bank account? No one ever asked you, because you were a child, unable to read at the time. But just before he died, Frank Fallon told you the numbers, and you also memorized them."

•

"I wouldn't buy it," Anna had told Killian flatly when he explained what they were doing. "Neither will the old man."

Killian had looked up at the ceiling then, letting his breath out in slow exasperation.

"Mrs. Bower, I frankly don't give the proverbial flying fuck what you believe. We've spoon-fed this story to the old man's followers over a very long period of time. He's swallowed it. That's what this whole brouhaha is about. He's convinced you know those numbers, and he'll lead you to believe he can kill your husband, your daughter, or both, in order to get you to give him that information."

"Or else he's spoon-feeding you," was Anna's opinion.

But what other explanation was there? And was the CIA any less vile than Reinheit for putting the value of an artifact above Jake Bower's life?

And not only Jake's life but her own. Was there really a file on her? She'd asked Killian point-blank and he'd refused to answer. Did the CIA as well believe she was Goebbels's daughter, or was it all smoke and mirrors? Even as she fenced with the old man, Anna knew that he wasn't the only enemy.

•

"We know what those numbers mean, Anna," the old man was saying patiently. "There is no mystery to us, except why Fallon, a nobody, was entrusted with such a secret. The only explanation is that one of the two men who brought you to him in Berlin must have told him, and his superiors questioned him about it later. What is mysterious to me is why you never pursued the meaning of those numbers yourself."

"Maybe I did." Anna shrugged. She managed to make her face grim, her voice flat, as if trying to decide where to hide now that her great secret had been discovered. "Maybe I thought if the CIA couldn't figure it out—"

The old man was chuckling to himself again.

"It's so ironic, you know. You and your Jew-husband have spent how much effort over how many years poring over documents, tracing down leads, trying to find the Amber Room, when the key was right there in your memory."

Now! Anna thought, steeling herself. "What are you talking about?" she demanded, hoping her voice was shrill enough.

She watched the triumph gleam in his eyes as he saw what he interpreted as her loss of control.

"You really do not know, do you?" He beamed at her, his eyebrows raised, his thin lips unpleasantly moist.

"What? You're going to tell me it's the number to a Stasi file? Ridiculous!"

"No, that would be an anachronism too foolish for anyone to believe. But let us suppose that, with typical German efficiency, someone during the war wrote down an address, but in a numerical code. If one could decipher that numerical code, one would have the address, most likely in Berlin, of one of those responsible for bringing you to the Americans."

•

Margarethe waited until Johann was comfortable, his feet up on the mismatched ottoman, then began unlacing his shoes. He looked as if he were about to object, but didn't have the strength.

"Did it go well?" she asked at last.

"The child is safe," he answered. "The Americans will see that she's taken care of."

"I could have cared for her, you know," she reminded him; the topic was not new. "Passed her off as my own. A change-of-life baby, or a grandchild."

The thought amused him. "She doesn't look anything like you."

"What does that matter? Half the children in this city are being raised by people not their parents. I'd have kept her safe. They'd never have found her."

"They would have found her," he said, ending the conversation. "Killed you, and taken her. It could not be risked."

"I suppose not," she said sadly, looking away as she eased his shoes off. He thought for a moment she might cry, but then he knew she wouldn't. He watched her hunch her shoulders, heard her sigh. The eyes that met his had tears in them, but she would not let them fall. "Poor little one. I'll miss her!"

•

The woman in the cellar! was Anna's first thought. She no longer remembered where she had heard the story first, might never know if it was true. Intrigued in spite of herself, she sat back in her chair.

"An address," she said, repeating the old man's words.

Karen, invisible, is clenching her fists as hard as she had when she witnessed Anna's ordeal in the closet. The answer is here; she can feel it.

"The address," the old man said, "of an individual who would later come to have a file in the Stasi archives, for whatever reasons. Antigovernment protests, black-market activities, or simply because the Stasi loved to keep records. If we can find this person's file, it will contain another document, taken from that coded address, which will lead us to the last known whereabouts of the Amber Room."

Anna suppressed any sign of amazement. Killian was right. The old man had swallowed the entire story, with all of its implausible and unnecessary complications. All that was left was for him to ask her for the numbers, for her to stall until threatened, and then to pretend to yield. Had she stalled long enough? They'd taken her watch when they came for her at Peter's house. She had no idea what time it was, even if it was day or night. Was it enough time for Peter to get to Jake?

Then something else occurred to her. What if even the story of the woman in the cellar was a legend, a figment of the Agency's imagination implanted in Frank Fallon's sodden brain, to be used to manipulate his adopted daughter decades later?

No, she couldn't think of it. Something about her past had to be true. As if from very far away, she heard herself speaking. She would milk it as long as she could, but eventually she would tell the old man what he wanted to hear.

•

Karen finds that by turning herself in a certain direction, she can avoid watching what transpires in the Museum. Because she already knows what Anna's going to say. In one reality, Anna is her creation, after all. So while Anna's spinning out her legend for Opa, Karen needs a quiet place to think.

Yes, Gentle Reader, she's still caught between Here and There, and yes, she is alone. But it's no longer blue screen all the way down. She is peopling it with her characters, and they're guiding her. A few more pages now, and she'll know exactly what to do.

What does a good writer do, after all, but live inside her characters' skins, ask herself if she would, could, do the things they do, if they are authentic? If she can do that in fiction, why not in real life? It's not as if it hasn't happened before. The only difference is, there are no jellyfish on this beach.

But how to go about it? Slip somehow back into Margarethe's life, persuade Johann not to give the child to the Americans? How the hell did Johann know Anna's identity anyway? Is she really Goebbels's daughter? Is that what the scene in the Berlin cellar was all about? Had Johann been sent to oversee the child's whereabouts? Sent by whom, for what purpose? Was Margarethe somehow involved? Was that the reason she and Karen and Fuchsia had been loitering near the Zoo *Flakturm*, where the old man said the Trojan Gold was hidden (could the Amber Room have been concealed there as well?) after curfew, in the middle of the worst of the shelling, looking for Johann?

Karen's head is starting to spin. What to do? If she can infiltrate Anna's reality somehow, perhaps find Margarethe somewhere in Anna's mind, slip back into Margarethe's life and maybe—maybe what? Maybe something. At least she'd be back on Earth, with Johann/Govannon.

And what about her own life, the life of a Karen yet to be born? If Govannon could only choose one human life (and, she reminded herself, he's chosen Jake for this go-round), would he be able to free her from Margarethe after she had done . . . well, whatever it was she was going to do?

No. Too risky. Explore all other options first. There was no guarantee that even borrowing Margarethe for a little while would change anything. Hadn't she learned that before? And how many times had she gotten tangled up in a narrative wrapping around itself like a Möbius strip and going nowhere when the only solution was to give her characters their heads and let them guide her?

Sometimes the hardest thing of all to do is nothing.

•

"There, now. Don't you feel better?" Opa asked Anna, stroking her forehead with one arthritic hand. He was close enough for her to smell the schnapps on his breath. "If only you had trusted me from the beginning, how much easier this would have been for us all."

"I will feel nothing until I have Jake back," she rasped, as if her throat hurt. Well, it did. She had shouted, she had wept, she had pleaded. How could she trust him? she had demanded. What if the numbers didn't lead him to the

Room, and he decided she had deceived him, and killed Jake? What if he found the Room and killed Jake anyway, for spite, and because he was a Jew?

He had countered each of her arguments by saying "The Room is only the beginning, Anna. Even more important is for you to trust me, and to believe in what I am doing."

Finally she had given him what he wanted, on nothing more than the promise that Jake would be returned to her once the Room was found. The deception was complete.

•

"Hold it!" she'd told Killian when he reached this part of the narrative. "Let's assume for a moment that everything actually goes as planned, which is a large enough assumption in itself. Let's assume I manage to stall Reinheit long enough for you and Peter to retrieve Jake and get him out of harm's way. Reinheit uses the magic numbers to retrieve a Stasi file that leads them—where? You're not telling me you actually have the Room?"

"No, I'm not telling you that," Killian acknowledged, impressed with how far ahead she had thought this through. "But they're going to think we do."

"And then what? You lead them into some sort of ambush, with me in the middle of it. Even if you do have a man on the inside, if they think I've led them into a trap—"

Peter, she remembered, had gone very quiet about then. Before Killian's arrival, she and Peter had meant to find Jake and then—what? Lie low? Elude a band of neo-Nazi terrorists as well as the CIA? Out of the question. Uncomfortable as it was, this was the only way.

"You're the heir apparent, Mrs. Bower. They won't harm you."

It was the only thing the other one—Silent Sam, as Peter would come to call him—would say the entire time he was there, but it was said with the same kind of fervent belief Anna encountered now in Opa's followers.

Now she played the scene for pathos, shuddering all over until Opa withdrew his hand and moved painfully away from her.

She watched him out of the corner of her eye as he settled himself ponderously in his chair. As if on cue, one of his "children"—Anna was beginning to recognize them, had made a point of asking them their names, making eye contact, being friendly, playing the Stockholm syndrome—brought him his medication.

"Opa, may I ask you something?" she asked when the door closed and they were alone again.

Her use of the name visited him with an almost childish glee. "That is the first time you have called me this!" He beamed at her. "I cannot tell you how delightful it sounds from your lips! Though you must admit, old as I am, I am not old enough to be your Opa. But, please, ask."

"What is your fascination with the Amber Room? Is it only because of the connection with . . . with my father?" *There!* she thought. *I've said it!* "That aside, I really don't see—"

He waved one hand dismissively. "Pure pragmatism, my dear. Once it is ours, we will offer it to the Russians, for a very large sum of money. The money will finance our campaign in the next national elections."

As simple as that! Anna thought, amazed that she could have thought it would be anything else.

"Interesting," she said coolly. "Who's your candidate?"

"You are."

EIGHTEEN

"Poor little one," Margarethe said. "I shall miss her."

"Poor little one," Johann agreed, though he wasn't thinking of the child. Had he been so caught up with his concern for her that he hadn't had time to really notice her caretaker?

He'd been attracted to Margarethe from the beginning, though she was quite different from the sort of women who had haunted his past, mournful women like the mother he barely remembered, clingy, manipulative women whose sole talent was that of survival, regardless of the cost to the men they clung to. Perhaps it was that Margarethe was the very opposite—staunch, plainspoken, virtually without guile— that had drawn him.

He drank her in with his eyes as she looked up at him, the strength of her jaw, her straight shiksa's nose, the hidden fire of the hair twisted up now in two practical plaits wound round her head. Why had he never noticed her eyes before? She had worn glasses in the beginning, he remembered. The lenses had been smashed, the frames hopelessly twisted, when she saved the child from the falling debris in the cellar. No way to replace them in occupied Berlin. How nearsighted was she? Did she suffer from eyestrain, headaches?

An almost overwhelming affection for her washed over

him momentarily. This was not the time for attachments. After years in hiding, he fancied himself beyond loneliness or even the desire for companionship. His war had been spent letting go, first of those who died or disappeared, now even of those who survived. The little girl with the big dark eyes had moved him more than he wanted to admit. Seeing her in the American GI's arms was almost too much to bear. Johann had turned and walked away so quickly that Timothy could barely keep up with him.

Now Margarethe's mere presence was threatening his composure. No. No more attachments. Not now, maybe not ever. He had come here to tell her the child had been delivered to the Americans, nothing more. Then why was he still here?

"Is it true?" Margarethe asked him. "Was—he—really her father? Or was it just some fantasy of the mother's? I wondered where she got those clothes, but still. She could have been any rich man's mistress."

"The rumor is sufficient," Johann said. "Sufficient to put the child in danger of being used by any number of factions."

"So you and Timothy took it upon yourselves to decide she would be safer out of the country. In principle, I agree. Neither of us has to imagine what could be done with that sort of information here." Margarethe rubbed her arms, as if against a sudden chill. "The madness does not end just because the war has. And at least in America she will have food, medicines, a chance at a normal life."

"As much of a chance as any of us, I suppose," Johann conceded.

•

Watching, Karen is at a loss. It's not as if she can't keep the story lines straight. Both realities are happening simultaneously within the Museum, but in the kind of stop action that transpires in fiction, so that it's possible to cut between the two without missing anything. But she can feel the pull of Govannon's personality as much in Johann as in Jake. It's as if he is proving without a doubt that he can be both simultaneously.

Which one will he choose? Does he have to choose either? Can he choose one of the earlier avatars? Is he already committed to the choice, or only taking each life for a test drive?

Karen wishes she knew what was going on. The itch to do something, anything, is almost overwhelming. But what?

•

Peter had waited until they were actually inside the caves to shake Killian. It was practical. Killian had the car keys, as well as Peter's documentation. Besides, he didn't want to lose him completely, just long enough to talk to Jake first.

If he listened very carefully, he swore he could still hear Killian back in the chamber known as the Cathedral, arguing with the tour guide in very bad German. Ridiculous, he realized, since he'd traveled at least a mile of tunnel since giving Killian the slip. But he could hear the conversation in his mind.

His friend *aus* Japan lost was, Killian was insisting. Immediately a search must be begun. Killian's usual turf was farther north. He spoke flawless Russian and Latvian, Lithuanian with a Russian accent, and enough Estonian to get by, but his German was atrocious.

Try English! Peter thought, ducking through one of the lower passages. *The guide probably speaks it better than you!*

The guide was politely reiterating that he recalled no such friend from Japan, that a close tally was kept of the number of tourists who entered the caverns so that no one would be left behind, if the American gentleman would be so kind as to return with the rest of the tour, he could be assured at the entrance that his friend was accounted for.

Peter grinned, in spite of the seriousness of the situation. His hide-in-plain-sight act had worked yet again. He hadn't run a caper like this in years, and it made him feel like a kid again. Maybe once they got back, assuming he wasn't on Killian's permanent shit list (he never for a moment harbored the thought that they might not get back), he'd ask to be put on active again.

Right now, time to pay attention. The passage opened out above his head so that he could not only stand upright again but could shine his flashlight on the beginnings of the names marked on the walls. He began speaking, softly at first, but letting his naturally deep voice roll out ahead of him.

"Jake, it's Peter. I know exactly where you are, because Anna told me. I'm alone for the moment, but there's an Official Person on my tail, and he's going to have to get to both of us soon. I know you're not armed, at least you don't have a gun, but I wouldn't put it past you to try to brain me with a stick or a shovel or something, so I wanted to warn you that I'm on my way, as much for my own protection as yours."

He stopped, waited for the echoes to precede him and gradually dissipate. He had seen the afterglow of a lantern being extinguished, and knew that he was close.

•

Jake had seen the flashlight, had heard the footsteps where he couldn't hear the drip of water, except at night. He'd assumed there was a good chance that someone would come for him before he decided to emerge on his own, and the likelihood was that it was someone sent by Anna, if not Anna herself, someone he could trust. But what if it wasn't?

For the first time it occurred to him how foolish it was, hiding in a cave. Never mind the sheer physical inconvenience, hadn't he in essence trapped himself? He had no idea what direction they would come from, if come they did, nor any way of knowing who they were or how many before they were upon him. Now it was too late. Of all the choices he could have made, why this one?

He had shut off the lantern the instant he heard the sound. Now he wondered if it was better to simply stay silent, motionless, hoping they would not find him, or to strike before they could.

With what, you fool? Thomas Mann? Jake almost laughed aloud. The book *was* heavy enough to kill someone.

•

"Jake?" Peter had stopped talking, stopped walking, for at least a minute. He could be as silent as a cat when he wanted to be, but had chosen to make enough noise to announce his approach. Now he wondered if that had been wise. Jake would have expected him to be virtually silent. Or would he?

"What's the password?" a voice demanded from the place where the light had gone out.

There was no password, there never had been. The thought that his old friend would in fact brain him with a shovel if he didn't think of one made Peter laugh out loud.

"Thank you!" he heard Jake say. The light flickered on again. "Come ahead."

"How could you be sure it was me?" Peter asked breathlessly, after they'd pounded each other on the back a few times and he'd made sure Jake was all right.

"Are you kidding? Anna says you ought to patent that laugh. Let's get the hell out of here. I want a shave and a hot bath and a hot meal, not necessarily in that order. . . ."

It was hard to tell by lantern light, but Jake seemed none the worse for wear. Pale and a little haggard, his beard grown in to mountain man, if not quite biblical, proportions, but clear of eye and mind.

". . . and thank God I don't have to spend another night with Thomas Mann. What is it?" Jake straightened up to his full height, his therapist's instincts reading into Peter's silence.

Peter told him what had happened in his absence, and what was supposed to happen next. He had barely finished when they saw a light bobbing toward them from the opposite direction.

"Dr. Bower?" Killian's voice, unsure of itself.

"I'm not here yet!" Peter whispered, clasping Jake's shoulder before fading back the way he came.

"W-who is it?" No mean actor, Jake put just enough fear into his voice. He also started shuffling through his things, as if looking for something to clobber an intruder.

"My name is Killian," the agent said, coming around the bend, flashlight in one hand, ID in the other. "CIA. Just like in the movies." He gave Jake the ID to study while he caught his breath, straightened his spine. "I did have Peter Kato with me, but he's decided to play ninja and go off on his own. Probably trying to get to you first for reasons I'm not too clear on, and probably lost somewhere, which will screw things up considerably if we don't find him in time. He didn't take into consideration that all I had to do was ask the right people where the refugees had hidden during the war."

"And the bribe you slipped the tour guide didn't hurt." Peter managed to look even more out of breath as he jogged the last few yards from his tunnel, as if he'd only just arrived. "Jake, my God, it's good to see you! Are you okay?"

They went through a second take of their original reunion some minutes earlier. It looked genuine enough to fool Killian.

"Actually, Peter, I wish you'd have more faith in me," the CIA man said. "You know the Agency doesn't need to bribe anyone. Here, Dr. Bower, let me help you with that." Jake had begun rolling up his sleeping bag again. "By now your lovely wife has told the people looking for you where you are. We'd like to get you settled in there before they arrive. . . ."

•

How much longer? Anna wondered. The car was a late-model Mercedes that devoured the autobahn at a steady purr. The eager young men had preened over the stereo/TV combination, the wet bar, even an onboard computer which, if this were a spy novel, Anna thought wryly, might come in handy. She ignored all of it, watching the scenery stream by as if it contained some clue.

The journey seemed unending. All she wanted was to be reunited with Jake. When at last she was, she knew, it would have to give the appearance of being almost anticlimactic.

"You will divorce him, of course," Opa said as they left the safe house which, she finally ascertained, was somewhere on the outskirts of Hamburg, a favorite breeding ground for terrorists. It was very early morning of a gray, drizzly day.

"Of course!" she'd answered, somewhat impatiently. "But what happens to him even then?"

The old man shook his head. "Do you still doubt me?"

"No. But if I'm to be your candidate for Chancellor"— she tried not to choke on the absurdity of it—"there's the question of a background check. It might be easier to 'disappear' a Jewish ex-husband and a *Mischling* daughter—"

She stopped herself. Why give them ideas? If the Agency's

plan didn't work . . . for the first time she allowed herself to think of the alternatives. When the old man patted her hand absently, she had to steel herself not to recoil.

"Would I risk losing your affection? No, my dear, I must have you completely on my side or not at all. Your past life will be offered to the media in its entirety, then explained away. Surely you know that was your father's great gift. Many of the founders had mixed blood, you will recall. Heydrich's mother, for example, was a Jewess. And there was the question of the Führer's grandfather. All the more reason why he was only the puppet for the true genius, the power . . ."

The old man's jaw went slack for a moment; he almost seemed to drool. Epilepsy? Anna wondered. Outside the window, signs gave the distance to Berlin. They would drive through the city, west to east, to where the Stasi files were kept. Those files were in the process of being moved, she knew, out of their former headquarters, which was to be turned into a museum, into larger warehouses in the eastern suburbs, where they could be sorted and painstakingly catalogued, a process which was expected to take years. There was probably not an East German citizen alive who did not have a Stasi file.

I was born here, Anna thought as they entered the outskirts, but the words were meaningless. The city she had left as a child was nothing but rubble; she could not expect to recognize any thing in the rebuilt and now reunited and still rebuilding city of Berlin. She turned away from the window to see that the old man had recovered from his spell.

"Youthful indiscretion, the wiles of the Eternal Jew seducing an innocent young woman." His moist lips worked over the words as if no time had passed. Neither the driver nor the other passenger, another Hitler Youth clone seated in the fold-out seat facing them, appeared to notice his lapse. "There is much material there which will only make you more sympathetic to our listeners.

"He will have to stay out of the public eye, of course, your former husband. A quiet retirement somewhere in the country, I think. Not possible to return him to America. The journalists, you know. He might let something slip. As for your daughter, she may continue with her musical career, as long as she remains apolitical. You see? Nothing to worry about."

Anna smiled weakly, settling into her coat as if for a nap. Safer than staring into the face of madness for too long, thinking of the possibility of Jake under house arrest somewhere off a dirt road in the middle of nowhere, Angelica accompanied everywhere lest she speak out of turn. While her eyes were closed, Anna's mind was racing.

She had followed Killian's instructions, told them Jake was using Tony Nunn's passport and biding his time in one of the hotels in Postojna. The old man was delighted to know this.

"We have researched this, you see. We knew about his connection with the caves. What we did not know was the identity of the man who died in the car in his place. But we would have ascertained that eventually."

"I'm sure you would," Anna had said evenly.

Before he left her alone in the summer house that night, Peter had assured her he would contrive to be with Jake when the time came. She had no idea how he would arrange that, but it wouldn't be the first time Peter Kato had managed the impossible. The man Jakob Bauer would require a brief car ride back to Trieste, Opa informed her, then a charter flight to Berlin, where she could see him again, if the number on the piece of paper sewn into the lining of a child's coat proved genuine.

•

A dull prewar brick building with far too many windows, rather than the cinder-block sameness of Soviet construction, the former Stasi headquarters probably had as many levels underground as above. Pale green corridors, offices with parquet floors and beechwood furniture, open-doored lifts that led to row upon row of metal shelves packed so close together that two people could not pass each other, even sideways, in the aisles between them.

Most of the shelves were emptied now, ghostly with dust and with a distinct sagging in the middle from the sheer weight of paper the only evidence of the plethora of human data they'd once held. That data was now consigned to canvas sacks, tossed into corners as if they held nothing more important than potatoes, and Anna's heart sank. If "her" file was in one of those sacks instead of still on the shelves, what hope was there of finding it?

•

"It's still on the shelf," Karen hears herself saying aloud. "Three aisles over, where the shelves haven't been emptied yet. Midway down the aisle, lefthand side, second shelf from the top. You're going to need a ladder."

Hell, if she were writing this, that's where it would be. As to how these characters are going to figure that out, let's leave that offstage. In fact, let's cut to the chase. Fade out, fade in, and, file in hand, we find ourselves on the main floor and on our way out through the entrance foyer, when:

Enter Jake Bower, *Übermenschen* to the right of him, *Übermenschen* to the left of him, and somehow Peter Kato at his side. No, we're not going to explain how Peter's managed to convince the Bad Guys to let him tag along. If we'd been contracted to write a proper thriller, things might be very different. But we're not being paid to write a thriller. We're barely being paid to write an s/f novel. Be grateful, Gentle Reader, we've been able to take you this far.

Anna's meeting with the man she loves is, under the circumstances, quite subdued. She must not let the Legend of Anna Goebbels (see John le Carré for the etymology of "legend" vis-à-vis espionage) be compromised by any display of what she really feels for this man she will have to set aside, after all, if she is to run for Chancellor of Germany. This is the natural order of things on the planet where Opa comes from.

She embraces Jake briefly, asks if he's all right, but there's nothing on her face. Jake, who's lived with her through prior traumas, reads her meaning and plays his own role, the weary and slightly disoriented older man, sleep deprived and not at all sure what's going on. Don't, Gentle Reader, believe it for a minute. Remember who Jake is, in addition to being Jake. He knows precisely what Anna's about.

There is also an exchange of not exactly pleasantries but introductions between Jake and Opa. Their eyes lock in a manner of silent, wintry combat, each recognizing the other out of past history, and each concerned with making his own position clear. Difficult to say which one breaks the stare first or if they both do it simultaneously, but it is Opa's bad knees that force him to move off first, giving whispered orders to his followers that it's time to follow.

Bathroom breaks for everyone, then off into three cars, one each for each of the "guests." We're off for the Polish border. As we leave Berlin, we find our way somewhat obstructed by recent road construction. Signs inform us that the project is the work of the Nordic Construction Company of Sweden, contractors, paving a straightaway from the German border to Moscow which is estimated to take ten years. It is emblematic of the hope that the future will not produce another Hitler or Napoleon who will drive his troops into the teeth of a Russian winter.

Anna has been assigned once more to ride with Opa. She studies the old man's face as the car continues east. He'd said he was on the eastern front. Was any of it true? Was he thinking how murderous those frozen kilometers had been more than half a century ago, and how many companions he had lost in the retreat?

Don't invest him with even this much humanity! she cautioned herself, mindful of her last glimpse of Jake as they bundled him into the car behind hers, the surreptitious thumbs-up Peter managed to give her before being unceremoniously shoved into the third car.

Killian hadn't told her what to expect at their final destination, and Peter hadn't been able to tell her anything more, but she could foresee a standoff, at least. She also still had not had any sign from Killian's "man on the inside." All she could do was play the role she'd been assigned. She had never felt more helpless.

•

In a town in what was once the Russian-occupied part of Germany, with a name, Gentle Reader, you probably couldn't pronounce and, interestingly enough, on the route a convoy carrying a heavy load might have taken in an attempt to get from the ruins of Königsberg Castle to Berlin, there is an abandoned villa that had been converted into working-class apartments under Soviet rule, and more recently abandoned, the tenants relocated, while its prewar owners petitioned to have it restored to them and the courts haggled it out.

The basement was a midden. Squatters had taken over the boiler room, convenient to the back-alley entrance in case the *Polizei* came nosing about. Rotten mattresses and a funk of urine, spliff, and takeout food were all that remained of them for now; they could smell authority before it was round the corner, and had melted out of sight.

One wall seeped constantly, ancient rust stains suggesting plumbing so far beyond repair it was held together only by the sediment built up inside. A jumble of old lumber, some with nails protruding, intermixed with rags, fragments of brick and cinder block and shattered floor tiles, formed an obstacle course down the center, and the party picked its way over it carefully, all but Opa, who remained just inside the doorway, knees locked, leaning on his cane. One of his "children," the one Anna knew as Klaus, stood beside him, protective.

Five others, she noted, including the woman who had done the cooking and who now, Marlene Dietrich–style, wore the same suit-and-tie uniform the men wore, leaving no doubt that there was a shoulder holster under the suit jacket. Seven members of Reinheit, Jake and Peter and herself. How the hell was Killian going to separate them without someone's getting hurt?

"Over here!" someone said, scattering her thoughts.

Not surprisingly, the lights didn't work. But enough ambient light streamed through the kicked-in windows to show a great deal of, well, something, stacked against another wall. Could that be the back of a picture frame?

It was. Disregarding her keepers, homing to art in any form, Anna pushed past everyone and pulled the thing loose. A tarnished gilt frame, moldy paper backing, a rusted wire that had strung it to a wall, decades of dust. More stacked in front of it, less dusty for having been in its lee. Extricated, turned around, they were, well, paintings.

Oils, recent ones, in Anna's terms, none older than she was. Daubs of pretentious abstracts, knockoffs of Impressionists, with far too much Monet. Anna stopped pulling at them after the third or fourth; there were perhaps a dozen altogether. Her face showed disappointment.

"Stage sets," Peter said, nodding toward the jumble of lath-and-canvas constructs leaning with their backs to them, perhaps six deep and taking up the back half of the cellar where the light was dimmest. "The paintings were probably part of some revival, some drawing-room comedy."

"Illusion," the old man said breathlessly in English, picking his way stubbornly over the refuse, with Klaus half carrying him in places. "Another false lead."

"Perhaps," Jake answered, and not for the first time Anna was startled at how easily the two seemed to concur on the little things. "Still . . ."

The humming in her ears that had begun in the D.C. restaurant when Peter first began to explain was suddenly stilled. It was enough to make Anna reel. Instinctively Jake steadied her with a hand on her elbow. Moving the rest of the paintings aside, oblivious to the dust on her hands and clothing, she touched the canvas back of one of the flats.

"Can we move this?" she asked of no one in particular.

Young blond *Übermenschen* have their uses. With much grappling and grunting and not a little awkwardness, several of them managed to extricate the flat Anna indicated from the others and swing it around a hundred eighty degrees.

"What's wrong with this picture?" Anna whispered to Jake and Peter when it was clear the others hadn't noticed anything.

"Don't give them anything," Peter whispered back. Jake

was silent, but his eyes were sparkling. "Make them work for it!"

"What are you whispering?" the old man demanded. His hearing, at least, had not been damaged by age.

"Nothing." Anna shrugged. "What do you see?"

Peter was right, a drawing-room comedy. An ornate eighteenth-century room, with damask-covered walls and cream-painted trim and an excess of broken and tarnished brass fixtures. Victorian wallpaper and an empty window frame with brackets for what would undoubtedly have been heavy velvet drapes. During the performance, a stagelight with a leaf-patterned gobo, perhaps, would have suggested sunlight through trees for act I, a different light with a blue gel transformed the world to night for the finale.

" 'I am a sea gull . . .' " Peter suggested. " 'No, no, that's not it!' "

"Foolishness!" the old man pronounced it. "A stage set, as you say. *Macht nichts.*"

"If you say so." Anna shrugged again.

"Put it back," the old man ordered.

"It's very heavy," one of the *Übermenschen* murmured, and that was when the light dawned.

"It is canvas and wood only," another said in fractured English. "How is it so heavy?"

Opa caught Anna's eye. "Perhaps, my dear, you can tell us."

She hesitated for only a moment.

"Does anyone have a pocket knife?"

Dietrich's clone produced a Swiss army knife from a trouser pocket. As she passed it to Anna, she held the handle a little longer than necessary and, unnoticed by the others, winked.

This, then, was Killian's "man on the inside." Anna would

follow her lead when and if something happened.

"Thank you," Anna said, and went to work.

She chose a bit of molding where the paint was already peeling and began to scratch at it. Within moments its true nature emerged. Not wood, but a translucent golden material that glowed with an inner light. Tearing a piece of the damask free, Anna revealed not plywood or canvas, but intricately carved and fitted amber-colored piecework. She stepped back and let the others judge her handiwork.

"Hidden in plain sight!" Peter grinned.

Two of the Hitler youth began counting the flats still stacked against the walls.

"Twelve, Opa," one reported.

Twelve out of the original eighteen panels. Impressive considering the thousands of miles they had been transported, the bombing, the fire, the rumors of bits and pieces turning up here and there over the years. Everyone seemed to be holding their breath, waiting for Opa to make some sort of statement.

"Brilliant!" he pronounced it. "Brilliant!"

The look of triumph on his face was chilling. After a lifetime of false hope, his dream of empire was about to be fulfilled.

Handing his cane to Klaus, he took Anna by the shoulders, embracing her.

"All because of you, my dear. All this because of you!"

Then all hell broke loose.

---⊶∞∞⊷---

NINETEEN

Have you ever wondered, Gentle Reader, how human activity must appear to the eye of God? Even staying "in the moment," as acting teachers say, on a single time line, the input must be staggering. As Killian's people make their move and Reinheit decide to resist, and orders are shouted, shots fired, and bodies move too quickly for the human eye to take it all in, less than a block away a group of boys kicks a soccer ball around and through the muddy puddles left by the morning's rain, a man who left work early complaining of flu makes furtive love to a woman not his wife, who is less concerned with what he's doing between her legs than with whether the tights she washed in the basin that morning and hung over the shower rod because it was raining outside will be dry enough for her to wear tomorrow, and trees fall in the forest around the world, even if only God and the squirrels can hear them.

The boys hear the shots and make laughing reference to some American movie playing at the local cinema before they resume their game. The naked man leaves off his thrusting and sweating for a moment and immediately thinks of what his wife would do to him if she found out; his cock shrivels and he curses sharply. His companion yawns, rolls out from under him, and shambles to the loo, squeezing the sodden toes of her tights dubiously.

Back in Berlin, where Hitler's bunker lies buried beneath a children's playground, and once upon a time when a physical as well as philosophical wall separated East from West, fifty-seven people crawled to freedom through a tunnel two feet high and two hundred fifty yards long, from an outdoor latrine in the Soviet sector to the basement of a bakery in the West, and far from the sound of this particular gun battle, a straight-backed elderly woman strides through one of the city's Jewish cemeteries with a purposefulness that belies her years.

Passing the mausoleum of Bernard Schwarz, with the broken stained-glass window in the roof where Jews in hiding concealed themselves in the rafters during the war, she finds the grave she is looking for. Wiping the rainwater off a wrought-iron bench with a dish towel which, ever practical, she has brought with her in her bag, she sits, tucking a strand of still-auburn hair under her hat, and remembers.

•

"Poor little one," Johann said, studying the curve of Margarethe's neck thoughtfully. He wasn't thinking of the child. Margarethe began to massage his feet. He had been walking, it seemed, all day, once he and Timothy had parted company. The sensation was soothing, but it also disturbed him. "Please don't do that!"

"Why not?" When she smiled, everything fell away from her, widowhood and middle age and war and deprivation, and she might have been a girl of seventeen. "Afraid I'll turn you into a hedonist?"

"No." He slid his feet off the ottoman onto the floor, sat up straighter, trying for dignity. "Afraid you'll discover I have only one pair of socks, and they're full of holes and not all that clean."

"Easily remedied," she said, disappearing into the bedroom. He heard her rummaging. She came back a moment later with a pair of good lisle socks. "At least some things the Russians had no use for. There are underclothes, too, even a couple of shirts, though they may be too small for you."

"Your husband's?" He had been killed, Johann remembered her telling him, in the third year of the war.

"Yes."

He sighed, defeated, taking the socks from her but making no effort to put them on. "You'd give me your life if I asked for it, wouldn't you?"

"Are you asking?"

His answer was a baleful look. She suddenly remembered something else.

"Would you like a bath? The water was turned back on again this morning, and Timothy has actually cadged some coal from somewhere to get the ovens going. He plans to reopen the bakery. Some deal with an American supply sergeant, not entirely kosher I'm sure, but there is water, and it's hot. I haven't had a hot bath since—"

She had started to remove his tattered socks. He leaned forward and took her wrists, and then her hands.

"Don't," he said gently but firmly. "I'm not an invalid. And don't remove any more of my clothing unless you promise to share the bath with me."

Her laugh was deep and throaty. "And then—?"

He squeezed her hands, mirrored her smile. "Then I suppose I will let you turn me into a hedonist."

She hesitated for only a moment. "This isn't meant just to take my mind off the child, is it?"

He stood, still holding her hands, drawing her upright with him and taking her in his arms.

"This is meant," he said between kisses light as butterflies, "to show you what I've wanted to do since the night I met you, but couldn't as long as the child was here."

She understood. There was no privacy. There had been a door to the bedroom once, but the Russians had used it for firewood. She and the little one had shared the big iron bed, and she had soothed the child's screaming nightmares with songs and fairy tales almost every night.

"I wonder who will chase away her nightmares now?" Margarethe said, half to herself.

Now, with the child gone, the bed seemed overlarge for just one person. Margarethe took Johann's hand and led the way into the bathroom.

•

The tub was a great clawed monster, deep enough for both of them. He sat at one end with his knees tucked up and she climbed in at the other end, their legs interweaving like pale saplings in a paler marsh. The solitary bulb in the bathroom fixture had burned out long ago and could not be replaced; a gibbous moon through the panelless window above the tub augmented the yellowish light from the hall through the open door, and more often than not they found each other by touch as much as sight.

True Germans, they concentrated first on the serious business of getting clean, having to refill the tub twice before the grime of the grieving city was washed off and drained away and they were both pink and scrubbed (and, bless you, Timothy! Karen thought, the water still ran hot) and the mirrors were steamed over and Margarethe's coppery hair, freed of its nest of pins, streamed down her back like mermaid hair, and tiny individual droplets glowed like pearls as the moonlight splashed the white of Johann's beard. By then they had each touched every part of the other, and so when he lifted her hips and eased himself into her beneath the waist-high water it was as if it was where he had always belonged.

"The war is over. . . ." she murmured later, stroking his chest in the suddenly not-so-big iron bed, her voice hoarse from the myriad other sounds she had been making. "And the drought as well."

•

"I never mourned my husband the way I mourn you," Margarethe says, standing before the headstone with its cold facts, name and dates, and a passage from the Torah. "Odd, isn't it, when you aren't really gone? I talk to you every day, even when it's too cold to come here, and I still hear your voice in my mind. It's the touch of you I will miss, always. Well."

She kisses her fingertips, rests them on the stone for a long, affectionate moment, then goes home.

•

"Okay, people, let's be sensible," was the last thing Killian said, his German remarkably improved in moments of crisis. "If we start shooting, we could damage the Room. Then everybody loses."

Killian, you bonehead, that's just the kind of Götterdammerung his kind feeds on! Peter thought as Opa shouted "So be it!" and the Walther in his palsied hand fired the first shot, winging Killian, whose own first shot angled up into the ceiling beams, spraying everybody with dust and splinters before cooler heads prevailed.

Sorting it out afterward, it was the local police—virtually every one of them, except for one dark-haired Silesian transplant, all but interchangeable physically with Reinheit's blond young men—who ultimately restored order. What happened, as nearly as Peter could recall, was this:

As Opa embraced Anna in his moment of triumph, Killian's "man" on the inside, whose name actually was Marlene, moved suddenly toward the smaller woman and pushed her out of the line of fire, having gotten a signal from Killian, who was crouched at street level peering in through one of the broken windows as his "troops"—the aforementioned local policemen, ten in number—suddenly swarmed out of nowhere in the dark cellar, positioning themselves so that each had a clear line of fire toward at least one member of Reinheit if it came to that. The young *Übermenschen*, it seemed, were too new at this game to have thought of posting a guard.

At about that same instant, Peter shoved his Reinheit watchdog against a nearby support pillar and moved toward Jake before anyone thought of using him as a human shield. That was when Killian made the mistake of trying to remain in charge while simultaneously trying to jump through the broken window without ripping his suit or damaging his knees. Which was about when Opa hauled the Walther out from under his jacket and fired it once before the ancient weapon jammed.

There were two more shots, Peter stated during his debriefing, Killian's and one other, or maybe it was three. He couldn't be sure. It might have been only two, followed by echoes in the low-ceilinged cellar. And, no, he couldn't tell who fired them in what order; it all happened too fast.

When it was all over, there were more than enough policemen to handcuff the Bad Guys and march them off, two officers assigned on either side of Opa, who couldn't walk very well without his cane, Marlene was still hovering protectively over Anna, Killian's jacket and shirt were ruined, and he'd have an interesting scar running right through his right tricep to show off to his grandchildren someday, and Jake Bower was dead.

•

"No!" Karen screams. She is not a screamer. But she has seen Margarethe at Johann's grave, and now watched as Jake was killed. Where is Govannon? Escaped again, as he did in Avaricum? She'd screamed then, too.

"Someone has to die here," says a voice behind her. "I don't know why, but I know it has to be."

Karen doesn't think. She turns her back on all of the mess and throws her arms around him.

"As long as it isn't you!" she murmurs into his chest.

He rests his chin on the top of her head. "Really? Do you really care so much? I'm just a collection of molecules."

"So's everybody!" Karen wipes her eyes. "What's your point?"

•

My point, Govannon thinks but cannot say, cannot say because to do so would be perhaps to unduly influence Karen's decision making at the one point where her decisions must be purest, *is that my many avatars have loved many women in their times, but the I of me is drawn to you when it is least convenient for it to do so.*

You do not know me, yet you do. Do not know in what form I may or may not appear without my human guise, but do not care. You have seen through me to the I of me, and that is what you love. How is such love possible? And what am I to do?

I have no time to love you! Yet I do.

•

"My point," Govannon says, "is that we're not in Tir na Nog anymore."

They are in the Museum. Don't read that sentence too quickly, Gentle Reader. If you do, you'll be tempted to say:

Oh, big fuckin' deal, like they haven't been bouncing back
and forth from the Museum to Someplace Else throughout
this entire novel as some sort of hokey transitional plot de-
vice, and aren't we sick of it!

Okay, try to pay attention here: Karen's been bouncing
back and forth. Govannon just got here.

So there.

For her part, Karen can't stop smiling. She's not sure she
can stand much more wear and tear on her emotions, but
the only thing that matters to her is that Govannon's Here.
Back on Relict, his point of origin, which not only means
that he doesn't have to die just because Jake does, but it's
half of what needs to be accomplished.

"Okay," she says, rolling up her metaphorical sleeves.
"What happens now?"

•

It's not up to Govannon. The tape's been rewound and they
are back in the cellar of the abandoned villa again (if it isn't
chickens, Karen thinks, it must be a cellar). Take Two.

There were two more shots, Peter would state during his
debriefing, or maybe it was three. He couldn't be sure. It
might have been only two, followed by echoes in the low-
ceilinged cellar. And, no, he couldn't tell who fired them in
what order; it all happened too fast.

When it was all over, Marlene had swung Anna around
behind another support pillar and was pressing her between
her own body and the wall, but with the sort of superhuman
strength that such moments evoke, Anna managed to twist
free of the younger, stronger woman on an agenda of her
own. She did not need to see Jake to know he was in the
line of fire. Instinctively she screamed, and the young swine
who'd decided he owed it to the cause to kill at least one

Jew was startled enough to slew toward her instead, and this time it was Anna who was dead.

•

"You're not as upset this time," Govannon observes. Is he judging her?

"It would explain why one version of Anna was out of synch when I met her," Karen says woodenly. "And I suppose if—when—I go back to Earth, there'll be no record of Anna's ever having been on *Nightline*." It's very hard for her to speak right now; even breathing is an effort. "And, no, I'm not as upset, because there's nothing I can do about it, because the more real the production values get, the more unreal this whole thing seems and, frankly, because it isn't you. I'm sorry for Jake because he's lost the woman he loves, but I'm not going to apologize for my feelings. You've made your point. I'm not ready for this. I'm only human. Maybe you're right. I have overstayed my welcome. I've gotten you back to Relict. Maybe it's time you sent me home."

For the first time she's able to look at him, and what she sees are tears. She reaches up and touches them off his cheeks with the tips of her fingers.

"Is that for Anna?"

"No. For all of us. There's no resonance," he explains. "Wherever TQ are, if they still are, I can't bring them back. Which means eventually the energy they left here, starting with this"—he gestures at the walls of the Museum, where the film has stopped, freeze-framed, with Anna's death— "and ending with the food in the refrigerator, will dissipate.

"I've been weighing options. I could remain here. Enough of my human avatars knew enough about agriculture. I could manage to grow enough to feed myself, I suppose, at least until my own personal energy also drained."

"What does that mean?"

"It means I'll lose this form, revert to what I was before. And I don't even remember what that was."

He turns away from her and she sees his shoulders shake with grief, as Jacob the Brewer's had when his Elspeth died. In that life, Karen had brought him out of his grief with a touch of her hand. That wasn't enough this time. What was?

Finally, all a writer has is words. "That's why you've been weighing your human lives," she suggests. "To choose which one you'd live out to the end."

He squares his shoulders, faces her. The tears are gone.

"I can still go through my Gat. Maybe more than once, but I don't dare risk it more than once. I have been weighing all my lives, trying to decide which one is safest, not for me but so as to have as little impact as possible on human history."

"Pretty difficult," Karen muses. "Since every one of your avatars seems to have been a lightning rod for some sort of turmoil."

"Rather like you," he starts to say, that wave of affection taking hold of him again. He could not, must not, let his feelings for her influence his decision. Couldn't he?

"Oh, for pity's sake!" Anna says, shattering the mood.

She steps down from the screen, à la *Purple Rose of Cairo,* and stands with her hands on her hips looking at them both. Stage blood from the bullet wound in her throat runs down her neck onto the collar of her coat.

"Shit!" she says in a most un-Anna-like voice, noticing it for the first time. "That's gonna leave a stain. And I really liked this coat. Anybody got a handkerchief?"

Between Karen and Govannon, it's difficult to say who's more surprised by this development. Having gotten no response from either of them, Anna slips back into the screen for a moment, retrieves her purse, and digs out some Kleenex. Wiping the blood away, she stalks over to Govannon and, practically standing on tiptoe, takes his chin in her hand and tugs none too gently on his beard. "Wake up, Santa Claus. It's I."

It's I. Had to be a TQ, Karen thinks. No one else would speak that way.

Wait a minute. Anna is a Third Thing? Suddenly it all makes a perverse kind of sense.

"Hadron," Govannon says glumly, as if seeing her for the first time.

"It took you long enough!" Her voice is harsh where Anna's was melodious, and she has this annoying habit of standing with her hands on her hips and her head thrown back, as if to compensate for her diminutive size. "How many more clues did you need?"

Karen's feeling distinctly left out of this conversation. She doesn't say anything, but she can't help clearing her throat.

"Sorry!" Govannon says, taking her elbow gently and bringing her closer to Anna—er—Hadron, which is the last place in the room she wants to be. "My ex-wife," Govannon explains in a tone that in a human male would have been sheepish.

"One of them," Hadron corrects him.

"Figures," Karen says, offering Hadron her hand to shake, but the smaller woman is distracted.

" 'Scuse me a minute, hon," she says, stepping back into the wall. "I've got a scene to finish."

•

When it was all over, there were more than enough policemen to handcuff the Bad Guys and march them off, two officers bracketing Opa, who couldn't walk very well without his cane, Marlene was still hovering protectively over

Anna, Killian's jacket and shirt were ruined, and he'd have an interesting scar running right through his right tricep to show off to his grandchildren someday, and Peter Kato was looking at the blood that had run down into his shirt cuff with a strange detachment.

"Guess I'll never play the violin again," he quipped. In a *grand jeté* that would have made Nureyev proud, our hero had leaped across the room to shove Jake out of the path of the bullet meant for him.

"Always have to be the fucking hero!" Jake chided him, his voice gruff as he pressed his handkerchief in place to staunch the blood. "You're lucky. It's just a graze. An inch closer and you'd have stigmata."

"Stigma," Anna couldn't help saying. Accuracy was her way of processing fear.

"Already got one of those," Peter remarked. "The Jap in America: A Memoir . . ."

Anna punched his shoulder lightly, then threw her arms around both men. "All of this for a heap of tree resin!"

"Amazing what human beings will kill for, isn't it?" Suddenly Killian was a philosopher. Waving off Marlene, who had come to tell him a doctor had been found to tend to his arm, he looked down at Peter with grudging respect. "Faster than a speeding bullet," he said, then winced with pain. "I want to thank you all for your help. We'll take it from here."

"Just a goddamn minute!" Anna said, and now it is Karen the writer's turn to wince. Anna has been tough, resourceful, resilient through all of this, but Hadron's personality is intruding here, and it's all Karen can do to keep from yelling "Cut!" As if any of them would pay any attention to her anyway.

"Mrs. Bower," Killian was saying. "Here's the plan. We've got agents going through Reinheit's database right now, and over the next few weeks we'll be reeling in members and sympathizers all over the world. Quite a few upstanding citizens are about to be publicly embarrassed.

"The Room is going to be airlifted to the States for safekeeping. You and Dr. Bower will get an official pat on the back for your efforts, and in time a joint committee of officials from the U.S. and the German Republic will give the Room back to the Russians with a great deal of diplomatic flourish, but your involvement is ended as of now. We've arranged for the best hotel suite in town. It ain't the Hilton, but you'll be comfortable overnight. Tomorrow you'll need to be debriefed before we fly you home. Right now, let's discuss your finder's fee."

Killian staggered a little, as if the pain or the loss of blood was finally getting to him, allowing them the briefest glimpse of vulnerability before he locked back into spook mode. Wincing again, he fumbled in his jacket left-handed and produced a manila file folder, a smear of fresh blood on the cover.

"Sorry about that!" he managed between clenched teeth, as Marlene force-marched him to where the doctor was waiting.

Inside the folder was a printout, a three-page e-mail, the first page nothing but strings of code, the second and third pages containing the Russian text and English translation of a one-paragraph forensics report.

"Waiting in Opa's e-mail when we broke in," Killian said as the doctor cut away his shirt and urged him to hold still, *bitte*. "One of the local *Polizei* had his laptop with him, so we had it forwarded."

Anna skimmed the official verbiage. Antigenic comparators of Blood Sample A with Cadaver Tissue G . . . results inconclusive.

Cadaver Tissue G so badly deteriorated that no definitive similarities between samples taken from several sites and Blood Sample A could be made. Conclusion: Negative.

" 'A legend for a girl,' " Killian said, smiling bleakly. The doctor was almost done.

Anna looked at him with the beginnings of respect.

"I'm not a complete dolt, Mrs. Bower. Even an American spy can read le Carré. Maybe more American spies *should* read le Carré. First order of business when I get back to Langley is the shredding of a certain file that never should have been taking up space in the first place. Cadaver G is dead. We intend to see he stays that way. No known connection between him and any other living person. Case closed. Case, in fact, never existed in the first place. Deal?"

"Deal," Anna said, and there was nothing more to do but head for home.

•

"You're looking awfully smug," Peter remarked the next day as the flight attendant took their lunch orders and the Airbus rose above the cloud cover. "Free at last, huh?"

"Not only that," Anna said, "just wait till the experts have a closer look at the Room . . ."

•

"It turned out to be a fake," Hadron says for Karen's benefit, stepping out of the screen again, which fades to black. "When the experts examined it, it turn out that the 'amber' was actually a clever mix of copal, a much younger and more common and therefore far less valuable substance than amber, and polyester resins—"

"—a cheap amalgam forgers have used for centuries as a

substitute for the real thing," Karen finishes for her. "So if I were writing this, I'd say that what you guys found in the basement was most likely a reproduction created for a Soviet exhibit in Stalin's heyday, stored in East Germany at the end of the tour and, like so much loot within the Soviet system, forgotten.

"The real Room probably did not survive the war. And because the big plan to donate it back to the Russians fizzled, and because Anna and Jake were sworn to secrecy, nothing ever came of it, and the first time you got any notice was when you found those oil paintings and ended up on *Nightline* a few years later."

"Brava!" Hadron says with that ironic twist to her voice, and not for the first time Karen wonders how she managed to sustain the act as Anna. "What a dutiful little researcher you are! But you're also dangerous. Your fictions have an alarming propensity for turning out to be true."

"Only in alternate universes." Karen shrugs. "Besides, my books never leave the warehouse, so your secret's safe with me."

"You joke," Anna said, "but this is deadly serious."

"It is to me, too." Karen's chin is stubborn. "Unlike you, I only have one lifetime. And I've invested it in a career no one cares about, in books no one will ever read. I realize that's trivial compared to the universes you dabble in, but—"

Govannon has been watching the two women squabble, chuckling to himself. But enough is enough.

"Will you excuse us for a moment?" he asks Karen and, taking Hadron by the elbow, says, "We have to talk . . ."

TWENTY

Karen will never know what it was the two of them talked about when they slipstreamed offstage, leaving her alone in an empty Museum on an uninhabited planet with nothing but her thoughts which, after she's run out of words, are all any writer has left, after all. None of her business, anyway, what went on between a man and his ex-wife. One of them.

Some climax. Anticlimax. One hundred thousand words, only two exploding spaceships, and those off-camera, and nary an elephant or a magic sword in sight.

Stop it.

She wonders if she ever really knew Govannon at all, or whether he, like Hadron, was just playing a role, and maybe he's as self-absorbed and mean-spirited as Hadron, and maybe Karen was just a character in his script. Interesting juxtaposition, the Writer Written. She'll examine all of that when she gets back to Earth, because it's clear now, as it wasn't before, that this is where her journey ends. Karen, mere human, goes back to Earth while Govannon and Hadron go off to save the universe, or at least their particular corner of it.

This is the end, beautiful friend. Karen's seen enough *Star Trek* movies to know all about the needs of the many and first best destinies. If there are two TQ, there are probably others. And if Hadron's found Govannon, then the two of them will have to find the rest. After that, Karen supposes, Govannon will continue to do what he does best, slip into certain humans' souls whenever they need the courage to save lives or sacrifice their own.

Wherever there's a Govannon needed to offer his life to the Celtic gods, or a Johann to save children from the Nazis, even a Jacob who brews the best beer in Plantagenet Christendom to rescue a little girl injured by a pitchfork, he'll be there. Maybe there are other Gats for him to travel, other worlds for him to work his magic in. For all she knows, entire civilizations are depending on him. Who is she to pout at a time like this?

Still, she can't help feeling abandoned. It was she Johann was making love to as much as Margarethe, the same as but different from Govannon in Avaricum; she hugs herself, cherishing the afterglow. She knows, too, that it was her fiction which served as the metaphorical string through the labyrinth that brought him home, and that as he continues to weave, like a fisherman mending his nets, a time-net möbiusing through past/present/future, it is at least in part her doing. Isn't that enough? Frankly, Scarlett, it isn't. It is, as Margarethe said, the touch of him she will miss the most.

"When is it my turn?" she asks the blank walls of the Museum softly. When they refuse to answer, she shouts it. "*When is it my turn?*"

Silence.

•

Hadron and Govannon are still arguing when they return.

". . . what you did was totally reprehensible!" Karen hears Govannon say. "What if they had succeeded?"

"Hitler might have won the war?" Hadron waved it away

with the back of her hand. "That's been done, and badly, in several people's fiction. There's a plan outside of this, or weren't you aware?"

Govannon stops in his tracks. "No, I wasn't. No one told me."

" 'No one told you'—! Takes a woman to figure it out. Come on. Let's get started. We've got work to do."

Hadron seems only now to notice that Karen's still here.

"I suppose you're wondering what's going on."

Karen adopts an offhand attitude of her own. "I've figured out most of it."

"You only think you have!" Hadron snorts, with that superior tone that's really beginning to get on Karen's nerves. "I'll tell you this much: There was a theory extant long before the War Between that, without our intervention, the individuals we inhabit couldn't withstand the ordeals the conditions of their society or their unique position in it forced them to endure. Something as simple as 7616Mycelia's staying alert long enough to notice the culture mutate, or something as complex as Anna's situation. Do you honestly think Anna would have lived through even the first kidnapping without going insane, if I hadn't intervened?"

Karen considers the Anna she has come to know through the bifurcate reality of her own fiction and what's known in some parts as real life.

"As a matter of fact, yes, I do."

"Well, whatever!"

"What did you mean about there being a plan outside of this?"

"That's not for you to know!" Hadron says sharply, annoyed that she's slipped and allowed Karen to hear that part.

"Unless I figure it out in the next book."

"According to you, there isn't going to be any 'next book,' " Hadron reminds her.

Karen's wearing that stubborn look. "Not as far as the people who pay me five cents a word are concerned." She catches Govannon watching her with sly admiration, and suddenly having to study his toes to keep from laughing. "As for the rest of the world . . . well, we'll see about that."

"Whatever," Hadron says again, and Karen wonders if she's ever played a book editor. But Hadron's dismissed Karen and turned her attention to Govannon. "Let's go. We've got work to do."

Govannon is looking more thoughtful than usual, hands in his pockets, eyes on the ground. When he finally looks up, his eyes are for Karen, though he speaks to Hadron.

"You go on ahead. I'll be right with you."

"Mocheril . . ." Hadron begins, but he turns on her with a look that, even though Karen can't see it, she knows is dangerous. Hadron gives ground and vanishes somehow, possibly slipping through the wall of the Museum, maybe just winking out. This sort of thing is so commonplace by now that Karen's not paying attention. She's too busy thinking: *Mocheril?*

"One of my earlier names," he admits sheepishly. "Guess I forgot to mention it. Which I suppose makes you wonder what else I've forgotten to mention."

"It doesn't matter," Karen says, although it does. "So you're going with her." It isn't a question.

"For now. I'm a time traveler, Hadron's a space traveler; she's been to more than human worlds. She believes that between us we may be able to trace the resonances of some of the others, slip-slide back the way they went, and maybe find the rest of them. One by one, if necessary, but it's a start."

"Heading them off at the past," Karen suggests.

Does he actually wince?

"You've been spending entirely too much time with me!" he says. Taking her chin in his hand, he tilts her head up and opens her mouth with his own.

•

"How do you feel?" Johann asked as he and Margarethe lay tangled together in the big iron bed.

He had marveled at the rosiness of her skin when she'd emerged from the bath and, naked and light as a girl, led him to her bed. Now he marveled at the way one small, perfect breast fit exactly into the cupped palm of his hand.

Margarethe laughed her throaty laugh before she answered. "I didn't know I had so much energy! Or that I could make such sounds. I never have before. Never."

"I'll bet you've said that to all your lovers. You're sure you weren't pretending?" he teased her. "Just trying to please an *alte Kocker* like me?"

"You aren't old," she said, kissing his chin through the close-cropped beard. "You are immortal."

He laced his fingers through her hair, cradled her head. Immortal? Six million of his people were dead; he would have to be. There was so much more to do.

•

Some years later, or is it only on a different time line, a little girl with auburn hair sits up in a hospital bed studiously making paper chains. Four days ago she had her appendix out, or did she run afoul of a pitchfork? The day nurse for the Pediatrics floor has told her in no uncertain terms to "Stay in that bed or else!" after she has, in a single afternoon, managed not only to wander into the contagious ward but to be found playing hide-and-seek in a pile of cardboard boxes waiting beside the incinerator to be, well, incinerated.

She's colored all her coloring books and doesn't care for what's on the TV in the playroom, from which she's now been banished anyway, if she's not allowed out of bed, and she is *bored*. Her belly doesn't hurt nearly as much as it did before and just after the operation. As a matter of fact, the dressing is beginning to itch, and she's been warned to leave it alone after the day nurse caught her peeling off one corner of the adhesive to try to peek at the scar.

"I just want to see it!" Karen protested. "Dr. Butler says it looks like a zipper. I want to see."

"Leave it *alone*!" the day nurse scolded. "Goodness, you're a handful. I'll be glad when you can go home."

"Me too!" Karen piped up.

To which the nurse said: "You're entirely too smart for someone who's only seven years old!" before she walked away shaking her head.

She couldn't go home until Monday, which Karen knows is two whole days from now, and she's not sure if she can stand it.

Then she remembers the paper-chain-making kit her grandmother bought for her to keep her out of just the sort of trouble she's been getting into. She sets about licking the ends of the little multicolored strips of paper to make them stick together and form the loops of the chain.

In less than no time she's all but buried in yards and yards of paper chain. The day nurse is so impressed she'll hang them on the doorways of the all rooms in Peds, remarking proudly to anyone who commented on them. "One of our little patients did that. The little tomboy with the red hair. She's a wild one; it's all we can do to keep her in bed. Guess it's true what they say about redheads. . . ."

Only when they've been hung up does Karen notice that some of the loops are twisted funny. She must have been in too much of a hurry when she did them. The nuns in her school said only God was perfect, but Karen tried, she really did. She became obsessed with those twisted ones, staring at them from her bed. It wasn't bad enough that she was bored and restless and couldn't wait to get out of here, but those twisty ones really annoyed her.

Under virtual house arrest, feeling sleepy, Karen watched the paper chains möbius about themselves, in a place where there was no time. When she dreamed, she dreamed of baby dragons, blind and pale against the dark.

·

"What did you tell the Americans?" Margarethe asked the next morning, over ersatz coffee and fresh rolls, the latter courtesy of Timothy's ovens, whose aromas reached them from the courtyard three stories below.

"American. One only. A hapless Irisher with captains' bars," Johann muttered, realizing he was saying too much. "We told him her name and that her mother had been killed in the bombing, nothing more. He will invent the rest. Which does not mean it won't be true."

Margarethe's smile was bemused. However long she might know this man, she would never entirely understand him.

"He didn't ask who you were, or whether she had a father?"

"We didn't give him time. He seemed more concerned that she might have some disease."

Margarethe shook her head. Americans!

"So he doesn't know about—" she started to say, but Johann touched her lips with one finger, ostensibly to brush a crumb away, but she understood the gesture. "Forgive me. It is only a rumor, after all. But it is the reason she must be taken out of the country."

"Margarethe . . ."

She loved the way he said her name.

"No more. You're right. We both have much work to do." She went into the bathroom to pin up her hair. When she emerged he had washed the chipped coffee cups and was lacing his shoes. "Will you come back tonight?"

He looked up at her under his eyebrows. "Do you wish me to?"

She shrugged as if it weren't important, as if she didn't know that, with the city divided, he could no longer hide in the cemetery, had no permanent place to stay.

After all he has been through, all he has done, Margarethe thought, he deserved a comfortable place to lay his head, at least. But if she said as much, she knew he would become stubborn and refuse her.

"You're free to do whatever you want," she said lightly.

He straightened his back, held her shoulders, brushed her lips lightly with his own. "Tonight, then. If I can."

•

Jeremiah may have been a bullfrog, but Proteus was a sea god. Sometimes known as the Old Man of the Sea, though not to be confused with Poseidon, who was the Boss God in those parts, Proteus was more of a magician, a shape-shifter, though his different forms were for his own purposes, not the amusement of others. Only when deceived or threatened with violence did he change himself in the presence of others, and then only to escape his tormenters.

Proteus anguinus, on the other hand, is a pale, eyeless, gilled newt, which has no known predators, and is extant only in the waters of the Adelsberg Caverns in what is now Slovenia.

(It's true, you could look it up. What, you think we're good enough to invent this stuff?)

While parts of the Adelsberg have been extensively explored and mapped—by the nineteenth century someone had even thought to hang chandeliers in some of the larger rooms, and run a narrow-gauge railroad over a mile long so that the ladies could admire the stalactites without exerting themselves; symphony orchestras performed there—no one really knows how deep they go or how far they extend.

For all we know, those caverns could extend under most of the European mainland and well into Asia (small wonder that for every extant tale of fairies there is also one of trolls) and, if not as far as another planet, at least to a small village in Bohemia named Salzheim, where the Salt Routes and the Silk Road once met, a place where magic happens.

If such a thing as the Amber Room ever existed, it might be hidden in any of the miles of salt mines that were first dug in the Bronze Age. Amazing stuff, salt. The air inside a salt mine is dry, bacteria free, completely preservative. Just about anything can be hidden safely in a salt mine, and it will be as if time stopped.

And if once upon a time and time again, a stranger emerged from the dark wood in the vicinity of one of those mines and shifted himself into a shape most humans would be comfortable with, the ancients would have said he was immortal, and who's to say their interpretation was any less scientific than ours?

•

Well, there you have it, Gentle Reader. The kind of people we work for aren't going to let us take this story any further, so this is as far as we can take you here. Check the author's Web site if you can, though. (If you don't have a computer, your local library does. You may even find the author's books there while you're at it.) You may find some surprises.

AFTERWARD

Karen wakes from a sound sleep, the lyrics of an old Doors song following her to the surface. It is still dark outside. The alarm—which she hadn't set last night, knowing she would wake ahead of it because she's nervous about missing her flight—reads four-thirty. The flight leaves at seven. There'll be virtually no traffic this early. The fact that it's pouring out won't slow the car service driver one bit; he'll have her at Newark in less than twenty minutes.

In her dream she'd been swimming with Govannon—um, Mocheril (oh, hell, he'll always be Govannon to her, her own private Thunderer)—and they were blind.

She's been wondering what she's going to do with the rest of her life. She knows she has to get out of New York. Back in the day when editors still paid for lunch, it seemed essential to be here, on the theory that if they could meet you, put a face and a personality with the words on the page, they'd be more amenable to buying your work. No more. Time to move on.

The Day Job, typing medical reports at two dollars a page, is portable. She can freelance, work at home, live close to the bone anywhere in the country. Somewhere in California seems appealing. Mild winters, none of that murderous East

Coast humidity. Her kids can spend their vacations with her. Her friendships extend around the globe and even offworld; there's no reason for her to stay here.

She'll think about that tomorrow or, to be accurate, after the weekend. For now, she has a flight to catch for Portage, Indiana.

Hot shower, cold rain, water running down the shower curtain or the closed windows of the cab, rushing down a mountainside on a distant world where bare rock transforms itself before the eye into cultivated gardens, trickling relentlessly through underground caverns where live the dragon's young.

Mocheril, the locals call them, the closest translation being "burrower into wetness." They swim together, she and Govannon, luminescent-pale in a darkness as profound as the sound of one hand clapping in the forest, long eel-like bodies undulating side by side and over-under, blind to the universe, seeing only each other. Can a newt know happiness? Protean proteus, shape-shifter. A lesser god, called sometimes Thunderer . . .

Karen yawns, pays the driver, drags her suitcase to the check-in counter. She hopes she can sleep on the plane, but doubts it. She's been thinking of abandoning the con scene, especially if she has to fly so early in the morning, but she committed to this one over a year ago, and can't let her constituents down.

It's pouring in Portage, too.

"So glad you could make it, hon!" One of the organizers, a breathlessly overweight man named Tim, speaks to her as if he's known her for years. Karen finds this not at all strange. He's read her work, which is the best of her, why not?

"Wait till you see who else is here . . ." He leads her into the autograph room. "I'm so pleased with myself, you have no idea. I've snagged not one but three of the guest stars from the original show. If I do this long enough, I'll get everyone who's ever been on *SpaceSeekers* . . ."

SpaceSeekers, the anomalous little '60s sci-fi show that was the reason Karen began writing science fiction in the first place. *SpaceSeekers*, whose equally anomalous half-alien science officer Benn had been her high school heartthrob, though he wasn't the only one. She'd thought the guy who played the Quirinian was a hunk. And even though she'd never seen him in anything else before, she'd recognized him the minute that angular face appeared on her TV screen. Like hearing voices on battlefields, it had seemed normal to her at the time.

Something about him, whether it was the sculpted planes of jaw and cheekbones, the crispness of his diction as he pronounced a death sentence on Captain Stark, whose ship had invaded Quirinian territory, had been so familiar she even knew there was something different about his hair.

"The makeup girl went crazy over it," he would tell her later. "She spent hours teasing it into all those little ringlets. I think she must have had a crush on me . . ."

Who wouldn't? Karen thinks, watching him work the crowd thirty years later. It's all come clear to her at last. The dark wavy hair is silver-white now, the lines of the face are sculpted deeper, but the hands and voice and eyes are the same, in any time or venue.

Later he will tell her of his many selves, not only actor, writer, artist, director but, like one of his many avatars, psychotherapist as well. For now, as she watches him sign autographs, she finds she is also being watched.

"My God, you're beautiful!" he says in that oh-so-familiar voice. "Where did you get that face?"

You should talk! Karen thinks. *TQ of a thousand faces.*

Hello, you, she thinks. *I've known you all my lives.*